BOOKS OF THE SHAPER: VOLUME III

SEVEN SORCERERS

JOHN R. FULTZ

orbit

www.orbitbooks.net

ORBIT

First published in Great Britain in 2013 by Orbit

A CIP catalogue record for this book
is available from the British Library.

ISBN 978-0-356-50083-6

Typeset in Garamond by M Rules
Printed and bound by Clays Ltd, St Ives plc

Papers used by Orbit are from well-managed forests
and other responsible sources.

MIX
Paper from
responsible sources
FSC® C104740

Orbit
An imprint of
Little, Brown Book Group
100 Victoria Embankment
London EC4Y 0DY

An Hachette UK Company
www.hachette.co.uk

www.orbitbooks.net

For John M. Waggoner,
a Giant among Men

Dramatis Personae

Vod the Giant-King – Former ruler and rebuilder of New Udurum, City of Men and Giants; slayer of Omagh the Serpent-Father; sorcerer and legend; also known as Vod of the Storms; drowned himself in the Cryptic Sea

Gammir the Wolf (formerly Fangodrel of Udurum) – Vod's adopted bastard son; his true father was Gammir the Second, Prince of Khyrei, who was slain by Vod; also known as Gammir the Bloody, the Undying One, and the Black Wolf; former Emperor of Khyrei

Ianthe the Panther – Former Empress of Khyrei; grandmother of Gammir; an ageless sorceress; slain by Vireon and Alua at the fall of Shar Dni; reborn in the body of Maelthyn of Udurum; also known as the White Panther and Ianthe the Claw

King Vireon of Udurum – Son of Vod and heir to his sorcery; ruler of New Udurum; all the power and strength of a Giant in the body of a Man; also known as Vireon Vodson and Vireon the Slayer; crowned as King of All Giants after the fall of Angrid the Long-Arm

Queen Alua of Udurum – Ageless sorceress married to Vireon; mother of Maelthyn; known for her mastery of the white flame magic; slain by Ianthe the Claw

Maelthyn of Udurum – Deceased daughter of King Vireon and Queen Alua; consumed by Ianthe's sorcery at the age of seven

Dahrima the Axe – Blonde-haired Uduri (Giantess) who once served Vod the Giant-King; now she serves as one of the Ninety-Nine, King Vireon's personal guard of Uduri spearmaidens; often considered Vireon's "right hand"

King D'zan of Yaskatha – Ruler of Yaskatha; reborn from a state of living death by the sorcery of Iardu and Sharadza after reclaiming his father's usurped throne; also known as the Sun Bringer

Sharadza Vodsdaughter – Vod's only daughter and heir to his sorcery; Princess of Udurum; apprentice of Iardu the Shaper; former Queen of Yaskatha and First Wife of D'zan

Emperor Tyro of Uurz – Twin brother of Lyrilan; swordsman of renown; also known as the Sword King; ordained as Emperor of Uurz after banishing his brother from the Stormlands

King Lyrilan of Uurz – Twin brother of Tyro; scholar and scribe; also known as the Scholar King; former co-ruler of Uurz who fled to Yaskatha after being framed for the murder of his wife and banished from the Stormlands

Queen Ramiyah of Uurz – Wife of King Lyrilan; born in Yaskatha; slain in Talondra's plot to make Tyro the uncontested Emperor of Uurz

Empress Talondra of Uurz – Wife of King Tyro; born in Shar Dni and survived its fall; recently slain by Lyrilan's newfound sorcery as revenge for the death of Ramiyah

Lord Mendices of Uurz – Warlord of Uurz; Tyro's chief advisor and military tactician; willing co-conspirator with Talondra in the plot to frame and banish Lyrilan for the murder of Ramiyah

King Undutu of Mumbaza – Nineteen-year-old ruler of Mumbaza; also known as the King on the Cliffs and Son of the Feathered Serpent

Khama the Feathered Serpent – Ageless sorcerer whose true form is that of a great feathered Serpent; fostered the founding of Mumbaza, advisor to its Kings, and protector of its long peace

King Angrid of the Icelands – Lord of the Frozen North; ruler of the Udvorg clans (blue-skinned Giants); slain by the behemoth of the Khyrein marshlands

Varda of the Keen Eyes – Shamaness in service to King Angrid; blessed Vireon with the slain Angrid's crown, making him King of All Giants

Tong the Avenger – King of New Khyrei; a former slave who led a revolution assisted by Iardu the Shaper and a horde of the blind subterranean creatures known as Sydathians; also called the Slave King and Tong the Liberator

Iardu the Shaper – Master of Shapes; an ageless sorcerer reputed to live on an island in the Cryptic Sea

Zyung the Almighty – Ageless sorcerer and "God-King" of the Zyung Empire; seeks to conquer the Land of the Five Cities with his Holy Armada; also known as the High Lord Celestial

Sungui the Venomous – A unique being of alternating male and female aspects; one of Zyung's High Seraphim, a legion of ageless sorcerers who serve as the enforcers of his empire

Vaazhia the Lizardess – Ageless sorceress dwelling in the ruins of a forgotten city beneath the Stormlands

Indreyah the Sea-Queen – Ageless sorceress who rules an undersea kingdom of "sea-folk" from her hidden coral city; also known as the Mer-Queen

Prologue

The Earthborn

(as extracted from
The Fifth Book of Imvek the Silent)

The two brothers met high above the world on the peak of a black mountain.

They were not true brothers as Men understand the term.

Nor were they true Men, or anything like them. Not yet. They were more like two great winds that sculpt the faces of mountains and stir the seas to wave and tempest.

This world was not their home, for they were born of distant stars. Yet their kind had lingered here since the continents were mounds of cooling magma between boiling oceans. The world had cooled now, and the brothers had risen above the others of their kind. They had replaced the towering chaos of the previous age with a kind of stillness and order.

Now they looked upon the green and fertile lands of the great continent below. Their eyes roamed beyond the purple horizons, past the golden deserts, across the vast swamplands, and even to the shores of the Cryptic Sea that divides the earth. They gazed into the low places and the high, observing the tiny things that climbed in the great forests and came down to wander the emerald plains.

"See how these brave little creatures take to the land," said the elder brother. "They have learned the secrets of fire and carving stone."

"They are clever indeed," said the younger brother. "I have watched them for a long while now. They are unlike the many species our kind has created, for the earth itself has made them. Yet I cannot say for what reason."

"Our own creations were made only to amuse or serve us," said the elder. "Yet these Earthborn seem to have their own sense of purpose. They are driven to master the land and they commune with its essence. Perhaps they know secrets that even we do not guess."

"Yet see how they gather in distinct bands and make war upon each other. They build and grow strong, only to destroy and become weak again. The cycle continues and they are unable to break it. They have great potential, yet they remain blind to it. There is no unity among them, therefore they may never achieve the greatness that is their inheritance."

"We must give them aid," said the elder. "With our guidance they will grow wise and their numbers will flourish. If we teach them to overcome their own base nature, they may one day reach the destiny for which they were born. On that day we will know the answer to this mystery, brother."

"I have reached the same conclusion," said the younger brother, watching two tribes of Earthborn slaughter one another over a narrow strip of hunting ground. "We must take their form and walk among them. We shall be sages, oracles, and voices of wisdom, shaping them gradually into something greater. Urging them with kindness toward their distant fate."

The elder brother's breath was like thunder falling from the mountain. "No," he said. "This is not the way. They are violent predators by nature; they will not understand our advice. We must take the shape of their Gods, conquer them, and force them to live according to the dictates of order. This is the only way to ensure lasting peace among the Earthborn."

The younger threw up his arms like flames dancing upon the mountaintop. "You are wrong, brother. If you do this you will crush the spirit that makes them unique. They must remain free to find their own way. You cannot force them to enlightenment, you must lead them. A mountain is not made in an instant; it is sculpted by the elements over the course of many ages."

"These creatures will battle one another to extinction long before they gain the wisdom of which you speak," said the elder. "As the younger, you must follow my words."

"I will not do it," said the younger. "You would trample the garden that you seek to grow. Can you not see the flaw in your vision?"

"I will trample only those weeds that would spoil and choke the garden of peace. Otherwise the kindest blossoms will never bloom."

"Then we must part ways," said the younger brother. "Go you into the west and build your garden as you will. I will travel east and begin my shaping of the Earthborn into something greater than their origins. Let us meet here again after an agreed period of time and compare the works we have accomplished. In this way we will discover whose philosophy is the wiser."

"Let it be done," said the elder brother.

And this period of time they agreed upon was five hundred years as Men reckon it.

Five centuries later the two brothers met once more upon the mountain's summit, and now they each wore the shapes of Men. The eyes of the elder brother were twin stars, and the skin of the younger brother was the color of burnished gold.

"I united six great warring tribes," said the younger, the winds of the upper earth tearing at his silver beard. "With my guidance and their own adroit skills they constructed three fine cities of granite and marble. I have achieved much by offering insight without conquest."

"So there is peace among your peoples?" asked the elder.

The younger frowned, and a gray rain fell upon the pinnacle. "For a while there was," he said. "Until two of these cities joined forces and destroyed the third, enslaving the survivors. Later these two cities warred upon each other as well, until only one was left. Yet it is a fine, tall, and proud city. There are philosophers, poets, dreamers, sages, and minstrels among the warriors and builders."

"So there is still war in the west?"

"Sadly, there is."

"I unified eight mighty eastern tribes," said the elder, "by killing their chieftains, casting down their temples, and making myself their only God. They have built a city of white towers and a temple-palace that bears my visage. In my name the people of the white city conquered ten more tribes in the surrounding lands. Now there are two cities that worship me. I have also enlisted a great number of our own kind to serve my endeavors. In doing so, they serve the destiny of the Earthborn. I ask now that you join us, brother."

"So there is peace among your peoples?" asked the younger.

The elder smiled and the rain turned to sleet, crowning the mountaintop with ice. "Not yet," he said. "For my holy armies march to conquer all the tribes of the world. They pursue a dream of grand unity that will result in ultimate peace and order."

"So there is still war in the east?"

"Yes, along the growing frontier of the Holy Empire. But peace is our aim."

"Then we are both closer to our goal," said the younger brother. "However, neither of us has yet achieved it."

"My philosophy of unity through conquest is superior to your gradual reshaping," said the elder. "For my people possess three great cities unified by a single cause. Your people possess only one city, and they have no greater purpose."

"It seems to me that these three great cities truly belong to you, brother," said the younger, "instead of to the Earthborn who built them. My people's city belongs wholly to them, and each one of them is free to find his own purpose. Your people possess neither peace nor freedom."

"Still we cannot agree," said the elder. "We must go back into the world below and continue our work. Let us meet here one more time, when another five hundred of Men's years are passed. Then we will see once and for all whose philosophy is the wiser."

"Let it be done," said the younger.

And they soared upon stormwinds into the realms east and west.

One last time the brothers met upon the frozen summit of the mountain. The world below had greatly changed in the second five hundred years. The Earthborn now inhabited every climate and domain of the great continent. Their villages and temples sprouted from plain, riverbank, mountainside, desert, forest, and seaside. They plied the deep waters with nautical vessels that harnessed the wind, and they tamed the beasts of earth and sky.

"See here," said the younger brother, who was a bright flame upon the mountain's summit. "I have fostered eight more cities among the Earthborn, built by their own hands and belonging wholly to them. For a while they warred upon each other, but now these nine proud capitals have signed peace treaties, uniting distant lands by the words and deeds of their wise Kings. They have mastered the metals of the deep earth, harnessed the land to feed their masses, and developed written languages capable of profound expression. There is beauty and wisdom in their songs and their creations, despite their adherence to the ancient ways."

"So there is peace among your peoples?" asked the elder brother.

"To a point," said the younger. "The nine Kings still make war upon the barbarian tribes of the north and south, seeking to force the worship of their own Gods upon the heathens. Yet the cities have achieved peace between themselves. The Earthborn have grown as a species and will continue to evolve toward unity and peace for all Men."

"So there is still war in the east?"

"Yes, along the borders of north and south."

"I rule over twenty united cities who call me their God and Master," said the elder. "A thousand of our own kind serve my vision now, delivering my justice and decrees through their formidable power. My empire is strong, and it has grown to encompass all the lands of the west. My generals look to the east, north, and south, where they see the strange Gods worshipped by your people. Soon we will move eastward and bring order to the rest of the great continent."

"So there is peace among your peoples?" asked the younger.

"There is," said the elder. "For I have given them no other choice."

"Yet the west will make war upon the east in the name of peace."

"Yes, for ultimate peace can only come with ultimate conquest. When all cities and peoples are united under my name, the Earthborn will be freed from their predatory origins. Even your eastern barbarians will be part of this great dream I have fostered. As you can see, brother, my philosophy has proven the greater. I ask you again to join us, for my Earthborn realm will soon swallow your own."

The younger brother rose up like a whirlwind of light and fury. He smote the elder and cast him from the mountaintop, which crumbled beneath them and released its inner fires. The blazing blood of the mountain poured along its sides, melting its icy crown. The elder brother cast the starlight of his eyes like arrows into the flesh of the younger, burning him terribly. Then he cast the younger into the molten center of the mountain and shouted these words after him:

"You may sleep in the depths of the earth if you wish while I go to conquer the lands your shaping has failed. Or you may rise up and serve me as do the others of our kind. If you still wish to aid the Earthborn and one day discover their destiny, there can be no other way. Confront me not again, or I will devour you as the stars devour dying worlds."

The elder brother departed the broken mountain and returned to his empire.

After a while the younger brother crawled from the flaming pit and walked toward the nearest of his eastern cities. There he saw the western armies swarming across the plains and casting boulders at the marble walls. The city burned like the broken mountain, and its people refused to surrender, so they died in great numbers.

The younger brother unleashed his wrath upon the invading horde, but an endless succession of conquering legions came over the horizon. A storm of death and destruction fell upon the peaceful eastern city, wiping it from the earth.

The younger brother would not give up his dream of reshaping the Earthborn into something greater by preserving their free will. Their wild spirits must evolve according to nature and time, not be forced into false progress. He had seen Men steal the spirits of proud stallions by breaking them, and he loved his people too well to let this be their fate. Men were not beasts to be corralled and enslaved. They were the Children of Earth, and their descendants would be its inheritors.

They called him the Shaper, and they knew well that he was no God, for the Gods remained deaf to their pleas while the conquering hordes marched on. An Age of Blood and Fire had begun, and the Gods of Men neither noticed nor cared.

The Shaper gathered about him all those who would listen. He spoke of the false God that was coming to break and enslave them, the mighty numbers of the Conqueror's armies, and the terrible powers at the Conqueror's command. Running always just ahead of war's red tide, the Shaper led his followers to the next eastern city, and the next, until he had assembled a multitude of families from each of the nine eastern realms. Yet there were multitudes who refused to flee, choosing instead to stay and defend their lands against the advancing western empire.

The Shaper led his people to the sea, where a fleet of vessels was constructed from the wood of an ancient forest. They sailed across the arc of the world, leaving the great continent to the mercies of the western hordes.

It is not known how long the People of the Shaper lingered upon the Cryptic Sea, or how many of them died in the perilous crossing. Yet with the Shaper's constant guidance, and a deep patience born of wisdom, they came at last to a new continent on the far side of the world.

This was the Land of Serpents, and life there was not easy.

Eventually the Stoneborn, who were called Giants, rose up to cleanse this land of its monsters, driving the People of the Shaper south and claiming the north as their own. There was no place for Men in the Giantlands, yet mankind thrived south of the Grim Mountains.

Still there were wars among Men, yet five great cities rose proud and shining.

The Shaper's dream endured, although at times even he needed to be reminded of it.

Nor was he the last of the Old Breed to foster a kingdom in the Land of the Five Cities.

1

Those Who Listen

Beneath an arbor of fig trees they lay at sundown, discreet as any other pair of lovers. Above their tender exertions starlight kissed leaf and blossom. The interplay of lean arms and legs mimicked the woven branches of the trees. An age-old dance of heat and flame, stoked by the friction of supple bodies.

How many eons had passed since they learned the glorious secret of *joining* without subsiding, *giving* without loss, *sharing* without weakening? Nations had risen and fallen and risen again since the gaining of that mortal skill. A savage continent had grown into a bright empire since that primeval day when they took on fleshly bodies and learned to share them.

Only the stars themselves were more ancient, blinking above the gnarled branches, casting no judgments on the lovers. During such rare moments they recalled for a time the ancient truth of those stars and the freedom of the dark gulfs between them.

Sungui had taken her female aspect this evening, knowing that Mahaavar scorned its opposite. From lips to breasts to hips, even to the tips of her toes, he praised her womanhood with kisses and soft caresses. As a male she could only have been his comrade, a fellow philosopher, and perhaps a drinking companion. There were many who felt a keen desire for Sungui's male aspect; yet the masculine form did not lend itself to intimacy in the same way.

So many of the Seraphim did not understand this: To assume *any* form was to endure its intrinsic vitality, to the point where form and purpose might be blended beyond all hope of separation.

So had the Old Breed been Diminished.

The lure of the world was strong. The temptation to join the realm of flesh and stone and soil was what had brought them here so long ago. It drew them downward, welcoming them into its deep folds and valleys, the churning depths of its seas, the rolling emerald of its forests, the pristine wastes of its desert lands. The beauty and power of the world itself had Diminished them all.

Zyung the Almighty had not been mastered by the earth. Instead, he had mastered it. Or so most of her kind believed, and his Living Empire proved it. The greatest among them had avoided the snare of the earth and its wonders. Zyung did not assimilate, he conquered.

Yet the empire that he built – that all of them helped him to build – even now drew him into itself, calcifying his existence, his very identity, like nothing else ever could.

Zyung was his empire; the Living Empire was Zyung. On the altar of his supremacy she had found the black shard of hope that was her deadliest weapon. She kept it hidden for generations, like a dagger tucked into the robe of a patient yet ambitious slave. No one else had seen the dark glimmer of its blade.

Soon she would show it to them.

The Garden of Twenty-Seven Delights lay in an obscure corner of the temple-palace complex, a labyrinth of trellised walls, sculpted avenues, and fountained walks. Orchards, arboretums, vineyards, and cloistered parks surrounded the garden. A white tower of five sides rose above the sparkling domes to block the view of the temple-palace proper.

The Holy Mountain, the faithful called it. Yet the citadel was not carved from any existing mountain; it was built by the hands of Men to stand as high and magnificent as any natural peak. The work of a million slaves, their tiny, broken lives scattered across the centuries. The stones of the soaring walls were mortared with their blood and bones.

Sungui recalled them swarming like ants across the unfinished ramparts of the flat-topped pyramid, swinging like a clutch of spiders from ropes as they sculpted the gargantuan face of Zyung on its southernmost façade. The last stone had been set, the last chisel laid down, more than five hundred years ago, yet the vision lived as clearly in her mind as if seen only yesterday. She avoided looking at that titanic face, both in the light of day and in the silver gloom of night.

In the same way that she avoided the carven face, she had learned to avoid the true face of the Almighty when it suited her purposes. The trick was to focus his attention elsewhere, as it had been for centuries now. The Almighty dreamed of the ripe, untamed lands beyond the Outer Sea. His growing obsession with the expansion of the Living Empire gave her the opportunity she had awaited since the City of Celestial Truth had been a mud-walled village alongside a stinking river.

Sungui arose from a carpet of grass and petals, donning a robe of iridescent silver. Mahaavar did the same, brushing purple blossoms from his shoulders. His shimmering vestment was identical in every way to her own. There were no distinctions among the High Seraphim. Another way in which Zyung reinforced their Diminishing: Making them equal.

All save himself.

None were equal to the Almighty.

She smirked at the moon, which the earth's shadow had divided precisely in half. Could there be an omen in that particular astronomic event? She had not consulted the moon charts when planning tonight's gathering.

They did not need to speak, Mahaavar and she. Their bodies had expressed everything in the ciphers of touch and sensation. The earthly manifestations of their eternal spirits. The complimentary nature of their bodies was their most effective communication. Mahaavar kissed her lips once again before leaving the garden; his were still hot and tasted of cinnamon.

Along the Path of Contemplation they walked, two silver-robes strolling in the unhurried way common to those in power. Slaves tending the nightflowers scurried from the path, prostrating themselves; the clacking of shears resumed as they passed. Guards in hawk-faced visors stiffened as the two High Seraphim walked by their stations upon garden walls and bridges. A nightingale sang sweetly among the clustered vines that hemmed the pathway. Sungui's bare feet on the polished marble made no sound; Mahaavar moved as quietly as she.

They passed through an arch of jade carved into a parade of winged children, and so came into the Grotto of Sighing Flowers. A breeze stirred the hems of their garments, the naked breath of great, pulsing blossoms. At the nearest of the Inner Walls, they paused while an alabaster gate rose to admit them. They entered the courtyard of the Thirty-Ninth Tower and crossed a lawn where white-barked trees harbored flocks of nesting doves. Only here, away from the ears of passing slaves and functionaries, did Mahaavar speak to her.

"How many do you expect?" he whispered.

"It does not matter," she said.

"Will they listen?"

"They have always listened," she said.

He said nothing, stifling his confusion.

"Yet they never—"

"Not yet," she said. "Such things take time. Longer than you could guess." She stopped in the middle of the courtyard, where the sound of cooing birds filled the branches. "Do you even remember how long it took to build the Holy Mountain? Do you remember – truly remember – how old you are?"

Mahaavar looked at the shadows swimming about the tree roots. A holy viper crawled through the grass, its white scales speckled with a pattern of scarlet diamonds.

"Sometimes," he said. "Sometimes I recall ... another life ... or lives."

She smiled and caressed his cheek. "They were all you, Beautiful Mahaavar."

Sungui turned and the pace resumed. Through a second gate of whitewashed oak and iron they entered a narrow corridor with recessed candles lining the walls. A slave carrying a bundle of cloth paused before them, lying flat upon the floor so that they might walk upon his back. Sungui and Mahaavar stepped across the man's bony frame one at a time. He neither groaned nor complained, although she did hear the complaint of his brittle bones. As they proceeded down the corridor, the slave was up again and carrying his burden in the direction from which they had come.

"Why here, in this mean place crawling with slaves?" Mahaavar asked. "It stinks of sweat and fear."

She breathed deeply the close air of the Slave Quarters. She smelled only sweat, soap, and the exhalations of simple cuisine. Slaves' cooking. Mahaavar was her spoiled lover, unaccustomed to walking in the lower precincts of the Holy Mountain. He was much like a boy, and she loved him for that as much as for their ancient and bloodless kinship. She allowed herself a lingering glance at his handsome face: high-set cheekbones, ebony hair, eyes blue as sapphire, the petulant mouth of a princeling. A lost and doddering God of the ancient world might look as fetching, were there ever any such beings. Adoring the beauty of his face, recalling the hot embrace of his body, she could understand why humans had created this notion of Gods.

Yet that was long ago, and all those imaginary deities had been slain, forgotten, or suffused into the essence of the High Lord Celestial himself. Zyung was their only God now. The one God they could believe in because he walked among them working miracles, casting dooms, spreading his gifts of pain and death. For thousands of years it had been so. And it might be so for thousands more.

Might be.

"Relax, my love," she told Mahaavar as they descended granite stairs. "Do you predict the Almighty's eyes will turn from dreams of western conquest to search out the catacombs where his slaves dwell?"

Mahaavar grinned. "Your cleverness amuses me. His Holiness would never expect to find a single one of his High Seraphim in such a place." Sungui nodded, strands of her dark hair whispering against the flared shoulders of her vestment.

Curtains of steam wafted in the damp air. A corridor of unadorned stone led them into an underground gallery dominated by a great, square pool of murky water. Young slaves tended two hearths where flames licked about hot stones. As the two High Seraphim entered, a terrified boy dropped a burning rock he was lifting with a pair of iron tongs. It fell steaming to the floor between his feet, glowing like a miniature red sun.

Several adult slaves were bathing in the pool. Their faces lit with surprise, then abject fear. They rushed up out of the pool, grabbing towels to wrap themselves and shuffling the bath-tenders out of the chamber with a series of bows, prostrations, and nervous words. In a few seconds the chamber stood empty but for the two High Seraphim in their glittering robes, perspiring in the steam.

Sungui raised a finger to her lips, ensuring Mahaavar's silence. They did not have long to wait. Four dark archways glimmered silver as ten more High Seraphim entered the chamber to stand about the abandoned pool.

Sungui's eyes greeted each of them in turn. Damodar with his shaven skull and large ears, nose pierced by a hoop of sacred platinum. Eshad, whose impressive physique shamed even that of Mahaavar, cords of muscle coiled beneath the bright skin of his robes. Myrinhama, whose golden hair fell to her waist, and whose almond eyes were golden as well. Gulzarr and Darisha, who had been lovers for centuries, ageless and inscrutable behind faces of serene beauty. Durangshara, portly as any spoiled merchant, who took his joy from the fruits of the earth and his pleasure from the howls of slaves. Johaar and Mezviit and Aldreka, who could be triplets they were so alike in form, taste, and bearing. And finally Lavanyia, whose hair was a mound of sable silk piled atop her lovely head. She reminded Sungui of the great lionesses that roamed the Weary Plains to the south. She could also be as dangerous, as bloodthirsty, and as unforgiving as one of those proud beasts.

Of them all, Lavanyia would be the hardest to convince.

They used to be so much more. So much greater. Some of them remembered this. Others Sungui had to remind. A single decade or less was all it took for the world's allure to smother and calcify these spirits who lingered in its fertile bosom. Yet Sungui had long ago found an advantage over her fellow Seraphim. Each of them had chosen a gender long ago and embraced it. She refused to do so. The flux of her aspects and the shifting of her form was her last defense against the tide of earthly influences that threatened to rob her of her true self.

"Brothers and Sisters," Sungui began. "The time has come to remember." She nearly sang the words, so soft and melodious was her tone. She had learned how to charm them, imitating the ways of comely humans. It was partly why they all loved her. She catered to their whims, their secret delights, their hidden natures. She knew them better than they knew themselves. They knew her as two beings, twin aspects, and so she carried mystery and beauty with her like precious stones.

She raised her hands as if to embrace them all. They took graceful steps about the edge of the pool, gathering into a close circle. Mahaavar stood at Sungui's left hand, staring at the faces of the conspiracy he would join.

Sungui sensed his eagerness. Mahaavar did not understand that there was no real sedition yet. No blasphemy. There was only this small group. Those Who Listen. There were only her words and these listeners' undeniable need to hear what she would say. They had not gathered like this in several years. Yet years passed like days for their kind. There were a thousand more High Seraphim across the Living Empire who knew nothing of these assemblies. Yet an idea must take root in the minds of the few. Later it might spread like wild vines across the ranks of the Celestial Ones, and they might finally awaken from this worldly dream.

These listeners were enough for now. The early seeds of a future forest.

The contracted circle gleamed with curious eyes. A ripple of light flashed across the silvery robes. Sungui bowed her head.

"In the time before time's advent, we moved between the stars," she said. "They were our mothers and fathers, our blazing progenitors. We sailed the vast ether and swam the oceans of eternity. Now we gather once more to recall the truth of what we are. We look back. We look inward. We listen once more to the music of our ancient selves, that it may remind us, reshape us, restore us."

"Hold," said a liquid voice. Sungui raised her eyes to the leonine face of Lavanyia. Never before had a listener interrupted her guided meditation. The lioness stared at Sungui, as did the rest of the circle. Even Mahaavar's eyes were upon her now. A chill crept up Sungui's spine.

"There is an Ear among us," said Lavanyia. Her onyx eyes did not leave Sungui's own. The eyes of the others darted nervously from face to face, peering into the shadows for any slaves that might be eavesdropping. There were none.

Sungui sighed.

"I am aware of this," she said.

"Then speak not another word until it has been removed," said Lavanyia. Sungui stood transfixed by her imperious beauty. She longed to turn her back on them all and so reassert her dominance of the gathering. Yet she only stared at Lavanyia and blinked.

"Now is not the time," she said.

Durangshara chuckled, his loose jowls quivering. "Shall we wait until His Holiness hears of this and annihilates us one by one?"

Mahaavar laid his hand upon Sungui's shoulder. His touch was firm yet gentle, as his lovemaking had been earlier. "A spy among us?" Mahaavar asked. "Let me kill him, Sungui. To prove my loyalty."

Sungui ignored the tightening of her stomach, the quickening of her pulse. She did not want this. Not tonight. She had hoped this ceremony would turn the Ear to her own purposes. Yet she knew the danger of such a gamble. The Almighty saw all there was to see in his realm, and the only way to avoid his gaze was to hide in the lowest of places, nooks and crannies that were beneath his attention. Hence the Slave Bath, where her listeners stood at odds in the fading steam.

Her eyes narrowed as she leaned toward Lavanyia. An unspoken challenge beamed in the eyes of the lioness. Lavanyia would take control of this revolution before it ever grew to fruition, if only she could recall the truth as well as Sungui. Yet Lavanyia could not. How she must envy Sungui's retention of identity while all those around her continued to Diminish. Perhaps Lavanyia even suspected that it was Sungui's double aspect which made her less susceptible to the Almighty's dominance. The lioness could not control the listeners, so she sought instead to control the speaker.

The moment of challenge seemed endless. Sungui might have turned away, but she did not. Her upper lip curled. A ripple ran across her body beneath the bright vestment. A familiar passion rose from her groin into her stomach, nearly burst from her throat. Her jaw-line shifted, her nose grew hawkish, her shoulders expanded, and the muscles of her arms, legs, and chest swelled. Manhood rose like a granite obelisk, rushing through flesh like angry blood, and she grew somewhat taller. At the same time she drew from the left sleeve of her robe a dagger of black metal, hilt crusted with rubies, blade etched with dread sigils.

Lavanyia did not flinch at the appearance of the weapon.

Sungui's female aspect was entirely gone. He stood utterly male and defiant amid the circle now. The iron blade glinted like the torch flames dancing in Lavanyia's eyes.

Mahaavar's hand dropped from Sungui's shoulder; he backed away from his transformed lover. Always discomfited by this shift. So locked into the role written for him by the Almighty that he did not even recognize the single nature of one who wore a double aspect. Mahaavar would not kiss, touch, or whisper any gentle words to the male Sungui, though perhaps secretly he fancied the blasphemous idea.

Lavanyia did not blink at all. There was no element of fear on

her splendid face. The maleness that had emerged so swiftly drew
Sungui toward the lioness with invisible chains. Suddenly Sungui
desired her, wished to conquer her stubborn femininity in the way
that men have always conquered women.

"Sungui," insisted Mahaavar. "Let me kill whoever—"

Mahaavar lost his words as the dagger's blade plunged into his
chest. It sank deep, and the hilt slammed against his skin with a
meaty slap. He staggered backward two steps, but did not crumble. His eyes fell to the ruby pommel protruding from his breast
like a piece of bizarre jewelry.

Sungui stepped forward, placing himself between the listeners
and the Ear.

"I had hoped to reach you." Sungui's male voice was deeper,
heavy with the weight of regret, laced with the poison of pity.
In his female aspect he would weep over Mahaavar. Yet now not
a single tear escaped his eye. His male aspect was used to
tragedy, remorse, and the spilling of blood. It thrived on such
sustenance.

Mahaavar's lips moved but he made no sound. Neither did he
fall to the wet stone floor of the bath chamber. He stood bleeding
and mouthing soundless pleas. Sungui avoided his eyes, looking
instead at the faces of Those Who Listen. Lavanyia did not smile
with her lips, but with her eyes. She gloated over Sungui's
remorse. She had driven Sungui to this moment, given him no
choice in how to handle Mahaavar's treachery. As soon as word of
their gathering reached Zyung from the lips of Mahaavar, they
would all be caught in the trap of the Almighty's awareness.
Hiding their fellowship from His Holiness then would no longer
be possible.

I probably could not have turned Mahaavar anyway.

The thought ran through Sungui's mind as if dropped there, a
cold stone rippling the waters of a still pond. His male aspect was

forever justifying the cruelty of its actions. This is how Men lived. He leaned close to Mahaavar, who stuttered and trembled. Mahaavar could not fall, nor could he move in any other way.

"I have aligned the metal of this blade with the Ninety Aspects of Higher Being," Sungui whispered. "Your position in this universe is now *fixed*, the last shred of freedom left to you by Zyung torn away ... until the stars shift themselves into new patterns."

Mahaavar's eyes grew large, terror bleeding from his wound along with dark blood.

"We could keep you this way for eons," Sungui said, "trapped between the edges of life and death."

Durangshara laughed, a metallic chortle. So very cruel, that one.

"Yet I pity you, Mahaavar," Sungui said. "Instead of this lingering punishment, we will accept you in the Ancient Way." Mahaavar's wet eyes closed. Sungui reached a hand to grab his throat and sang the tones of an ancient song.

The hand released the neck, and Mahaavar fell at last. His body clattered against the stones, no longer made of flesh and blood. The Ear was now a bone-pale statue, a perfect effigy of himself, dead of eye and limb. Sungui licked a finger and rubbed it along Mahaavar's petrified cheek. He brought it to his tongue and tasted the salt. Bitter and strong as any earthly salt.

Sungui grabbed the salt figure's wrist and broke off the entire hand with a snapping sound. He raised it to show his fellow High Seraphim that the consumption was ready. Each of them came forward, male and female, reaching down to snap off an arm, a foot, a thigh. The head was divided three ways into odd-shaped blocks of grainy salt. They broke the salted Mahaavar into a dozen white lumps, shoving each of them into their mouths, and chewed at the chalky substance.

Sungui frowned.

How have I lost them so soon?

"We are Diminished in his presence now for ten thousand years," said Lavanyia. "To live as a bright spark in the shadow of his divinity is far better than the darkness of annihilation. We must remain Diminished."

"You fear him," said Sungui. His voice was broken gravel. Anger gnawed at his heart.

"Of course we fear him," said Damodar. "We listen ... we remember ... but we are not fools. If you believe this invasion will weaken him, or enable your treason in any way, you are very much mistaken."

"Perhaps the fate of Mahaavar lies too heavy on your soul," offered Darisha.

The salty remains lingered on Sungui's tongue. "No!" he spat. "Let me show you more. Let me share another vision of our former greatness. You will see that *he* is no greater than any of us. And all of us together—"

"Would stand no chance," said Durangshara. His beefy hands rose in a dismissive gesture. "His will made us what we are. His will can unmake us. All talk of rebellion must be forgotten, scoured from our mind as the remains of Mahaavar shall be washed from this floor."

"They why did you come here?" Sungui faced the fat one, defying his arrogance with a puffed chest. "Why listen to me at all?"

Silence ruled the chamber. The crackling of flames in the sconces.

It was Myrinhama the Golden who finally answered. Her voice was honey and sunlight.

"We listen because we must remember," she said, "as an adult remembers the joys of childhood ... the time of innocence when the boundaries of reality did not yet exist. We listen to honor what we once were, and what we are now. Yet the grown woman does not seek to become a girl-child again. Children have no power, and they are meant to grow . . . to *become*. There is no going back, Sungui."

How could he make them see past this conditioning? This was the earth working its magic on them. Zyung's order took its power from the cycles of nature. Birth, Death, and Rebirth. These cycles did not apply to the Old Breed. They never had. Until Zyung had chained their kind to this world and so made them part of it.

The others nodded at the perceived wisdom of Myrinhama's words.

"You are all fools," Sungui said.

Durangshara chuckled. "There is only one fool among us here. We indulge you, Sungui. Yet consider what we have said today. You cannot hide your true self from His Holiness forever. Before he discovers your ambition, we will ourselves send you to salt."

Sungui picked up the black dagger, stained with the pale residue of Mahaavar. He whirled to face the fat Seraphim once again, thrusting his chin forward.

"There is no threat within you," Sungui growled.

Durangshara leaned back only a hair's breadth. His glinting eyes followed the salty blade.

Lavanyia spoke again, her voice calm as night. "Durangshara means only that you must forget this treason, Sungui. You will not find peace until you do so."

Sungui sheathed the dagger in the sleeve of his robe. The eyes of Those Who Listen followed him as he walked toward the arched exit.

They listened, yes. But they did not hear.

He would have offered some final word of defiance, but the chance was stolen from him.

The gray brick walls began to tremble. A rain of dust and pebbles fell from the ceiling, and the waters of the cooled bath grew confused with ripples and splashing. A torch fell from its sconce and extinguished itself in the bathwater.

Above the trembling of rock and soil and water, a tremendous note rang clear and powerful. The peal of the Great Horn, the voice of Zyung himself, giving at last the signal that was fifty years in coming. For a generation now, sons of the empire had labored to fulfill their fathers' dreams of the coming conquest. The Holy Armada had been expanded and the ranks of the Almighty's armies had swollen. The preparations for this westward expansion had captured the attention of the Inner and Outer Provinces for as long as any living man could remember.

Now it had come, on this night of all nights. The night of Mahaavar's consumption.

The Almighty's horn cast its thunderous knell across the Divine Province, and its din would roll on the evening currents into the lands beyond, igniting the cities where his flame-eyed visage loomed over Kings and Caliphs alike.

The time had come.

The Great Horn called them all to war.

The Invasion of the West was begun.

With a fleeting glance at the resigned listeners, Sungui ran from the chamber, leaping the prostrate forms of wailing slaves. Rising from the catacombs, he entered a courtyard and bounded up the heart-spiral of a tower, toward a series of arched stone bridges. This high route would bring him quickly to the dread-nought landing bay.

Again his designs Diminish me.

There is no escape from it.

No time to convince Those Who Listen that Lavanyia is wrong.

No time for treason.

Today there was only time to serve Zyung.

The Holy Armada would sail the wind.

2

The Shaper

What is time?

A series of curtains rippling and waving, each one a doorway into past or future. There are many futures. Often I reach for the nearest curtain and pull aside its gossamer fabric, gazing into one of these possible futures. Yet there are so many curtains exactly like this one, shrouds against futures that might be, or will be, or should never be.

At times I fail to pierce the veil of the future, and then I can only stand at the curtain and listen to the echoes of what has not yet come to pass.

What is space?

An infinite void sparkling with the energies of creation. An ocean of glimmering stardust spread across the gulf, taking on shape and form, spilling into comets and spheres and nameless singularities. Endless patterns, spinning through infinity. There are many worlds, worlds within worlds, and yet there is only the one in which I sit and contemplate the angles of possibility. This is the world I chose long ago to inhabit, revere, and sculpt into something greater.

This is my world.

Men call me the Shaper.

Yet there is another world on the other side of this one. In fact, the two worlds are one and the same, two halves of a whole. Yet in many ways they could not be more different. Until yesterday the Kings of Men and Giants did not know that *another* Shaper exists. I have also shown them the true shape of their world . . . a sphere . . . and given them a vision of what is to come. Yet I fear that they will not be able to withstand it.

The Old Breed came into this world when it was young. Our home was the vastness between the stars. Even I cannot remember what drove us from the infinite into the bosom of this tiny mote. We fell as thundering tempests, raging winds, and flaming meteors into the primal seas. We crafted continents and raised up the basest of organisms, birthing sentient races to worship our greatness. We toyed with these early species, casting them into terrible wars, smiling at the grim temples they erected in our honor, laughing at the mortal doom which inevitably came. The curse of Blood and Fire and Suffering. It fascinated us, this mortal delicacy, this predilection for pain and death. Sometimes we slaughtered entire empires and rebuilt them, as a child plays with stones. We reigned over an Age of Chaos.

We strode across the world as its dark Emperors, weaving histories and legends, watching them fade in the mists of time, and we grew bored. Some of us returned to the vastness of the starry gulfs, while others Diminished into the world itself. We became seas, mountain ranges, glaciers, volcanoes, and ceaseless winds. Others fell lower, taking on the forms of those we had created for our own amusement; we exploited our status as monarchs and holy beings among the young races. Tired of playing with the world and its peoples as separate entities, we *became* them.

And we began to forget ourselves.

Now we forged nations and empires from inside the menagerie

we had built. We walked in the bodies of those who came before Men, and each time the red plague of war came and struck us low. We warred among ourselves to prove whose creations were superior. We warred out of boredom and fickle emotions. We lost ourselves in the pain and pleasure of a small existence. Now we were tied to this tiny world, and so we destroyed and rebuilt it again and again.

Now we had learned too much of mortal existence. It had changed us as surely as we had manipulated it throughout the ancient epochs. We began to forget one another, to find our own solitary places to sit and dream away eternity. But not all of us slept.

In the wake of a great slaughter, the one I call my brother came to me. We were no more true brothers than we were true Men, yet there is no other word to express our common origins. He called together the last of the Old Breed who lingered among the mortal realms. A thousand of us gathered like clouds above the plain of blood and bones where the ravens feasted.

The time has come, said my brother. Soon he would take the name of Zyung. *The Earthborn have arisen, and they are not of our making. The time of chaos and destruction must end. Now it is plain to me what must be done: This world must be tamed so the Earthborn might prosper. A lasting order must be built. An ultimate domain that cannot fall, a Living Empire that will bring an end to strife and warfare. On this day I will begin shaping this world into an eternal paradise. Who will join me in the pursuit of this great dream?*

These are only my memories.

They sometimes fade like night vapors in the light of dawn.

It might have happened differently.

Most of my brothers and sisters chose to serve Zyung. His Living Empire grew across the great continent. He pruned the tribes of Men as a gardener prunes a vine. His shadows cast by his bright light fell across realm after realm. Men called him their God; they conquered and slaughtered in his name.

As the Living Empire grew, I witnessed the death of free will, the elimination of curiosity, the stamping out of higher thought among the Earthborn. Zyung's everlasting peace could only be gained by enduring a long age of death and domination. I saw proud peoples become little more than slaves, choosing servitude over annihilation. Always the same choice he offered them, and always the dead outnumbered the living.

One day there would be no more death, no more conflict. There would be only Zyung, who would be the world itself, and all those within the world would be Zyung as well.

So I faced my brother and denied him. A handful of the Old Breed joined me in this. Some were eager to shirk the chains of obedience, while others dreamed of forging their own empires as they had done in past ages. There were not many of us, and so we could not stand long against the growing power of Zyung. We built a fleet of ships and gathered a host of Earthborn from the last of the free nations. We led our people across the Cryptic Sea and found a lesser continent on the other side of the world. The tribes we had saved were free to roam its interior and build their own kingdoms.

Yet our new home was haunted by the great Serpents of old. So I raised up the race of Giants from the stones of the earth and set them to slaying the Old Wyrms. Once this was done, our transplanted tribes flourished, eventually giving birth to five great city-states. I will not describe the long ages of each kingdom's birth and evolution, yet all the while Zyung's empire grew and grew across the trackless ocean.

A thousand years ago Zyung conquered the last of the lands on the far side of the world. The ancestral lands of the peoples known as Uurzians, Yaskathans, Mumbazans, Sharrians, and Khyreins were now gone, replaced by the homogeneity of the Living Empire. Yet the descendants of these five noble tribes have long forgotten their true origins. To them, the Land of the Five Cities is the entirety of the world itself.

For such a long time I labored to keep them ignorant of the truth.

Now that truth can no longer be denied.

In his quest to build a paradise that encompasses the earth itself, Zyung is coming.

Now the Kings of this land are united at last. Now they must face the Living Empire and I must face my brother. I do fear the greatness of his power. Yet I knew that one day this conflict would fall upon me. For a time I gave up on saving the Land of the Five Cities from Zyung's dominion. For so very long I had tried and failed to rid mankind of its lust for war. I nearly lost the hope of ever doing so.

Man was doomed to struggle, bleed, and die. There was no hope of changing his essential nature, which was that of a warrior, a direct manifestation of his predatory instinct. I had grown weary of trying to change the Earthborn.

It was the heart of a single brave girl who gave me the strength to try again.

Sharadza.

I clutch at my stray thoughts now and force them back toward Zyung.

I love her.

Now is not the time for such illusions.

The gray-green ocean simmers beneath a scattering of stars. A bank of stormclouds hides the sinking sun, harbinger of the darkness to come. War is a storm that clouds the affairs of Men as well as those who are more than Men. There will be great suffering.

I hover, legs folded, above a crag overlooking the Golden Sea.

The evening winds whip at my robes and make the blue flame upon my chest flicker. The black city of Khyrei smokes with ten thousand feast-fires behind me. Its people celebrate their liberation at the hands of Tong the Avenger, a slave who became a revolutionary. As their new monarch, Tong sits restless upon his throne. He must rebuild a fractured kingdom into something better and stronger, a nation freed from the ancient grip of Ianthe the Claw.

Ianthe had crossed the world with me long ago, fleeing Zyung's power. I was a fool for her charms, which blinded me to her wicked nature. In many ways, she was far worse than Zyung, yet I had set her loose upon the new continent to stoke the fires of the Earthborn's worst qualities. She became a conqueror, a parasite, a tyrant. To rid the world of her was as difficult as changing the essence of the Earthborn. Yet now her dark kingdom has at last been stolen away from her, and she has left it behind.

I see it now, clear as the rising moon: Ianthe has returned to Zyung, taking Gammir with her. They will feed him many secrets about my half of the world. Ianthe, who built kingdoms and destroyed them on a whim; who revels in the blood of innocents; whose pattern was blended with that of the predator. And Gammir, who was once perhaps her equal, but now is only her slave. Yet both of them will be little more than slaves in Zyung's world. There is no room for anything else there.

In the Khyrein harbor the double fleet prepares for a morning launch. I might weep for the fools who are doomed to die beneath those sails, but I do not have the luxury. The regal swanships of Mumbaza sit alongside the Yaskathan triremes, an impressive assembly of no less than seven hundred warships. Tong has pledged another hundred Khyrein reavers, newly liberated and pledged into his service. This brings the total close to one thousand vessels.

The Southern Kings think their combined fleets invincible. They are good men, but they are fools. Even after I split the veil of the future and showed them the Hordes of Zyung only days from landfall, they still deny the truth of their weakness.

When those ships sail in the morning, each man on board will be sailing to his death.

One can bring a Council of Kings together, yet still fail to make them listen.

So I sit above the darkening sea, striving to peer deeper into the corridor of the future. Which veil hides the truth from me? I must offer these brave Kings something more before they sail off to die. For the first time, I wonder exactly how much I have Diminished, living among the Earthborn for so long. Perhaps that single glance of what is to come, the golden cloud vision that I offered them, is all that I am capable of giving. Still I must try.

The moon rises, split in half by the earth's shadow, and no longer can I see the future clearly. The veils are too thick. Too numerous. This has always been difficult, for the future is nebulous and unformed. Yet now it becomes impossible.

Perhaps it is Zyung himself who obscures my vision. Surely he has not forgotten me, or the exodus which I made possible so long ago.

In the war room of Khyrei's black palace, near to the ruins of Ianthe's tower, the Kings and their advisors had gathered before sunset. They had all seen the golden cloud on the previous day, the vision of overwhelming forces that had sent even resilient Tyro into a delirious fever. Now they had gathered again, this time to decide a course of action.

How I had hoped they would listen to me.

Yet they are Kings, used to getting their own way.

Prideful Kings, some of them, who would rather face death directly than run from it.

Undutu of Mumbaza, barely nineteen years old, spoke the loudest. This was no surprise to me. "We have assembled the greatest fleet in history," said the young King. "The only thing that has changed is our enemy." His eyes, darker than his ebony skin, flashed with boyish bravado. The other Kings saw this naïve ignorance as nothing less than raw courage.

"Well spoken," said Tyro, King of Uurz, before I could correct the Mumbazan. "The war we intended to fight against Khyrei shall now be against Zyung. If the wizard's vision is true—"

"You know it is true," Sharadza interrupted him. I avoided looking at her emerald eyes. It would not do to be seen fawning over the former Queen of Yaskatha while her husband sat at the same table. "The great horde approaches. You saw it in Iardu's vision."

D'zan, King of Yaskatha, rubbed his unshaven chin. A platinum crown sat heavy upon his brow. He knew my powers well; he had no cause to doubt the vision. "Iardu," he said, "you showed us a vast armada that sails upon the air, and in numbers far greater than even our combined forces. Yet what can you tell us of this God-King's weakness? How may we best face these invaders?"

The faces of the Kings fell upon me. Brave Tong, whose reign had begun only three short days ago, relied on a quick-witted translator to speak with these royal visitors. Vireon, King of Udurum, sat silent as stone, his great arms folded, a quiet storm brewing in his eyes. He wore now the crown of Angrid, a circlet of heavy iron set with a trio of sapphires; it made him King of All Giants. Tyro was the ambitious Emperor of Uurz, his golden breastplate gleaming bright with emeralds. There was no trace of his earlier wound, or the mad fever that my potions had dispelled. I had worked to assemble the Kings here. Now I must make them listen to me.

"If Zyung the God-King has a weakness," I said, "it can only be found in his obsession with bringing order and peace to this world. A legion of sorcerers works at his command, supporting the great empire that took him millennia to build." I sighed and rose to pace about the council chamber. The walls of black basalt were hung with tapestries of Khyrei's bloody history. "You rulers of six kingdoms must band together as never before. You must fight as one, or there can be no hope for victory."

"You tell us what we already know, Shaper," said Undutu. His white smile beamed at me, yet his words carried no trace of mirth. "This man is a wizard, not a warrior," he said to his fellow Kings. "The fighting of war should be left to soldiers, generals, and Kings."

"How can we fight such sorcery?" D'zan asked. "Our ships sail on water while *they* own the sky!"

Sharadza looked at me. Her face was lovely in the soft light of a dozen lamps.

Tell them our plan, she said without speaking. I nodded.

"Only a sorcerer can defeat a sorcerer," I said. "This old adage is true. Therefore I have asked Khama the Feathered Serpent and Sharadza Vodsdaughter to accompany me on an errand of utmost urgency. We will find the Dreaming Ones, the sorcerers who have lain hidden for ages throughout our world, and convince them to join us against Zyung. I know not how many will pledge to our cause. Yet we three alone cannot stand against Zyung's ranks of High Seraphim."

"You're leaving us?" asked D'zan. "On the eve of this great invasion?"

Sharadza turned to the man she had married and left. I wondered if she still loved him.

"We have little time, but there is no other choice," she said. "We will try to return before the invasion force makes land. Until then you must prepare your troops for what is to come."

"Sit here and wait for death?" Undutu rose from his chair, a fist wrapped about the hilt of his cutlass. "No! This is not the way Men protect their homes. We must sail to meet this Zyung. In three days our ships can make the Jade Isles. There we can form a vanguard against these invaders."

"Would you sail into a hopeless battle?" asked Vireon, speaking for the first time. All eyes turned to the man-sized Giant-King. "What hope have you of bringing down this aerial fleet? My sister speaks truly: We must stay and fortify. To meet Zyung's armada at the Jade Isles would be folly."

"Listen to the Giant-King," I encouraged them. "Let the battle be fought here, at the edge of our continent, far from your great cities. Khyrei itself is already battle-scarred. Tong has only a fraction of its former fleet to offer, but here he has the aid of the fierce Sydathians. You must fight this battle on land, not on sea."

Undutu's eyes narrowed. He turned to Khama, who looked as though he might be the Mumbazan King's grandfather. Perhaps he was. Khama has always kept his own secrets.

"There is only one wizard whose words I trust," said Undutu. "Khama, what say you?"

Khama met my own gaze with a look of sorrow. He had avoided sending Mumbaza to war for centuries, yet that time of peace was at an end. I knew he loved the young King as a man loves his own son. He knew as well as I that Undutu sought the glory of battle to prove his manhood. I wondered, not for the first time, at the wisdom of letting warriors be made into Kings. Khama lifted a goblet and drank deep of the red vintage of Tong's hospitality.

"I will follow the will of my King," said Khama. "The time of long peace is done. This saddens me. Yet the quickest route through the maze of war is a straight line. If you wish to face your enemies, Majesty, then I will accompany and aid you as always. Even unto death."

My patience had reached its end. I slammed my palm against the table, displacing several cups of wine. My throat ached for a drink of the heady stuff, but I had foresworn it. Now was not the time for drunken self-pity. Now was the time to speak sense to those who chose not to listen.

Undutu faced D'zan, his fellow southern King. Their fleets had circumnavigated the continent in anticipation of a great bloodshed at Khyrei, yet it was not to be. Despite a few isolated sea battles, their bloodlust had not been quenched.

"Do you remember the words of our treaty, D'zan?" asked Undutu.

D'zan nodded, refilling his own goblet. "If Mumbaza sails for the Jade Isles . . . " – he paused to quaff the wine – "then Yaskatha sails with her." His green eyes turned toward me, then to Sharadza. "Honor demands it," he explained. His voice was weary.

Tyro saw his moment. "So be it," he declared. "The double fleet will meet the invaders at Ongthaia while the armies of Uurz, Udurum, and Khyrei fortify the coast. Do I speak for you in this matter, Vireon?"

The Giant-King nodded. Both monarchs of the north turned their faces to Tong, whose translator strove to keep up with the conversation. After a moment Tong's pale face broke into a smile. He spoke in his native Khyrein, his message delivered by the translator: "My true friends, our nations will stand together against this Conqueror from the world's far side. In the red fury to come, let our peoples forge a friendship that will outlast the terrors of war. Although our forces are in disarray and will take some time to assemble, Khyrei stands with Uurz and Udurum."

"No!" The word burst out of me. I looked from kingly face to face. I felt like a raving old man in the midst of foolhardy youths. "If you do this, if you split your forces, your fleets will be crushed.

Three kingdoms will be conquered before Zyung ever sets foot on your soil. Are you prepared for this?"

"Then give us a weapon, Shaper!" demanded Undutu. "Your power is great! Make us mighty. Is there nothing you can do to help us besides speak of doom and death? Give us an army of demons to fight for us. Give us tactical advice that we can use if nothing else. Will you help us resist this horde, or run off and leave us to our fate?"

I looked to Khama, whose face was apologetic.

"The Dreadnoughts of Zyung will not break easily," I said. "They are creations of sorcery. Demons will only betray mortal Men, King Undutu. I will not unleash a plague of them on this land that is already beset with so many horrors. I will ... attempt ... to view the future again. To see something that might aid you in this foolish gambit."

"The rage of my winds might tear these dreadnoughts from the sky," said Khama. "Drown them in the sea."

I stared out the chamber window at the double fleet arrayed in and around the Khyrein bay. So many lives. So many deaths.

"Perhaps," I admitted.

Undutu smiled. "We have the Feathered Serpent with us," he boasted. "All is not lost."

Tyro drained his goblet. "A warrior fears not death," he said. The old saying that led generations of Men into giving up their lives for rash causes: It was at the same time a foolish yet wise statement. Death was not to be feared, but neither was it to be sought after in the name of something as useless as *honor*. If only the Earthborn Kings could see this, it might have ended differently at the council.

A servant bustled about the table refilling the wine cups.

"I will provide your fleets with nine black hawks," I told them. "Bring me nine of your most clever soldiers. They will be your eyes upon the seas." By this they knew I would reshape the soldiers into the forms of hawks for tactical advantage.

"Come with us, Iardu," said D'zan. "With your power and Khama's at our side, we will give the God-King pause. Perhaps we can even defeat him."

I shook my head. The Flame of Intellect flared indigo below my beard. "You listen but you do not hear. Our only chance of resisting this invasion lies in gathering this land's sorcerers to oppose the thousand who serve Zyung. This is what I must do, if there is to be any hope of survival."

Undutu turned his head and rolled his eyes. Too young to know truth when he heard it. Eager for the spilling of blood and the seductive songs of death.

The servant refilled the Mumbazan King's cup.

"I am going with Iardu," said Sharadza. "We will wake the Dreaming Ones." My heart raced when she said my name.

"We leave at first light," I said.

"As will our fleets," said Undutu.

I shook my head. There was no reaching sense with a young King who wished more than anything to be a warrior. I did not understand Khama's willingness to indulge the boy's death wish. Yet Khama was of the Old Breed, and we had built this world apart from Zyung, along with those others who came across so long ago. I must respect his decision.

The servant stood now at Tong's elbow. From the waist of his robe a dagger of green jade appeared. He thrust it at Tong's breast. Tong's powerful legs propelled him backward, knocking over his chair and sending him to the floor. The dagger failed to find its mark.

The translator yelled for a guard while the assassin leaped upon the fallen Tong. I raised a hand to still the would-be slayer. Yet before my spell was cast a white wolf sprang across the table and collided with the knife-wielder. Sharadza. She shredded the man's wrist with ivory fangs, keeping him on the floor with the sheer weight of her wolfish form. The dagger fell from useless fingers. Tong righted himself as guards rushed into the chamber, and Tyro picked up the jade dagger.

"A Deathbringer," muttered Tyro, studying the stone blade and the purple hue of its poison. "I have not seen such a dagger since Olthacus the Stone was killed by Khyrein assassins behind the walls of Uurz."

Tong did not chastise or interrogate his attacker in the presence of his fellow Kings. Guards dragged the man kicking and screaming from the room. Only those who spoke his language heard his words: "Death to the False King! The Claw shall return! Death to Tong!"

The translator righted Tong's chair and the King of New Khyrei resumed his place at the table. He spoke again through the interpreter: "It seems that not all the Royal Houses approve of a Khyrei free of slavery," he said. "This is a minor problem that we are looking to solve soon. Until then, Ianthe's cult of assassins has found some new master."

"A pity the Deathbringers do not serve their King with such fervor," said D'zan. "I do not envy you, Tong. There are no assassins lurking in the palace at Yaskatha."

Tong nodded his understanding. "The traditions of Khyrei are long and deeply held," he said. "Not all of them will change so quickly." Sharadza had taken on her womanly form again, and Tong took her hands in his own. "Thank you, Great Lady," he said.

Sharadza bowed low before him, though she did not need to do so. There was pride and something far more dangerous surging in my heart. Vod's daughter was everything I had hoped she would become, and so much more.

Thus the council had ended, with a decision to divide our forces and an attempted regicide. There would be more such attempts before Tong managed to quell the rebellious nature of every last Royal House. A revolution does not end in a single day. Like a war, or a disease, it can linger and cause vexation even in the midst of triumph.

Now I sit overlooking the beach, trying to catch another glimpse of the future. I have only until the sun rises and the ships of the southern kingdoms sail off to meet their doom. If only I can offer them something more, one more piece of vital information or a morsel of victory-to-come. Then I might leave them to their fates with a tad less guilt weighing upon my shoulders.

Briefly I had considered going with Khama, waging war upon Zyung at the Jade Isles. Yet in my heart I know that this is a fool's path. Zyung's armada will not be stopped by any mortal fleet. The only possible effect of this advance confrontation is to weaken the invasion force before it makes landfall. And perhaps it will buy me a bit more time to gather a few sorcerers willing to stand against Zyung's legion of High Seraphim; something which may not even be possible. For these merest advantages the Kings will sacrifice a thousand warships and countless lives.

The future waxes cloudy and obscure before me.

Rain sweeps off the sea to drench my robe and hair. Still I hover above the breakers, peering into the murky depths of time.

I see the double fleet, aligned in a tight arc about the Jade Isles. I see fires dropping from above and soaring from below. I hear the screams of dying men and beasts.

I see the decimation of the fleets, the burning timbers and sails, the broken men impaled on foreign lances, drowning in red waters ablaze. The face of Zyung peers back at me with eyes of solar fire.

One last thing I see before I turn from this futile task: A pile of blackened ruins that used to be a city. By the coastal valley and its sluggish river I recognize it as Shar Dni. Where the remnants of the dead city have lain for thirty years, there gathers a mass of shadows, ancient and hungry. Long have they slumbered beneath the blood-spotted stones, after feasting on the blood and souls of innocents during the city's doom.

Now I see a pale citadel rise from those ruins, a towering edifice of shattered stone and a mountain of ground bones. It grows from the scattered debris that used to be temples, streets, the husk of a charred palace. There at the scene of Khyrei's greatest crime, Zyung will create his beachhead. About this citadel of bone, his legions of Manslayers and Seraphim will gather and spread across the land like locusts. The ruins of Shar Dni will be the seat of the God-King's power when he arrives. The carven image of his imperious face dominates the upper half of the structure, and the smokes of a hundred thousand flames fill the valley.

The eyes of Zyung's stone-wrought visage flare bright enough to blind me.

I see nothing else.

Sharadza finds me then, a white seabird flapping to perch upon my shoulder.

Sunrise comes soon, she says in the language of birds. *We must go.*

Yes, we must go and rouse those of the Dreaming Ones who will stand with us. If any will do so. Sorcerers cannot easily be swayed. But first I must share what little I have seen.

"Go and find Vireon," I tell her. "No doubt he sleeps among the tents of his warriors, if he sleeps at all. Tell him this war will begin at the ruins of Shar Dni. Tell him to move his armies north along the coast. The Sharrian valley is the key. We will perform our task and meet him there as soon as we can."

She flies off to deliver the message, conscious of its deadly significance.

Perhaps I will tell her that I love her before Zyung puts an end to us.

Who knows what we will be after he has reforged us in the fires of his will?

We might become his slaves, or worse. He might bless us with annihilation.

Even we, the Masters of Shapes and Patterns, we who cannot truly die, might be robbed of our very existence. His is the power to make it possible.

I should tell her before it is too late.

Why can I not say the words?

3

The Axe

For three days the armies of Men and Giants marched north along the Golden Sea coast, and for three days rain fell from the leaden sky.

In a double line they marched, like twin Serpents winding along cliff tops that grew ever higher as they left the drowned marshlands. The head of the first Serpent was Vireon Vodson. As tall as any of his Giant cousins, he stalked through the mud. The purple cloak of Udurum flapped at his shoulders, and the crown of iron and sapphire gleamed rain-slick on his head. Behind the rippling hammer-and-fist banner paced an entire legion of blue-skinned Udvorg Giants armed with spears, axes, swords, and maces of northern steel. A hundred and twenty pale-skinned Giants of Uduria marched at the center of the great Udvorg line. In their wake trudged the twenty-nine Uduri who used to be their wives and lovers.

Dahrima the Axe walked in the midst of the sullen spear-maidens, glad today of the distance between herself and her King.

Behind the Giants came the Men of Udurum, eight legions strong, even after their losses in the Khyrein swamps. The first of these legions was cavalry, hardy northmen armored in plates of blackened bronze with spears of Udurum steel bright as silver in their fists. Greatswords hung from their waists or upon their broad backs. They rode tall warhorses of sable, gray, or piebald coats. Behind the riders marched Udurum's infantry, twenty thousand soldiers, spearmen, and archers. At their center rolled supply wagons stuffed with barrels of freshwater, corn, salted pork, dried fruits, and Khyrein foodstuffs for which they had no name – all gifts of the black city's new King.

The head of the second Serpent, which moved alongside the first, was Tyro, Emperor of Uurz, also called the Sword King. He rode a trotting black charger that kept him beside the marching Giant-King. Tyro's crown was a masterwork of gold and emeralds, his gilded breastplate bearing the sun-sigil of Uurz. On his banner a similar sun cast yellow rays across a field of green, and not even the pelting storms could dim the brightness of that standard. Tyro's broadsword hung between his broad shoulders, and his cloak was a perfect replica of his royal banner.

Nineteen legions of Uurzian soldiers marched behind the Sword King. The foremost and rearmost legions were comprised of cavalrymen similar to the Men of Udurum in all but colors. Whereas Vireon's train was black and purple, Tyro's was green and gold. Tyro commanded more than twice the number of archers, horsemen, swordsmen, and lancers as the Giant-King. Nearly sixty thousand warriors had followed Tyro from the City of Sacred Waters; yet the Sword King had none of the Giantkind in his service. Each one of Vireon's Giants, or Giantesses, was worth two companies of human soldiers, if not more. Therefore, Vireon's forces were accounted greater and far deadlier than Tyro's, despite the discrepancy in raw numbers.

Dahrima marched in silence, gazing often across the storm-wracked sea on her right, or into the tangled forest of the High

Realms on her left. Now and then she wandered close to the edge of the sea cliff and felt the absurd urge to leap from it into the turbulent waters. Already she was drenched, as was every Man and Giant marching northward; the rain had found its way beneath her bronze cuirass and settled into the fibers of her cloak and tunic. It would have settled into her skin and softened it as well if she were not an Uduri with skin hard as stone.

She felt pity for the Men of the legions when she looked upon their miserable faces. They did not have the hearty constitution of Giants and could not ignore the damp, the chill, and the discomfort of such weather. The blue-skinned Udvorg were used to bitter ice and terrible cold; for them these southern storms were hardly noticeable. Each evening at the setting of camp, and all through the sodden nights that followed, Men gathered about their tent-fires, shivering and huddling together for warmth like hairless wolf-pups. Meanwhile, the Udvorg and Uduru gathered around barrels of cold Khyrein ale, laughing at the thunder and the sea winds that swept the coastline.

As for the Uduri, the Giantesses gathered about Dahrima as if she were their captain, although no such rank existed among them. They were pledged to serve Vireon and the City of Men and Giants. They had given their males the blessing of absolution years ago, urging them to go north to the Icelands and mate with the blue-skins' fertile women in order to save the dwindling Uduru race. The Uduri had remained in Uduria and taken a vow of service to the King, although a handful of them had wandered into the wilderness and disappeared instead.

They were barren women, yet potent warriors. The Ninety-Nine Uduri found satisfaction not in the roles of mothers and wives, but as elite guardians of Vireon's house. When Vireon had led his forces south to make war on Ianthe the Claw, forty Uduri had remained to watch the walls of Udurum. Twenty-nine had

recently met honorable deaths, either while protecting the King
and his family before the southward march, or while battling the
Swamp God west of Khyrei. Ninety Uduru had died in that
battle, along with four hundred Udvorg and their King Angrid.
Vireon now ruled over all Giants, both pale- and blue-skinned.
The leviathan of the marshland had also claimed the lives of many
brave Men. Dahrima had gained a new respect for the warriors of
Uurz and Udurum after seeing their valor in the grip of such a
colossal horror.

On the evening of the third day's march the signal came back
through the line. The two armies would halt here for the night,
perched between raging sea and highland forest. The Uduri gathered around Dahrima, as they had done on the two previous
nights. She led them toward the cliff's edge where the mud was
less deep and the ground was mainly crags of mottled stone. She
leaned her great axe and longspear against an outcropping of granite and sat down with her back against the rock. Her spearsisters
did likewise. The moon was lost behind stormclouds and the rain
poured as steadily as ever. She heard the crashing of waves against
the strand far below the precipice. She studied the tangle of black-
barked trees standing a half-league inland, wondering what
mysteries lay in their green shadows.

The Men passed tents, bedrolls, and provisions forward along
the lines and their camp slowly took shape. The first cookfires
were kindled beneath canvas tarps. Giants did not bother with
such formalities. When they did erect tents, they simply picked
the nearest spot of level ground and made it their home for the
night. Some of the Udvorg wandered toward the forest to hunt
nocturnal game, while others cracked open ale barrels or wrestled
for the amusement of their fellows.

Dahrima watched the group of Uduru mingling with the blue-
skins. She recognized Boroldun the Bear-Fang, Magron Irontooth,

and Kol the Stumbler. Dressed in the crude furs and fanged neck-laces of the Icelands, they were practically Udvorg now. Only their pale skins and dark eyes separated them from the blue-skins. Curiously, she had noticed a lightness creeping into the skins of the Udvorg for weeks now. The longer they stayed out of their frozen realm the paler their blue hides were becoming. She imag-ined that their crimson eyes were dulling as well. Perhaps if they stayed out of the ice and snow long enough, the Udvorg would lose their pigmentation and become indistinguishable from their Uduru cousins. Did that mean the hundreds of Uduru who remained in the Icelands were slowly turning blue of skin and red of eye? These colors could be merely signs that Giants adapted well to any environment.

"You speak little these days," said Chygara the Windcaller. She sat down against the same stone Dahrima had chosen. The other Uduri sat or lay at rest about them, some already sleeping, others watching the angry sea thunder at the base of the bluff. Merelda the Flamesinger walked off to meet with an Uduru that Dahrima recognized as Ugroff Elkslayer. He had been Merelda's mate years ago, before she sent him north to spawn children with blue-skinned Uduri. Most of the spearmaidens had never taken husbands, only a series of lovers. Yet Merelda had pledged her love to Ugroff when they were young. Perhaps Ugroff had only joined this southern crusade for the chance to see his first wife again. Dahrima wondered if his second wife longed for him in the king-dom of snows.

"I have little to say," Dahrima told Chygara.

Chygara's long braids were corn-yellow like Dahrima's, and she wore bands of silver about them. A thin scar upon the Windcaller's left cheek marred her fine face. She leaned her shoul-der against the pole of her spear, which she had planted in the dirt between her knees.

"We no longer march at the King's side," said Chygara.

Dahrima shrugged. "My spearsisters are free to march where they will."

Chygara smiled. One of her upper incisors was missing, the result of some ancient brawl. "Before we reached the black city you would not leave Vireon's presence," she said. "Now you keep yourself apart from him. Your sisters wonder why this should be."

"My sisters should mind their own fates," said Dahrima. Here it was then. She had wondered how long it would be until one of them brought up their repositioning in the ranks.

Chygara stared at her. Other faces glanced her way as well: Atha Spearhawk, Gorinna the Grin, Vantha the Tigress, Shaigra the Shieldsplitter. Why must they pry into her private thoughts? She was not their leader, not by any law. They followed her of their own free will, as she followed the Giant-King. Their vows were to serve Vireon, not Dahrima. She owed them no answers. Let them go forward and march at Vireon's heels like a pack of hounds if they wished to do so.

Alisk the Raven offered Dahrima a tankard of dark ale, her broad hand cupped over its top to keep out the rain. Dahrima took it, drank half its contents, and wiped her lips with the back of her hand.

"Five nights now," said Alisk, "the blue witch shares Vireon's tent." She chewed at a piece of dried beef.

"What of it?" asked Dahrima. "Why tell me what my own eyes can see?"

Chygara and Alisk exchanged a glance. Their eyes flashed in the rain. The smells of horse manure, Mansweat, and saltwater floated on the wind. Beneath it all Dahrima sensed the musky reek of the Udvorg. They stank less now after three days of rain had washed their cloaks and tunics of matted fur, but still she could not get her nostrils free of their scent. There were so many of them.

"Varda of the Keen Eyes has taken your place," said Chygara. "This is the cause of your sorrow."

Dahrima shook her head, slinging rain from her braids. She drained the rest of the tankard. "Foolish girls," she muttered. "You are too long without coupling so you invent stories and gossip."

"If this is not true," said Alisk, "then why do we march among these smelly blue-skins instead of at the King's side?"

"March where you will!" Dahrima spat. She stood up, grabbed her spear and shoved the handle of her great axe through the loop on her belt. Lightning danced above the distant forest. "Speak no more of this to me, else I crack open your thick heads."

She trudged into the rain, leaving her sisters behind. Men and Giants watched as she passed through their clustered camps, heading toward the open woodland. By the time she reached the edge of the encampment the scent of warming stews and the smoke of cookfires had replaced the stench of the blue-skins. Dahrima's stomach growled, but she had no appetite.

The dark trees grew taller as she paced toward them. The sounds of the sea faded behind her. The forest had looked more impressive from a distance; there were no mighty Uygas growing here. The mightiest of the skinny trees stood twice as tall as Dahrima, and the floor was an endless tangle of vine and root, leaf and brushwood. She enjoyed the splintering of undergrowth beneath her boots, the wholesome smell of green growing things. Her spear pushed hanging branches and broad leaves out of her path as she trudged through the gloom. When her eyes grew accustomed to the darkness, she found a thick carpet of moss near a small cascade of whitewater. She sat down on the wet moss and rested her back against a tree bole.

Vireon had changed greatly since he had slain the Swamp God. Since he had found his true stature. Dahrima always knew that he possessed the soul of a Giant, even though he had stood barely taller than the Men of Udurum. Now Vireon's true inheritance had manifested; his father's sorcery ran in his veins. Now he was a true Giant in both spirit and body. Yet it was more than his physical nature that had changed.

It began with the death of his wife and daughter. Ianthe the Claw had taken them both. The sorceress had masqueraded as little Maelthyn for seven years. The child itself was a living lie, the product of Ianthe's sorcery quickened in Alua's womb. Vireon's cherished daughter was never real, only a cruel joke spun by the Claw. Dahrima had seen the Giant-King weep when the truth fell upon him like a maiming blade. She too had endured the deep pain of that terrible discovery. Dahrima had loved Maelthyn, watched over her from the moment of her birth. Many of her spearsisters had perished trying to save the child and its mother. Yet the Claw, once revealed, had eluded Vireon's justice.

Vireon tracked Ianthe to the Mountain of Ghosts. Dahrima followed, and more of her sisters died there. With the stolen power of Alua's white flame, the sorceress had crossed the sky and returned to Khyrei. So Vireon summoned his legions, gathered the Lord of the Icelands to his cause, and marched south with the Sword King of Uurz. In the stinking swamps west of Khyrei they faced a behemoth that killed hundreds of Giants and thousands of Men. Vireon's unleashed power had finally crushed the monster. Dahrima had been there to pull the senseless Vireon from the mire and dress his wounds.

Yet it was Varda of the Keen Eyes who had given Vireon the crown of Angrid, making him King of All Giants. Several nights later Dahrima found them lying together inside her own tent. That was the moment she realized how much her King had truly changed. Now that Vireon stood as tall as any Giant, he was a true King in the eyes of the blue-skins. The scheming blue-skinned witch had to have him for her own. Had Vireon already forgotten Alua, his beloved Queen? Had he forgotten Dahrima too, who followed him without fail through blood and death and terror?

Perhaps the blue witch had cast a spell upon him. When Varda sat the iron crown upon his head, she must have stolen his heart. A false magic, a curse to bend the new Lord of Giants to her will. Now she shared Vireon's tent, and Dahrima avoided the Giant-King.

It must be a spell, she decided. How else could he bear the frigid touch of the blue-skin harlot? Had Varda influenced the actions of King Angrid in exactly the same way? That must be the secret of her power. Dahrima hated her, as she had begun to hate the sour stench of the Udvorg males. Why did the blue-skin women not march to war with their men? They must be too busy raising the new children fostered on them by the Uduru. Were those children blue or pale-skinned? How many more blue-skin warriors had stayed behind in the Icelands? Less than two hundred Uduru had been willing to walk the path of war with Vireon. Were they so happy in their icy hovels, gathered about the cold flames with their squealing babes and blue-skin wives?

The gurgling of the whitewater lulled Dahrima to sleep, and she awoke to another gray dawn. Gathering axe and spear, she stalked back to join the spearmaidens. The double army was breaking camp and preparing for another day's march. The rain fell as steady as ever, and the Golden Sea was a dull expanse that matched the color of the roiling sky.

"Dahrima the Axe!" A Man's voice called to her from the edge of the Uduri camp. She turned to see a herald in the black-and-purple livery of Udurum. "His Majesty Vireon wishes to speak with you in his pavilion." Dahrima's sisters gave her queer looks that she tried her best to ignore. *Let them think what they will. I am the only one with sense enough to see what the blue witch is doing.*

She followed the herald through the ranks of yawning Udvorg. The Giants pulled themselves from the mud and drank mouthfuls of rainwater caught in their bronze war helms. The stink of them filled her nostrils as she walked. A few called out to her, complimenting her golden hair or challenging her to a wrestling match. She had made it clear that she had no interest in lying with any of them, but still they persisted. Before the march to the Sharrian ruins was complete, she would have to break one of their jaws to make her point. The first one who touched her without permission would regret it.

Her own people knew better than to tease Uduri in such a way. When an Uduri wished to lie with an Uduru, she let him know. Best not to bother her about it beforehand. Dahrima had no wish to lie with any of them either, not even Hrolgar the Iron-Foot, who had been her lover many times before the migration. That was ancient history, and Hrolgar had an Udvorg wife and two children waiting for him in the Icelands.

Vireon's pavilion stood before her now, the standard of Udurum billowing atop its center pole. Instead of the usual two Uduri placed before the entrance, a pair of Udvorg spearmen stood there. Another way the blue-skins had replaced Dahrima and her sisters. She wondered why Vireon would summon her now after ignoring her for three days.

The herald directed her toward the big tent but went no further. Dahrima expected the Udvorg guards to stop her, but they only stared at her with their blood-colored eyes. She pulled back the flap and strode inside. A blue flame danced in an iron brazier. Vireon's greatsword and crown lay upon the bed of furs, yet the Giant-King himself was nowhere to be seen. Instead, Varda of the Keen Eyes stood waiting for her.

"Where is my lord?" Dahrima asked.

"Your King," Varda corrected her. "Breaking his fast with Emperor Tyro."

Dahrima paused just inside the tent. She studied the witch's narrow eyes, her long black mane of hair, wild and uncombed as usual. Most Udvorg hair was the color of snow, but the witch's was dark as midnight. A bronze ring hung from Varda's nose, and twelve more just like it pierced her ears. The scars on her cheeks were angular and purposefully made. Dahrima found them exceptionally ugly. Scars should be earned in battle, not crafted by one's own hand. Usually the witch wore a black wolf-skin cloak, but inside the tent she was dressed in a corslet of boiled leather, an Uurzian skirt of plaited bronze, and a band of silver across her forehead. Her blue feet were bare upon the damp carpets.

"I was told that Vireon summoned me," Dahrima said. She wished to leave. The company of the blue witch was not something she could long endure.

"He did," said Varda. She picked up her long black staff and a blue flame ignited at its tip. "You are to remain here until he returns. It will give us a chance to talk."

Dahrima bristled beneath her breastplate of dark bronze. "I must go . . . "

"Will you defy the Giant-King's orders?" asked Varda. "You will stay, Axe."

Dahrima nodded her head and lowered her eyes. Looking at the witch's cold beauty gave her a curious pain that she could not identify.

"Vireon tells me the Uduri have been his private guard for years," said Varda.

Dahrima nodded.

"Yet on this coastal march your sisters travel with the Uduru instead of marching alongside their King."

"My sisters march where they will," said Dahrima. "I do not command them."

Varda smiled. Her crimson eyes widened a bit. "Yet they follow you," she said. "They flock to you like great, golden birds."

Dahrima's fist tightened about the haft of her spear. Was the witch trying to make her angry? Did Vireon truly summon her, or was this some trick meant to humiliate and chasten her?

"We march with the King's forces," said Dahrima. "We have fought and died for him. We will fight and die again. We are his true servants. This we have sworn."

"Yes, I have heard tell of this oath. The Ninety-Nine they call you. Yet how many are left?"

"Twenty-nine marchers," said Dahrima, "and forty guarding the walls of Udurum."

"So few . . ." The words of the shamaness were full of mock sadness.

"What does His Majesty wish of me?" Dahrima asked.

"He wishes for you and your twenty-eight sisters to go home," said Varda. "Enough of the Uduri have died in his service. Vireon does not want to see more death among the spearmaidens. Take your sisters and return to Udurum. Keep its walls strong and unbroken. Leave today."

Dahrima could not prevent a growl from escaping her throat. "I do not believe you."

Varda's eyes blazed red while the flame atop her staff flared a deeper blue. "You will hear it from his own lips when he returns. You should be grateful. We are to face untold dangers from this invading horde. Perhaps you think the Uduri are expendable because they are incapable of childbirth. I can assure you Vireon does not share this view. He wishes to protect the last of you."

Dahrima spat upon the carpet. "We are warriors! A single

Uduri is worth three Uduru. We march where we will, and we have sworn to march with Vireon. We will fight."

"Will you defy the orders of your King?"

"If we must."

Varda stepped closer. Dahrima's knuckles itched. She longed to pull her axe and cleave the witch's skull. "Listen to me," said Varda. "Vireon is done with you. Take your sisters and go now, or lose the honor that is all you have left."

Dahrima gritted her teeth. Her breath came heavy and loudly. For a moment, she could not speak.

"I know what you are doing," she told the witch. "You seek to rule Vireon's mind as you ruled that of Angrid. I will not allow it."

Varda laughed in her face. "You are mad and hopeless, Axe. Vireon has made his choice. Go now, or risk my anger." She turned her back to Dahrima and walked toward the bed of furs. The crown of iron and sapphire glittered there, waiting for its King to return and set it upon his head. It was Varda's tool, the keystone of her spell.

"First you steal our mates," breathed Dahrima, "and now you try to steal our King."

The witch whirled about and waved her blue flame. A blast of wind and ice caught Dahrima in the chest, encasing her in a thin layer of frost that burned like fire. Dahrima grimaced and slammed the haft of her spear against her breastplate, knocking the frost loose.

"Witch!" she cried, moving closer to Varda. "Poisonous harlot!"

Varda's staff moved again, knocking the spear from Dahrima's grip.

Another blast of cobalt flame sent Dahrima clattering to the ground. A thick and heavy sheath of ice engulfed her chest and upper legs. Varda stood above her now, staff raised as if for a killing blow.

"Beg my forgiveness," said the witch. "Or die."

Dahrima swept her leg across Varda's knees. She shattered the ice about her middle with spear and fist as the witch fell upon the carpet. Dahrima rolled into a standing crouch and pulled the great axe from her belt.

Varda screeched like a bird of prey, pulling herself upward with the black staff. Dahrima kicked it across the tent. The blue flame extinguished itself. Varda leaped upon the furs and pulled Vireon's greatsword from its scabbard. The blade gleamed silver-blue as the two Giantesses faced one another. Rain pelted hard against the canvas ceiling.

"I do not need the cold flame to take your life," said Varda. "I will cut out your heart and feed it to the wolves."

"You would cut out the heart of Vireon," said Dahrima. "But I will not let you."

Varda lunged forward. The greatsword clanged against the axe's double blade. Purple sparks flew across the tent.

Someone pulled back the tent flap and Dahrima saw the faces of the Udvorg guards peering at her. One of them shouted something. Varda sprang forward again, blue flames streaming from her open mouth.

The sword would have taken off Dahrima's head if she hadn't ducked below its arc. She raised the axe to counter a downward slash and kicked at the witch's flat belly. Varda flew backwards across the tent and the canvas tore from its moorings. The shamaness lay in the mud with the demolished pavilion wrapped about her body. Dahrima could have rushed in and finished her at that moment, but she stood fuming instead. The witch used Vireon's blade to cut herself free of the canvas, then stood to face Dahrima.

A ring of grinning Udvorg surrounded them now. The blue-skins clapped their hands, stomped in the mud, and shouted to their fellows. This was a fine sport for them, watching two Uduri – the blue-skin and the pale-skin – battle in the rain. Where was Vireon? Dahrima could not see the Sword King's pavilion; a wall of grunting, drooling Giants closed her off from everything except her foe and the driving rain. Thunder shook the High Realm.

Varda rushed her with the big sword raised high. Dahrima side-stepped the blow and brought her axe down instinctively. She felt the shock of a meaty impact before she realized what she had done. The world seemed to slow in that moment, as if time itself were frozen beneath the witch's ice. The greatsword splattered into the mud, followed by Varda's limp body. Her head, sliced cleanly from her spouting shoulders, rolled across the ground to rest at the toe of Dahrima's boot. The bloody eyes stared up at her. A whisper of blue flame died inside the open mouth.

Varda's blood was the deep purple of Udurum cloaks. It mingled with the brown mud, turning it black. A swathe of violet spray stained Dahrima's legs, but already the hard rain was washing them clean. The Udvorg looked on in shocked silence. The sound of the storm filled Dahrima's ears until a familiar voice cried out from beyond the ring of gawkers.

Vireon came shoving his way through the blue-skins, his black tunic and hair drenched by the rain. His crownless head lowered to examine Varda's corpse, then rose to meet Dahrima's gaze. He looked upon her with a wordless sorrow.

"Dahrima?" He said her name once, but she barely heard it beneath the pounding rain.

She could not bear to see what emotion would flood Vireon's face next, so she turned and pushed her way through the mumbling Udvorg, knocking many of them into the mud. She ran while thunder and lightning tore open the sky above the cliffs. Horses and Men rushed to get out of her way. She passed the green-gold pavilion of the Sword King without looking back, running north along the shore.

The words of Varda rang in her head as she fled: *Vireon is done with you.*

She came to a high crag and leaped from it into the driving wind. She seemed to fall forever, sinking toward the gray ocean. In her right hand the great axe was already washed clean of the witch's purple blood. A reflected flash of lightning danced across its blades as she fell.

Finally the frigid water accepted her; she plunged into its dark depths.

She contemplated death by drowning. She might let herself sink to the bottom of the sea and stay there forever, a proper penance for her crime of rage. She had betrayed her King. She had seen it in his eyes as Vireon stared at her over the corpse of his lover.

She sank deeper into the peaceful bliss of the waters below the storm. It was so quiet down here. Yet now she heard herself thinking, and her thoughts were loud as thunder.

Vireon is done with you.

No. Varda will not haunt me in this way.

She earned her death with those words. Let the Udvorg moan the loss of their shamaness. Vireon will be free of her spells now. Free to rule both his kingdoms as he thinks best.

With a single stroke of her axe, Dahrima had freed him.

With her crime and her shame, she had restored his liberty.

Her feet met the sandy ocean bottom. The last bit of breath escaped her lungs as she pushed herself upward. Her head and shoulders broke the surface, and she sucked in rainwater along with precious air. She swam toward the rocky shoal. Far above and beyond the lip of the precipice, the morning smokes of the camp rose into the sky and disappeared.

Dahrima walked out of the sea and ran northward along the beach, axe in hand.

I have disgraced myself. Yet I have sworn the oath.

I will serve Vireon.

Let my sisters return to Udurum if they will.

I will not.

I cannot.

Neither could she march with the Udvorg any longer. They would hate her now, and they would call for her head to pay for the witch's. A life for a life, that was the way of justice for both Uduru and Udvorg. Vireon might even give it to them.

Perhaps the blue-skins would indeed have her head someday. But not today.

A great invasion was coming. Vireon still needed her. The first battle would be fought at the ruins of Shar Dni. She sprinted north along the strand, leaving behind the twin armies that crept along the cliffs.

He needs me.

She ran against the sea winds, and the rain pelting her face mingled with salty tears.

4

The Feathered Serpent

Khama missed the days when he was a simple herder of goats. For twenty years he had enjoyed that blissful existence on the yellow plains west of the Pearl City. During that time he had been only a Man, with a loving wife who bore him four perfect children. He missed the sweet winds playing over the tall grass, the bleating of his docile herd as he led them to water, and the serenity of the open sky. He missed Emi's brown face and soft lips, the laughter of his children and their warm hugs.

Goats were so much easier to guide than Men.

He might have lived in domestic bliss on his tiny farm for decades more, might have forgotten his ancient past completely, if the two hawks had not come south from the Land of Giants. One of the hawks was Iardu the Shaper, the other his disciple – daughter of the dead Giant-King. It was Iardu's prismatic eyes that made Khama recall the truth he had hidden from himself. Iardu's soft voice woke him from the dream of tranquility he had woven so carefully about his family.

All dreams must end eventually, as all dreamers must awaken.

Khama stood upon the forecastle of the *Bird of War*, wrapped in a fluttering cloak of scarlet feathers. The calls of sailors and soldiers mingled with the songs of low-flying seabirds. A powerful wind filled the white sails of four hundred Mumbazan swanships, a wind Khama had summoned himself and kept steady for three days. Three hundred Yaskathan galleys glided among the swanships, the silver Sword and Tree insignia bright upon their crimson sails. Nearly two hundred black-sailed reavers, newly pledged to the Slave King of Khyrei, served as rearguard for the southern fleets.

Soon the emerald hills of the Jade Isles would dot the eastern horizon. Khama hoped the combined fleet was not too late. The Hordes of Zyung approached the island chain even now from the far east. If the Jade King were a wise man, he would surrender to Zyung immediately and accept the yoke of his rule. By doing so, he would save thousands of lives. His island folk, never a warlike race, might prefer slavery to slaughter. They were more like goats in that way than the people of Mumbaza or Yaskatha. However, the Jade King would have little choice in the matter if Undutu and D'zan reached his court before Zyung. They would persuade him through mighty orations, chests of gold, and implied threats if necessary, to join his small fleet with their own. Khama sighed and breathed deeply of the marine air, dreading the battle that would ensue.

Since that day eight years ago when Iardu had caused Khama to remember his own history, the herdsman had given up his agrarian life for a palatial estate near the palace of Undutu. There his family dwelled in luxury and privilege. All save Kuchka, his oldest son, who had attended the College of Sages before joining the cavalry legions of Undutu. Khama was thankful that his warrior-sage son had not joined the royal navy, or he would be on one of these ships right now, and sailing toward a grim fate.

In the past eight years Undutu the Boy-King had grown into a strapping young man, a brash lion eager to prove himself by cutting down foes and winning glory. Two years ago his mother's regency had come to an end as Undutu reached his seventeenth year. On that same day Khama's position was elevated from Chief Advisor to Prime Vizier. Undutu had needed his advice more than ever as his mother's fading health kept her from the throne room. The voices of generals and diplomats filled the young King's ears constantly, but always he came back to Khama when making important decisions. Undutu had never known his father, a victim of the plague while Undutu was yet an infant, so he came to view Khama in a paternal light. Khama, too, saw the King as more than his liege. At times Undutu seemed more like Khama's son than the fiercely independent Kuchka. The King of Mumbaza was often called Son of the Feathered Serpent, but only Khama knew the irony of that honorific.

Tuka and Bota were both well into their teenage years now, strong boys showing much promise. And little Isha, Khama's only daughter, was twelve. All three spent most of their time with tutors, or in the company of other highborn children. Khama wished he knew them better, as well as he had come to know Undutu.

Undutu's tutors had filled the young King's head with stories from the Age of Heroes, legends from the Age of Walking Gods. The King's martial instructors, General Tsoti chief among them, had honed his gift for swordplay, spearcraft, and war strategy to the point of obsession. This had begun well before Khama had come to court. For years now he had persuaded Undutu to avoid the call to war; the Sword King of Uurz made ceaseless overtures to the King on the Cliffs. Each year it had become more difficult to sway the young lion with the wisdom of peace. When the King of Yaskatha at last joined the Sword King's crusade to conquer Khyrei, Undutu had gone deaf to Khama's words. There would be war, and Khyrei would finally pay for its long list of crimes.

Yet the Slave King had arisen before the Legions of Uurz and Udurum had arrived. There was no longer any need to assault the black city, for Gammir the Reborn and Ianthe the Claw were vanquished at the hands of Sharadza Vodsdaughter and an army of vengeful slaves. Word of the aborted siege had reached Khama before the southern navies reached the shores of Khyrei. But Khama remained skeptical until Undutu's flagship had docked at the Khyrein harbor; then he saw that Iardu the Shaper had been behind the entire affair.

Iardu had awakened Khama to the reality of his own past years ago. And now he had called together the Kings of the Five Cities and awakened them to the reality of what was to come. He showed them Zyung the God-King, Lord of the Living Empire, and his hordes of Manslayers. After three thousand years, Zyung's mighty hand was finally reaching across the world. A great invasion was coming. It wasn't until he saw Iardu's vision that Khama realized how inevitable this war had become. Long ago Khama and Iardu had led their peoples to a land where the Living Empire had no foothold. Khama had fostered Mumbaza, a kingdom based on peace and freedom; he had worked hard to maintain its peace and advised every King of the Pearl City's lineage. Yet all of it was about to end, unless the Hordes of Zyung were repelled.

Undutu would get his chance to be a hero.

The Son of the Feathered Serpent would not sit idle and await invasion. As any hero from the sagas would do, Undutu must sail his fleet to meet the invaders on the open sea, carry the fight to the aggressors. King D'zan agreed, despite the Shaper's disapproval. Iardu's manipulations had come to an end; he could no longer trick the assembled Kings into following his advice. So the fleets had sailed eastward, and Tong the Avenger had contributed his own navy to the armada. The Khyreins were only too glad to avoid persecution by pledging themselves to the Slave King and his allies. The two hundred black warships with their devil-head prows had been scourges of the Golden Sea when Ianthe and Gammir had ruled. Now they would serve well in the coming battle, if only as fodder for Zyung's dreadnoughts.

This would not only be a battle of Men and metal, flesh and blood. A second battle would determine the true course of events. A battle of sorcery. Khama contemplated the immense sky-ships that carried Zyung's legions and the flocks of flying lizards that supplemented their numbers. Soon he must begin to weave spells for his King and the double fleet. For now, he stood at the prow of the flagship and watched the fleets slicing through the waves.

Undutu approached from midship. Sunlight glinted on his peaked silver helm, its white ostrich feather dancing in the wind. The King's dark, muscular arms were bare except for the golden cobra torques wound about his biceps. A vest of pearly scale mail covered his broad chest and midriff. His cloak was whiter than the ship's sail, and the golden insignia of the Feathered Serpent was stitched upon it.

"What do you see, Khama?" asked the young lion. His right hand lingered on the golden pommel of the cutlass at his belt.

"I see blood," Khama said. "The Golden Sea stained to crimson. The Jade Isles flaming and littered with corpses. Drowning men and crying mothers."

Undutu frowned. "I thought you were behind me in this war."

"I am," said Khama. "What I see is the truth of war, the reality to which heroes, soldiers, and even Kings, are often blind until it is too late."

"Ah," said Undutu. "So it is the future you see. Like Iardu's golden cloud. Tell me you see a victory for us."

The wind tore at the feathers in Khama's headdress. He turned to face the King. In the bright eyes, broad cheeks, and handsome smile he saw the face of Kuchka flash for a moment.

"I cannot do this," said Khama. "Yet I can tell you that there are many futures, as there are many roads a man may travel to reach his destination. He may find each of these several roads, but ultimately he must choose only one."

"And how does a man know he has chosen the right path?"

Khama shrugged. "He discovers this when he reaches his destination."

Undutu laughed at the wind. "I ask for sorcery and you give me philosophy."

"I will give you more than that, Majesty," said Khama. "I will give you hurricanes to cast at these sky-ships. I will give you knowledge and power and wisdom. I will give you the Feathered Serpent in all his glorious fury."

Undutu clapped him on the back. "I know you will, my friend. Look at this armada. The warships of three nations joined together. Soon to be four! There has never been anything like this assembly in all of history."

Now it was Khama's turn to frown. "Not in *your* history, Majesty. Yet there are many lands ancient and powerful that lie beyond your own. The Land of the Five Cities is a tiny thing compared to the Living Empire of Zyung, whose history goes back ten thousand years."

Undutu leaned against the railing. The ship's figurehead, a great swan head with a curved neck, loomed above him. "Tell me of this history," said the King. "Tsoti tells me it is wise to know one's enemy."

Khama smiled. "Nearly three thousand years ago, long before I had taken the shape of a Man, I guided Ywatha the First across the Cryptic Sea to the wild land he would name Mumbaza."

"My venerable ancestor," smiled Undutu. "Every boy knows this story."

"Yet have you ever wondered where the First Son of the Feathered Serpent and his people came from?"

Undutu's brow knotted. "The Ancient Land . . . a place of curses and monsters."

Khama smirked. "So grandmothers tell their children. Yet the truth is this: A great continent lies beyond the Cryptic Sea, and also beyond the Golden Sea, for as you've learned our world is a sphere. Like a golden ring, it doubles back upon itself until the beginning is the end and the end is the beginning. This great continent is many times the size of our own. Entire seas are found within its borders. This is the land where Zyung built his empire, and now it bears his name.

"Ages ago the God-King began the campaign of conquest that would build this empire. He knew it would take thousands of years to subdue all the realms of the great continent, but being an immortal, this did not concern him. He gathered together those of the Old Breed who would take up his cause and began to topple the capitals of minor kingdoms. With each kingdom that fell to him, he gathered more power, more legions, and more fuel to feed the fires of his great dream."

"What was this dream?" asked Undutu.

"The same as it is now," said Khama. "To remake the world in his image. To remove free will and conflict and individual thought and replace it with his vision of perfect unity. To rid this world of all those who would oppose him and create an empire of slaves living as one beneath his tread. There would be only one King and one God for the world. Zyung would be both. In the name of peace and order he slaughtered millions. His empire grew slowly, but it crept like a disease across the great continent.

"Your own ancestors, the People of Ywatha, lived free and wild on a great plain called Orbusa. A land of wild oxen and crystal streams, silver grasses and fertile soil. They built no cities, erected no walls, kept no armies, for they had no enemies. Until the legions of Zyung came and razed the villages, cast down their wooden idols, and enslaved the proud tribes of Orbusa. I had lived among these tribes for generations. They had built a temple for me from the holy wood of the sacred *ahbroa* trees. They worshipped the Feathered Serpent as their deity, though the wisest among them knew that I was not truly a God. Yet I was their protector.

"One of the Old Breed had come to me a century earlier, urging me to quit the silver plain and take my people across the ocean. He led his own tribe of refugees, survivors of Zyung's early conquests, and promised a new land across the waves where the God-King's legions could not reach. I should have listened then, but it was a century later when the Manslayers of Zyung reached Orbusa. Only then, watching my people cut down and their fields set to the torch . . . only when the conquerors burned my beautiful temple and forced me to wrath . . . only then did I hear the wisdom in what Iardu the Shaper had said to me. More of Zyung's legions would arrive to replace the ones my power had annihilated. I had no wish for further slaughter. I only wanted to protect those I loved. An exodus was the only answer.

"I gathered together the surviving tribes of Orbusa and ordained Ywatha as their King. We marched toward the shores of the Cryptic Sea. Many were the hardships and sufferings of the Orbusans as they migrated. Once we came to the edge of the great continent, we built ships from the wood of an ancient forest. For long months that tiny fleet endured the waves and the storms. Many were lost to the ocean's wild hunger.

"I flew ahead of the ships and found the lesser continent that Iardu the Shaper had promised. His people had fanned out across this new land, yet none had claimed the golden lands beyond the Pearl Cliffs. There I advised Ywatha to build his new capital, and there his son Ybondu was crowned as the Second King. Before Ywatha died, content that his life had been most fruitful, he named this new land Mumbaza.

"I served Ybondu and his people as I had served their ancestors. I aided them through early wars and kept them safe from plagues and famines. I tried my best to secure peace for them. Before the Usurper Elhathym returned to Yaskatha eight years ago, Mumbaza had enjoyed a hundred years of unbroken peace. Nor was this the first era to be blessed with the absence of war."

Khama sighed. "Yet always war returns, as our tiny world spins among the stars. Perhaps it is an inevitable part of what we are. You, me, the Old Breed, all of us slaves to unknown forces that drive the universe. Now Zyung rules the entirety of the great continent, and he reaches across the Golden Sea for the Land of the Five Cities. Now we must go to war again, or choose to be slaves."

Khama had almost forgotten all of this during his two decades as a goatherd. Taking the form and life of a simple man, he had almost *become* that man. Part of him was glad that Iardu had shaken him from the peaceful dream, while another part resented the Shaper for robbing him of a few more years of bliss. Yet Khama could never abandon the people of Mumbaza. He loved them deeply, and they were all his family. He could no longer hide them from the blazing eyes of Zyung. Now they must stand and fight. They would live as a free nation, or die as a legend of freedom. Khama would die with them if he must. He would not give himself to the sway of the God-King's power. Not in the past, and not now.

I will never serve him. Better to face annihilation.
Iardu must feel the same way.

Khama wondered if the Shaper would truly find others of the

Old Breed to stand and oppose Zyung's invasion. How many of the Dreaming Ones could be awakened? How many of them would make a difference in the face of ultimate power? How many of them even still existed as entities separate from the living world itself?

Khama had no answers to these questions, so he refocused his thoughts on the battle to come. The first strike in the final war for freedom. Many of these ships would perish, and thousands of Men would die. Yet the Feathered Serpent would do what he could to protect the dream of his beloved Mumbaza.

Undutu's face was grim. He stared at the blue waters rushing past the prow of his flagship. The *Bird of War* and D'zan's *Kingspear* led the triple fleet.

"Zyung was once of the Old Breed?" asked the young lion.

"He was the greatest of us all," said Khama. "Also the cruelest."

Undutu swallowed. Perhaps he regretted rushing toward the invaders so readily. Yet it was too late now. The King could not change his course.

Undutu waved his hand toward the horizon. "Bah! This tyrant is only another sorcerer. Let the people of his great continent crawl before him like insects. We will face him and die like Men. We will tear his ships from the sky and make his Manslayers scream like weeping children. He may destroy us, Khama, but he will *remember* us."

Khama grabbed the young lion by his shoulder. He smiled.

"Do not forget that Iardu stands with us," he told the King. "Even now he travels with the Vodsdaughter to enlist more sorcerers. Together we will stand against Zyung as none have ever dared to stand. Remember too that nothing ever truly ends. Life and death are twin illusions."

"And honor?"

"Honor is what defines us."

Undutu nodded. His own honor would lead him to victory or death; he was prepared for either. A surge of pride swelled in Khama's chest. Here was a King who truly deserved to be called Son of the Feathered Serpent.

Wake them, Iardu. Wake them all, as you awakened me.

Through our sacrifice you will have the time you need.

The nine black hawks of Iardu's creation were dispatched on the day of the triple fleet's launch. Eight of them ranged far and wide across the Golden Sea, searching for signs of the God-King's airborne forces. After three days only the ninth hawk returned, the one sent as messenger to the Jade Isles.

The bird dropped out of a bloody sunset to perch on the forward railing. Sailors sent word to Undutu's cabin that his envoy had returned. Khama came up with him to speak with the hawk that was a Man. He did not like the choice of form the Shaper had chosen.

Hawks always bring trouble.

If his own sorcery could weave and warp others' flesh the way Iardu's could, Khama would have changed the soldiers into seabirds. Yet the Feathered Serpent's magic was confined mainly to his own person and the realms of wind, storm, sun, and cloud. Iardu had called him a Creature of the Air. Once there were others like Khama, but they were lost in the rushing depths of time.

The black hawk bowed its head and screeched a welcome as the King and his Vizier drew near. It spoke in a human voice, barely a whisper but easily understood. Onyx eyes focused on Undutu.

"Majesty, I bring word from the court of Ongthaia," said the transformed one, using the true name of the island kingdom. Only in the Five Cities was Ongthaia referred to as the Jade Isles.

"Speak, last of my hawks," said Undutu. Khama steadied himself for dreadful news.

"An emissary of Zyung has arrived at the Jade King's palace," croaked the bird. "Robed all in silver, he stands at the King's side as an honored guest. He offers the Jade King a choice: Surrender to Zyung or face death."

Khama looked at Undutu. The young lion's jaw was firm-set.

"What was the Jade King's answer?" asked Undutu.

"I know not, Majesty," said the hawk. "The foreign emissary is a sorcerer. He knew me for no natural bird and caught me with his bare hands. I feared he would snap my neck, but instead he gave me a message for you." The false hawk screeched again, as if it would rather take to the sky than deliver the words of the enemy's herald.

"Well? What is the message?" asked Undutu. He was angry. The young lion was too quick to anger these days. As a young boy he did not have this weakness. It was the weight of full Kinghood that had changed boy to man and set fire to his temper.

The hawk fluttered its wings. *"Turn your ships about,"* it said. *"Return to your Five Cities and prepare for the blessed peace of Zyung to fall upon you like the summer rain. There will be no further warning.* So the emissary spoke, Majesty." The hawk turned its glimmering eyes toward the clouds.

Undutu stood silent for a moment, then raised his head and laughed into the wind. "This servant of Zyung does not understand us, Khama. We must educate him."

Khama nodded. *We will all learn a lesson that only spilled blood can teach.*

"Your work is done," Undutu told the hawk. "Rest now and eat well. Soon we reach the isles and soon after we meet our enemies."

The hawk's feathers began to fall out as its form lengthened, swirled like dark smoke, and took once more its true shape. The dusky-skinned soldier, freed now from Iardu's spell, sank to one knee before Undutu then trundled off to find clothing, armor, and weapons. Khama supposed the man was glad to be back to his true self, even on the eve of war and death.

"We must deal with this emissary," said Undutu.

"He may have already persuaded the Jade King to turn against us," said Khama.

Undutu stared into the darkening horizon. "We shall have to be more persuasive."

Khama bowed and took himself below decks to find his rest. Tomorrow the fleets would arrive at Ongthaia, and there would be little time left for sleeping. Unless death itself could be counted as slumber. Of that unwelcome sleep he was sure there would be no lack.

Ongthaia was a chain of thirteen islands, each one larger than the last. Six of them possessed wide harbors where ships from the Five Cities and the Southern Isles came to trade mainland goods for green stone, yellow spices, woven silks, and black plum wines. Villages of thatched dome huts sprouted thick as palm trees on every island, but the only proper towns were found on the harbor isles. The kingdom's capital city, Morovanga, rose from the shoulders of a dormant volcano on the largest isle. Its double walls were of black basalt, but the towers that stood within were built all of sparkling jade. The greatest of those spires rose from the Jade Palace, where King Zharua sat upon a throne made of that same far-famed stone.

The harbors were full of ships from the mainland, all identifiable by the colors of sails and standards flying from prow and mast, yet Khama saw no sign of invaders' ships. No looming dreadnought floating in the clouds above the green palace. He wondered how the emissary of Zyung had come to Ongthaia. Perhaps he flew under his own power. He might even be one of the Old Breed. Khama could remember few of their names after so many ages.

The royal harbor of Morovanga was crowded with vessels, mostly Jade Isle traders. The *Bird of War* and the *Kingspear* had entered the harbor with an escort of six ships. The rest of the triple fleet assembled itself in a crescent that enclosed the western side of the great island. Ongthaia kept no warships among its own fleet. The Jade Folk traded peaceably with every country – even Khyrei during Ianthe's rule – therefore they had no need of armies or galleons of war. However, their traders were big and sleek, with massive hulls that could hold half a legion if required. In previous ages those holds had carried slaves, and the Jade Isles had built their early reputation in that unwholesome trade.

Some recent ancestor of Zharua's had received a message from the Sea God that slave-trading was an unholy practice, so that noble monarch outlawed it forevermore. Khama believed there must still be an illegal black market for slaves here. The Jade Folk still kept slaves for themselves, but they no longer bought or sold them with outsiders. On these islands slaves were simply the lowest form of social class. The poorest of the poor were born into it, yet any of them could gain freedom through years of hard work and loyalty.

Khama wondered how many slaves staffed the great Jade Palace as he walked through its gates in the company of Undutu and D'zan. A company of Mumbazans in white cloaks and plumed helms followed them, as well as a cadre of Yaskathans in chain mail and crimson tabards. As a sign of respect for the Jade King's court, they carried no spears. Yet each warrior retained his sword, curved cutlasses for the Mumbazans and longblades for the Yaskathans, all worn at the waist. The Yaskathan King was the sole exception: D'zan carried a greatsword on his back. The Sun God's mark was set into the scabbard with a pattern of rubies and diamonds. Khama carried no weapons at all; it had never been his custom to bear arms. Word of his powers usually assured a peaceful reception wherever he traveled. Perhaps this would not be the case with an emissary of Zyung waiting inside these viridian walls.

The procession had wound through the narrow streets from the royal harbor, drawing the stares of curious Jade Folk and the smiles of scampering children. Sages and merchant lords watched the mainland Kings from the balconies of their green towers and the eaves of garden walks. There were few horses on the Jades, so most of the wealthy here traveled on slave-borne litters. The poor walked, and those who could afford beasts of burden rode shaggy yaks with curved horns. A squad of guardsmen mounted on these curious beasts had greeted Undutu and D'zan at the wharves, guided them on the quickest route through the metropolis, and now granted them access through the King's Gate.

The city itself smelled of sea winds, ripe citrus, and the smokes of spicy cooking. Within the walls of the Jade Palace these odors were replaced entirely by incense redolent of jasmine and purple lotus blossoms. Murals in a thousand colors decorated every surface, from floor to walls to ceiling. Precious stones gleamed in swirling arabesques and glyphs between pillars of smoky quartz, ruddy chalcedony, or the ever-present jade. Slaves in gaudy robes dropped to their knees as the mainland Kings passed through the palace halls.

Tiny red monkeys skittered up and down the pillars wearing jeweled collars. Young nobles gathered the tittering beasts on their shoulders and made way for the foreign delegation. A sense of urgency hung in the air stronger than the smoke of incense that burned in ubiquitous braziers. Sunbeams fell through cleverly designed skylights, bringing the colors of the palace to life in all their splendor.

King Zharua was a fat man with tiny eyes. He sat upon a throne of pale jade – what else? – carved into the likeness of a thir-teen-rayed sun above his round head. His hair was black, cut short, and his eyes were dark slits above brown cheeks and a tiny chin. A wisp of mustache fell from either side of his broad-lipped mouth. A necklace heavy with topazes and opals hung on the breast of his silk robe, and his tall golden collar rose higher than his golden crown. Khama marveled at the crown's simplicity, given the opulence of everything else in the Jade King's domain. A single emerald was set directly at the center of Zharua's fore-head.

A black tiger slept at the Jade King's feet, its collar chained to a ring at the base of the throne. A bevy of beautiful women lay upon cushions spread across the royal dais. Zharua kept a harem that was the envy of the world. Beauties from every kingdom lounged about the monarch and his tiger; they stared at the visiting Kings with heavy-lidded eyes. Yet many of these con-cubines were natives of the Jade Isles with flowing black hair and olive skin. Khama had heard an old saying: "To be born beauti-ful in the Jade Isles is to be the King's treasure." Now he saw the truth of the adage. He thought of Emi's dark eyes staring into his own, and he looked from the harem girls toward the emissary of Zyung.

The pale man was tall with a bald head and large ears. His eye-brows were white and bushy, the only sign of hair on his head. A ring of platinum hung from his long nose, which overshadowed a wide mouth. A long robe of silvery substance hid most of his lean body. Sunlight flashed across the rippling fabric. His long-fingered hands were crossed before his waist as he offered the Southern Kings a passive smile. He stood to the immediate left of Zharua's throne, bare feet visible on the middle of three broad steps.

Zharua called for padded chairs to accommodate his visitors. Slaves rushed forward and soon Khama found himself seated between Undutu and D'zan. He declined the goblet of dark wine offered him by the slaves; the young Kings followed his example.

"This is a rare honor," said Zharua. He looked at them with a mixture of worry and awe. "Not only does the legendary Feathered Serpent grace my court, but two mainland Kings." His voice was soft yet powerful enough to dominate the hall, which was built to amplify his speeches. His Ongthaian accent was barely noticeable; he was the Trader King, and he spoke all the dialects of the mainland superbly. In his younger years, Zharua had traveled to each of the great cities. Khama remembered a much thinner version of the Jade King meeting with Undutu's father some twenty-five years ago.

"We are grateful for your hospitality," said Khama. The Southern Kings had agreed that he should speak for both of them to begin negotiations. "Surely the Jade King knows why we have come."

Zharua nodded, his double chin bouncing. "I received your hawk messenger," he said. "My trade captains have brought word of your great fleet. Is it true that the Five Cities have achieved unity after centuries of feuds and squabbles?"

Khama nodded. Undutu and D'zan bristled in their cushioned seats. "It is true. The threat that we now face threatens to destroy us all. Your realm lies in the path of that threat. The Hordes of Zyung approach from the other side of the world."

Zharua's eyes shot toward the silver-robed emissary, then back to Khama. "I am pleased to introduce the esteemed Damodar of the High Seraphim. Envoy of the God-King. Voice of the Living Empire."

Damodar bowed his hairless head for the briefest of moments.

Khama did not meet the envoy's gaze. Before he could respond, Undutu spoke.

"Has this bald mouthpiece offered you the chance to be the God-King's slave? Has he swayed you with polite words to give up your isles and your people to Zyung? Or have you chosen to stand with the Five Cities?"

Khama frowned inwardly. *The boy's temper will be the death of him.*

Zharua's eyelids fluttered. He was not used to being addressed in so loose a manner. "Son of the Feathered Serpent," he said. "King on the Cliffs ... Master of Pearls ... the fire of your youth exceeds your courtly decorum. Still, these are troubled times, and I attribute your rudeness to the sense of urgency you must feel."

"I, too, am a young King," said D'zan. His green eyes blazed. The hilt of the Sun God's blade rose above his right shoulder. "Yet we both are schooled by those far wiser than ourselves. We speak plainly because there is little time. We extend to Ongthaia the goodwill and martial protection of the Five Cities. We also bring a tribute of gold and jewels. Our triple fleet stands ready to oppose these invaders. Will you stand with us?"

Beads of sweat glimmered on Zharua's round face. His eyes flittered to the face of Damodar. Instead of the Jade King, it was Zyung's envoy who answered.

"The Great Zharua has not yet answered the Almighty's offering of peace," said the envoy. "Though his time for reply grows short."

Khama spoke before either of the young Kings could. "What offer has he made you, Zharua? The choice to die as a King or live as a slave? There is no true choice here ... only a veiled threat."

Zharua nodded. A slave fanned him with a great peacock feather at the end of a gilded pole. "Damodar tells me the God-King brings three thousand great warships."

"*Holy Dreadnoughts*," corrected Damodar. "Each carrying a thousand armored Manslayers."

Zharua swallowed a lump in his throat and downed a cup of wine offered by a female slave. Khama sensed fear hanging about the Jade King like an invisible fog, a stink of desperation. Could these numbers be true? Iardu's vision supported the claims. Best not to consider this conflict in terms of numbers. The Manslayers were only Men. It was the God-King's sorcerers that were the true threat. This Damodar must be one of them.

"Three million soldiers," said Zharua, his small eyes growing wide. "Can you imagine this, Feathered One? The forces of this Living Empire dwarf those of the Five Cities combined. And Damodar tells me there are yet more – legions of knights who ride the skies on the backs of scaly beasts . . . "

"*Trills*," said Damodar. "Twenty thousand, each driven by a skilled Manslayer. The Almighty's empire is beyond anything established on this side of the world. There is no standing against his will. Yet he would rather have your loyalty than your blood."

"We will tear your ships from the sky!" said Undutu. His hand was already on the hilt of his sword. Khama knew he longed to cut down the emissary. D'zan sat in silence, perhaps stunned by the numbers revealed by Damodar's boasting. He might now regret sailing east with Undutu's fleet.

Damodar smiled as one who indulges a child's foolishness.

Zharua seemed at a loss for words. How could he refuse an offer that was his only certain chance at continued existence? The Jade Islanders were not warriors. Perhaps their healthy trade would continue, even increase, under the auspices of the Living Empire. He did not realize that the true price he would pay, that all of his people must pay, would be their very souls.

Khama stood up. "Great Zharua," he said, "perhaps you should remove your lovely concubines and eager servants that we may speak more openly."

Zharua waved his hand and the ladies rose from their cushions in a jangle of jewelry and rustle of silks. They followed the slaves from the hall, one of whom led away the black tiger by its chain.

Khama stepped closer to the nervous King. Damodar's eyes followed him closely, the eyes of an adder moments before it strikes. "Know this, Majesty," said Khama. "This man offers you death, not life. The death of your freedom, your sovereignty, and the independence that has made the Jade Isles a true power in the world. His master will replace your crown with a yoke; your temples will be cast into ruin and your Gods forgotten; your people will no longer be able to earn their way from slavery to wealth because all of them will be slaves to Zyung. Those who resist his smallest command will be slaughtered without mercy. The God-King cares nothing for individual lives, only for his all-consuming Order.

"I know these things because I have walked the shores of the Living Empire. Long ago my own people fled Zyung's hordes. I have seen lakes of blood spilled in his name. There is no other choice but to stand against him. If we must die, we will die together with honor. To do otherwise is to accept the slow death of all you hold dear. Look into my eyes, Great Zharua, and know that I speak the truth."

Zharua did stare into Khama's eyes. His fear did not lessen, but an understanding dawned in his mind. Khama urged it to grow as a man fans a fire to greater heat. Zharua's lips quivered, but he made no sound.

"Enough!" said Damodar. For the first time the envoy's composure was shattered. He stepped between the Jade King and Khama. The sparks of an unrevealed power glimmered in his eyes. "You speak of matters that border on heresy. You pour words into

Zharua's ears like a poison to murder his wisdom. I see now that
you are a sorcerer."

"As are you," said Khama.

Damodar uncrossed his lean hands. They hung limp at his sides
now. His silver robe shimmered. "Perhaps the battle for Ongthaia
begins right now," said the envoy.

"It does," said Khama.

A bolt of lightning crashed through the glassy panes of a
skylight. It struck Damodar with a clap of thunder. Zharua shuddered on this throne. Undutu and D'zan leaped backward, tossing
their chairs to the floor.

Damodar's struck body did not fall. He stood steaming in his
splendid silver vestment, a grimace distorting his face for a
moment. Then he laughed long and loud, perhaps at Khama, perhaps at his own fleeting pain.

Khama's flesh flowed like water, taking on a dozen different
colors as his arms and legs merged with his torso and a riot of
feathers sprouted. The two Southern Kings drew their swords, as
did every man of their escorts. The guards stationed about the
Jade King's throne rushed forward to shield Zharua with their
bodies.

Damodar should have been a mass of charred flesh. The proof
of his Old Breed power was evident in the fact of his surviving
Khama's strike. Now the Feathered Serpent coiled his serpentine
body across the length of the hall. The maw of his triangular head
bristled with fangs. He raised the black stinger at the end of his
tail, broad nostrils flaring and steaming.

The silver sorcerer was quick. He leaped above the Feathered
Serpent and shot a bolt of green flame from his open mouth.
Khama's plumage ignited, black smoke streaming from his elon-
gated body. His forked tongue shot out to constrict the envoy, but
Damodar grabbed it with a flaming fist and nearly ripped it out

by the roots. Khama roared in agony and his roar became a peal of thunder. Men dropped their spears and clasped hands over their ears. Damodar's body slammed into the wall high above the marble floor.

The Zyungian did not fall. He hovered before the cracked palace wall as mortar dust rained upon the carpets below. Khama launched himself at the sorcerer. His snout caught Damodar in the chest and tore through the shattered wall. He burst into the sky between the jade towers with Damodar clinging to his jaws. Freed of the palace confines, Khama could now bring the full force of his power to bear.

Damodar's eyes were silver-gray like his raiment, and blood trickled from his mouth. "You cannot survive his coming!" shouted the envoy. "We are all but sparks about his great flame!"

The envoy released his hold on Khama's snout and fell toward the streets of Morovanga. The Feathered Serpent coiled about in mid-air and belched a streak of lightning hotter and brighter than the one he had called from the clouds. The bolt found Damodar as he fell. This time, however, the lightning struck a sphere of light that enclosed the envoy's body like gleaming crystal.

Khama sped toward him on currents of hot wind, but the radiant bubble arced toward the eastern coast of the island. Damodar was no longer falling; he was flying. He shouted back at Khama, who struggled to overtake him.

"There are *hundreds* of us, Khama! We are the last of the Old Breed! All of us serving *him*! You have a few more days to think on this ... "

Khama opened his maw to spew another thunderbolt, but the sphere of light shot away with terrible speed. Soon it was lost over the eastern horizon, where Khama saw only the green waves of the Outer Sea. Somewhere beyond that horizon, not too far from him, the Hordes of Zyung were winging their way toward the Jade Isles and the Land of the Five Cities.

You have a few more days . . .

Khama turned his wingless body back toward the island chain, a few smoldering feathers falling free of his leathery flesh. New ones grew instantly to replace them in shades of scarlet, emerald, azure, and gold.

A matter of days. The God-King's forces are near.

Damodar's power was undeniable. He could have stayed and fought Khama to a standstill. Perhaps he would have even won. Yet he fled instead back to Zyung to fulfill his mission and report Zharua's answer. The Jade King's decision had been made for him.

There are hundreds of us . . .

Khama soared above the Jade Palace as the islanders pointed and stared against the sun to catch a glimpse of him. He swerved and spiraled for a few moments below the heavy clouds that marred the blue sky, then sank head first toward the hole he had made in the Jade King's roof.

In the throne room the soldiers had sheathed their weapons. Undutu and D'zan stood close to Zharua's throne. They spoke in tones of assurance and comforted the Jade King with statements of bravado. Great Zharua wept on his green seat, nodding his head at the words of his allies. He seemed relieved that the weight of an impossible choice had been removed from his shoulders. Yet now he must face the consequences of rejecting Damodar's terms.

Khama sank to the floor on a soft current of wind and resumed his manly shape. His cloak of crimson feathers had been altered; it now bore all the motley shades of his serpentine plumage. Singed feathers and shards of glass littered the carpets and pillows.

The faces of all three Kings turned to hear Khama's next words.

"Zyung is coming."

5

Daystar

In the dreadnought's heart chamber Sungui tended the Ethus Tree with thought and sickle. The tree's bark was the color of burnished gold and smooth as a shark's skin. Sungui floated among its maze of branches, wrapped in the earthy smell of the amber leaves. Its trunk was as wide as a merchant tower, its branches thick as arching bridges. The gleaming roots coiled seamlessly, like the branches, into the chamber's floor and walls. The difference between branch and root was found only in the clusters of foliage growing from the former. Over the course of decades the tree had grown this ovoid chamber to cocoon itself, as it had grown the keel, hull, decks, and masts of the airship that was its extended body.

Sungui had fostered this particular tree himself, from seedling to fully formed dreadnought. He felt strangely secure nestled inside its network of yellow limbs. His heartbeat and the tree's own pulsing essence achieved a synchronicity similar to that of a mother tending a child. Yet, dwarfed by the tree's colossal stature, Sungui felt more the child than the caregiver. In the presence of the Almighty he often felt this way, yet Zyung's presence was a paternal force; the Ethus Tree seemed more like a silent mother. Sungui did not remember having any true parents.

New sprigs constantly sprouted from the interlinking branches. If left to its own free will the Ethus would continue to manifest larger and more complex structures. The carefully sculpted shapes of dreadnoughts were guided by the thoughtforms of tree-bonded High Seraphim. Many of Sungui's kind had bonded with two or three different Ethus Trees, yet he had refused to weaken his union with the *Daystar* by adding another ship to his heart-mind. This was the flagship of the Almighty himself. Sungui's charge was to ensure that it kept a form and substance that outshone the rest of the Holy Armada.

He raised the silver sickle and sliced a three-foot sprig from a vertical roof branch. Sap like honey dripped along the blade and pattered upon the curled roots below. A twinge of pain shuddered through the tree and along Sungui's fingers; a momentary sensation of discomfort, soon replaced by numbness. The amber leaves rustled.

"Be still," Sungui whispered, as one might speak to a horse being fitted for shoes. "A few more, my darling. We are almost finished."

The tree responded with a silent rush of understanding. Sungui regretted the small pains that pruning caused the Ethus, but it was necessary to maintain the *Daystar*'s physical perfection.

The dilemma of preserving the Ethus Tree, the Almighty had told Sungui, *is the dilemma of preserving the Living Empire. Sometimes one must remove a limb in order to preserve the integrity of the body. When we destroy a rebellious city or depopulate a riotous province, the process is much like pruning the unwanted branches of the Ethus. A moment of quick pain leads to years of peace and order.*

Sungui placed the severed branch, still leaking its golden lifeblood, into the basket in his left hand. Several more branches lay there, results of his morning's work. The tree seemed to understand the need for these moments of pain, though it could not prevent itself from sprouting more needless sprigs and stems. Its very nature was to grow beyond all orderly shape, so the High Seraphim worked constantly to preserve the shapes of the Holy Dreadnoughts.

In his most private moments, Sungui wondered if the same was true of mankind. Perhaps mortal beings could not help but erupt in sedition and treason every once in a while. This must be their nature, as the Ethus Tree's nature was to grow into a glorious yet chaotic tangle of woodflesh. Without Seraphim to tend and prune the Living Empire, it would grow into chaos, and nature would inevitably destroy it.

Sungui dismissed this line of thought as something his female aspect might ponder more readily. Duty was the soul of his male aspect. Questions about the worthiness of his position among the Seraphim sank like heavy stones into the black depths of his subconscious. He knew they would emerge to trouble him once more as soon as his aspect changed. This did not worry him, as so many other qualities changed when that metamorphosis occurred. He had accepted that, as the Ethus Tree had accepted the need for its weekly pruning.

"There," he said, tucking the final cutting into his basket. "All finished." He placed a slim hand upon the golden trunk. Warmth radiated from the bright bark, and a shudder of contentment rattled the leaves about him. Sungui closed his eyes and reached out to the rest of the ship through its living core.

Winds rushed across the curved hull, sliced by the bladed keel. The massive hold lay silent and stuffed full of provisions. Above it sixty slaves pulled upon oars to flap the two sets of canvas wings extending from the sides of the ship. The snores of another hundred and twenty slaves rattled the sleeping chamber on the same

deck. At midnight the oarsmen would change shifts. The power
of the Ethus Tree itself levitated the dreadnought vertically, but
it took the beating of these wings and the sweat of slaves to drive
it forward through the air. Conjured winds in the sails added
speed, but the true mobility of the armada rested on the backs of
these honored slaves. Such oarsmen were pampered and well fed,
almost a separate class of slave royalty. Their strength was aug-
mented by alchemic elixirs brewed for this purpose.

On the next deck above the oarsmen, hundreds of Manslayers
honed their blades, oiled their armor, and spoke in anxious voices
about the battles to come. Above that level the quarters of sailors
and Lesser Seraphim ran the length of the ship. Finally, the upper
deck vibrated with the steel-shod steps of Manslayers sparring or
keeping watch, the tread of busy sailors, and the footfalls of slaves
preparing meals in the ship's galley.

In the forecastle the palatial cabin of the Almighty himself was
empty of his presence. Holy Zyung stood near the mainmast,
directly beneath the rippling violet sails stitched with the likeness
of his flame-eyed face. Next to him stood Red Ajithi, the flagship's captain. The two were speaking, but Sungui could not hear
their words from the heart chamber. He imagined the Almighty's
eyes scanning the western horizon of the sea, perhaps looking
beyond the waves toward his goal. Zyung must see further than
any of those who served him. Perhaps he saw his future victory
lying beyond the heavy clouds.

Sungui sensed the familiar presence of two others next to his
sovereign. The Black Wolf and the Pale Panther walked always at
Zyung's side these days. His favorite new pets. The Wolf he called
Gammir, the Panther Ianthe. He named them his allies, but
Sungui knew them to be little more than traitors. Both had aban-
doned their kingdom in the Land of the Five Cities and come to
Zyung's side as fawning turncoats. At times they walked in the

shapes of man and woman, but they seemed to prefer the bestial forms. Or perhaps it was Zyung who preferred those forms. Visible reminders of their true nature?

Black Wolf and Pale Panther were two important keys to the coming triumph.

Sungui removed his hand from the Ethus bark and floated downward through the leaves. He left the heart chamber through its single portal and climbed the spiral stairs to the door of his own deck. Walking the long hallway he approached two Lesser Seraphim on their way to the upper deck. They halted and bowed on either side of Sungui as he passed. Although the Lesser Ones were mortal, they were disciples of the High Seraphim, devotees of the minor sorceries allocated to their kind. Many served as dreadnought captains in the armada. These two were part of the thirty or so who served Zyung directly, thus their presence here on the Holy Flagship.

The deck's central corridor was a broad tunnel of seamless yellow Ethus wood. At its far end Sungui opened the door to the alchemical laboratory where Gulzarr and Darisha worked amid an array of crystal decanters, glass tubes, cauldrons, and braziers. The pair were lost in their work, beautiful and serene as always, brewing potions and elixirs for the potency of slaves and vitality of the Manslayers. Sungui sat the basket of Ethus trimmings on a workbench, along with the curved sickle, and departed without words. The leaves and sap from the trees were highly effective in the endeavors of alchemy. The alchemists had even brewed a delicious mead from the sap, one only the High Seraphim and Zyung himself were permitted to drink. The couple's work now, on the edge of the invasion, was focused on more practical concerns.

Sungui climbed another spiral stairway to emerge on the middle deck. The fierce winds grabbed his hair and tossed it about his head. Manslayers in scalloped plates of steel and spiked helms paced the deck with tall spears clutched in their gauntlets. To either side of the hatch stood a row of Trill stables; every dreadnought had facilities to house twelve of the bronze-beaked sky-lizards, though only half of these were occupied at any one time. The stables were empty now, the Trill Knights having taken their mounts into the clouds for maneuvers. The winged beasts must fly daily or they grew restless and hard to control. They also caught seabirds as fodder on these flights, requiring less of each ship's supplies to feed them. The reek of Trill feces stung Sungui's nostrils, but the wind quickly tore it away from him.

Captain Ajithi remained standing near the mainmast, studying a map scroll while the great sail thundered above him. Zyung had left him alone there. Sungui supposed the Almighty had returned to the privacy of his great cabin. Red Ajithi had earned his way up through the ranks of Manslayers to dreadnought captain by quelling three separate revolts in the Outer Provinces during his thirty-year service. The man was in his fifties now, and still wore his polished breastplate, shoulder guards, and skirt of silver scales. He had forsaken the beaked helmet of the Manslayer for a turban of purple silk that matched the ship's sail. An onyx gemstone large as an egg sat in the fabric above his forehead, and his waist-length hair was completely bundled into the turban. A curved greatsword hung upon his back, its pommel set with a ruby that matched the size of his turban's onyx.

Ajithi looked up from his map as Sungui approached.

"The pruning is complete," Sungui told him.

Ajithi nodded. "His Holiness wishes to speak with you in his chambers," said the captain. Sungui returned the nod and watched him march immediately to his command chair high on the quarterdeck. Like the entire ship, the captain's chair was an extension of the Ethus Tree, a chair-shaped conglomeration of lesser branches woven specifically to accommodate a man-sized commander. Nestled into its curved comfort, pillowed by orange leaves and surrounded by the pointed tips of curling limbs, the captain communed with the tree as well as any Seraphim. During the regular pruning sessions most captains vacated the command chair to avoid sharing the pain of the tree. This was a luxury the pruning Seraphim themselves could not enjoy.

Ajithi wrapped his hands about two curling sprigs at chest level and resumed control of the vessel. A faint smile grew on his lips as his tree-bond returned. Sungui knew the warmth of that bond, and he envied the captain's right to avoid the tree's pain. Yet because Sungui felt that pain which no captain deigned to endure, his bond with the Ethus was the stronger one.

Sungui turned about and headed for the forecastle. The wind whipped at his silver robes and chilled his bare feet. Beyond the far railings at left and right, banks of gray clouds rose like billowing mountain ranges. A few Trills and their riders could be seen darting through those clouds. The bulk of the Trill Knights flew behind the flagship, but the lizards would pursue tasty avian prey with great speed before returning to the ranks. Knowing when to indulge a Trill's appetites was a large part of commanding such a mount. Sungui had not the talent for it, but he admired the warriors who dedicated their lives to mastering the lizards.

Below the cloudscapes a green ocean simmered with white-capped waves. Three weeks the Holy Armada had been flying, and still no sign of land. The sea below must be truly vast. Yet they must be close to the other side of the world now. Sungui could feel it, as he had felt the entirety of the ship while communing with the Ethus at its core.

He stood now before the double doors of Zyung's quarters. As tall and grand as any palace portals they stood, engraved with holy sigils and the flame-eyed face of Zyung. The doors were made thrice the height of a man to accommodate the Almighty's great size. Rarely did Zyung reduce himself to the size of a mortal, though it was easily within his power. The multitudes needed to see that their God was a massive and imposing figure. Two hulking Manslayers stood before the portal, one on either side. They bowed as Sungui approached, uncrossing their barbed spears and pulling the doors open.

The Almighty's council chamber was as large as a provincial King's throne room. It spread across the entire width of the forecastle, with oval windows admitting rays of sunshine through colored glass. The ceiling was high and vaulted, supported by eighteen pillars of amber wood. Each pillar was shaped into the form of its own tree, although these were merely extensions of the great Ethus Tree below. Tapestries of jeweled silk hung along the walls or separated the front of the chamber from the sleeping quarters at its far end. The Almighty's personal slaves scurried about the room carrying pitchers of wine and water, sweeping the rich carpets, and preparing platters of foodstuffs for their lord and his visitors.

Zyung's gigantic form sat in a larger yet less ornate version of the captain's command chair. Before him sat a table of polished obsidian scattered with oversized scrolls, leather-bound tomes, maps, quills, and goblets. A circlet of flawless platinum held back Zyung's black mane. His skin was polished bronze, and his silver robe was the exemplar upon which all the robes of the Seraphim were patterned. His eyes were miniature suns, his chin a block of marble. A chain of black opals glittered across the slab of his chest.

Before the high table, in seats built to accommodate their lesser sizes, sat the three advisors who had already arrived: Lavanyia with her mound of sable hair wound in golden wire; Gammir the Black Wolf in his slim human form, and Ianthe the Pale Panther in her womanly shape. Ianthe's skin and hair were pale as milk, her nails sharp as talons, her lips red as blood. Her beauty rivaled even Lavanyia's. She stared at Sungui with feline eyes. No longer did he imagine Lavanyia as a lioness of the plains; the feral nature of Ianthe dispelled all notions of Lavanyia as a predatory creature. Ianthe still looked every bit the cat, even when shaped as a woman. Gammir's black hair and eyes likewise maintained their lupine aspect, although he was unexpectedly handsome. Sungui wondered if the two expatriates were related in some way.

Lavanyia's presence was surprising. She tended the Ethus Tree of the *Flametongue*, and had never set foot on the *Daystar* until now. Yet she stood first among the High Seraphim, so the Almighty must have summoned her for some reason. Perhaps a new strategy had been devised for the coming invasion.

An empty chair waited for Sungui. He bowed to the Almighty and settled himself in its cushioned seat. Both of the expatriates wore the silver robes of Seraphim. Were the Wolf and Panther to be counted among the ranks of the Holy? It must be so, for only Seraphim were permitted to wear such garments. Sungui would not be foolish enough to question the Almighty's wisdom on the subject. The four guests sat meek as children before an imposing father.

Zyung regarded them with eyes hard and bright as diamonds. His voice was the rolling of distant thunder. One did not simply *hear* the Almighty's words, one *felt* them resonating in the bones that lay beneath flesh and skin.

"Tender of my Ethus Tree," said Zyung. "Your work does not go unnoticed. Would that I had another thousand with your skill at woodcraft."

Sungui bowed his head. The eyes of Lavanyia fell upon him, but he felt the gazes of Gammir and Ianthe most keenly. Their stares were leaden weights upon his shoulders.

"I live only to serve His Holiness," Sungui said. The words were ritual, the only proper response to such praise.

Zyung waved one of his great fingers and a network of chromatic lights spread through the air between his guests. In a moment's time the colors resolved themselves into a map, one with which Sungui had some familiarity. Yet now the map bore details and reliefs that had never existed in previous versions. It hovered before them, a vision of the continent to which they were heading.

"While awaiting word from Ongthaia," said Zyung, "I have learned much from the Wolf and Panther. Before your eyes stands the Land of the Five Cities in more detail than any have seen until now. I have discussed our strategy with my generals and decided upon the most favorable tactics. We shall establish the seat of the Extended Empire here . . . "

Zyung's finger pointed to a stylized city etched upon the floating light-map, the representation of a metropolis with tiny towers and domes encircled by a high wall. It sat upon the eastern shore of the greater land mass. "Here lie the ruins of Shar Dni, destroyed eight years ago by the wrath of its enemies Ianthe and Gammir. These ruins are uninhabited save for ghosts and blood spirits. It lies in a fertile valley at the mouth of a mighty river. There are abundant croplands for our slaves to work. Our legions will be well fed. Here we will build a new Holy Mountain from the shattered stones of the dead city."

Sungui scanned the lands beyond the valley of Shar Dni. To its north lay a continent-spanning range of high mountains. Beyond that, the forests of the Giantlands and the city called New Udurum. To the valley's west lay the broad plains of the Stormlands, marked with the gold-green city of Uurz. South of Uurz stood a mighty cliff labeled as the Earth Wall, and beyond that a realm of untamed wilderness. In the southern half of the continent he counted three great cities: Mumbaza and Yaskatha on the western coast, and Khyrei on the eastern coast directly across the Golden Sea from Shar Dni's ruins. Two peninsulas of rugged mountains and volcanoes hemmed the Golden Sea to north and south. The Jade Isles of Ongthaia did not appear on this map. The Almighty must believe them unimportant to his invasion. A few stepping stones to cross on the way to his true prize.

"Holiness, what of this Khyrei?" Lavanyia pointed at the city. It gleamed with dark purple light. "Should we not establish a foothold there as well to secure the southern half of the continent?"

Gammir shifted in his seat. "That is *my* city," he said, glaring at Lavanyia with a wolf's inscrutable calm. His eyes shifted to Ianthe and he corrected himself. "*Our* city. A revolt of slaves and sorcerers has temporarily removed it from our power. His Holiness has promised to restore it to our care. We shall rule it in his name."

Lavanyia stared at Sungui. Her look said: *These traitorous fools should not be here.*

Sungui offered her the slightest of smiles.

"Khyrei will be spared until we have conquered the Stormlands," said Zyung. "Then we will send legions south with Wolf and Panther to take back their city. A few of the High Seraphim will join them. When Khyrei is secure, these southern forces will move upon Yaskatha and Mumbaza. Yet our greatest concerns at present are these two northern cities. Uurz must fall first, followed by Udurum, City of Men and Giants. The Giant-King's armies must be destroyed when he comes to the aid of Uurz, as I am told he will surely do. Without the power of the Giants, Udurum cannot stand for long."

"You speak of sorcerers, Wolf," said Sungui. "How many are there to oppose us?"

Ianthe laughed and answered for Gammir. "A handful of the Old Breed," she said. "Iardu the Shaper struggles to rouse more of them, but most will continue to languish in their long sleep."

"Yet there were enough to steal away your southern city," said Lavanyia.

Ianthe's eyes focused on her. Sungui expected bolts of flame to leap from them and reduce the highest of the High Seraphim to ash. The Pale Panther only smiled.

"We did not yet stand in the grace of the Almighty when this happened," said Ianthe. "By his power we will shatter our old foes. In his presence we grow mightier than ever."

"Indeed," said Lavanyia. Her eyes returned to the glimmering map.

"When we reach the Sharrian valley," said Zyung, "the High Seraphim will conjure up these blood spirits and bind them to aid us in the siege of Uurz. The Lesser Seraphim will begin construction of the new Holy Mountain and a city to serve it. Any slaves taken from the interior will be sent to work there. What was once Shar Dni shall stand again as New Zyung, Heart of the Extended Empire."

Zyung's listeners bowed their heads in a simultaneous gesture of understanding.

"Lavanyia, Sungui, you will travel among the Seraphim tomorrow and dispense these new commandments. When you have accomplished this, report to me your success. We have only a few more days until we see the Isles of Ongthaia. After that, a single day will bring us to the Land of the Five Cities."

Again the four heads bowed. The floating map faded like a snuffed torch. Sunrays gleamed in Zyung's great eyes. Or perhaps they beamed *from* his eyes. Sungui could not be certain which was true.

"Rejoice, my children," said Zyung. "You will bring abiding

peace to a realm that has known only war, strife, and chaos for
ages. Through these mighty works of ours, future generations of
Khyreins, Uurzians, Yaskathans, Udurumites, and Mumbazans
will know the bliss of ultimate order, the strength of holy unity,
and the sweetness of a universal harmony that spans the entire
world. Rejoice, for the future of mankind grows brighter with
every league we travel."

Sungui could not help smiling at the brilliant truth of the
Almighty's words. The others also shared this breathless awe. Here
was the naked joy of Zyung's presence: the absolute conviction
that the world was made better by his very existence, and that
your part in the great drama was to help him spread that ecstasy
across the earth. Power brought Order; Order brought Peace; and
Peace brought Bliss. Zyung and his Seraphim were about to unite
the world as it had never been united in all its long, bloody ages
of struggle. First there must come a great pruning, then the Tree
of Empire would grow stronger and healthier than ever.

A final round of bows preceded a goblet of highborn wine for
each of them. Then the four were dispatched from mighty Zyung's
presence. On the windy deck outside, nothing much had changed.
The *Daystar* sailed through the sky with the Holy Armada trailing behind it, three thousand Holy Dreadnoughts filling the blue
heavens in all directions. The great flock of Trills spread itself
between the airships, flapping leathery wings, and the armor of
knights riding on their ridged backs gleamed bright as diamonds.

Sungui breathed deeply of the cool, fresh air. He let the winds
caress his face like the gentle fingers of a lover. Gammir and
Ianthe went down the main hatch where the comfort of their quarters waited. Surely there were others among the Seraphim who
resented the presence of these newcomers, but to voice opinions
on the matter might bring one in direct conflict with Zyung's
wishes.

Lavanyia lingered at the railing of the middle deck, her eyes searching among the dreadnoughts for some unspoken sign. Sungui joined her, sensing that she wished to speak.

"I do not trust these traitors who often wear the forms of beasts," she said, her eyes still on the armada. The rattle of sails mingled with the sound of the *Daystar*'s flapping wings. "It is said they drink the blood of slaves."

"This is true," Sungui told her. "Six days past a galley slave was burned nigh to death in an accident. Captain Ajithi ordered a spearman to put the wretch out of his misery, but the Black Wolf came instead and took the wounded man away with permission from His Holiness. Later I witnessed the Manslayers toss a charred and shriveled corpse into the sea. There was not a drop of blood left in the body. Sergeant Mhirondu tells me they have requested more slaves' blood, but His Holiness denies them. Yet they will be allowed to drink their fill in the coming battles."

Lavanyia sighed. "Blood magic," she whispered. "There is no place for it among the Celestial Ones."

Sungui offered a half-smile. "Apparently there is."

Lavanyia's dark eyes turned to Sungui. She caressed his face with her soft palm. "Be wary of them, Sungui. When they are no longer of use to His Holiness, we will rid ourselves of them."

"With the Almighty's permission," said Sungui.

"Of course," said Lavanyia. She kissed his cheek and floated beyond the railing, winds tearing at her silver vestment. He watched her glide gentle as a seabird past the *Serpentine* and the *Steel Heart*, alighting finally on the deck of the *Flametongue*. He lost sight of her among the armored figures pacing there.

The armada flew directly toward the setting sun. Shades of scarlet, pink, and gold bled from the clouds into the sea. Sungui watched the last of the sun's disc sink beyond the horizon, and the first stars blinked to life in the purpled sky. Darkness covered the ocean and a yellow half-moon emerged from a bank of clouds. Lamps and braziers came to life across the top decks. The Trill Knights brought their screeching mounts back to the stables of their assigned ships, driving them home with prodding spears and vocal commands. Slaves came forth with hocks of raw meat to feed the lizards. The familiar odor of Trill dung filled the middle deck, and the sound of snapping beaks shod in bronze.

Sungui took a last look at the armada trailing behind the *Daystar* before going below. In the darkness the Almighty's great fleet resembled nothing less than a constellation of stars rushing across the darkness. Sungui descended the middle stair and entered his cabin, where slaves brought a meal of roasted fowl, seasoned rice, and assorted fruits. When the remains of his repast were removed, Sungui hung his silver robe on a peg near the cabin door and practiced evening meditation by the light of a tallow candle. In the morning he must travel across half the armada to deliver the Almighty's instructions. Tonight a calm mind and deep sleep would serve him best. He lay upon the pillowed cot and closed his eyes, denying himself the opportunity to yearn for his comfortable bed and spacious apartments in the Holy Mountain.

As he hung upon the edge of sleep, an image of poor, salt-doomed Mahaavar leaped into his mind. The specter followed Sungui into a dark dream where she wore her female aspect and lay with Mahaavar again in the Garden of Twenty-Seven Delights. In waking life Sungui had to choose either male or female form, but the sleeping mind was both at once. The emotions of both aspects mingled and merged in a way they rarely did during conscious moments.

The Almighty had taken no notice of Mahaavar's disappearance. He was not the first of the High Seraphim to be found unworthy, sent to salt, and consumed by his kind. It was likely that he would not be the last. The High Lord Celestial had more weighty matters on his mind, and a thousand other High Seraphim to serve him.

In the dream Sungui the woman made love to Mahaavar on a bed of crumpled flowers. Yet at the moment of climax, Mahaavar turned to salt. Sungui cried out and woke abruptly in the dark cabin, still entirely male. He blinked into the darkness and realized that he was not alone. He might have been startled by this realization, but he was strangely unmoved for some reason. Warm hands moved across his chest. The scents of jasmine, rose, and lavender. A lithe, pale form lingered next to him on the edge of the cot.

Sungui whispered a word of flame and the candle on his bedside table ignited itself. A woman's round, heavy breasts hung before his face. Above them Ianthe's white tresses framed her exquisite face. Ruby lips smiled at him as her palms explored the muscles beneath his taught skin. Her eyes were black diamonds reflecting the candlelight.

"Sungui . . . " She whispered his name like a spell. "I want you."

Sungui sat up, taking her wrists in his strong hands. She did not struggle or resist him.

"You wish to drink my blood."

Ianthe laughed. "The wine of your veins is far too rich a vintage for me," she said. "I do not drink the blood of allies . . . only enemies."

And slaves.

Her breath was honey-sweet in his face. He had expected the breath of a carnivore. Suddenly he became fully conscious of her nudity and his own. Already his body was responding to her presence. Her hips were wide, her legs long and slim. She was pale perfection.

"We cannot do this," he told her. His words contradicted the promise of his ready loins.

"Why not?" she asked. "Gammir is not my lover. He is my . . . heir."

She is of the Old Breed, like us.

Yet, unlike most of us, she is not fully Diminished by the will of the Almighty.

She is ageless and full of mysterious power.

"I am told the Seraphim often take lovers among their own kind," she said. "And that your last paramour is no longer among us." Her lips hovered close to his. Her hot breath quickened his pulse.

"I am not . . ." A rushing flood of lust washed away his words and thoughts.

His hands fell to the softness of her breasts.

His eyes closed tightly, as if he were staring at the sun.

"Do I please you?" she asked. Her lips smothered his before he could answer. Heat surged to the limits of his body. He grabbed her narrow waist and pulled her close. The world and all its powers were lost as he fell into a red dream.

When their lovemaking was finished, the candle guttered low. She lay wrapped in his arms, cheek resting against his chest. Had she worked a spell to enchant him? Or was it only that ancient enchantment that all women possessed? He could not be sure. The pantherish aspect of her nature had shone through in her savage mating. He lay spent and exhausted. Sleep stole his awareness, despite a growing sense of alarm.

She woke him with kisses before the sweat had dried on their bodies. Starlight through the porthole of his cabin told him it was still deep night outside. Where he had been exhausted, he was aroused once again. Her taloned fingers worked a tender magic on his flesh.

"You were marvelous," she said. "A most glorious lover."

He returned the praise. Yet he did not tell her the whole truth, that her skills had eclipsed all of his previous lovers. Through ten thousand years of carnal delights, he had experienced nothing like her. Already he craved more.

"Is it true that you alone among the Seraphim," she asked, "assume both male and female forms to suit your moods?"

His hand lingered on the warm curve of her waist. Her snowy tresses smelled of lilac and rosewater. "I possess both aspects," he said. "But in truth my moods are most often determined by which aspect I wear. Temperament follows form, as form follows function."

She cooed into his ear and wiggled in his arms. "Never have I found such an enticing lover," she breathed. "Show me!"

Sungui shook his head. None who shared his body had ever made such a request. As a male he took female lovers, just as his female aspect enjoyed a variety of male lovers. The idea of mingling the two for a single paramour seemed strange. Perhaps forbidden. The Almighty would not allow it, of that he was certain.

"Please," she begged, touching him in places he could not resist. "I wish to make love to *all* of you, Sungui. I can find this thrill nowhere else in the world. I have loved women before. You will see that I know how to please both your aspects equally well. Let me do it."

Why should it be such a strange thing? He was a being of double aspect. Why not share it with her? Why should his intimates not experience the fullness of his being? Already the female aspect slumbering within him leaped at the idea. The female Sungui was rebellious, defiant, and adventurous. To do this thing that had never been done before was a quiet rebellion against the established order. Zyung's order. The thought excited him, grew in his chest and loins until he could no longer contain it.

Ianthe glided away to watch him change. The hard planes of his body softened to supple curves. His cheekbones and chin receded, growing smaller and more feminine. His neck lengthened and smoothed, as did his legs and arms. A pair of firm breasts sprouted from his chest, smaller than those of Ianthe but no less beautiful. The hair upon his body vanished except for the tangled black mane that grew soft as silk, and the matching eyebrows. Soon the female aspect had banished all manly elements from the body.

Sungui lay bare and splendid in the candlelight. She blinked her heavy-lidded eyes at the amazed and curious Ianthe. Wordless, their bodies joined together in a wholly different yet strikingly similar passion. The Pale Panther taught Sungui the secret arts of pleasing a woman, something only her male aspect had considered until this moment. If this was some arcane spell the pale sorceress had woven, then Sungui was entirely lost in its grip. She no longer cared. They spent the remainder of the night wrapped in an urgent bliss as fresh as new-fallen snow, yet hot as dancing flame.

When the first rays of a gray dawn crept through the porthole, Sungui rose to wash herself in a basin filled by mute slaves. Ianthe lay propped on one elbow, watching her every move. In the corner of Sungui's vision the Khyrein seemed once again to be a great, white cat staring at her. Sungui accepted a platter of cheese and mangoes from her body-slave, and brought it to the cot. Ianthe's ebony eyes haunted her with memories of the night's splendors.

They fed one another slices of yellow fruit and shared juicy kisses as the morning light grew bolder, filling the cabin with a golden glow.

"Why do you serve Zyung?" Sungui asked, sitting on the cot's edge.

Ianthe smiled. "Because I must," she replied.

Her feline eyes whispered another message: *I am using him to get what I want.*

"The Seraphim resent you and Gammir," Sungui said. She reached for a comb to run through her rumpled locks. "They feel you do not belong. You do not *believe*."

"Do you believe?" Ianthe asked.

"I *remember*," said Sungui.

"What do you remember?"

Sungui lowered her lips to her new lover's ear. She whispered what she could not say aloud. "Freedom. And power."

Ianthe placed a hand on her thigh, tracing invisible patterns with a black talon. "These things can be yours again."

Sungui shook her head. "A few of the High Seraphim remember their true power, but still they fear Zyung. We are all Diminished in his presence. This will happen to you as well."

Ianthe laughed. "I serve him, this is true," she said. "Yet I refuse to be Diminished."

Sungui touched the pale oval of Ianthe's face. "So did we all, until we no longer could resist. I have tried to stir them, to restore their greatness, yet I alone retain this independence of thought. Perhaps it is because of my dual nature. I serve, yet I defy. I am a perfect union of opposites."

Ianthe kissed Sungui's lips, one last ember of the fires that had blazed between them.

"What do you truly want?"

Sungui's eyes were bound to Ianthe's black diamonds. She hesitated.

"To be as I once was," Sungui said. Her body trembled. "To be free of this Diminished state. To rule, to roam, to build my own empire. To love and slay and tear down mountains if they offend me. To walk this world as *he* walks it. Fearless and invincible."

"I sensed this the moment I saw you," said Ianthe. "These dreams are your birthright. You will have them, Sungui."

"How?"

"I will aid you. We will both aid the Almighty in taking his new lands, then we will steal them away from him. He is no greater than you or I. You will see . . . "

Sungui did not believe this. But she wanted to. She yearned for it to be true. It had haunted her dreams for centuries. Longer. Yet none of Those Who Listened would truly hear. She had been alone in this private turmoil for so long, it had become an invisible chain that constricted her body in both its aspects, dragging her down with the weight of ages.

Now, for the first time, she might break that chain. She was no longer alone.

She would steal back the power that was rightly hers, and the world would no longer be slave to Zyung's peace and order.

"What of Gammir?" Sungui asked.

Ianthe grinned, stroking Sungui's chin. "Your beauty is unsurpassed," said the Panther. "I am sure you can persuade Gammir to join our plans. Go to him tonight, as I came to you. Be sure to wear your female aspect."

Ianthe stood to pull on her silver robe.

"What of the Almighty?" Sungui said. Her heart beat faster, as it had done during the night. "What if he should discover us?"

"Zyung cannot hear our words or taste our minds," said Ianthe. "My own power prevents it. Speak to no one of this save Gammir." She gave Sungui a lingering kiss before departing.

Sungui pulled away, wiping blood from her lower lip. Ianthe had bitten it.

Ianthe licked her own lips. Her eyes said: *You may have me again, in both your aspects.* Then she was gone, leaving Sungui alone in the cabin, a coppery tang on her tongue and drop of red staining the breast of her silver vestment.

Blood magic.

She changed her robe and decided to remain female as she

toured the dreadnoughts to deliver the pronouncements of Zyung. Memories of Ianthe's body and the phantom sensations of her touch lingered throughout the day.

In the early afternoon Damodar returned to the *Daystar* from Ongthaia. Wrapped in a luminous sphere of power, he emerged from a bank of dark clouds. Sungui had just returned from her own duties, so she came to the middle deck to greet him.

Damodar's lean face was troubled; the remnants of rage still simmered about his eyes.

"Has the Jade King surrendered?" Sungui asked.

Damodar ignored her, but she knew the answer.

"I must speak with His Holiness." Damodar stalked toward the Almighty's cabin. When the great doors closed behind him, a peal of thunder shook the sky. The captain was barking orders to his crew. Men rushed to secure lines and masts while Trill Knights brought their flapping beasts in early. This was no weather for the winged lizards and their riders to brave.

Ahead of the flagship, the horizon was a mass of dark, churning clouds split by jagged veins of lightning. A wall of cold rain engulfed the decks, and the wind grew fierce. It moaned in Sungui's ears like the howling of conjured devils. Thunder rattled the sails and drowned men's voices.

"*Hurricane!*" called the captain from his high seat.

The *Daystar* sailed into the rising storm.

6

The Dreaming Ones

North we fly, in the shapes of white eagles.

We do not pause for sleep, or food, or rest. We do not speak, although there are many questions Sharadza would like to ask me. There are many things I would like to tell her.

Now is not the time.

"Our first ally lies deep in the Frozen North," I told her before we left New Khyrei. She had turned a puzzled face toward me. Her emerald eyes sparkled, so like those of her mother.

"Is there a member of the Old Breed among the Udvorg?" she had asked. The blue-skinned Giants roamed the high plateaus of the Icelands. A great force of them had followed her brother south in his campaign against Ianthe the Claw. Yet many Udvorg tribes still roamed the tundra, or held the icy palace of Angrid that now belonged to Vireon.

"Not the Udvorg," I told her. "Far beyond their hunting grounds we must go. To the shores of the Frozen Sea at the top of the world."

She knew the urgency of our need and she asked no more questions. She had already delivered my message to Vireon and Tyro. The northern armies prepared to march along the Golden Sea coast to set up defenses in the Sharrian valley. Before they reached the shattered remains of Shar Dni, we must enter the white realm where even the Udvorg did not go.

Never had we flown so fast, or so far. I feared her strength might not be great enough for the long flight, and that she might slow me down. I would not leave her in any case. Yet I need not have worried. The tips of her wings were never far behind my own.

On the second day of flight we soared over the Stormlands. A continent of shifting clouds hid the fields and rivers from our eagle eyes. We flew higher than the storms so the angry winds would not impede our progress. On the third day we crossed over the Grim Mountains, sailing past frosty peaks and dark valleys where shadows danced. The bones of Serpents moldered in deep gorges. Beyond the mountains we passed over the City of Men and Giants. How long had it been since Sharadza had visited the city of her birth, seat of her brother's power? No doubt she wished to dip between its ebony towers and walk its bustling streets again. Perhaps she longed to visit Vod's tomb and lay a wreath of flowers at its door. Yet she said nothing of these desires. The time for returning to Udurum would be later, when the fate of the continent and all its peoples did not lie upon our shoulders.

As the mighty towers dwindled behind us and the colossal forests of Uyga and pine covered the world below, I recalled the tavern in Udurum where Sharadza's word – and her deep green eyes – had awakened me from a cynical slumber. She had stirred me to action, demanded that I help her stop a war before it started, and would not accept my protests of futility. I had worn the shape of a disheveled old winesop for so long, walked the cities telling stories for handfuls of coins, that I had nearly forgotten my true self. Her father had condemned me twenty years earlier for manipulating his life to suit the needs of the world. Vod's harsh words and his anger had haunted me. I no longer wanted to be the Shaper. So I became Old Fellow, a spinner of yarns, and a drunk. Yet that was not me at all.

How ironic that Vod's own daughter was the source of my rebirth. She had come to me begging to be taught the rudiments of sorcery. In this I had complied at last, although hiding my true identity from her. She saw through my disguises. In that squalid drinking house, she roused more than my true self from its dark dream of shame and regret. She returned me to life as surely as the warm sun brings forth the first blossom of spring.

All that I have done since that day to prepare the Land of the Five Cities for the coming of Zyung is because of her. Sharadza Vodsdaughter became my apprentice, my muse, and my friend. She had agreed recently to stay on my island, since she could no longer tolerate life as the spurned Queen of Yaskatha. Perhaps one day she will love me as I have come to love her. Yet we must stand against Zyung and repel his hordes, or that sweet dream will never come to pass. Like millions of others, it will die to be replaced by Zyung's dream of absolute order.

On the fourth day of our flight we passed the White Mountains and looked upon the vast ice fields where bands of Udvorg hunted mammoth and elk. The crystalline palace of the Ice King glimmered at the western edge of our sight.

By the end of the day we approach a range of glaciers big as mountains, the glittering ramparts of the Frozen Sea. Here I circle downward toward a peak of icy shards as Sharadza follows me. The northern horizon is an unbroken plain of whiteness, an ice-capped ocean whose depths have never been explored by Man or Giant. In all the world there is only one thinking entity who has swum below those thick crusts of ice and seen the dark secrets of the polar sea.

To find her, we have come all this way.

In the north-facing wall of a mighty glacier yawns the mouth of a jagged cave. Our wings bring us to the narrow ledge of blue-green ice that hangs before it. The wind blows bitter and frigid across the snows that mantle the cleft. Our bodies shift from eagle to man and woman. Sharadza stares into the ice cavern, seeking to penetrate its blue shadows. Then her eyes turn to me and I feel her trepidation. Our thin robes and sandals grow into thick furs and boots. Still the cold bites into my bones. Icicles form instantly in the long, dark tresses of her hair. The wind rattles them like brittle bones.

"Do not be afraid," I tell her. The blue flame flares on my chest, yet it is not an earthly flame so there is no heat from it. I walk through the deep snow at the lip of the cave. I offer Sharadza my hand and she takes it. Even in this barren place where the chill of death hangs over us, even through the thick leather gloves that cover our fingers, her touch brings a glad warmth. We enter the cold cavern together.

"Who would sleep in such a forbidding place?" Sharadza asks, her voice a whisper. The roaring winds are left behind us as we advance between the walls of ice.

"Not all of the Dreaming Ones are truly asleep," I say. "They may have simply lingered in a chosen role or shape for too long. They have effectively *become* the roles they have been playing. This is the danger of assuming any form; wear it too long and it subsumes your true nature. Recall Khama the Herder of Goats, whom we were forced to remind that he was the Feathered Serpent. Some of the Old Breed have enjoyed their long sleep for too long. They do not wish to be awakened. They might greet us with anger, or refuse to recall the truth."

"What can we do in such cases?" she asks.

I conjure up a long staff from the ice to help me navigate the uneven floor. It feels cool and solid in my right hand, while Sharadza clutches my left.

"We can only try," I tell her. "Try to make them remember who they really are."

I do not mention the particular dangers of waking the long sleepers, especially the one who lies at the far end of this cavern. There are other factors at play here. Some of the Dreaming Ones did not choose their forms, but fell into them as mortal men fall into unwanted dreams.

"What is that smell?" Sharadza asks.

The bones of devoured walrus and seal lie scattered on the cave floor, some buried beneath the ice. My blue flame flares again, shedding cobalt light across the back of the cavern, and Sharadza sees the answer to her question. She gasps.

"This one *does* sleep," I whisper. "Yet no longer . . ."

A colossal mound of white fur rises above our heads. On either side of us great claws rest upon frosted rock. A pair of great eyes dark as obsidian and rimmed with pink flesh opens to regard us. A black snout sniffs at us as the mother of all snow bears awakens. A rumble rises in its throat and icicles fall from the cavern roof, splintering about us. The she-bear is large enough to swallow us both whole.

Its maw opens, displaying yellow fangs long as swords and a pink tongue wet and dripping. Hot breath washes over us, reeking of marine flesh.

I raise the staff of ice and send the Flame of Intellect coursing through it like a torch. The great she-bear blinks and the blue fire dances in her black eyes.

"Ytara!" I call her by name, using the oldest one I can remember. "It is Iardu, your cousin. I bring you the gifts of memory and light."

The she-bear growls, shifts its massive bulk. Sharadza squeezes my hand. She must be afraid, but she shows no other sign of it. Perhaps she recognizes something in the great she-bear's eyes. She was always a clever apprentice.

The beast rises on all four legs, shedding ice from its back and sides. It sniffs at us, regards us with eyes full of curiosity. And hunger. Either she will remember her name, or she will try to devour us. I stand ready for either.

The white she-bear speaks in the voice of a woman. The language is ancient. One I have not heard in ages. It is a language spoken only by sages and sorcerers.

"I do not know these names," she says. Her tongue slides across her black snout. "Yet your voice is familiar." The she-bear settles herself before us, laying her head upon one massive paw. Her ebony orbs shift to Sharadza. "I know your beauty . . ." The voice is uncertain. She has lost much. Rather, much has been stolen from her.

"Ytara is your name," I say. "Though you have known many others. Do you remember Shayakatha? Ymbriss? Anyarom? All these names mortals have called you. Do you recall your long journey southward? Do you recall the warm jungle and the kindly folk of Omu?"

The she-bear growls. "Dreams . . ." says the woman's voice. "Dreams of a golden sun and purple blossoms . . . a city among the trees."

"Yes!" I encourage her. "You remember Omu the Green City. Many were the temples built in your honor there. The simple folk of Omu worshipped you as their Goddess in another form than this one. I visited you there long ago. You were most happy. Until the Pale Queen came and stole it from you. Then you fled north, back to this lonely land from whence you came."

The she-bear roars. I am stirring unpleasant recollections now. Sometimes the deepest memories bring the deepest pain.

Sharadza releases my hand. She stares at me instead of at the Bear Goddess.

"The White Panther . . . " says the she-bear.

I nod. "That was the first time she stole your life and loved ones," I say. "The first time you faced Ianthe the Claw."

The she-bear gnashes her fangs. "I remember this name," rumbles the voice, more bear than woman now. I must be careful. "I remember my enemy . . . "

"Wait!" I say, raising the bright staff to catch her eyes again. "There is one last name you must recall, for when you lost it you lost everything. Again you manifested here, in the sanctum of your power, where you ruled before the coming of Man."

The she-bear is silent. Columns of antediluvian stone glimmer inside the luminous walls. The ice-swallowed remnants of a forgotten temple.

"*Alua.*" Sharadza says it before I do. She sees it clearly now and knows who we have awakened this day. "You were Alua, Queen of New Udurum. It was my brother who named you this. He found you roaming the Icelands in the shape of a fox who became a woman. He loved you, and he helped you find your lost memory. Do you remember him?"

The great she-bear blinks at the Daughter of Vod. Its eyes fall to the floor, pressed downward by the weight of loss.

"*Vireon* . . . " says the she-bear.

"Yes," I say. "What else do you remember?" I do not want to speak of her lost daughter. The girl-child who was Ianthe's ruinous lie.

The she-bear slumps to the cave floor. "Nothing else . . . "

"The White Panther tricked you," Sharadza continues. "Once again she stole what was yours. Can you not recall this?"

"She stole your life," I say, "and your power, your white flame. I see now that the Claw has also stolen much of your memory."

She should remember more than this. The hollowness inside her is Ianthe's doing. Still, we only need to stir enough memory to bring her with us.

I glance at Sharadza. A tear slips from her eye, freezing solid upon her gentle cheek. I want to reach over and wipe it away. I resist the urge.

"You are Alua!" Sharadza shouts. "Wife of Vireon! Queen of Udurum! You cannot have forgotten this."

The she-bear's shaggy bulk shrinks.

"You are of the Old Breed," I remind her.

It is no longer a hulking beast that stands before us. It is now the slim figure of a woman with blonde tresses hanging the length of her waist. The only remainder of the she-bear is a great white pelt hanging like a cloak from her shoulders. Beneath it she is naked, bare feet pale upon the icy ground. Yet she does not shiver.

"*Alua.*" She repeats her name, and now the feminine voice fits the body. She speaks in the common tongue of the Five Cities; the language of traders and diplomats, scholars and Kings.

Sharadza rushes forward and grabs her in a tight embrace. Both women weep. How much does Alua truly recall, and how much as Ianthe erased forever? I cannot say.

Alua raises her hand. A white flame erupts in the center of her palm.

I cannot help but smile at this display. Sharadza laughs, wiping frost from her cheeks.

"Names ... faces ... a few torn fragments of dreams," Alua says. "These are all I have. I have lost so much ... " Her tears flow freely now. She lets them fall. They turn to motes of ice before they reach the cave floor.

"Come with us," I tell her. "Stand with us in the battle that is coming and face the Claw one last time. She is the enemy of us all, and she serves an even greater enemy. Come with us and make Ianthe pay, for she has twice wronged you and those you love."

"My name is Alua," she says, as if finally convincing herself.

Her sense of loss is deep. I feel it opening like an abyss inside the core of her being.

"Yes." Sharadza cradles her hands.

A blast of white flame surrounds us. Encased in its blazing light, we burst from the cave and rise into the blue vault of sky. No longer must Sharadza and I flap our weary wings to fly.

Inside the flaming sphere Sharadza grabs my hand as well. Her glistening eyes stare into mine with a flood of released emotions. Her brother will rejoice when he finds that his beloved wife still lives. Vireon could not know how difficult it is to slay a true sorceress.

Yet we cannot seek Vireon yet. Sharadza knows this too.

More of the Dreaming Ones must be awakened.

A white comet hurtles south above the frozen world.

Inside the cocoon of white flames Sharadza speaks softly with the reborn Alua, whose look is that of a child being lectured by a kindly tutor. Her memories are only fragments, but she quickly understands the immediacy of our danger and the urgency of our mission. The name of Zyung she does not remember. I do not wish to burden her reintegrated mind any further, so I describe his horde and his goal. It is enough for Alua that he has allied with Ianthe the Claw. That above all else makes him her enemy.

The lands below rush by as we watch them through the sphere of pale fire. Once again we cross the Grim Mountains, yet at a speed that far exceeds that of our eagle forms. Alua weaves a garment for herself from the white flame. It cools and congeals to the smooth consistency of silk, and she keeps the cloak of snowy bearskin as a reminder of her most ancient aspect. Her dark eyes, too, remind me of the great she-bear.

She listens quietly to our voices, flashes of recognition igniting in her black pupils. Yet her mind is still clouded. Ianthe stole far more than her white flame. She has not spoken the name of Maelthyn, the daughter born of her womb and Ianthe's sorcery. We do not have the heart to remind her of this terrible crime. Perhaps she will remember everything in time, and what a torrent of pain will follow that memory. Yet for now I need to keep her focused on the task at hand.

"Our destination lies northwest of Uurz," I say. Alua's head turns and the flaming sphere arcs westward above the Stormlands. "Some leagues east of the Western Flow, yet many leagues south of Vod's Lake. There we will find a series of green mounds dotted with ancient stones. A great city stood there long before Men came to the Desert of Many Thunders." I take Alua's hand and show her a mental image of the grassy mounds. They are all that is left of the nameless city.

In a few short hours we have crossed from the top of the Frozen North into the very heart of the Stormlands. I see the Western Flow glimmering silver below us. I guide Alua toward the scattered mounds. There are tiny villages on the green plain here. All this land was black desert before Vod worked his great spell and slew the Father of Serpents. Yet no villages sit close to the low mounds that we now approach. A soft rain falls from thinning clouds, and rays of sunlight stir rainbows to life above the steppe.

The globe of white flame descends to earth. It fades, leaving Alua, Sharadza, and myself amid the tall grass. Cool winds rustle my robe, and the honest scent of wet earth fills my nostrils.

Like the burial mounds of lost Kings the seven hillocks rise about us. Dense thickets of thornwhistle and starflower grow upon their crowns. Toppled obelisks of worn granite lie here and there between the mounds, covered by emerald moss and purple lichen. The blocks are so old that only the faintest remnants of glyphs and sigils are visible in the pitted stone.

"What is this place?" Sharadza asks.

"It has no name," I say. "Rather its name has been lost for ages. These crumbling stones were once the foundation of a metropolis older than any on this continent."

I walk between the obelisks, touching each of them in turn. Some are merely the remnants of foundation stones that once supported walls as large as those of Udurum or Uurz. My touch extends through the porous rock into the soil beneath. It is not long before I find the one for which I am searching. I mumble a word of power and the slab rises from the loam to float in the damp air. Tendrils of moss and creeper vine hang from it, dripping rainwater into the rectangular hole that has been revealed.

"Come," I say. Sharadza and Alua follow me down the ancient steps into the womb of the earth. The concealing obelisk lowers itself behind us, sealing the entryway once again. The blue flame gutters on my chest, turning the rough-hewn walls from dirty brown to shades of azure. The light is not enough for Alua, so she conjures another white flame to dance in her palm. Sharadza keeps her silence as we descend.

At a certain depth the crevices of the stairwell are still filled with black sand from the desert that used to lie above. Sigils and hieroglyphs run along the walls in clever patterns. Another dead language, this one inscribed in stone. A human skull lies in a corner where the stairwell turns in another direction. The smells of fungi and rotted bones prevail here; there is only darkness outside our sphere of pale bluish light.

At last we reach the bottom of the long stair and enter a grand cavern. A forest of eight-sided pillars stands carved from floor-to-ceiling stalagmites. Nameless ciphers and icons swirl across the surface of these columns. The floor is of natural stone as well, yet graven smooth except for faded murals and cryptographs. I remember this place full of light and life, but it is the blurred memory of a dream that might or might not have been real.

My companions follow me into the depths of the pillared vault. We stop at the mouth of a great, dry well encircled by runes that I recognize. The marks of protective sorcery. Standing above the dark shaft, I sing the notes of an ancient song. My voice echoes among the pillars, travels across the dusty floor, and sinks into the well. By the time my song is done, twenty pairs of yellow eyes stare at us from the darkness between the pillars.

The Nameless Folk have us surrounded.

They creep forward, silent as cats. Curved blades glimmer in their fists. Dark veils cover the lower half of their faces, and hoods hide the tops of their heads. They offer us only the glare of their reptilian eyes. Some carry loaded crossbows of dark wood. I am surprised to see such recent advancements in weaponry here.

Alua's white flame surges but a glance from me dispels her alarm. Sharadza stands against my shoulder. I can almost feel the questions lingering on her tongue. She has learned to be patient; a necessary trait for any sorcerer.

"*Vaazhia*." I address them with the name of their creator. It is the only word I need to say. One of them motions me forward. I walk in the direction indicated by his raised blade. Sharadza takes Alua's hand and reaches for my own. The thick gloves are gone now, and her touch is a pleasant heat in my grasp.

We pass through an archway guarded by two stone demons with chipped teeth and empty eye sockets where great jewels once sat. The Nameless Folk enclose us, part escorts, part guards. They lead us on without voices (for they have none) through shadowed galleries and twisting hallways, always downward into the earth by stone ramp and stairway. We navigate a narrow ledge, pressing our backs against cobwebbed stone and glancing into an abyss of windblown darkness. More stairwells await us beyond the gulf, and we come at last to a massive cavern with a river running swift through its middle. An arcing bridge of stone carries us over the whitewater; tall torches along its length blaze with orange light, despite the clouds of wet mist rising from below. This must be the same waterway that runs beneath the palace of Uurz, or at least one of the Sacred River's tributaries. On the far side, another arch accepts us and a corridor leads us into a realm of dancing flames.

The walls of a great hall glisten with constellations of raw diamonds. Braziers of ancient iron burn hot with the leaping flames. Hundreds more of the Nameless Folk mill about the polished floor, peering from behind columns of green beryl and yellow quartz. All of them wear the veils that show only their yellow eyes, and they are all so very similar. There are no children or young ones among them, as there are no elderly. This does not surprise me.

Our armed escort leads us toward the far end of the hall, past the yawning mouths of corridors agleam with half-light. This is the nexus of their sunken city, the heart of a nameless kingdom that few living beings know exists. There are no books in any of the Five Cities' libraries that speak of this place, no stone tablets that record its history. Only one entity survives who remembers the glory of this lost city when it thrived in the sunlit world an eon past. Her gaze falls upon us now.

She sits upon a tusked throne made from crystal and the bones of mammoth Serpents. The nameless ones bow before her dais. I sink to one knee and my companions join me. She regards me in silence as I raise my head to speak.

"Greetings, Vaazhia, Queen of the Nameless Realm," I say. "It has been far too long since last we spoke." I use the common tongue because I know she understands it. Not even she remembers the long-dead language of her own kingdom.

Vaazhia's eyes gleam bright as rubies with vertical pupils of ebony. She sits tall as an Uduri upon her throne. High cheekbones dominate her shapely face, and her full lips are purple as the skin of fresh grapes. Her tall forehead sweeps back into six horns that rise from her skull like a crown of yellowed ivory. A flood of night-black hair flows from the top of her head to cover her shoulders and breasts. Strands of jewels shimmer upon her arms and legs, where the scales of her scarlet skin reflect the glow of firelight.

"Shaper." I am relieved to see that she remembers me. Her forked tongue darts from between her lips and slides back into the hollow of her mouth. "You have not visited me since the black desert ruled the lands above. Are these your daughters?" Her eyes shift to examine Alua and Sharadza.

"These are my honorable companions," I say, emphasizing the last word. I introduce both women at length. Vaazhia was always impressed with formalities and courtly etiquette. Reminders of her lost Queenhood, perhaps.

"I am most honored to meet you," Sharadza says with a curtsey. "Your hidden kingdom is . . . quite lovely."

Alua's only greeting is a silent bow of the head. "You are of the Old Breed," Vaazhia says to her. She recognizes the subtle signs of our ancient kind. Her eyes return to Sharadza: "And you carry the blood."

"My father was Vod, King of Giants, Breaker of the Desert," says Sharadza.

Vaazhia's eyes widen. She leans forward in her great chair. "Yes. I see him in your face, girl. Yet I knew him by another name. And his father I knew better than he did. Yet too short was his stay in my company. This cannot have been so long ago . . ."

"Only a few decades," I say. "Time is an illusion that fools us all, cousin."

Vaazhia looks at me as if seeing me for the first time. She nods, her eyes glazing with memories, or the shreds of memories. A silence falls upon the chamber. Even the orange flames, fueled by her sorcery, are without sound.

I break her reverie by speaking her name again. She blinks like a viper.

"Do you recall the name of Zyung?" I ask. The lizardess nods. "A great war falls upon the world above, and Zyung has become our enemy. We seek your aid in opposing him and those of our kind that he commands."

Vaazhia laughs. "The world above does not concern me," she says. "Long ago I enjoyed life beneath the sun and stars. This is my world now and I am content. My children take what I need from the fields above, and there are none to challenge my rule here."

"Your ... *children* ... are known only as brigands and river pirates in the world above," I remind her. "When they raided the desert they bore the stigma of nomads and the hatred of civilized folk. Now they are the scourge of the Stormlands, and still held in contempt for it. Do you not wish for allies, for respect, for companionship?"

"I have companions," she says, spreading her arms wide to indicate the Nameless Folk. They stare at us, silent as mushrooms.

"I know the truth of these nameless ones," I say. "They are creations of your sorcery, nothing more than phantoms designed to resemble those you once ruled here. In the world of the living they are nothing less than scavengers and thieves, all in service to an unknown sovereign. They neither think nor feel. You are *alone* here, Vaazhia. Yet you need not be."

The lizardess stands, towering twice my own height. Sharadza takes a step back. Alua does not move.

Vaazhia opens her mouth wide, baring fangs like those of a cobra. "You insult me, Shaper . . . " The earth rumbles beneath our feet and sand trickles from the vaulted ceiling. The flames in her braziers rise higher and brighter. Serpents of fire dance there, ready to leap and devour us.

"No," I say. "I bring you a gift called truth." I step closer to her, drawing her gaze lower. The long talons of her fingers curl on either side of me. "Far too long have you wallowed in the sorrow of your own memories. The world you built here died long ago! Yet you can build another. Do not waste your immortality sitting in the dark, lost in a prison of remembrance. Live, Vaazhia! Rise up and discover how fine and beautiful the world has become! I will help you!"

Her rage subsides. She does not weep, but sinks back into her throne. The braziers return to their calm state of illumination. She sighs, sweeping her gaze across the throng of phantom folk who have served her for millennia. Vaazhia's curse is not to forget, but to remember. I must break her of it. I reach out with the invisible coils of my heart, hoping to reach her own. Eager to make her believe that something other than this futile existence is possible.

"How can I do this?" she asks. Her voice is that of a despairing child.

"Let me – let us – show you how," I say. "You are of the Old Breed. You can remake yourself as you will. Come and see the world that lives green and golden above you. Fangodrel's world." Vaazhia loved Vod's father Fangodrel, if only for a little while. When he refused to stay with her in this sunken realm, it only confirmed her despair. Yet Fangodrel was but a taste of the world that had moved on without her. I know she longs for more of that sweet flavor.

"There is so much goodness to discover in the world," Sharadza says. "Light and love and the laughter of children. The gleam of sunlight on water and leaf. The breath of night and the glimmer of stars. So much more . . . "

Vaazhia sits in silence for a long moment.

The nameless ones collapse into piles of black sand and coarse cloth. They will no longer raid the ships of the Western Flow and the villages of the grassy steppe. They were nothing but mindless drones that served the will and appetites of Vaazhia. Now the lizardess must learn to serve herself.

"Tell me more of Zyung and this war," she says.

In the coral palace of Indreyah the Mer-Queen we are received without ceremony by a cadre of Sea-Folk guards in scalloped armor. Alua's flaming sphere has carried us far over the Cryptic Sea, and as we plunged into the blue waters I replaced it with a sphere of sunlight and fresh air. Once I was welcome here, but those days are done.

As we sank into the great chasm and left the aquamarine light behind, Vaazhia asked me a question that I could not answer. "Do you really believe your former lover will aid you in this struggle, Shaper?" The lizardess was blunt. The waters rushed by us in a swirl of bubbles. The purple glow of the anemone forest lay directly below us. Eels and schools of silver fish darted by our sinking globe of light.

"She may hold little love for me these days," I said. "But she is quite fond of Sharadza."

Alua and Vaazhia turned to the Daughter of Vod. Vaazhia had reduced her size to stand no taller than any of us. Her crimson orbs blinked with curiosity.

"I once visited her palace," said Sharadza, "to reclaim the bones of my dead father. Later she aided me against a sorcerer who had imprisoned me."

"You have lived a most interesting life for one so young," said the lizardess. Of course, she had lingered for an eon in the cellars of a dead city. Having Sharadza as a companion would be good for her. The Daughter of Vod had given me a new passion for life, and I was sure she would do the same for Vaazhia. If we all survived the coming of Zyung and retained our individual natures.

We descended among a multitude of gliding sharks, rays, and squids toward the avenues of the coral city. Spires and domes glimmered below like constructs hewn from monolithic emeralds. Shades of crimson, turquoise, and azure danced amid the incandescent marine gardens. The Sea-Folk swam thickly here, where streets and plazas were home to phosphorescent anemones, gardens of kelp, and groves of deepwater flora.

Curious crowds of the silver-scaled folk encircled us, staring with the amber orbs of their eyes. The sharp tines along the middle of their backs and on the tops of their heads twitched nervously. Some brandished tridents or harpoons of whale bone. Indreyah's people were a cautious breed; the people of the dry lands had exploited the ocean's riches for as long as there had existed divers, swimmers, and seagoing vessels. The Sea-Folk had good reason to fear the air-breathers of the world. I could not begrudge their lack of hospitality.

As we sank into the palace courtyard, pitted walls of crimson coral rose to hide the city from us. Indreyah's finny warriors came forth to surround us with the points of their fishbone spears. Their captain rode on the back of a harnessed black shark and carried a crystalline blade. He spoke in the bubbling language of the Sea-Folk, and among our group only I understood him.

I addressed him by name, in my own language, yet by my conscious magic he understood my words. "Captain Aoliooyulp, you look well. Take us to the Queen if it pleases you." He knew that my request was in truth a polite demand. Aoliooyulp had known my anger before and had no wish to draw it upon himself again.

I was not always so level-headed in matters of the heart, or so cautious about releasing my rage upon those about me. One of my many faults. Indreyah had discovered most of them during my time in her watery kingdom.

So we enter the coral palace under heavy escort and are brought before the throne of sculpted sapphire. Indreyah the Mer-Queen leans back against the great oyster shell that rises from her high seat. The lambent jewels of a hundred lost kingdoms encrust the dais below her webbed feet. Strands of dark hair float about her silvery head, evoking an image of black flames. The topaz orbs of her eyes flash directly at me, as if she does not see my three companions at all. I do not wait for her to condemn me with words or compel me to leave. Before she can do either, I sink to both knees and spread my arms wide within the tiny sphere of air.

"Great Queen of the Sea," I begin, "my old and dear friend, most beautiful of all creatures beneath the waves, ruler of the coral kingdom and keeper of the Great Pearl. My heart rejoices to see you again."

Indreyah does not reply to my obvious fawning. I must play the fool here to disarm her; better to draw her amusement than her scorn. It is a fine dance that requires a perfect balance of charm and flattery.

The Mer-Queen's eyes settle upon the ladies behind me. "Sharadza of Udurum, Daughter of the Great and Honorable Vod." She smiles, baring teeth bright as pearls and sharp as fangs. "*You* are most welcome here."

Sharadza performs her royal curtsey and offers a smile that is worth far more than my own words. "It has been too long, Majesty," Sharadza says. "Since last we spoke, I have gained and lost a Queenhood. I am no longer of Udurum, though my heart still dwells there. Allow me to present Alua, Queen of Udurum, wife of my brother Vireon, King of Giants. Perhaps you have known Alua by another name long ago, for she is of your kind. And this is—"

"Vaazhia," says the Mer-Queen. Recognition glimmers in her yellow orbs. "My cousin."

The lizardess bows and her forked tongue darts in and out.

"I did not know you still lingered among us," says Indreyah. "Yet I am glad to see you."

"Empires may rise and fall," Vaazhia says, "but the Old Breed are forever. Your realm is one of beauty and splendor."

Indreyah turns her gaze upon me again. I remain kneeling before her dais, knowing that to do less would be unwise. "Iardu, what scheme of yours brings these great ladies together?"

I smile at the subtle nature of her insult. "No scheme but urgent need, Queen of Coral. Zyung has finally reached across the great water. He would conquer the Five Cities and all their peoples. I would not trouble you if the circumstances were not so dire. I come on behalf of Sharadza and her kingdom, as well as the kingdoms of Uurz, Yaskatha, Mumbaza, and even dark Khyrei, to ask for your support in the greatest struggle of this age."

The Mer-Queen's bubbling laughter fills her throne room. Her soldiers and courtesans join in her mirth, unsure of the reason for it.

I look at Sharadza, who understands what I need her to do.

"Majesty," Sharadza says, "Iardu speaks truly." She describes the Hordes of Zyung, the legions of Manslayers, the vast armada of airborne dreadnoughts. She elicits the threat of Zyung as eloquently as I could have done myself, perhaps even better. The Mer-Queen listens attentively and says nothing to interrupt her. Sharadza finishes her well-spoken plea and the Sea-Folk watch her as if they too understand. Perhaps some of them have studied the dry tongues.

"I have no wish to battle with this God-King of the Dry

Lands," says Indreyah at last. "I remember the power of Zyung from the time before Man walked the continents. Let him rule the world above the waves if that is what he wishes. He is no threat to me. If what you say is true, he will bring peace and order to the kingdoms of the Five Cities. If he wishes to parley with the underwater realm, I will speak with him as an equal. Yet I do not think he cares for my deep kingdom. I will not condemn my people to fight a war that does not serve their interests. I am afraid that you have wasted your time in coming here, though you are always welcome, Daughter of Vod."

"Indreyah . . . " My tone is pleading. "You are far more than the Queen of the Sea-Folk. You are of the Old Breed! Do not forget what this means . . . "

"I am what I wish to be," Indreyah says. "As are we all."

Her amber eyes smolder with pent flames.

"Is there nothing I can do to sway you?" I ask. "I returned your great pearl years ago. Do you still begrudge me so?"

"I begrudge no one," Indreyah says, spreading her long webbed fingers. "I will not seek war when there is nothing to gain from it. Only fools and madmen do so. Perhaps you should consider negotiating with Zyung instead of forsaking his dream of peace."

"I have already achieved peace between the Five Cities!" I almost lose my temper. She has to see the tragic irony of what befalls us. "There is peace now above the waves – for the first time there is no war among Men! Ianthe no longer rules Khyrei. There is a chance for a new and brighter world here, far from the oppression of Zyung's empire. A dream I never thought possible has been fulfilled only to face extinction from the other side of the world. I cannot let everything I have worked so long to build be crushed beneath his heel."

"Everything you have built?" She mocks me. "Your manipulations are like those of Zyung, yet you realize it not. How many

Kings have you tricked into following your designs? How many Men and Giants have given their lives to your scheming? How many lost races and crumbled kingdoms? You speak of freedom and liberty, but you have always been a tyrant where it concerns your personal stakes."

The remnants of old arguments have risen like hungry krakens to tear at our hearts.

"You never did understand me," I tell her.

"I have spoken," says the Mer-Queen. "You may stay here as honored guests, or depart on the moment. But I will not join your war."

Sharadza is silent. She knows there is nothing more to be said.

"Time grows short," I say. "We cannot linger. There is one last ally we must try to win."

Indreyah glides from her throne to hover above our airy sphere.

"Go then with my blessing," she says. Then to Sharadza, Vaazhia, and Alua: "Return to me when you have no favors to ask. I would enjoy your company."

"If we live to see victory," says Sharadza. "I promise that I will."

The Mer-Queen glides into a shadowed hallway, followed by a coterie of silver-scaled attendants.

The air inside our glowing sphere has grown thin. The guards lead us into the courtyard where I will the sphere to rise, taking us as fast as I dare toward the surface. I had hoped Indreyah's fondness for Sharadza would win her to our cause. I should have known better. Like Vod himself, the Queen of the Sea-Folk would never forget or forgive the ways in which I had wronged her.

"I am sorry," says Sharadza, her hand on my shoulder. I can only smile at her. I promise myself now that I will never give her cause to hate me as Indreyah does. As Vod had done.

"You plan to seek the Maker of Mountains," says Vaazhia, guessing my next move.

I nod a silent confirmation.

"You would disturb his long sleep?" she asks, reptile tongue darting nervously. "Do you not fear risking the wrath of Udgrond?"

I cannot lie to her, or the others.

"Yes," I say. "I do. But we have little choice."

"Who is Udgrond?" asks Sharadza.

"The Maker of Mountains," I answer. She need not know more at this time. Our sphere breaks above the waves, and Alua weaves the white flame about us once again.

I close my eyes and look inward, seeing a vision of the Jade Isles wracked by typhoon and wave. Beyond that scene, cleaving the very heart of Khama's wall of storms, the Holy Armada of Zyung approaches. Khama and the Southern Kings will not long delay him. I cannot dwell on the hundreds of ships and the thousands of lives that will be soon lost. Instead, I plant a vision of our destination into the mind of Alua, and the flaming sphere carries us across the sky.

For a fleeting moment I consider sending my companions across the continent to join Vireon's forces in the Sharrian valley. Or to the Jade Isles, perhaps to lessen the inevitable slaughter. Then I realize that all our powers might be necessary in this current endeavor. We must go together if we are to have any hope. We have only a day, perhaps two. Three at most.

"And where does one find a Maker of Mountains?" asks Sharadza.

I want to take her in my arms and hold her close, but I cannot do this.

Instead I answer her question.

"At the blazing heart of the world."

7

Valley of the Dead

The sea cliffs lay far behind her. The land spread green and flat to the west, and the Golden Sea reflected sunfire to the east. Dahrima walked between the two worlds of steppe and ocean, alone but for the parade of memories in her head. Her boots left deep tracks in the wet sand. The sound of the rushing surf had become a soothing refrain, a song of water meeting earth that rose and fell in ceaseless rhythm. Somewhere leagues ahead of her the River Orra rushed along the haunted valley and poured itself into the sea.

Once it had been called the Valley of the Bull, when its slopes were filled with terraced croplands. In those days not so long ago the towers of Shar Dni stood white and strong between the blue temple-pyramids of the Sky God. Dahrima had never seen it in person, only in colorful landscapes adorning the halls of the palace at Udurum. Queen Shaira, Vireon's mother, was born a Sharrian and retained the pride of her heritage. Dahrima did not know Shaira well – certainly not as she had known Vod himself – but she understood Shaira's love of her homeland and respected her for it. Scenes of the Sharrian valley were common throughout Vod's palace, whether rendered in oils, woven in tapestries, or crafted into stone murals. Men said the deep green of the valley's grass could be seen in Shaira's eyes. Sharadza Vodsdaughter had those same eyes, though she was a child of Udurum.

Shar Dni was only a pile of cursed ruins now. Ghosts and devils were said to roam the valley. Perhaps these rumors accounted for why no living men had resettled the valley after Gammir and Ianthe destroyed and plundered it. Dahrima recalled the blood-shadows that had crept into Vireon's chambers and fed upon the blood of her spearsisters. The ghosts had nearly claimed Dahrima's life as well, but Vireon had saved her by driving out the witch who wore the shape of his daughter. Dahrima could not imagine the pain of losing a child to such dreadful sorcery. Vireon had lost Alua as well. This war had begun with bloody betrayal inside the Giant-King's house, and the revelation of Ianthe's rebirth inside poor, doomed Maelthyn.

Vireon had lost all that he loved on that night. The burden of a King was heavy, and loneliness was his usual recompense. Dahrima realized days ago that it must be loneliness, an unshakable sense of loss, that had driven Vireon into the arms of Varda. Even cold arms must provide comfort to one who suffered as Vireon did. Yet Dahrima, in a fit of rage, had robbed her King of that small comfort. For this she hated herself, even though she knew that Varda's comfort was a false one. Nothing more than a strategy for gaining Vireon's trust.

Dahrima would atone for her crime somehow. She must stay alive at least long enough to do this. Let Vireon's justice fall upon her if it must, but first she would stand against his enemies. She may have broken the vow of service with her hands, but not with her heart.

He needs me.

On the second day, her flight had turned into a scouting mission. She decided on reaching Shar Dni before the forces of Uurz and Udurum. Alone she could run faster than any marching legions. Let her spearsisters stay behind and march with the Udvorg – they had not sinned against the blue-skins. If Dahrima had stayed, her sisters would have risen to protect her from any reprisals. Slaying Varda was a matter of personal honor, every Uduri would argue. This was the way Uduri had always settled their conflicts, with strength of arm and, if necessary, naked steel. It was Varda who drew steel first and thus sealed her own fate; otherwise the witch might have endured only a sound beating. Of course, the Udvorg might not see it this way. Perhaps Vireon would not either. Yet by moving ahead and scouting the way for the northern hosts, Dahrima could still be of service. When the battle began, she would be there, ready to slay and die for her King.

Her running had slowed when she approached the harbor town of Allundra. At the foot of the Earth Wall it nestled above a small bay. Trading galleons from all the great cities were moored at its wharves, along with a dozen Jade Isle traders. There were even a few Khyrein reavers docked there, having escaped the revolution that placed the black fleet into the service of Tong the Avenger. They were likely pirates now, expatriate seadogs who would rather sail the main preying on merchant vessels than pledge fealty to the King of New Khyrei. Allundra was a haven for any ship that dared its port, no matter its nation or purpose. The town had long been neutral in affairs of state, even allowing Khyrein slavers access to its taverns and warehouses. Though it lay at the southeastern edge of the Stormlands, it was not claimed by either Uurz or Khyrei. Despite Allundra's important position as a crossroads for seagoing merchants, it was little more than a haven for smugglers, pirates, and outlaws.

Dahrima had not liked the smells of raw fish, human waste, and rotting seaweed that wafted from the seaport. The jumble of red-tiled roofs leaked a thousand gray smokes. She decided against braving the muddy streets to seek ale and fresh meat. Instead she rested until sundown and ran on, skirting the edge of the town. She crossed the inland road under cover of night.

The following sunset she discovered a cluster of fishing villages girding the delta of the Eastern Flow. Tiny two-man boats dotted the ocean here, and children in brown tunics played along the beaches. These settlements seemed more wholesome than Allundra, but again Dahrima hid herself from those who might gawk at a lone Giantess and carry word of her far and wide. She waded across the delta by moonlight and sprinted away from the villages.

The next day rains rolled off the sea, cool and heavy. Dahrima slept a little beneath a crag of chalky stone overlooking the waves. She was far enough from the river delta to avoid the fisherfolk. Upon waking she killed a hare with a throw of her knife, and built a small fire to cook it before resuming her northward run.

Another day of moving along the coast brought her to a sheltered cove, where she stopped to pick oysters from the shallows. She ate them raw and drank from a rocky stream feeding the inlet. She slept there in the damp shadows of the cove.

Now she walked the eastern edge of the Stormlands once again. Looking out across the peaceful turquoise waters, she could not envision the great armada sailing above it. Perhaps Zyung's forces had already reached the haunted valley. If so, Vireon must know. This was another important reason why she must scout ahead. What human could travel as far and as fast as she could with as little nourishment or rest? Knowing that she was close now, Dahrima picked up her speed. Her memory of maps was keen, and she estimated that another day of running would bring her to the Valley of the Bull which was now a valley of death.

The sun was an orange disk of flame hovering at the blue sky's zenith when Dahrima topped a ridge and found her destination. The land fell away from her in graceful curves, green and pleasant despite the rumors of evil that hung about it. The broad, flat valley narrowed as it approached the seacoast. The Orra was a silver ribbon winding from misty highlands to pour itself into the sea at the mouth of the vale. Dahrima had left the rain behind when she departed the oyster cove; this was no longer the Stormlands with its daily showers. Yet plenty of white clouds floated above the valley, reminders that storms were not unknown here.

Across the silver river lay the shattered stones of Shar Dni. In the eight years since its doom, the city's jumbled remains had been smothered by a multitude of mosses: green, brown, ochre, yellow, and azure. In the bright sunlight it seemed a scattering of jewels lay among the weedy pavements and toppled walls. The great stones that were not covered by moss had faded from white to gray, and nothing remained of the city's towers but the jagged stubs of splintered foundations. They stood here and there among the devastation like the toothy stumps of fallen Uyga trees. No trace of the blue temple-pyramids remained, or if they did the creeping mosses had blanketed them entirely.

White gulls flew in flocks above the river, picking fish from the shallows. The rotted husks of warships and trading vessels lay half buried in sand about the crescent bay. One pointed prow stuck up from between the reeds of the delta, the rest of its bulk having been swallowed by mud. When Dahrima looked carefully, she saw the white glimmer of scattered bones beneath the moss and weeds.

A great arched bridge of stone had once straddled the river, connecting the western road with the threshold of the city gate. A few of the bridge's great stones protruded from the river's placid surface. Only the eastern and western ends of the crumbled bridge remained intact, each one arcing now into thin air. All the Sharrian wall gates were gone, leaving hollow gaps in the disintegrating ramparts. The damp sea air ate away at the mortar slowly. In a few more years what sections of the city wall that remained would be nothing more than piles of broken stone, like the rest of the city.

Dahrima was pleased to see that the grasses of the valley were as verdant and healthy as legend insisted. She walked down the hillside toward the shattered bridge. The ruins did not seem haunted from this vantage. Sad, perhaps, but not cursed. It reminded her of Old Udurum when the titanic Serpent-Father had reduced it to rubble. Yet the Valley of the Bull did not fill her with the foreboding and unease she had expected.

Memories of Old Udurum played through her mind as she waded across the cool river. Thirty years as Men counted the calendar had passed since the oldest enemy of Men and Giants had risen from beneath the Grim Mountains to destroy the old City of Giants. In those days the Uduru dwelled apart from their small cousins, as they had for three thousand years. Fangodrel the First, father of Vod, had ruled the city then. Those were days of lasting peace, long hunts, and endless revelry.

Dahrima had lived for eight centuries behind the walls of Hreeg's City. Often the wilderness of Uduria had called her to the hunt. She had known a dozen lovers in those days. She had never blamed King Fangodrel for the curse of barrenness that had fallen upon her kind. The wise among them said it was mighty Hreeg's fault, for the original Giant-King had driven Omagh the Serpent-Father back into the deep earth without killing him. Sleeping in his underground haunt for two thousand years, the Lord of Serpents had dreamed a curse upon Giantkind. The curse of gradual extinction borne by the Uduri. Sterility.

When Fangodrel's first son was born, an exception to the growing curse, the City of Giants had erupted in celebration and song. Yet it was only a few days later that the infant Vod was stolen away by a great black eagle. King Fangodrel had trekked south for years to search for him. While he was away, new Serpents began to crawl out of the mountains and devour Giants. Fangodrel returned eventually to stand against Omagh himself, when the Serpent-Father awoke from his long sleep and fell upon the city. Fangodrel had failed to find his lost son, and he failed to protect the city from Omagh's wrath. Vod's father died in battle, impaled by one of Omagh's great fangs, and the behemoth tore the city to pieces.

Thousands of Uduru had perished in that battle. The race was already dwindling in numbers due to the lack of birthings, but now multitudes were crushed, burned, and devoured by Omagh and his brood. Dahrima had killed Serpents for days on end, and like all the Uduru she learned to skin the beasts and use their black scales for armor. In the end it was Ghaldrim the Golden who saved them all. He gathered the last of the Uduru, some twelve hundred Giants, and led them south into the lands of Men. Ghaldrim was the first to realize that there would be no reclaiming shattered Udurum with such tiny numbers. The Serpent-Father made his nest in the piled ruins, large as a mountain, while Ghaldrim led the Uduru across the mountains into the Desert of Many Thunders.

If Ghaldrim had not led the Giants to assault the gates of Uurz in their desperation, Vod would never have discovered his lost heritage. The Uduru would never have regained their lost King. And Vod would never have marched north to slay the Serpent-Father, in the process altering the shape of the world and giving birth to the Stormlands. Vod later rebuilt Udurum stronger than it had ever been, and he opened its gates to Men.

Dahrima had lain with Vod when he rediscovered his Giant heritage. Soon after their night together, he won rulership of the Uduru from Ghaldrim. She had hoped Vod's royal seed in her belly would give her the child that she had never been able to conceive. But not even Vod's magic could quicken her empty womb, and her charms were not great enough to hold his attention for long. Vod loved a human girl; he had even taken the form of a Man to win her hand. Shaira of Shar Dni would bear his strong sons, not Dahrima the Axe.

Vireon had been the proud result of Vod and Shaira's union. Dahrima understood now that it was all for the best. If she had claimed a child fathered by Vod, he might never have taken Shaira as his Queen. Then Vireon would never have been born to unite the Uduru with their cousins the Udvorg. He might not now wear the crown of Udurum, as well as that of the Udvorg. Vireon was in all ways the Son of Vod, heir to greatness. The King of All Giants.

The greatest honor in Dahrima's life had been to serve him.

She walked among the mossy stones of the dead city while the sun sank toward the sea. The shadows grew long and she found an arch of pale granite under which she might sleep. There was no sign of creeping bloodshadows, foreign ships, or other threats. She would wait here for the armies of Vireon and Tyro, watching the sea for signs of enemies. She would run and carry news of Zyung's arrival, should it come before Vireon's. She was the Giant-King's eyes in the valley of death.

In the glow of twilight she began a search for wild game among the stones. Instead she found the imprint of a human foot in a bed of orange moss. It was freshly made, and she sensed the odor of Mansweat on the breeze. She could not be sure if there were more than one set of tracks, but she knew now that she was not alone in this forsaken place.

There was no trace of hare, squirrel, or other wildlife among the ruins. It was as if animals avoided this place altogether. Except for the seagulls that came close enough to fish in the delta. The absence of game was not as troubling as the presence of a man, or men, in the dead city.

She lay beneath the arch, pretending to take an early sleep. The sun hovered low above the purpling ocean. Shadows filled the nooks and crevices of the ruins. It was not long before she heard the scrape of a foot upon bare stone. Something climbed a nearby block of granite large as a fisherman's hut and crouched atop it. Dahrima felt the subtle caress of eyes upon her.

She opened her own eyes just enough to catch a glimpse of her observer: a man-shaped silhouette limned in twilight. It squatted like an ape on its stony perch. A glint of metal or precious stone glimmered below its round head.

She heard shallow breathing now. Smelled the stench of filthy flesh.

Her knuckles tightened about the handle of her knife as the shadow leaped.

The armies of Uurz and Udurum set camp for the night on the plain southwest of the Eastern Flow. The glow of a thousand cook-fires painted the tents in shades of red and orange. The moon cast its silver across the tall grass and the distant ocean. Tyro sat in a folding chair in his royal pavilion drinking yellow wine from Yaskatha. Mendices had taken a cadre of Uurzian soldiers into the cluster of fishing villages to purchase fresh seafood, vegetables, and hearth-baked bread.

The sound of grumbling and laughing Giants wafted over the tents to the Sword King's ears. Vireon had furnished them with a hundred kegs of ale when the armies passed Allundra. All it took was red meat and good ale to keep the Giants happy.

Unlike the dour, grim-faced soldiers of Uurz, the Udvorg did not dread the great battle that lay ahead. While the Uurzians oiled their blades, sparred, and mended the straps of their armor, the blue-skinned Giants continued to jest, sing, and wrestle about their fires. A visitor to the camp would never know the Giants had lost both their King and their shamaness. The Udvorg were not mourners.

Yet Tyro had heard their complaints to Vireon, and he admired the grace with which the Giant-King dismissed their concerns. Losing Varda of the Keen Eyes was a personal inconvenience for Vireon, but he proclaimed it an Uduri affair. Dahrima's slaying of the blue witch was just by Uduri Law, which allowed for personal duels. When Vireon had replaced Angrid as King of the Udvorg, his word had become incontestable. In private, Vireon brooded over the loss of the two Giantesses who were foremost in his confidence. Dahrima, the murderess, had fled into the sea, or along the northern coast. No one seemed quite sure which was the case. Tyro did not question Vireon's judgment on the matter, although if Dahrima had slain one of his own warriors, the act would have had far greater ramifications.

Tyro propped his feet upon the low table. Two days of nonstop riding from the bottom of the Great Stair had not made up for the time lost by marching inland to use it. Yet there had been no other way to get the northern host down from the High Realm into the bosom of the Stormlands. The Udvorg might have climbed down the Earth Wall – in fact several of them did so on a dare – but the Men and horses and supply wagons could only return the way they had come in the first place. Tyro took solace in the fact that the legions were far closer to the Sharrian valley now than to Uurz. Another three days of marching should bring them to the ruins.

Vireon's faith in Iardu's word was unquestionable, so Tyro kept any doubts to himself. The wizard had said Zyung would beach his horde at Shar Dni rather than Khyrei, so Tyro had little choice but to accept this northward journey. Mendices warned him constantly against taking the Shaper's council, but Mendices did not trust the Giant-King either. Tyro had thrown in his lot with Vireon and increased the power of Uurz by doing so. Now was not the time to second-guess or defy Vireon's decisions. Whatever their Kings' personal squabbles might be, Uurz and Udurum were at their mightiest when allied. In truth, Tyro cared little whether they fought a battle among the Sharrian ruins or on the shores of Khyrei. Now that the black city was no longer an enemy, these invaders would serve well to test the mettle of the northern forces. Fighting a common enemy would strengthen the Uurz–Udurum alliance even further, as well as bringing glory to the victors for repelling the greatest invasion in history.

The few Khyrein ships anchored at Allundra had quickly raised their sails and taken to the sea when the vanguard of Giants came marching out of the Earth Wall's shadow. Tyro had enjoyed watching the black reavers flee like a startled flock of crows, yet it had reminded him of the triple fleet that sailed to intercept Zyung at Ongthaia. There had been no word since its departure. Had the battle been joined there yet? Would the Kings of Yaskatha and Mumbaza return alive to bring knowledge of their common foes, or were the Southern fleets doomed as Iardu had said they would be? Tyro did not know the full power of Khama the Feathered Serpent, but perhaps it would be enough to win at least a small victory. In his heart, Tyro did not believe they would save the Jade Isles. But if they could weaken the floating horde in some significant way – tear a few ships out of the sky and kill a few thousand Manslayers – that would provide some edge in the coming battle.

Since Varda's death, Vireon had ridden in silence on a black warhorse, something he could only do at the size of a Man. When camp was made each night, the Giant-King brooded in his royal tent. Tyro had tried to speak with him three times, but in each case Vireon proved tight-lipped and surly. Let the Man-Giant work through his grief, Tyro decided. When they reached the dead city, Vireon must break his silence for a council of strategy. No use having that discussion before they set eyes on the landscape and evaluated its tactical resources.

So Tyro sat alone tonight and enjoyed the wine, occupying his thoughts with memories of Talondra. It had been many weeks since he departed Uurz. He imagined that her taut, brown belly would be lightly swollen by now. He looked into the future, imagining his son as a young lad learning the art of swordplay. Tyro would teach Dairon the Second himself if, Gods willing, he survived this war. His own father had entrusted Tyro's training to old Lord Zormicus, who had done a fine job. Yet Tyro remembered wishing the Emperor would enter the training yard himself and show his son the proper way to hold and swing a sword. Or at least observe his son's progress from time to time. However, Dairon the First had been far too busy running the affairs of Uurz to sit and watch a boy swinging a practice blade. Tyro promised himself that he would put his son first. Matters of state should never interfere with matters of family.

This reminded him of Lyrilan, and the bitter power struggle that had seen his brother exiled and his sister-in-law murdered. He poured another cup of wine from the flagon and drank deep. The irony of his own considerations was not lost upon him.

I had to put the good of the realm before Lyrilan. There was no other choice.

I will never do this with my own son.

Perhaps Mendices was right. Tyro's best course of action might be to bring his legions back to Uurz and secure its walls, letting the Men and Giants of Udurum face the onslaught of Zyung by themselves. If he did this now, Tyro was certain to reach home in time to witness the birth of his son. If he maintained his present course, however, he might never see the boy. In the final analysis, it was a question of honor. He could not abandon Vireon without disgracing himself in the eyes of Udurum and its people, including the great folk of the Icelands.

Suddenly a new thought struck him: How many Giants remained still in the Frozen North? How many more legions of them could Vireon summon to fight for him? This was another reason why Uurz must remain allied with Udurum. If Zyung's horde was as massive as Iardu's vision showed it to be, the Land of the Five Cities might need more Giants to come to its aid. Putting aside the invasion of Zyung, Vireon might also be the only thing standing between the wild Giants and the gates of Uurz. Better to fight alongside the King of Giants than to oppose him, even if the war was costly. Having the united Giantlands as an enemy was unthinkable.

Tyro stood to unbuckle his breastplate when the sound of beating hooves cut through the clutter of camp noises. Someone spoke in a loud, urgent voice. A mount whinnied as it was led away to be groomed and fed. A soldier entered through the royal pavilion's flap, his green cloak swirling in the evening breeze.

"Majesty, a herald arrives from Uurz."

Tyro nodded. He knew the sound of a herald's advent well. "Have him fed and washed. I will see him within the hour."

"My Lord . . ." said the soldier, his eyes steady upon those of his King. Tyro recalled that his name was Aerodus, or it could have been Aerion. The two men were brothers and much alike. Another reminder of Lyrilan. There were so many of late. "This herald has ridden through the night. He says his message cannot wait. He wishes to see you immediately, if it please you."

Tyro wished Mendices was back from his fish-buying to meet with the messenger. Politics never ceased to complicate his life, even hundreds of leagues away from the City of Sacred Waters. "Very well," he said. "Admit him."

Tyro settled back into his chair and filled a second copper goblet for the herald. Soon the man came stamping into the tent, mud and road-dirt dripping from cloak and greaves. He smelled strongly of horse, and the soiled state of his garments evinced several days of hard riding. An unkempt beard of several days' growth obscured his chin; without the green-gold livery of an Uurzian official he might have passed as a vagabond.

The herald sank to one knee, clutching his tarnished helm in the crook of an arm. He carried no scroll or missive that Tyro could see. The message must be a private one, meant only for the King's ears. Perhaps this was more than a political development that needed his attention.

"Rise," said Tyro. "Will you drink?"

The worn-out herald shook his head. His breath was heavy, his eyes weary. Tyro realized this could only be bad news.

"Majesty," the herald said. "I have ridden six days from Uurz to bring you ill tidings."

Of course. Tyro nodded. "Speak then," he said, taking another swig of wine. Someone must have died. Could the Green and Gold factions still be quarreling even after Lyrilan's humiliation and exile?

The herald would not meet his eyes as he spoke. "Empress Talondra . . . " His voice became a stammer. In the early ages heralds who brought bad news were often slain immediately. "She was found . . . "

Tyro's temper kindled. Let the man be brave enough to speak his message. Tyro was no barbarian chief to slit the throat of a loyal servant. Any man of Uurz should know that about him.

"Speak," said Tyro. A hollow hunger yawned in his gut. He had not taken supper.

"The Empress Talondra was found ... dead, Sire. In her bed-chamber. Seven days past." The herald kept his gaze fixed upon the faded carpets of the tent.

Tyro stood up and grabbed the man by his throat, pulling him to his feet. The hunger in his belly was replaced by a black claw ripping at his intestines. The rider repeated his message at Tyro's command. Tyro stared into his gray eyes, looking for signs of false-hood. The messenger wept, his tears carving channels through the grime of his worried face.

"I am sorry, Majesty," whispered the soldier. "By the Four Gods, I am so sorry ... "

Tyro dropped the man to the carpet. His own legs failed, but he found the seat in time to catch him. He drained the full cup of wine, spilling it on either side of his mouth.

"How?" he asked. There was no strength left in his voice. His eyes welled.

"No one knows," said the herald. "Her flesh and bones were ... *crushed* ... as if by a heavy stone, or a constricting Serpent."

Tyro grabbed the flagon and turned it to his lips. Wine poured bitter into his mouth while hot tears poured from his eyes. He tossed the empty bottle across the tent where it clanged off a round shield bearing the sun standard of Uurz. His head swam and his fists clenched. His body quivered with a sickening blend of rage and despair.

His wife and unborn son were dead. It seemed unreal. A night-mare. Was he lying on the cushions awaiting the return of Mendices and dreaming this tragedy?

Talondra. Crushed to death?

Sorcery. It must be. One of his many enemies. Could Zyung's magic have raced ahead of his armada to slaughter Tyro's family?

If so, why not slaughter the Sword King himself? Ianthe and Gammir had been destroyed by Iardu and Sharadza. Or so they told him.

My son will never be born.

He remembered Talondra's sweet face, her eyes bright as sapphires, her touch hot as flame. His tigress. His Empress. She had survived the Doom of Shar Dni only to perish behind the mighty walls of Uurz. Madness rose like bile from the core of his stomach and thundered into his skull. He must not go mad with grief. He must be strong. Still it rose, like the ocean tide rising in the evening to drown the sand. It could not be stopped. No more than rushing blood could be stopped spilling from sliced flesh.

The Emperor of Uurz fell to his knees and screamed like a wounded animal. The herald rushed from the tent, terror on his face, tears in his eyes. The silks and fabrics of the tent became a blur of colors as Tyro ripped and tore them to ribbons. The clanging of metal implements and the splintering of wooden furniture were drowned by his wailing. A ring of soldiers rushed into the pavilion, standing about him like gilded pillars. He hurled himself against their raised shields, banging at the embossed metal with his fists until his knuckles were torn and bloody. He knocked men down, but others replaced them. They did not touch him, or offer him comfort – what comfort could they offer a raging Emperor? – but simply allowed him to bellow his pain and batter at their metal until he fell spent upon the carpets and cried like an infant.

Mendices found him like that. The Warlord quickly dismissed the soldiers. "Any man who speaks of this will be executed!" spat the Warlord. These were the cruel words that penetrated the fog of madness and brought Tyro back to his senses.

Mendices righted the overturned cot and laid Tyro upon it. Like a father tending a sick son, he leaned over Tyro and poured cold water between his lips.

"She's dead," Tyro whispered. "She's dead."

Mendices held him fast as fresh sobs brought fresh convulsions.

Tyro did not recall passing from grief into slumber, but at some point exhaustion and the weight of loss pulled him under. He welcomed the blackness, but not the dreams of flowing blood, pulped flesh, and cracked bone that replaced the waking world.

He tossed and turned, and finally opened his eyes to the gloom of the reordered tent. Mendices lay snoring nearby on a pile of pillows. A single brazier lighted the interior, sending a trail of black smoke to curl about the hole in its roof. The great camp was oddly quiet beyond the walls of mud-stained canvas.

At first Tyro thought the herald had returned to stand at attention in the corner of the pavilion. He raised his head, blinking blood-rimmed eyes, and saw that it was not the herald at all who stood watching him sleep. It was none of his soldiers either.

The figure wore a robe of sable with runes stitched in green thread about the sleeves and neck. Emeralds glittered somewhere among the dark folds. A mane of black wavy hair framed the head like a hood. The face that stared at Tyro was his own.

The scale is balanced, said the apparition.

Lyrilan's voice.

Your wife and child have joined mine.

Tyro whimpered. He could not move arms or legs. To cry out was impossible. His broadsword lay upon the cushions ten handspans away. It might as well be ten thousand leagues from him.

Do not despair, brother, said Lyrilan. *You will see them again when you enter the valley of death.*

Tyro leaped up suddenly, as if a great stone had rolled off his chest.

Lyrilan was gone, if he had ever been there at all. The brazier's flame was dead.

The Emperor of Uurz sat on the edge of his cot and wept in the darkness.

Dahrima's fingers closed about the scrambling creature's neck. It squealed and tore at her wrist with dirty fingernails as she raised the knife. This was no creature of the shadow world who stalked her, but only a hairy, disheveled wretch. She hesitated to call it a Man; it gagged and screeched like a dying pig as she dragged it into the moonlight to get a better look.

"Please," gasped the creature. "Don't hurt me! Don't hurt me!"

The moon on its face showed her a round head, bald on the pate but sprouting a dirty brown beard about the mouth, jaw, and chin. Its sunken chest and limbs were hairy as well, but no more than some northerners she had seen shirtless. A loincloth of dirty rags was its only garment. The beard was matted with mud, dried insect husks, and possibly blood. It was the tiny, desperate eyes that assured her it was a human after all. They were tarnished green, almost olive, bloodshot, and full of darting madness.

She held the blade of her long knife before one of those eyes.

"Name yourself," she said in the language common to Men.

"I have no name," blurted the wretch. "I lost it. I lost it among the shattered stones." Foam dripped from his swollen lips. "I lost everything. I am nothing! Please don't hurt me."

Dahrima sheathed the knife but kept hold of the scrawny neck. "All right, Sir Nothing," she said. "Are there any more of your kind living among these ruins? Speak the truth and I'll not harm you. Lie to me and I will roast your flesh and crunch your bones between my teeth." She smiled to show him her teeth. Most humans south of the Grim were ignorant of Giant culture; this one might actually believe the old tales about Giants eating manflesh.

"Nobody!" said Sir Nothing. "They are all dead here. All dead . . . "

"Promise you'll not run away and I will release you," said Dahrima.

"I'll not run!" wheezed Sir Nothing. The olive eyes watered and pleaded. "I'll not run . . ."

She turned him loose and he fell back against the big stone, grasping his neck and drawing in ragged breaths. Below the tangled beard hung the gleaming stone she had noticed earlier. On a narrow strip of worn leather dangled a sapphire large as a robin's egg. Some sigil or rune was etched into its surface, but she couldn't make it out in the gloom.

Sir Nothing kept his ratlike eyes on her face. She loomed over him, and he smiled at her the way a child smiles at his doting mother.

"Such beauty . . ." he muttered. "Tall as the sun, bright as the sea. You must be the Queen of Giants."

Dahrima laughed. "Flattery will not work on me, Sir Nothing. Are you Sharrian?" She recognized the brown skin, the dark hair, the green eyes. She already knew the answer.

Nothing's eyes scanned the dark stones lying about them in jagged confusion. "I am of this place," he said. His voice was faraway now, the voice of an old sage. Or a madman.

"How long have you been here?" she asked.

"All my life, Lady," he replied. "I was born in the great palace that used to stand there." He pointed a bony finger toward the center of the ruins. A cold breeze blew off the sea and he shrank toward the earth with sudden alarm. "You cannot stay here! Oh, no . . . nobody stays here. They linger beneath the stones, you see." His voice fell to a guarded whisper. "*They still hunger.*"

Dahrima looked about the ruined landscape and saw nothing but the rising moon, the glimmering sea, and the hills of the valley being swallowed by darkness. If there were bloodshadows lurking in this place, they showed no sign of themselves. Perhaps they awaited the passing of the last rays of sun. The river glided through the gloom, a silent silver mystery.

"Come," said Nothing. "I will show you out of the valley. You cannot stay here. They will come for you. The night draws them out like crabs from the sea. Delicious crabs, crawling and feasting ..."

"If spirits haunt this valley," Dahrima said, refusing to move, "then why have they not devoured *you* long before now?"

Sir Nothing grabbed the stone hanging from his neck. "This!" He whispered. "My savior, my protector. I found it in the basement of a ruined temple. Oh, the temples were so grand here once. Sky-blue pyramids topped with pearly clouds ... Oh, the holy smokes that rose to honor the Gods!" He inhaled the night air, smelling memories. "They reeked of holiness and meadowflower, the sweet smokes. How I miss them, Lady." His voice had risen to a poetic timbre, but now it dropped again to a whisper. "This amulet belonged to a priest of the Sky God. I plucked it from his bones when the black slayers departed. I've worn it ever since. It keeps the hungry shadows from me, you see. Only me!" He drew away from her, suddenly afraid she would steal his magic stone. She understood then that it was a talisman, protection from evil spirits. At least to this deranged hermit. The sigil on its surface resembled a cloud.

"In the Giantlands we worship different Gods than Men do," said Dahrima. "Or perhaps they are the same Gods with different names."

Sir Nothing drew near to her foot like a fawning puppy, nuzzling her ankle. "The Gods have forsaken this place," he said. "But I have not. And I never will."

Dahrima wanted to push him away. His stink rose into her nostrils again. But she pitied him, so she endured his touch and his odor. The poor fellow had lost his mind long ago.

"Why don't you leave these crumbled stones?" she asked. "You would find fellowship and comfort in Udurum or Uurz. Are you not lonely?"

He leaped away from her, curling into a ball. "Don't take me away," he cried. "Please don't take me away! This is where I belong . . ."

"This is a place of death and foul spirits," she told him. He gazed at the stars now, perhaps not hearing her words. "You can have no life here."

Sir Nothing looked at her again, his eyes reflecting the moonlight. "This is my kingdom," he said proudly. He tried to stand up straight before her, but his crooked back would not allow it. His long arms hung at his sides, and again he reminded her of a southern ape. "I am the last royal heir, you see."

Dahrima smiled. "You told me you were nothing."

"I am the King of Shar Dni," he told her. "This is my realm. All the others are dead, but I still rule this place. The ghosts of my people serve me and call me Majesty. Nobody can hear them but me. They need their King."

Dahrima recalled the account she had read of the Doom of Shar Dni in Shaira's library. When Gammir and Ianthe led the hosts of Khyrei across the sea to raze the city, Vireon and Alua had arrived too late to save it. Yet they drove the conquerors out of the valley and took thousands of refugees back to Udurum. Andoses, the heir to King Ammon's throne, died in that battle. Andoses had fathered no children, so this madman could not be his heir. Unless he were some other relative of Ammon's.

"Tell me what happened," Dahrima said. She used the voice she might offer a child. Gentleness did not come easily to her, but she attempted it for the sake of the truth buried here. "Where were you when the Khyreins came?"

Nothing slumped into a bed of crackling moss. The shadow of

the broken arch obscured his face, but his dull green eyes glowed. "They locked me in a room," he said. "I screamed and yelled and cried . . . but they said I must behave until my cousin returned. He would be the new King. Ammon was his father."

"You speak of Andoses?"

He looked at her face again, his eyes growing wide. "Andoses the Brave," he smiled. "My cousin had gone to visit the Giants. Did you know him? Tell me you knew him, Lady."

Dahrima nodded. She had seen Shaira's nephew about the palace of Udurum when he visited, but had never shared words with him. She knew only that he had traveled south with Tadarus, Fangodrel, Vireon, and D'zan, and that he had died at the Doom of Shar Dni.

"Why did they lock you up?" she asked. "Were you a criminal?"

Silence. The night winds picked up, roaring through the valley.

"They said I was mad," he told her, "because of what I had seen. The Prince of Shadows did it to me . . . He should have killed me, you see, but he left me alive and mad. That was what they told me. I remember it, too."

The Prince of Shadows? He must mean Gammir.

"He came to visit my uncle the King. There were pirates in those days, you see. Horrid reavers spilling blood on the Golden Sea. Ammon – he was my uncle – wanted help from the City of Men and Giants. They sent Fangodrel, Son of Vod, to us then. Oh, he was a fine spectacle in his black mail and cloak of shadows. Yet he was terrifying, Lady. So terrifying . . . "

Fangodrel was the northern name of Gammir. He must have visited Shar Dni on his way to take the throne of Khyrei from his sorceress grandmother. Ianthe had called him to her side, urging him to murder his own brother, Tadarus. Fangodrel was not truly the Son of Vod. He was a bastard and the heir to Ianthe's blood magic.

"Tell me all of it," Dahrima asked.

"A feast!" Sir Nothing started. He danced a jig between the broken stones, then stopped and came near her with a whisper. "There was a feast to honor the Shadow Prince. But he did not want food. No, he wanted *blood*."

The madman wept as he continued. "My seven cousins were there, the daughters of Ammon. Such beautiful Princesses as you will never find elsewhere. And my brother Dutho – he was named Duke that year. He was at the feast too ... Oh, Gods, would that he were not. The Shadow Prince drank their blood, one by one. His army of shadows poured forth to strangle the guardsmen. My uncle – he was the King, you see – he died first. Oh, the screams of the Princesses were terrible. I still hear them when I close my eyes."

He did close his eyes then, lost in a dark reverie. Dahrima waited for him to finish the tale. Tears squeezed from beneath his eyelids, streaming to join the filth trapped in his beard.

His eyes flew open. "Blood! So much blood! The Prince of Shadows took their lives and their blood. I was the last. I begged him for mercy ... Oh, how I begged, Lady. He took pity on me. He chose not to drink my blood. *Tell them*, he said to me. *Tell them what happened.* His teeth were wolves' teeth. He sprouted black wings and flew away ..."

Sir Nothing cradled his head in the palms of his hands, fingers twitching on his scalp.

"They locked me in the yellow room after that. There I stayed, laughing and screaming. I had to tell them, you see. He had *commanded* me to tell them. Oh, the blood ... the blood. Then he returned with the Pale Queen and her armies of black metal. The city burned and fell to ash. Someone broke open the door of the yellow room. They tortured me. They had the faces of demons. Then they were gone and I was alone. There are no more left of the King's bloodline. I am the last."

"What of your father?" she asked. "Who was he?"

"He died at sea, battling demon-faced pirates."

Brother of Dutho. Nephew of Ammon. That made him Shaira's nephew as well. Dahrima did not know enough of Sharrian genealogy to guess his name. Vireon would know. Perhaps a name was all the poor wretch needed to end the spell of madness that held him here.

As if sensing her thoughts, he whispered a final confession.

"I was Pyrus, Son of Omirus."

Dahrima met his sad eyes and offered him a smile. She bent to one knee before him.

"Hail, Pyrus," she said. "Last King of Shar Dni. I am Dahrima the Axe. I serve Vireon, King of Giants and Men, Son of Vod, Lord of Udurum and the Icelands."

"Pyrus . . . " He repeated the name, as if remembering it again for the first time.

She stood then. Her courtly gesture had not impressed him. The memories must weigh too heavily on his broken mind. He had lived like a rat in these haunted ruins for eight years. He could not be older than thirty, though he looked closer to sixty.

"Are you hungry, Pyrus?" she asked.

He smiled at her, displaying rotted teeth. "There are plenty of fish in the river, Lady."

Pyrus seemed to forget the sad tale he had told as he led her through the ruins to the bank of the Orra. There he produced a crude spear from its hiding place inside a hollow log. He waded into the shallows and tried several times to skewer a passing fish. Dahrima was amazed that he could see so well in the moonlight. Yet he speared one and raised it wriggling from the water. He offered her another crooked smile as he climbed back onto the riverbank.

"I will build a fire," Dahrima said. She gathered enough twigs to serve and sparked them with a piece of flint from her belt. As she blew on the tiny flame to make it grow, Pyrus used a sharp rock to scale and gut his catch. Soon it was spitted and roasting above the flame. He watched it with an eager glee, licking his lips.

"Soon there will be great danger here," she told him. "A great foreign army sails toward this valley, and the Legions of Uurz and Udurum are marching to stand against them."

Pyrus ignored her words, intent on the cooking fish.

Dahrima gazed at the stars. The night was clear and the moon was bright above the valley. "It will not be safe for you to stay here much longer," she said. "Do you understand?"

Pyrus nodded his head and removed the spit from the cookfire. "It is done!" He tore a chunk from the fish and offered her the rest of it. She nodded thanks and accepted it. She would have to force him to leave the valley before the battle began. She put that unpleasant thought aside for later and enjoyed the taste of the fish. It was not bad, despite the lack of seasoning. Not a Giant's preferred fare, but it filled her belly.

After the meal they lay back and watched the stars. Pyrus hummed an ancient melody of the Sharrian folk. He nodded off and she followed soon after.

There was no way of knowing how long she slept before the darkness rose to wrap itself about her throat, arms, and legs. She came awake in its frigid grip, limbs of solid shadow reaching out of the ground to seize her with claws sharp as daggers. They raked across her flesh, tore the bronze corslet from her body, and stole the breath from her lungs. She strove to rise, to suck in air before she suffocated. Her fingers found nothing to grasp. The shadows were going to rip her apart and she could not touch them.

She gagged and kicked and rolled across the glowing embers. The bodiless claws tore at her stubborn flesh. An Uduri's skin was tough enough to turn arrows, but the bloodshadows would keep at it until her insides burst forth and her blood spilled out to feed them. Pairs of eyes like crimson coals hovered in the mass of living darkness, radiant with malice. A scream escaped her throat as the first set of claws pierced her shoulder. Another tore the flesh of her thigh. Every second, more of them found ingress to her flesh. They sucked at her seeping blood like a cloud of formless leeches.

She could no longer even squirm or kick. The shadows took on the shapes of wolves and gliding vipers, beating wings like a flock of bats about her captured body.

Something cold and hard met the palm of her right hand. Her fingers were shoved tight about it. A blue glow infused the air and the shadows dispersed in a fog of hissing and rustling half-shapes. Dahrima lay gasping and bleeding on the raw earth while the shadows converged nearby.

A high, moaning sound filled her ears. The sound of a man screaming.

She raised her fist and saw the object Pyrus had forced into her grasp. The blue stone worn about his neck. The Sky God's amulet. His only protection from the bloodshadows. She'd had none, and he had tried to warn her of this fact. Now the talisman's potency was proven.

Dahrima struggled to her knees. Pyrus lay beneath the feasting shadows, who no longer could touch her. His arms and legs twitched. He no longer screamed. The sound of crunching bones came next.

She crawled toward the mass of shadows, waving the blue stone amid the darkness. The blood drinkers flew into the night on leathery wings, taking with them the Last King of Shar Dni. Drops of red blood marked his passing. They fell like raindrops across the bed of moss.

"Pyrus!" She called after him, but her voice was only a parched croak.

Dahrima clutched the Sky God's stone and took up her great axe. Yet there was no foe left to fight, no enemy's skull to split. The man who had saved her life was gone, and she could do nothing to avenge him. There was no further sign of bloodshadows.

She tied the amulet about her neck and walked to the shore to wash her wounds. The cold saltwater stung her broken skin and revived her senses. No one was there to witness her shed tears for the noble madman, so she let them flow.

She sat on the beach until dawn, axe balanced on her knees, and watched the red horizon for signs of flesh-and-bone enemies.

Many Kings had died in this cursed valley.

Pyrus would not be the last.

8

The Whelming

For two days the islands of Ongthaia had known only wind, rain, and thunder. Great waves came barreling off the Outer Ocean, shattering the small boats of fishermen into kindling. Most of the foreign traders had departed for the mainland when King Zharua made his proclamation of war. His own fleet of merchant vessels had been quickly outfitted to join the Mumbazan, Yaskathan, and Khyrein warships. On the eastern horizon the clouds swirled black as night, and bolts of purple lightning flared ceaselessly.

Khama's willpower kept the worst effects of the storms from the islands. Yet every hurricane and typhoon he hurled across the ocean toward the Dreadnoughts of Zyung left a trace of itself behind, driving the hapless folk of the Jade Isles indoors. The populations of several lesser towns had braved the choppy waters to gain sanctuary behind the double wall of Morovanga City, but thousands remained on the twelve lesser isles. They found shelter as best they could in stone huts or hillside caves. The capital's walls would provide some security for Zharua's people, should the majority of Zyung's ships make it through the barrage of storms.

The Feathered Serpent coiled himself atop the volcano over-looking the Jade King's city. Khama stared deep into the raging tempests, searching for any signal of Zyung's approach. It was too much to hope his hurricanes would destroy all of the great sky-ships, or even half of the invasion force. Yet every single dreadnought that fell to his storm magic would remove a thousand Manslayers, as well as a few of the flying Trills, and maybe even a sorcerer or two.

In Zharua's war room two days ago Khama had sat with Undutu, D'zan, and a company of sea captains and generals. The Jade King himself presided over the strategy session, although he mainly listened to the advice of those who were skilled at war-craft, then passed orders to his own shipmasters. Zharua had pledged his vast fortune and every merchant vessel to the defense of the islands. Thousands of men worked on refitting the Ongthaian ships while their rulers met to discuss tactics. This would be the greatest conflict the Jade Isles had ever known. In fact, the greatest marine battle in all the history of the world. Khama had let Undutu speak for him at the council; the Son of the Feathered Serpent had a gift for inspiring Men to courageous deeds.

On the second day after the ousting of Zyung's envoy, the defending ships began to position themselves east of the island chain. With the addition of a hundred Jade Isle traders, the fleet now stood a thousand ships strong. Of course, each ship carried one-fifth the number of warriors as the colossal dreadnoughts, and no sorcerers among them. Beyond these grim facts, the ship-to-ship ratio still weighed three-to-one in Zyung's favor. Khama hurled more deadly storms across the sea, hoping to even those numbers.

The allied fleets were assembled in a great half-moon arc east of the islands. A wall of flapping sails and rippling banners.

Khama's concentration assured that none of them would be capsized by his storms. Yet the driving rain and whipping winds could not altogether be banished. All he could do with the forces of nature he had aroused was to focus them away from the isles and its protectors. This he did, and after two days he began to feel the strain of working such sorcery without pause. Still he would not relent. The tempests must rage across the distant seascape until Zyung's forces reached the isles. Only then would he refocus his efforts on more direct assaults. He was the single factor that gave his people any chance of victory, slim as that chance might be.

Perhaps Iardu will return with more of the Old Breed before Zyung arrives.

The thought was of some comfort, but Khama knew it was still too soon. This battle was being waged against Iardu's wishes because the Shaper already knew that he would not be able to gather a formidable force in time. It was Undutu and his impenetrable sense of honor that brought all of this to bear. The warrior code that belonged to his fathers, passed down to him from the tribal chieftains of the Ancient Land. A land that Zyung had crushed like so many others and remade into his own image.

Khama might have tried to talk Undutu out of this dangerous and near-futile course of action, but his duty was to support the decisions of his King. To advise, not to dictate. So he had done throughout the course of Mumbazan history. Khama reminded himself again that this battle would stall Zyung's advance, giving Iardu's mission more time to bear fruit. By the time Zyung reached the mainland, there must be a cadre of Old Breed sorcerers standing with the armies of the Five Cities. Khama forced himself to believe that the sacrifice of these fleets would be worth that time. Meanwhile, he would do what he could to balance the scales of war.

Undutu and D'zan stood upon the foredecks of their flagships, gazing into the black tempests. The Kings were too distant from the Feathered Serpent for him to set eyes upon them, but he saw the banners of the *Bird of War* and the *Kingspear* flying near the center of the great arc. Along the decks of every ship a hundred archers stood ready with arrows wrapped in pitch rags. Two iron braziers blazed beneath canopied rain shelters at the prow and middle deck of each vessel. The Mumbazan and Yaskathan forces had also treated the great bolts of their ballistae with pitch and oiled lengths of hemp rope. The Khyrein reavers possessed no ballistae, but their catapults were filled with oily spheres of pitch set to burn. The allied fleets would hurl fire at the sky-ships when they came within range.

Khama did not know if the dreadnoughts would burn, or if sorcery protected them from such danger. It did not matter; there was little else the seabound vessels could do to assault the aerial armada. The hope was to force them out of the sky so that ship-to-ship grappling and boarding would be possible. The invaders had more manpower, but the defenders would fight more fiercely; they were protecting their homelands and loved ones. Numbers were not everything – history was full of battles that had been won by outnumbered armies. Khama took some comfort in that fact as he stared into the thundering wall of stormclouds.

There.

A single pinprick of light amid the churning thunderheads. Not the flicker of lightning, but steady as a lantern moving through fog. Then another, and another, and a whole line of lanterns emerging from the tempests.

Across the entire horizon they appeared, spanning the length of the visible world. Orbs of glowing white radiance, like the sphere that had surrounded Damodar. Inside each great orb floated a dreadnought, gliding through the ravaged sky with triple sails intact. On they came, rank after rank of golden sky-ships wrapped in shells of gleaming sorcery. Leagues away still, they seemed tiny as model ships, yet Khama knew that each of them was three times larger than the greatest Yaskathan trireme. Seeing the dreadnoughts emerge now from his battery of hurricanes, he realized the truth: Not a single dreadnought had been lost to the storms. The magic of a thousand Old Breed, the most highly prized servants of Zyung, had protected them from harm.

The beating of war drums rose to Khama's ears from the Mumbazan warships at the center of the great arc. Their persistent cadence spread across the allied fleets, and men readied their arrows for igniting. "Not yet!" Khama could almost hear the captains shouting. "Let them draw near! Wait for the signal!"

At once the storms ceased. The rain disappeared and the winds fell to nothing. Khama withdrew his furious control and replaced it with the peaceful glow of sunshine peeking through the clouds. The armada of dreadnoughts sailed on through the sky, still encased in their sorcerous radiance. The sea grew still and golden as the stormclouds dissipated. Calm air was needed to allow the arrows and bolts of the fleet to fly true. Khama would throw winds where needed, to fan any flames devouring the sky-ships. If that were even possible. He would know soon.

The dreadnoughts grew larger. Their speed was unprecedented, far faster than any water-borne vessel. Yet they slowed as they came near to the islands, the northern and southern flanks of the armada curling about to encircle the thirteen land masses and the arc of warships. Here was Undutu's first tactical mistake. Assembling in the eastern waters did not provide a barrier to protect the islands; the lofty positions and great numbers of the dreadnoughts allowed them to completely encircle their enemies before the fighting even began.

The dreadnoughts were still too far out to attack or be attacked, and the spheres of light still enclosed them. But Khama could see now the glitter of spears and mail upon their decks – the rush of activity that preceded a strike on the forces below. The moment their protective shells fell, the airships would rain destruction upon Undutu and his allies. At that same moment the defenders would unleash forty thousand flaming arrows, seven hundred ballistae bolts, and two hundred balls of flaming pitch. As for what forces the dreadnoughts would deploy, Khama could only guess.

The circle of three thousand sky-ships grew tighter. In three concentric rings Zyung's Holy Armada now had surrounded the Jade Isles. Those in the innermost circle would be the first to attack – and only those on the east side of the circle would be in range of the aquatic fleets. Then Khama saw it: Along the eastern third of the circle all three ranks of dreadnoughts would be close enough to attack the allied fleets – assuming the dreadnoughts' weapons shared a range similar to those of the water-borne ships. There the attack must come first.

Along the sides of each dreadnought round apertures opened and tubes of black iron emerged, swiveling toward the lands and ships below. The sky-ships sank lower now, as they converged upon Ongthaia and its anxious defenders.

Khama tensed his coils, remaining hidden on the rim of the volcano. The enemy must not see him until he attacked. And he must wait until the moment those radiant spheres blinked out of existence. The sea was calm as glass, the wind had escaped to some other world, and the ward drums of a thousand ships counted the moments until conflagration.

Tighter grew the circles. The drums beat on, steady as eternity.

Behind the black walls of the Jade City, fifty thousand people cowered and prayed to the Gods of Sea and Sky for succor. Zharua was not among the ships; he was no Warrior King. He must be pacing the tops of his palace ramparts, hearing the drums, watching the convergence of his sky-borne enemies, and perhaps wishing he had accepted Zyung's offer of surrender. It was too late now. His fate lay in the hands of the Southern Kings and their valiant navies. As did the fate of all the Five Cities. In truth, all hope lay in the hands of Iardu the Shaper. If Khama believed in the Gods worshipped by Men, he would have prayed to them in that moment.

The circles tightened and lowered. The drums thundered.

The spheres of light faded and time ceased. The nature of the world itself seemed to shift, reality dilated, and the clouds inhaled the muttered prayers of men.

Khama launched himself into the air, a streak of rainbow flames. He raced toward the nearest of the sky-ships as the iron tubes spurted streams of white fire. The same liquid flames exploded from the irons along all three rows of the eastern dreadnoughts. In that same moment the war drums ceased, and thousands of flaming arrows flew toward the golden hulls. Khama was a bolt of light gliding between the rising and falling firestorms.

The sky ignited with a maelstrom of fires pale and orange and red as blood.

Khama's head struck the hull of a dreadnought as a wreath of lightning swirled along his Serpent body. The cries of dying men filled his ears beneath the splintering of wood and the booming of strange sorceries. He burst from the great ship's midsection like an arrow shot through an overripe pear. Armored bodies flew in all directions, and the airship lurched behind him. He sped on, cracking two of the three masts with his forehead, grabbing the third between his fangs. He vomited bolts of lightning along its length to engulf the shattered vessel and every living thing on it.

He snapped the mast off and spat it out as the sky-ship rocked and spilled toward the sea. A gargantuan tree fell in the midst of the plummeting wreckage and howling crew. The tree burned and withered even as the ship fell apart. A thousand armored warriors clutched at falling debris. A few escaped on leather-winged lizards, but not many.

Khama rose high above the dreadnoughts now. The eyes of captains, bowmen, and sorcerers rose toward him as he wheeled in the hot air. He would get no more surprise attacks. One of three thousand ships had died instantly from his explosive power, but now the enemy had marked his presence with weapon and spell.

Below the hovering armada great fires raged. Hulls were peppered with blazing arrows. Ballista bolts struck home, digging deep into the golden keels and trailing oiled ropes from the ships below. Men kindled those ropes and the flames shot upward to rush across the bottoms of the sky-ships. The Khyrein globes of pitch struck home as well, scorching hulls or burning tiny holes in the sides of dreadnoughts. The airships were far too large for the catapults to do much damage. The only true threat to the dreadnoughts' superiority, besides Khama's power, were the thousands of arrows spreading flame across their lower halves.

Khama sped outside of the dreadnoughts' circle to get a better look at the efficacy of their weapons. From each iron tube a bolt of brilliant flame raced like venom from a cobra's mouth, setting fire to whatever sea vessels it fell upon. The dreadnoughts were equipped with mechanisms of sorcery that hurled gouts of alchemical flame. At least twenty of these iron tubes sprouted on either side of every sky-ship, raining forty streams of enchanted fire upon their foes. Already half of the aquatic ships were burning, compared to a mere fifty or so dreadnoughts that were set aflame by arrow, bolt, or catapult. And the battle was only thirty seconds engaged.

Men leaped into the water to avoid burning to death, but the sorcerous fires burned atop the water. There was no escaping the devastation by abandoning ship. The dreadnoughts fired a second barrage of flames, and more warships ignited. Volleys of burning arrows rose from ships individually now. In the broadening devastation there would be no more simultaneous fleet-wide volleys launched upward. Scores of ships were now separated by flames, panic, smoke, and the chaos of battle.

Khama had no time to seek out the *Bird of War* to check Undutu's status. He hurtled toward another of the dreadnoughts. A blast of lightning flew from his tongue and set the airship's sails alight. The ship quavered and a hundred arrows flew at Khama from its decks. They bounced off the scales beneath his feathers as he plummeted. The two nearest dreadnoughts sprayed him with flaming alchemy as he passed, so when he struck his target it was as a flaming meteor. Men and wood went flying. Khama found himself immersed in the bowels of the great ship this time, without enough force to burst through its bottom hull. He looked through a shattered bulkhead into a womb-like chamber filled by another mammoth tree.

Among the topaz branches of the tree floated a woman in silver robes similar to those of Damodar. Another of Zyung's Old Breed slaves. She shouted wrath at Khama and unseen forces hurled his body from the pierced ship. He left a hole torn halfway through its decks all the way to its heart.

The trees are the source of power for these vessels.

He knew it instantly, whirling above the dreadnoughts to quench the flames along his coils. Why else would sorcerers guard and protect these trees? The tree's countless branches and roots, he had noted, flowed into the substance of the ship itself. The trees were the seeds from which grew the dreadnoughts, sculpted by the will of Old Breed magic. How could he use this knowledge to defeat the armada? An answer eluded him.

There was no time to consider it further as six globes of light rose from six different dreadnoughts to surround Khama. At the center of each radiance floated a silver-robed sorcerer. They glared at him with eyes of murderous calm. He recognized one of them as the very same envoy he had cast out of Zharua's palace.

Damodar and his fellow wizards, come to rip the Feathered Serpent apart.

Khama bellowed a gout of thunder at the silver-robes, scattering them like leaves. Yet more of them rose from the surrounding dreadnoughts. He could not count their numbers. He had never seen so many sorcerers gathered in one spot, not in all his eons of existence.

Below him the allied fleets were burning, the cries of dying men rising like ash to fill the superheated air. The dreadnoughts continued pouring their flame upon the aquatic ships, as fewer and fewer arrows rose from the crumbling decks.

How can it be over so soon?

Khama swirled in the air, weaving a pattern of cosmic energies as the floating silver-robes converged upon him. They cast bolts of starlight from their mouths and fingers, yet their power cascaded across the sizzling corona of his sorcery. Faster and faster he spun, releasing the core of his power, glowing like a second sun in the crowded sky, absorbing the blasts hurled against him, swallowing the pain, letting his physical form give way to the raw currents of sorcery that fueled his eternal spirit.

More of Zyung's sorcerers flew toward him, yet he barely saw them through the haze of his own unleashed potency. Finally he released all of it, exploding from the epicenter of his being. His fury washed across the sorcerers and the ships behind them, a tidal wave of light and gravity and the all-consuming fires of stellar destruction.

Khama spun and raged and erupted like a dying celestial body, no longer heedful of the screaming, the flames, the death that filled the bowl of the earth. He was the annihilation of planets, the yawning chaos at the heart of existence, an irresistible spark torn from the cosmic furnace in which all things must find obliteration.

Until . . .

A great dark hand fell about him, clutching and quenching the flame of his existence. Inside the fist of shadows he saw the glimmering of galaxies, the starfields of alien worlds glinting like diamonds in the palm of a black gauntlet. The mighty hand squeezed, crushing the life from him, extinguishing the inextinguishable, snuffing out his glorious blaze.

The titanic fingers opened, and Khama fell.

A smoking ember of charred flesh, dropping from the light of sun and sky into the cold embrace of salty waters. He sank like a speck of molten rock, cooling and coalescing, as the deep accepted his defeat in a way that he could not.

No! I will not suffer this!

A single word, or the blast of a mighty horn, sounded in his awareness.

Both the hand and the word belonged to Zyung the Almighty.

The sea became a void, full of dead stars and shriveled worlds.

Khama sank deeper, toward a bottom that may or may not exist.

Then darkness.

No.

I will not be vanquished in this way.

I am the Feathered Serpent.

I am of the Old Breed.

Zyung is not my master.

I have no master but my own will.

I choose to endure.

*

In a deep trench the light of Khama's intellect rekindled, a shimmering mote in the briny dark. Sand and coral and drifting strands of plant life mingled and merged with a passing school of fish. Pallid coils manifested across the seabed, sprouting feathers and scales.

His new eyes opened wide, shedding amber light across the ocean floor.

A shadow of his former self, weak and spent of all but his unbreakable intent, Khama glided among the shoals and underwater reefs. His head rose upward, guiding the rest of his body toward the higher waters.

First, the aquamarine glow of sunlight seen from below the surface. Then the crimson and orange glow of flames, and the white streaks of burning sorcery tainting the waters. Broken ships sank into the depths, still burning with unquenchable fires. The broken, drowned, and ragged bodies of sailors and soldiers drifted downward or lay among tangled beds of kelp.

By the hundreds, by the thousands they perished and sank to watery graves. Khama glided among them like a massive eel, skirting the hungry flames, searching by the light of his instinct for the *Bird of War*.

Zyung's attention was no longer focused on Khama, or the God-King would crush him once again. He must find Undutu before that happened. Find him and fly him from this great slaughter before it consumed them both.

The great arc of sea vessels was broken and scattered. The black reavers of Khyrei were wrecked and blazing; the Jade Isle traders were nothing more than floating splinters; the lean galleys of Yaskatha drifted in flaming pieces toward the sea-bottom; the alabaster swanships of Mumbaza burned brightest of all, refusing to go down even as the flames consumed them. Warriors leaped blazing and wailing into the waters, where floating fires scorched them as they drowned.

Nearly all of the thousands ships assembled by Undutu and D'zan were burning and broken. The rest would soon follow.

Khama saw the *Bird of War* floating in two pieces, each one upturned to bob upon the surface, pale flames eating at the bisected hull and boiling the waters beneath.

I am too late.

He surfaced into the last moments of the firestorm. No more flames rose into the sky, but still the burning alchemy rained upon the wreckage and flotsam. A deluge of cleansing fire meant to sweep all resistance from the path of Zyung. It had succeeded.

Khama lifted only his head above the surface, directly between the two halves of the *Bird of War*. The moans of doomed men wrapped in blazing sails tore at his heart like the claws of vultures. His eyes scanned the wreckage . . .

He lives!

Undutu clung to the scorched keel of the swanship. His crown and sword were lost to him, as was his mighty fleet and all its proud warriors. A score of burns marked his lean body, yet he shouted defiance at the dreadnoughts hovering less than a bow-shot above the waves. The airships had come in low to finish any survivors. As if in response to Undutu's raving cries, a gout of flame arced toward him from on high.

Khama grabbed the King's leg between his jaws, gentle enough to avoid harm, and yanked him from the ruined shard of hull. He pulled Undutu beneath the water as the surface ignited and the flotsam charred to cinders. There was panic in the King's face as the sea swallowed him, until he met the glowing eyes of Khama, who pulled him deeper still.

A globe of air bubbled from Khama's throat to engulf Undutu. The bleeding monarch, able to breathe again, pulled himself along Khama's skull to straddle the Feathered Serpent's neck.

Khama sped away from the devastation, heading for the black

roots of the nearest island. He stayed low to the seabed. *Let them believe they have slain both Serpent and King this day.*

Undutu wept and moaned, his fists dug into Khama's fresh plumage. The black waters rushed by as the thunders of battle faded behind them.

The foot of an island loomed before them now, a blue-green mountain rising toward the air and sun. Khama followed the course of the underwater crag, planning to surface only when he had carried Undutu west of Ongthaia. Yet something drew his attention toward the southern end of the isle. Someone was calling his name. A familiar voice. He reversed direction, swimming fast as a shark toward the sound that was more than sound.

The sea floor sloped upward, erupting in a beach of golden sand. Once again Khama raised his head above the waves. This time the head and shoulders of Undutu rose behind it.

"Gods of Sea and Sky!" Undutu cried.

A handful of figures lay panting and groaning where surf met sand. Less than a dozen men had reached the shore under the power of their own arms and legs. Only one of them stood to greet the Feathered Serpent; the rest vomited seawater or lay senseless and bleeding.

"Khama!" shouted the caller. He grasped a blade of black iron etched with the Sun God's sigil, which blazed in the sunlight.

"D'zan!" called Undutu.

Khama glided into the shallow water, where Undutu leaped from his back and embraced his fellow King. They stared across the waves, where less than a league from the shore the remnants of their routed fleets burned and sank. The sky was full of hovering dreadnoughts; throughout the battle they had held their concentric formation above Ongthaia.

Yet now another sound filled the air. The flapping of a thousand pairs of leathery wings. Flying lizards with gilded beaks descended from the center ring of sky-ships, skimming low above the shattered fleets. The Trills plucked men from the sea with beak and claw. Their riders, Manslayers in silver plate mail, skewered swimming men on hooked lances. Soon the devil-birds would reach the islands, where they would sweep and feast on these few survivors, then move inland to raze the towns. First they concentrated on finishing off the last of the naval survivors.

"We are lost," D'zan moaned. His eyes turned from Undutu to Khama, then to the burning wrecks and flocks of hungry monsters.

"Yet you live, Majesties," said Khama. He scanned the men who had reached the beach. One had already died, three were too injured to walk, and six others were wounded yet whole. D'zan had lost his crown as well, but somehow kept hold of his blade. He appeared unharmed but for a gash across his chest and a few burns on legs and cheek. Undutu's burns were worse, yet he bore them like a true King, without complaint. How they must pain him now that he was free of the cold waters.

Of the eleven survivors, all save D'zan were Mumbazans. Either Khama's favored folk were more powerful swimmers than the Yaskathans, or they were simply luckier. Perhaps these men had only made it here because their swanship was stationed closest to this island. But that did not account for D'zan's presence; he had sailed in the prow of the *Kingspear*.

Eleven men living. A hundred thousand dead.

Khama scented sorcery in D'zan's exhausted breaths. The Yaskathan King held ancient power within his young flesh. Perhaps it accounted for his surviving when no others of his kind had done so. How could he swim all this way with the weight of that blade on his back? D'zan's boots were caked with mud and seaweed, as if he had run across the seabed instead of swimming to shore. There was no time to explore the mystery now. It was a blessing that both Kings had survived this day.

The blast of a great war horn sounded above the islands. Thunder followed in its wake.

"Quickly," Khama told the two Kings. "Gather these men onto my back. We will not let Zyung take us this day. We must fight again on the mainland."

D'zan and Undutu exchanged a pitiful glance. They lived, yet their hope was dead. Perhaps they would choose to stay and perish with their fleets. Khama would not allow it.

"Hurry!" he growled. His eyes flashed and they obeyed his orders in a daze.

Undutu roused his countrymen with shouts, D'zan with the strength of his arms. Each of the survivors waded into the shallows and took his place upon Khama's feathery coils. Undutu climbed on to reclaim his place at the base of the Feathered Serpent's neck, and D'zan sat just behind him.

"Grab hold of the feathers!" Undutu ordered.

A vast roaring filled the whole of the earth as the echoes of the war horn died away. Khama knew it was Zyung who blew that terrible note.

The dreadnoughts and the flock of Trills rose high into the air once again, leaving those who had evaded them to die swimming or bleeding into the brine. The waters of the beach suddenly receded away from the island. Khama sensed wrongness in the air. He flew west above the waterline as the reverse tide ran away from the island's shores.

The green slopes of hills and jungles passed by in a blur, and he skirted a cluster of villages on the island's southern coast. The waters there had flowed away too, exposing the crusted hulks of ancient shipwrecks.

Khama flew on winds of his own making, as fast as he dared. He could not risk the Kings or the last of Undutu's men being swept off his back. Yet he raced ahead of disaster, and he knew it. Behind him a cataclysm was brewing like one of his storms, though far more deadly.

The thirteen islands dwindled behind him, and the Armada of Zyung became a swarm of specks against the blue sky. Only when the God-King's forces seemed tiny and harmless did Khama slow his flight and whirl about in slow arcs to watch doom fall upon Ongthaia.

The sound of a great voice boomed across the waves, but the meaning of its words did not carry this far. It rang like distant thunder in syllables of condemnation.

The men riding on Khama's back called out to their Gods or hid their faces like frightened children when they saw the great wave rise up. A massive wall of blue-green seawater towered above the island chain. The fleet of dreadnoughts had risen toward the clouds. The mighty wave slid beneath them toward Zharua's kingdom.

The God-King's wave swept over the isles as a tide sweeps over pebbles. On it came, unstoppable in its wrath, driving toward Khama. He flew westward again, doubling his speed. Undutu and D'zan wailed in the rushing wind. Few men had seen such a sight and lived. They would never forget the whelming of the Jade Isles.

The great wave dwindled slowly as Khama hurtled westward before it. Soon the coast of the mainland continent appeared on the horizon, a line of purple cliffs with the peaks of misty mountains at its southern and northern tips.

Khama spun about one last time and cast his far sight across the ocean. He was glad the men he carried could not see across the hundreds of leagues, for they were spared the worst part of Zyung's punishment.

Khama saw the islands battered and torn by the tidal wave,

lying still in the shadow of Zyung's dreadnoughts. A greater flock of Trills descended to pick over the flooded and smashed towns of the twelve lesser islands. Perhaps some of the islanders yet lived, those who had sheltered in the high caves and mountainsides.

Of the last and greatest island, the seat of Zharua's power, where walls of black basalt had failed to protect the Jade City, there was nothing left. The Jade King's defiance had drawn the ire of Zyung, and a terrible penalty had been paid.

Khama understood this as his far sight faded. He said nothing of it to Undutu or D'zan. No need to burden them further with the true depth of their loss. Not now.

Zyung had made the sea rise up to swallow the Jade King's island. Now there were only twelve isles left for the God-King to rule, and precious few subjects left there to enslave. None of this mattered to Zyung. His true prize was the Land of the Five Cities.

Khama flew toward the green coast of the Stormlands, where the Kings of Men and Giants prepared for the next great slaughter.

9

Duality

In the Almighty's council chamber ten of the High Seraphim stood in attendance, visions of silver between the golden tree-columns. The great table had been removed and Zyung's massive chair sat empty. Beyond the rustling tapestries at the chamber's far end, slaves prepared their lord and master for his audience. The shuffling of these attendants' feet against the smooth floor was the only sound.

Sungui was certain that Zyung kept them all waiting to make a point: They served him and must wait upon his every whim. In this they were no different than the servants who scrubbed his flesh, cleaned his robes, and served his wine. Even the High Seraphim were slaves in the Living Empire; they simply wielded more power than any other slaves. As the oarsmen of the dread-noughts were elevated above the rank-and-file servants, so were the High Seraphim placed above everyone else.

Still wearing her female aspect, as she had for days now, Sungui scanned the faces of those gathered before the makeshift throne. Of course Lavanyia stood foremost among them, being officially responsible for the actions of every other High Seraphim. Her black eyes were as inscrutable as her sable hair was perfect. Brawny

Eshad stood solid as stone in his silver raiment, the Warlord of the Holy Armada in all but name. Myrinhama stood near him, seeming to glow in the sunlight falling through the oversized portholes. Her gleaming eyes and hair were brighter than beaten gold, her tiny chin lowered in supplication. The alchemists Gulzarr and Darisha stood shoulder to shoulder; they dared not hold hands in the Almighty's presence, but their hearts were almost visibly entwined.

Four others waited with blank faces, hands clasped at their waists. Ondhi, Verrim, Tholduu, and Chariniha – Sungui knew their names but they were inconsequential. They were not among Those Who Listen. They had never come to Sungui's covert gatherings to remember their true greatness. They were completely lost in the Great Dream of Zyung. Diminished forever.

The Wolf and Panther were not here. That was good. Perhaps they had already slipped beneath Zyung's notice. He enjoyed their counsel as far as the Land of the Five Cities and its elements of possible resistance, but had not taken them fully into his trust. Ianthe claimed that she and Gammir remained Undiminished as they served Zyung. Her claim had to be true, or Sungui might not be here at this moment. The Almighty would know that she had plotted with – and lain with – both of them. Surely if he knew he would send her to salt, or imprison her at the very least.

Sungui noticed Lavanyia's eyes upon her, felt the feather touch of her mind searching for secrets. The First Among Seraphim did not fully trust her, but that was nothing new. If Ianthe's power could hide her ambitions from Zyung, it could certainly hide them from Lavanyia. Sungui kept her mind closed to Lavanyia, who eventually withdrew her mental caress. Yet her eyes lingered on Sungui until the sound of the Almighty's footsteps resounded behind the tapestries.

Zyung strode forth and took his place in the chair of curling Ethus wood. The branches sighed as they took the weight of his great frame. Tawny leaves sprouted about the chair in places, rustling against Zyung's silvery mantle.

"Eshad," spoke the Almighty. "Speak to me first of our losses." Sungui's skin prickled at the deepness of his voice, and her pulse quickened as it always did in Zyung's presence. So did the pulses of all those around her. Their eyes were transfixed by Zyung's glorious beauty, which was far more than a physical trait. His very aura commanded love, fealty, and a longing to please.

Eshad might have been Zyung's own son, so similar was he in bearing and appearance. Yet he was only a small reflection of the High Lord Celestial's greatness. Eshad spoke in a voice strong and firm with confidence. "Six dreadnoughts were lost to the power of the Feathered Serpent," he said. "From those six we managed to save seven hundred Manslayers and two hundred oarsmen. The Lesser Seraphim who guided these ships are wounded but they will recover. However, our greatest casualty is the noble Damodar, who flew too close to the Serpent's fury. His physical body was annihilated, yet I am certain he will return to us when his presence has fully manifested."

Sungui recalled the blazing singularity that Khama had become, his eruption of solar devastation. That was after he had physically broken two ships in half. She had never seen a single dreadnought brought down before this battle, not in the five centuries they had roamed the skies of the Living Empire enforcing its unity with light and word. The men in the pitiful fleets below had foolishly tried to set the sky-ships aflame with arrow and catapult, yet these weapons only scorched the hulls or marred a wing here or there. Even the lowest of the Lesser Seraphim could quench such terrestrial fires in moments.

The canvas wings were easily replaced. The Feathered Serpent and his power had been the only true threat in the Battle of Ongthaia. The sea vessels burned like matchsticks, and the men died like wingless sparrows cast into the sea. She remembered Khama from the ancient ages. He had always stood tall among the Old Breed, yet had never been part of Zyung's vision. Iardu and Khama had crafted their own dream of how the world should be. In this, they were guilty of the same artifice as Zyung.

Khama might have destroyed more ships – and more Seraphim – if Zyung himself had not intervened. His great, dark hand had snuffed the raging star that was Khama's quintessence. The one danger to the armada had dropped into the sea as nothing more than a scorched mote. Like Damodar, Khama would return when his spirit found some distant sanctum and reformed its physical shell. None could say where or when that might be. Damodar would manifest somewhere back in the Celestial Province, most likely within the Holy Mountain itself. Yet she doubted he would travel across the world on his own power to rejoin the armada. Unless Zyung were to specifically summon him, which was a possibility.

Zyung's eyes, brighter than the sun even at their most dim, shifted to Sungui. "These losses are of little consequence. Our victory here was assured and the resistance we faced was an act of foolish bravado. Yet we can expect more fools to rise up and challenge our advent upon the mainland. Khama has survived his humbling. He will join those who prepare to stand against us."

Now Zyung's eyes shed their gleam upon Lavanyia. "What of our prisoners?"

"None of those on Morovanga survived its sinking," she said. "Yet we have gathered some five thousand from the highlands of the lesser islands. All have pledged themselves and their families to serve the Living Empire. I have dispatched three Lesser Seraphim to remain here and construct a temple. When this is

done, a new King of the Jade Isles will be chosen from the survivors to rule in the name of the Almighty. As for the forces that
supported Khama's resistance, all were burned, drowned, or
devoured by Trills. Our foes died bravely, if stupidly."

Zyung nodded and turned his gaze to Gulzarr. "And how fare
our alchemies?"

"Our stores are not in the least depleted, Celestial One,"
answered Gulzarr.

"Seven hundred vats of liquid fire remain untouched," added
Darisha. "And the oarsmen we lost to the Feathered Serpent's sorcery mean extra elixir for the rest of them. When we reach the
mainland we can gather ingredients to produce more. We hope to
set up a foundry with the building of the new Holy Mountain."

Zyung asked Myrinhama for details of the surviving slaves' dis-
tribution. She summarized the dispersion of the oarsmen plucked
from the wreckage of the lost dreadnoughts. Their strength would
ease the burden on ships whose oarsmen were reaching the end of
their short lives. The drugs that gave them inhuman vigor tended
to shorten their natural lifespans, and the journey across the Outer
Sea had been their most taxing service yet. Still, Myrinhama
assured the Almighty that more than enough healthy oarsmen
remained to reach the mainland, where a few days of rest would
restore their vitality.

The other four Seraphim spoke of minor shipboard matters,
confirming what their lord must already know. Again Zyung's
blazing eyes turned to Sungui, but there was no question for her.
At least, none put into words.

"We sail at once for the ruins of Shar Dni," announced Zyung.
"There we will crush our enemies and build the seat of the
Extended Empire. Iardu the Shaper gathers forces against us, a
handful of Old Breed who remain defiant. We will cast them
down as we did the Feathered Serpent. This was no true battle,

but an act of deliberate insolence. A symbol of the true resistance we must soon face. Spread my word across the armada, as you are accustomed to doing. We will meet again when the mainland shore has been secured. Go now, all of you, to consult your captains."

The ten Seraphim bowed as one and turned to leave.

"Sungui, remain," said Zyung. "I will speak with you in confidence."

Sungui resumed her place of attention, ignoring the jealous glance of Lavanyia as she departed. The great doors closed, leaving Sungui alone with the Almighty.

This would be the true test of Ianthe's power. If she could screen Sungui's thoughts from Zyung's all-knowing gaze, it must be now. Perhaps he already knew of Sungui's verbal and mental treachery. This could be the day of her execution.

Her body began to change, almost instinctively morphing toward her more dutiful male incarnation. Her jaw began to pulse and lengthen as her chest grew smaller and muscle mass began its expansion.

"No," said Zyung, his voice a drum in her ears. "Maintain your female aspect, Sungui the Venomous. That is what they call you?"

She reversed the flow of her unbidden power, mastering her body once again, reinforcing her female nature and eliminating the masculinity that had begun to manifest. In a matter of seconds she was once more fully female. Her eyes studied the floor of living wood. Her bare feet upon it connected her with the Ethus Tree below, and she drew upon its deep calm to fortify her own.

"Some have named me that, Lord," she admitted. "A testament to my fierceness in both aspects, I am sure."

Zyung smiled. She was not looking at his face, but she felt the smile.

"Your duality is the core of your nature, child," he said.

I am as ancient as you are.

No, hide that thought. Think only of his greatness and your worthiness to serve him.

That is what he wants from you. Nothing else.

Silence hung between them. She feared him enough not to break it. Perhaps he was reading her mind in that very moment. He might do this without ever alerting her to his presence.

"Sungui." He said her name again, this time with a deep tenderness. Like the lazy thunder that still rolls when storm has departed. Or perhaps it was the sound of thunder looming in the distance, heralding the approach of the true storm.

"I know that you seek to betray me," said the Almighty.

Sungui's legs grew weak. She nearly fell. Her breath stopped for a second.

She would face obliteration with bravery, defiant as she had lived. If she must.

"Look at me," Zyung said, and she had no choice but to obey him. The flares of his eyes burned low, like simmering coals.

"Will you send me to salt?" she asked. "Devour me?"

"Perhaps I should," he mused. "But no. I will speak with you instead." At his unspoken command, a servant brought her a chair. She lowered herself onto its soft cushion.

What game is he playing now?

"You have two aspects, but a single heart," said Zyung. "And I know that heart well. You have served me with honor in the building of my empire. You have championed order and peace in all ways. You have killed in my name and built monuments to my glory. You were the first to foster the Ethus Trees which are the soul of my Holy Armada. Yet your uncertainty remains, a seed of doubt buried deep in your immortal being. I have often wondered what fruits will grow from such a seed."

Does he know of Ianthe's plans? Does he know of my involvement? He must.

As he must also know about Those Who Listen. Those Who Remember. But then why allow my continued existence?

This was not Zyung's way. It never had been.

Unless she did not truly know him at all.

"Why not destroy me?" she asked. The question burst from her. She regretted it immediately. Let him speak plainly, or get on with her annihilation.

He did not answer her question directly. "This great land that we have shaped is a construct built for unity, stability, and peace above all else. One deity serves all the peoples of the Living Empire, one set of laws, one governing body that sits above all others, and humanity thrives in a world free of incessant war and conflict. Yet all of this is but the extension of an *idea*, Sungui. A theory, if you will. The idea came from me, and most of the Old Breed adopted it. Those who refused to do so fled across the world, and will soon answer for their denial.

"Ideas are thoughts, and thoughts are the manifestations of power. All wise creatures recognize this truth. Yet what is the worth of the idea that is untested, unquestioned, taken on blind faith to be the ultimate truth of existence? I have kept you close to me throughout these millennia not because you are the most faithful disciple of my Great Idea. I have elevated you into the ranks of my foremost Seraphim not because of your fealty, but because you are the question that tests my resolve.

"You are the speck of doubt that floats upon the sea of my consciousness. You are the other side of the coin. No, you are both sides of the coin: A living embodiment of contradiction and duality. I value this quality in you, Sungui. That is why I allow you to doubt me, and to recall the greatness of your own past.

"If you, who doubts the truth of my empire, who second-guesses my conquering of the world and its peoples, who remembers that all of this is only an idea enforced by a single will, if you continue to serve me, then I know that my idea remains worthy. Now, as we prepare to spread our great peace across the second half of this world, I need more than ever to know that you stand with me, despite your doubts.

"The death of a few thousand in war is of no consequence compared with lives of millions who will gain peace from it. If we left mortals to their own rule, mankind would only annihilate itself with hatred and war. Its death will be long in coming, preceded by ages of suffering, blood, and slaughter. Nothing innocent can survive in such a savage world. Man is born of the earth like the beasts of the field, and he carries their vicious nature in his very blood. Yet there is also nobility and love and the potential for immortality there as well. We must foster this potential by denying the savage nature of these Earthborn. We are the preservers of mankind, the lightbringers, the scions of peace. This is the sole reason for the Living Empire's existence and expansion.

"You are not without compassion, child. In fact, because of your dual nature you love more deeply than all others. I have seen this. You are a creature not only of doubt, but of passion. In this you are much like those we fight to foster and preserve. I ask you to consider all of this as we spread our great peace to the Five Cities and its peoples.

"You want power, you want freedom. Yet these things are already yours, more than any other who walks my domain. I will not remove your doubt by recasting your spirit, and I will not consign you to oblivion. You must choose to serve me freely, and in doing so you will remind me that our cause, our Holy Crusade, is just.

"Before you answer, consider this as well: As the High Seraphim, who were once the Old Breed, are Diminished before me, so I am Diminished before my own creation. I *am* the Living Empire. The more of myself I invest to preserve it, the more I am bound into its existence. As a rich man is owned by his wealth, so I am possessed by my creation. We are inseparable. You and your brethren serve me, this is true. But I serve the empire, for the reasons I have told you. This is the true source of my divinity: The sacrifice of my infinite potential for the benefit of the world. My power is my empire, and my empire is my power. I serve mankind, as mankind must serve me. There is love at the core of all my crimes, sins, and devastations. This world must be made whole, and I make it so.

"Carry these words with you as you carry your doubt, Sungui."

Sungui's eyes were wet. How could she ever dream of betraying such a noble dream? Zyung's sacrifice was the light of the world. The hope for its future. What better cause to serve than this? There was none other, only the slumbering desire for the ancient freedom she had known in the days of Blood and Fire. Days when the Old Breed were dark Gods who toppled prehuman civilizations as children cast aside their toys. Zyung was among the first to tire of such sport, replacing it with his Great Idea. Yet Iardu had resisted him even at its birth, fleeing into realms where chaos persisted. What secret did Iardu know about mankind and its savage nature? Or was he simply selfish?

"What of Ianthe?" Sungui asked. "And Gammir? Do they serve you truly?"

Zyung frowned. The inner flames of his eyes grew brighter.

"Not yet," he said. "They serve themselves and believe that I do not know it. The Panther has ruled in defiance of Iardu for so long, she wishes only to maintain her power. Gammir is little more than her lapdog. Yet in serving their own desires, these two will serve mine as well. Their enemies are also mine, so they will aid me to regain their lost kingdom. Yet once their desires are fulfilled, they would of course betray me. Before that time comes, I will sway them to our cause. I will teach them to love me, and to love mankind. Failing that, I will end them. But not yet. They are of use to me. To us."

Sungui was still uncertain as to how much Zyung knew about her dalliances with the Wolf and Panther. Yet his words had moved her. His wisdom saw through the fawning words and false pledges of Ianthe, yet did his power see through the blinding screen of her own servitude? Perhaps he did not need to, for he already knew what to expect from Ianthe and Gammir.

"I will consider all that you have said," Sungui told him. "As I continue to serve your Great Idea, and your Holy Will." She bowed low.

"I know that you will," said Zyung. "You may go."

Sungui departed the council chamber heedless of the crewmen and warriors walking the upper decks. Her thoughts were cast inward, churning like the restless sea after the sinking of Morovanga. The High Lord Celestial was testing her – he had been testing her for ages. She suddenly realized how important her service was to him. This meant that her power was even greater than she had recognized. Yet still Zyung knew that he could obliterate her if she moved in open rebellion. That she had never done. There were none to join her in that endeavor, none who could overcome their fear of his matchless power.

That is, until the coming of Ianthe and Gammir. The Wolf and Panther feared nothing.

There was much to think about.

She went below decks to take her rest. The armada turned its prows westward once again. Tomorrow they would see the mainland, and the true battles would begin.

The seed of doubt continued to hum in her heart. It would

grow, like any seed, according to the forces that shaped and directed its power.

She met Ianthe after midnight beneath the branches of the flag-ship's Ethus Tree. The heart chamber was empty but for the tree and the six High Seraphim gathered between its curling root-walls. The ship was quiet save for the distant beating of its wings and the synchronized grunting of the night oarsmen. Sungui's senses were always amplified this close to the tree; she did not know if the others could hear these sounds as she did.

The armada was speeding toward the mainland. It was only a matter of hours until they touched ground where the stones of Shar Dni lay gathering dust.

This latest assembly of conspirators might have taken place on some other ship, further from Zyung's presence. Yet Ianthe and Gammir were restricted to the *Daystar*. The Almighty wished to keep them close, as he had kept her in his sight all these millen-nia. The Panther's power might screen her actions and words from Zyung, but evidently she did not wish to risk being able to hide her physical absence from the ship. Perhaps her screening only worked when done right under the Almighty's nose. It was a tactic Sungui herself had used in the past, although now she doubted that her own efforts at deceiving Zyung had ever worked. He had tolerated her ceremonies of remembrance instead of quash-ing them. Could he be tolerating Ianthe's plot as well?

In the shadow of the golden tree the Panther and her Wolf waited for Sungui. She was not surprised to see fat Durangshara standing there; the cruel one had responded to Ianthe's wickedness because it matched his own. As far as Sungui knew, Durangshara did not feed on the blood of slaves, but he enjoyed their torment. She was surprised, however, to find Bahlah the Young and Lochdan the Eye with Ianthe, for those two had never joined the ceremonies of Those Who Listen. Sungui had thought them hope-lessly Diminished. Ianthe's charms, it seemed, were formidable enough to sway even those who had never questioned their faith in Zyung. Sungui was once again impressed.

The Panther's flesh glimmered pale among the yellow roots of the Ethus. Her milky locks were smooth and straight, her eyes black diamonds. The power of those eyes rivaled Zyung's own, as the dark of midnight rivals the brightness of noonday. Gammir leaned against the tree, his lupine face more handsome than any of the Seraphim. Sungui had enjoyed her tryst with him, yet like most men he had no interest in her male aspect. Ianthe was the only lover who demanded pleasure from both Sungui's male and female forms, and the Panther had made that demand every night since the first. Sungui relished the fulfilling of that wish.

Zyung's words rang in her head like shards of dream lingering in a mind not fully awake. Since speaking with him three hours ago, she had meditated privately in her cabin, until Ianthe's sum-mons had arrived like a whisper of wind.

"I see our numbers have grown," Sungui said, nodding to the three newcomers.

Durangshara's robe glimmered as his great belly shook with chuckling. "I should have known Sungui would join your coven, Ianthe," he said. "Her ambition has been known to us for cen-turies." His eyes roamed across the curves of Sungui's body. He would never have her in either aspect. His brutal proclivities had always disgusted her.

Bahlah and Lochdan merely nodded. They were far more inter-ested in Ianthe's body than in either of Sungui's aspects. Gammir, however, stared at Sungui with a knowing smirk. He knew that she had found him irresistible, and he enjoyed the fact. She won-dered if Ianthe had lied about Gammir not being her lover. The two seemed well accustomed to decadence and depravity.

Ianthe greeted Sungui with a smile red as blood. "You spoke with the God-King?"

Sungui blinked. "We do not call him this," she said.

Ianthe threw her head back. "Ah, yes, the *Almighty*. Forgive me . . ." Her mockery brought another chuckle from Durangshara.

"*His Holiness* is also acceptable," said Sungui. "I spoke with him at some length. Though he did most of the talking."

"What did he say?" Ianthe asked.

Should I tell her that he does not trust her? Should I inform her that he expects – allows – my defiance? That he gives me license to make up my own mind, believing I will choose his wisdom over my own lust for power?

For some reason she could not yet identify, Sungui chose not to reveal everything.

"He spoke of trust," she said, "and our holy mission in the Land of the Five Cities. I believe he regrets the deaths he caused today, and those to come. Yet his resolve is unbreakable."

Ianthe stepped closer. "He does not suspect that you plot against him?"

He does.

"He does not," Sungui said. "Unless he hides it from me. He knows that he can use your ambitions to his own ends. He plans to fulfill his promise by restoring you to the throne of Khyrei. In his name, of course."

"Of course," Ianthe grinned. Her teeth were as white as her skin and hair, bright as pearls, the incisors sharp as tiny knives. Even in her human form, the Panther was never far away from her. "You see? I told you my sorcery would keep our planning from his awareness. Even now he cannot see or sense this meeting directly below his flying seat of power. Unlike you Seraphim, I remain Undiminished in his presence, and that is the soul of our coming victory."

"Tell me more of this plan," said Durangshara. "Exactly how will we depose His Holiness and divide his empire? There are too many High Seraphim, even for so many provinces, and not all of them will join us. What of those who refuse? Will they not tip our hand?"

Ianthe ran a single talon along Durangshara's fleshy jowl. He stood captivated by her eyes. "Patience and confidence is required, Sweet One," said the Panther. "There is one whose power nearly matches that of Zyung. Even now he prepares a force of Old Breed to confront and destroy your High Lord Celestial. You saw the might displayed by Khama, foolhardy as it was, and I can tell you that Khama will rise again to face us on the mainland. He will join with the one of whom I speak, the one Men call Iardu the Shaper. Others, too, have already joined him. He wakes them from their long dreams, stoking the fires of their power. I have misled your sovereign into believing this will amount to naught, but those who stand against Zyung will be formidable foes."

"Yet Iardu is your enemy as well," said Lochdan.

"Forever," said Ianthe, her hand falling to his lean shoulder. "Yet he believes me vanquished. His eyes are upon Zyung and this Holy Armada. All his power, and the powers of those he gathers, will be aimed at the God-King. This is a final confrontation that has brewed for ten thousand years."

"What must we do then?" asked Bahlah. "Join this Iardu in open defiance?"

"Perhaps not," said Ianthe, pinning him with her gaze. "It may come to that, but only at the very end. We simply serve Zyung as best we can until Iardu and his sorcerers strike. This might be in the Valley of the Bull, or soon after, but it matters not. We remain faithful – all of us – until the moment the Almighty needs us to engage these Old Breed. Then we do nothing. He will be out-numbered by the Undiminished who are rising to face him. Until then, we continue to win as many of the High Seraphim to our cause as we can. The Lesser Seraphim are of no consequence; they are little more than slaves trained to use small magics."

"I have seen the persuasiveness of your arguments and your sorcery," said Durangshara. "But still you cannot hope to gain the majority of the High Seraphim to our cause. The time is not long, and the Diminished are stubborn. Many would rather be sent to salt than betray His Holiness."

"Then they shall be!" said Ianthe, returning her attention to the cruel one. "While Zyung faces Iardu and his forces, our coven will move quickly among the Seraphim, salting those who refuse to join us. When our conspiracy is revealed in that moment of fire and fury, more of the Diminished will then choose rebellion over annihilation. By striking at the heart of Zyung's ranks when he needs them the most, we will increase his vulnerability to Iardu."

"And if Iardu's forces still fail to overcome Zyung?" asked Sungui.

"Then – and only then – we move against Zyung himself."

"You would have us join with your enemy?" Durangshara grimaced.

"To end Zyung, yes," said Ianthe. "The battle will tax Iardu, and he will accept even my aid if he thinks it means victory. When the God-King is defeated, we may turn upon the weakened Iardu and send him to salt. Along with any who still serve him."

"A clever strategy," said Lochdan, rubbing his pointed beard. "We let Iardu and his allies exhaust themselves against the Almighty, helping only if we must, then turn upon them while they have no strength left to resist us. What then?"

Ianthe spread her arms and stared up at the mass of limbs that was the living core of the *Daystar*. She closed her eyes, as if dreaming that perfect moment when both Iardu and Zyung were gone from the world forever. "Then you freed Seraphim will take your fine, golden ships back to the other side of the world and divide the Living Empire amongst yourselves. Gammir and I wish only to rule this side. The Land of the Five Cities is ours. Surely it ranks no more than two or three provinces when compared to the vast empire Zyung has built? There will be plenty for each surviving Seraphim to rule as he sees fit. And if some of you turn upon the others to claim their lands for your own, then let the strongest rule. Yet all of you will be God-Kings instead of slaves."

Sungui considered the ramifications of such a victory. The continent before them would suffer beneath the rule of Ianthe. She guessed that it was only Iardu and Khama who had stood between Ianthe and her domination of the Five Cities until now. With those obstacles removed, she and Gammir would reign over this far side of the world. The Living Empire, however, would be fragmented and ruined, broken into a chaos of scrabbling Seraphim who no longer cowered before the Almighty's unifying power. She knew Durangshara would not settle for a single province, no matter how large or wealthy. Others would feel the same.

It would be like the Lost Ages, the Ages of Blood and Fire. The Old Breed would once again rattle the earth with their steps. Zyung's precious order, his long-lasting and hard-won peace, would be less than a memory, his Great Idea proven false. War and savagery would reclaim the kingdoms of Man. This was the awesome price of free will, the dissolution of the Living Empire; the former Seraphim would feast upon its rotting corpse. The call of chaos and the thrill of destruction quickened Sungui's blood.

Remember the red feasts, the howling sacrifices and rivers of blood.

Remember the colossal temples and the roaring of multitudes groveling at your feet.

Remember when they worshipped you, not Zyung.

It will be that way again.

"One question remains unanswered," said Durangshara. "Those you plan to approach in these next few hours . . . what of the ones who refuse? One voice or stray thought is all it will take to alert His Holiness to our betrayal."

Ianthe licked her lips. "Have you so little faith, Sweet One?" She gave Durangshara a brief kiss. "Those who refuse me will never remember speaking to me."

Durangshara smiled and nodded.

"How will you move among the ships?" asked Sungui. "Can you hide even your absence from His Holiness?"

"Alas, no," said the Panther. Her face drew close to Sungui's, as if she would dare to kiss her too in full view of the rest. "I will remain here, where my spell continues to blind Zyung. My spirit will approach your brethren in ways my body cannot. I will taste the bloodflower and draw each of them into the Red Dream, where we will speak of regaining lost power. When next we gather, many others will join us. Those who remain beyond our reach will not recall my presence. Dreams, above all other dangers, are most easily forgotten."

"Tomorrow we reach Shar Dni," said Bahlah. "How many Seraphim can you visit in the few hours before dawn?"

"All of them," said Ianthe.

The conspirators nodded, exchanging pleased glances.

They departed as one, dispersing to their individual cabins and ships. Sungui longed to lie with Ianthe again, but the Panther would be far too busy tonight working her dreamspell. So Sungui went instead with Gammir and gave herself again to the Wolf's embrace. Gammir's lovemaking was only a taste of the blood and fire and chaos that was to come. When the Living Empire was carved into pieces and the Old Breed walked the earth in their full power once again, every night would taste like this.

I serve mankind, as mankind must serve me.

There is love at the core of all my crimes, sins, and devastations.

This world must be made whole, and I make it so.

Zyung's justifications rang in her ears still.

She drowned them in the rush of Gammir's hot blood, the fire of his caress, and the pleasures he rained upon her body like blows.

Somewhere nearby, Ianthe crept through the doorways of a thousand dreams.

10

The Maker of Mountains

The chamber is of black stone and carved from the island's native rock. Its door is iron, inlaid with runes of protection in silver, beryl, and opal. Outside its triple lock the most faithful of my children stands alert and ready to rouse me if any hostile force threatens the manor. Eyeni possesses the strength of a Giant in her leonine body. One would never guess the truth of her gentle nature from the size of her claws.

The eyes of her girlish face see not only the physical world, but also the world of spirits and ghosts. Her nose can scent the strands of any alien sorcery on the island, and her delicate ears can hear wind in the sails of ships up to a league offshore. Yet there are very few alive who would brave the ring of storms that surrounds my remote citadel. I expect no interruptions to the weaving of this great spell.

I have posted other servitors among the towers, gates, and courtyards, all of them less visible, less intelligent, and far more dangerous. Eyeni will be their eyes and ears, sitting before the door of my spirit chamber like a marble effigy before an Emperor's tomb. She will protect the living bodies of four souls about to leave the flesh behind. We will make a journey to a place where our physical selves cannot go. I would trust our security to no other being.

Sharadza lies on her back, the soles of her feet pointing toward the northern land of her birth. Vaazhia rests directly across from her, clawed toes aiming southward. Alua lies perpendicular to them both, as do I. Between our four pairs of feet the central mandala glows brighter as it anchors our spirits together. I have removed the Flame of Intellect from about my neck and placed its silver chain at the hub of this circle of power.

Before taking my place as the fourth spoke of the spirit wheel, I poured glyphs about the floor with a beaker of sea salt, then again with rich earth from a garden bucket. Finally, I wove strands of my own breath into lines of frost to complete the circuit. Fire, Water, Earth, and Air are now configured in their proper places. Now our bodies lie inside the circle, the last of its essential elements.

"Why can we not go directly to Udgrond?" Vaazhia had asked me. The white flame had carried us a short distance across the sea to my tiny island. "Surely this flaming sphere can carry us below?"

"Such a journey would take longer than you know," I had explained. "And it would be far too dangerous. The fires of the deep earth belong to Udgrond himself. Alua's flame would not burn there, at least not with its full power. There are places that have no entrances for physical beings, and we must defy all of them to reach the Maker of Mountains in his den. The great pressure and heat at the center of the world would destroy our flesh, sending our spirits back to our separate sanctums and scattering us for days, weeks, or months. And if we were to try it again, we would be caught in a loop of destruction and rebirth. The only way to approach the one we seek is through the spirit corridors, where physical dangers cannot harm us."

"Physical?" Sharadza said. "Do you mean there are *other* dangers we must risk?"

"Certainly," I told her. "The danger to our spirit-selves is limited, but ever-present. The spirit is the eternal core of our being. It can neither be created nor destroyed, although it can be drastically altered, captured, or consigned to unending torment. That is why we must go together, four spirits to represent the four elements of the living world. There is strength in numbers. We will endure the journey by combining our powers, and our ability to sway Udgrond to our cause will be that much greater."

"I remember this name," said Alua. Pieces of her previous existence, and the many lives that preceded it, had been returning gradually. "From the long Ages of Blood and Fire... When we were new to this world. I remember fearing him, yet I do not know why."

"There were many who feared him," I said. "For his wrath was great, and his fury shook the world. While his brethren walked the world playing games of creation and destruction with the young races, he tore apart continents and flooded the great chasms to create oceans. He was the wildest of the Old Breed, and his nature was never tempered by involvement with mortal beings. Some say he devoured entire worlds in his youth, long before this one came to our attention."

"If this Udgrond is so fierce and untamed," asked Sharadza, "why seek him at all?"

She was clever, my lovely apprentice. I was as proud of her intellect as I was annoyed by the question. "Because he has power that even Zyung will respect and fear," said Iardu. "And he has lain so long at the world's heart that his will must have weakened. I believe that with your help I can shape his thoughts into a pattern that will serve our goals."

"And make him a weapon to wield against the God-King," said Vaazhia.

"Not a weapon," I said. "An ally. This is our last chance to increase our strength before we must face Zyung. We must not fail."

I begin the ancient song, my voice rising to fill the locked chamber. The indigo flame leaps at the circle's midpoint. The voices of my three companions join with mine, a swirl of chanted harmony. A four-part mantra rises from our throats as our spirits must rise from our bodies. Our short practice has served us well. The chant continues, revolving upon itself like the turning of the world-sphere. The chamber fades beneath the rising light of the mystic flame.

There is no moment of jarring release, no sudden cleaving of form and spirit. Our souls simply rise, borne on the melodies ringing from our throats. The song continues until all four of us float above our prone bodies, looking upon our circle of power. At my mental cue, our disembodied wills cause our empty forms to cease the chanting.

We hover at the invisible gateway to astral regions now, seeing the world beyond the chamber as an interlocking pattern of bright auras. Seething colors without names or physical analogues revolve about us. The veil of material existence has been torn aside. We swim freely among the vapors of creation, as fish navigate the glimmering sea.

"So beautiful . . . " Sharadza's gaze lifts beyond the world to the miracle of celestial space, where planets and stars and galaxies glide and twirl, beckoning all of us into the infinite.

"No," I tell her in the wordless voice of a spirit. "We must go down . . . inward . . . not up and outward. Time enough later to explore the wonders of the universe. We seek the heart of the earth, my friends." I take their hands in mine, although none of us have hands in this form. It is our spirits that are linked, not our bodies. "This way . . . "

I lead them downward, through the solid rock of the floor, into the root of the island itself. Crystalline lights sparkle about us, the souls of stone and mineral and raw earth. We sink deeper, leaving the vast ocean and the tiny island above us. I lead them through vast caverns of quartz and shale and diamond. We descend through leagues of solid earth, four motes of light coursing through a world of lights. There is no darkness on this level of reality, only overlapping fields of intelligence, seas of atom and wave, the essence of the world's bones.

"All matter is an illusion," I remind them. "Nothing is truly solid. The only true reality is awareness, filtered and redefined by perception."

Great vaults of magma open before us, and we descend through liquid fires that blind us with their heat. We move faster, flying through pockets of molten earth, layers of magnetic energy, fields of frozen potential, caverns full of eyeless, pale things that scrabble and breed in the unbroken dark. Phantoms of living fire surge from molten seas, leviathans of flame with bones of liquid metal. We dive deeper, heading toward the heart of it all, the hub of supernal gravity and ultimate pressure that is the core of the earth itself.

The hidden seat of Udgrond's power.

The laws of time and space bend and warp this close to the core. This is why we have left our time-bound and space-bound selves far above, locked in the spirit chamber and guarded by Eyeni's keen senses.

Our timeless journey brings us at last to a great sea of molten silver. There, nestled at the center of a molten orb large as the moon, a titan sleeps. His body has become the earth itself, and we look upon his naked spirit, curled like a babe in its mother's womb. I call Udgrond *him*, but he is a genderless force of nature. That is the role he has chosen to play in the drama of this world's ongoing existence. My companions know this instinctively as we glimmer before him, a quartet of moths buzzing about the sun.

Calling upon the strength of my allies, whose spirit-selves are linked to mine, I send a great thought spiraling through the molten core to awaken the Maker of Mountains. It strikes him as a ray of starlight strikes a still pool, without ripple or wave.

Somewhere far, far above, the earth trembles.

Again I call out to Udgrond, and now the stellar sea ripples.

I might say that he opens his eyes, but that would not be accurate. His awareness opens, turns away from the long dream of continents and oceans and mountains and sliding tectonic plates. Earthquakes and tremors rattle the globe along its ancient faults.

Udgrond.

I name him, and so bring myself into the focus of his celestial glow. He gathers the molten silver as a King gathers up his cloak to meet guests in his throne hall. Giving himself form now, he dwarfs our minuscule spirit-selves with his immensity. His eyes are blazing suns erupting in a molten face. He might swallow us and return to his epochal dreaming. I cannot let this happen. Currents of fear and awe radiate from my companions.

Maker of Mountains, I call out to him. *Do you know your cousin?*

His memory is ancient and deep. His form becomes a silver immensity, stretching itself into arms and legs and head. Here, at the earth's blazing core, his size has no consequence. If he were to stand this tall and mighty in the world above, his very weight would crack its surface and send him plunging through its crust back to this place of compressed celestial forces.

Tiny spirits. He notices us. How long has it been since anyone has spoken to him via thought or language? He is beyond both, and my presence calls him back toward the ephemeral states of form and density. *Does the world end so soon? Must I awake to enter the void once more?*

No, I tell him. *The world yet lives, Udgrond. But it needs your help.*

His colossal bulk shifts. I do not think of the earth far above, shaking and trembling at his every twitch. I must convince him to take a less massive form so that he may leave this place and aid us.

I remember you, Iardu Starwing.

None have called me this name since the Age of Walking Gods. We were not Gods, which are wholly human inventions, but we might as well have been in that distant era.

Long have you slept here at the world's heart, I say. *And now I ask you to awaken, to join me in the raiment of flesh, and to walk the world above. Your power is needed, cousin.*

There is silence in the world's silvery core.

I wait for the significance of my plea to dawn upon Udgrond's waking mind.

I have made the mountains and seas, he says. *I am weary from it. I must rest. This is the place I have chosen. Let others walk the surface and play the games of Blood and Fire. This is not for me.*

He is stubborn, as I remember. Always he walked alone. I must sway him.

You have children in the world above, I tell him. *They are called Men, and they are the fruits of the earth you have molded. And there are Giants, born of the stones you cherish. And others, a thousand forms and shapes manifested from the earth's bounty. Will you not come and meet them? Bless them with your favor?*

Udgrond's mighty eyes scintillate, memories of the cold void appearing and vanishing.

What of the Ogvaeth, the Vequanad, the mighty Muthsaka? They, too, were my children.

All gone, I say. *Swept away by the winds of time. The world belongs to Men now.*

The Maker of Mountains does not like this news. The lost races he remembers are less than memories to those who inhabit the world-sphere now. I realize too late that I have upset him. He curls fists the size of asteroids, and certain volcanoes erupt across the globe.

Life endures, cousin, I remind him. *The depth and variety of its forms are unbounded. Yet Men are among its most brilliant creations, for they most mirror the Old Breed in thought and deed. Your long sleep has lasted long enough. The Age of Men requires your attention. I awaken you to help us in the final shaping of the world above. As your kinsman, I beg you: Rise up with us and walk the world again.*

Sharadza, Vaazhia, and Alua say nothing. They are stunned mute by the majesty of Udgrond's realm and the potency of his nature. That is all to the good. There is nothing they can say beyond what I have said. My will reaches out to the Maker of Mountains, strengthened by the wills of the three linked to me, and I shape Udgrond's thoughts toward my own ends.

Heed my call. Aid me in this last great Shaping.

A silver leviathan hovers before us in the molten light. He feels the pull of my magic, drawing him toward a more earthly form. Yet still he towers above us, eyes gleaming with unfathomable thoughts.

Udgrond rises through the core of liquid silver, dragging us along by the hem of his will. The earth parts for him, and the great heat grows less and less, until he bursts through the rock into a vast, steaming cavern large as a kingdom. Rivers of magma criss-cross its floor, and mountain-sized columns extend from floor to ceiling, alive with jewels in all the colors of earthly splendor. There he sits upon a throne carven from a single peak, studded with diamonds large as galleons.

His silver skin still burns, dripping and smoking across the great chair. We float before him like fireflies in a realm of ashy brilliance. The heat here is still too great for any flesh to survive, yet Udgrond's own flesh is molten metal. Our hovering spirit-selves are more comfortable in this flaming cavern than inside the magnetic singularity that was his resting place. Udgrond's mouth opens like the maw of a volcano, and he speaks with the sound of grinding continents. It is the original language, the syllables of raw power manifested into sounds.

"You have awakened me too soon, Iardu Starwing," he says. "This displeases me, for I have lost my dreambond with the earth. I no longer feel the winds that carve the face of crags, or the patient mountains who spew forth the fires of creation. I no longer feel the storms rushing across the face of the world, or the thunder of seas against the continents. You have separated me from the songs of the earth. My head is a hollow cavern now, filled only with fleeting shards of memory."

In the world above you will find all of these pleasures and more, I promise him. *Come see the results of your long dreaming, and help shape its final destiny.*

The silver titan's skin turns to black, gleaming with veins of scarlet where it still hasn't cooled. His eyes shed starlight across the deep cavern.

"I will go above," says the Maker of Mountains. "I will aid you, cousin. But my rest is not yet done. I will sit here and slumber lightly for a little while longer. When next I awake, I will ascend with you and see what the world has become."

No! You must come now, Udgrond, I insist. *Our time is short. Forces are shaping the world against us even as we speak. We cannot wait for your power. Our enemies will destroy us!*

"Then I will keep you here," says Udgrond, "where you will be safe from all enemies. None dare reach into my domain to harm you. Only sleep a little while alongside me, and all will be well."

No!

Udgrond raises his hand. Raw earth hurtles up from the cavern floor and down from the vault-roof, encasing our spirit-selves like flies caught in amber. The titan's eyes blink. His head of cooling silver nods upon his monolithic neck.

"Sleep now, as I do," he says. His voice is the very sound of sorcery. "You will be safe here until I awaken."

Already his power has fallen upon us. The rock turns to lucent crystal about us. We cannot move, for his power over us reaches far beyond the physical. His will is harder and more solid than the deepest diamond.

We are trapped in a column of quartz tall enough to span an ocean.

How long will he sleep? Sharadza asks me.

I should lie to mask my despair. But I cannot lie to her.

It could be centuries, I say. *The Maker of Mountains has forgotten the urgency of time, if he ever knew it at all. To him a hundred years is the blink of an eye.*

What can we do? Alua asks, her panic rising.

Free us, Iardu! demands Vaazhia. *We do not need this drowsy godling.*

She is right, says Sharadza. *This Udgrond is beyond us. Send us back to our bodies and we four will stand against Zyung. Khama will stand with us too. It will be enough!*

The last of the crystal freezes into place. The Maker of Mountains sleeps again, this time as a silvery behemoth upon his mountainous throne. I should have known he would not awaken all at once and rush to serve my whims.

I never should have tried to rouse him. My desperation has betrayed us all.

Free us now, Iardu, says Alua. Her distress is an unending howl inside our shared consciousness. I hesitate to tell them the truth, but I have little choice.

I cannot, I explain. *It is not this crystalline substance that holds us fast, but the naked will of Udgrond. We are caught in his dream. Only when he awakens again will we escape this prison.*

There is terror now, rising to suffocate our shared essence. I cannot calm them, no matter how hard I try. Their spirit-selves might scream and wail for years, making not a sound in the vast cavern of sunken fires.

The cacophony of our thoughts does nothing to rouse Udgrond.

After a while the screaming turns to weeping.

You have doomed them all, Sharadza says. *Vireon, D'zan, all our families and kingdoms. They will be lost while we linger here and slowly go mad.*

There is nothing I can say that will comfort her. I do not insult her by trying.

Udgrond dreams on, and we wait, hopeless and grieving.

Eventually the great dream overtakes even our thoughts, and the silent earth swallows the last of our awareness.

11

Invasion

Storms rolled off the leaden sea into the valley, smothering the dawn with a layer of furious clouds. Dahrima spent her second day among the ruins sitting beneath the arch of a broken wall, though it gave her little protection from the driving rains and fierce winds. She kept her eyes on the gray horizon, where sparks of lightning danced above the waters. A tall wave hammered the beach, followed by a second one that sank the reedy delta beneath the bay. The angry sea rushed forward, drowning the beaches and the ruined piers, licking at the base of the shattered city walls. Later the flood receded, leaving dead fish, marooned crabs, and mounds of seaweed littering the strand.

A few hours before sunset the clouds dispersed with unnatural quickness. The ocean calmed and eventually turned to blood as the sun met the rim of the world. No hungry shadows crawled out of the earth that night. Dahrima wore the Sky God's amulet so they slumbered instead, waiting for the next warm-blooded beings to enter the valley. She did not sleep, but kept vigil on the beach among the stinking piles of seaweed. She saw nothing but moon-light upon the dark waters.

In the first hour of morning the twenty-eight Uduri appeared atop the valley's western ridge. Their shields and braids glittered bright as gold against a tapestry of purple clouds. The Giantesses lifted their spears in greeting; Dahrima raised her axe in reply. She crossed the fields of tumbled stones to meet them at the riverbank while they waded across. It was good to see their faces again. The legions of Vireon and Tyro must not be far behind them. Dahrima silently praised both the Gods of Men and Giants – the Northern Kings would apparently reach the valley before the invading hordes.

Chygara the Windcaller stepped out of the river and embraced Dahrima.

"Sister!" Chygara's smile was full of broad, white teeth. "I knew we would find you here. You left your spear when you decided to take a swim." She offered the weapon to Dahrima, then pulled her own spear from beneath the straps on her back. Dahrima slid the handle of her axe into the iron loop on her belt and took up the lance. The weight of it felt splendid in her fist. She had missed it almost as much as she missed her spearsisters.

"It is fortunate that you arrive here in the sun's glow," Dahrima told them. "This place is cursed – haunted by flesh-eating devils that live beneath the stones. It is death to stay here after dark."

Alisk the Raven nodded. "We were told of the valley's dangers. Still, this is the place where the Kings choose to make their stand. The Feathered Serpent has returned to them. I'll wager Vireon counts on Khama's power to quell these restless spirits."

Dahrima turned her face to the flat green sea. "I have watched for two days, but seen no sign of the invaders," she said. "Only distant storms and mighty waves."

Chygara grimaced. "What you saw was the destruction of the southern fleets." She told Dahrima of the utter defeat suffered by the allied armada. Even the Jade Isles' ships had been destroyed, and the Jade King's isle sunk beneath the waves. There were few survivors; the Feathered Serpent had returned with only a handful of men. Among them were the Kings D'zan and Undutu. "They looked like death, Dahrima. The Mumbazan King is little more than a youth. He wept and howled for his lost navy. They say he blames himself for the slaughter and may die of shame. Only nine of his warriors returned."

"King D'zan fares little better," said Vantha. "He is sick with grief and will not speak a word since the rout. There were no Yaskathan survivors save him. Yet both of the conquered Kings choose to ride with Vireon and face the power of Zyung again."

Dahrima shook her head. "Iardu tried to tell the young Pearl King that he sailed to a futile doom. Undutu was so eager to face death, yet he did not truly understand it. Perhaps now he understands, yet at too heavy a cost. Has Iardu returned from his errand?"

"Not yet," said Chygara. "Vireon asks for the wizard at every dawn and dusk. I believe the Giant-King fears for his sweet sister. Sorceress she may be, but still he worries."

Dahrima shoved the butt of her spear into the mud. The wind played through her blonde locks. She had removed her braids to let her hair dry and forgotten to reset them. She must do this before the coming battle. If Vireon allowed her on the field at all. She hoped that she would not have to defy him in order to aid his cause.

Chygara must have sensed her thoughts. "Sister, we spoke with the Giant-King on your behalf." Dahrima frowned at her. "Listen before you get angry. Vireon understands the nature of the Uduri, yet also that it is not the way of Udvorg women. He knows that Varda took up his own sword and sought your head with it. He wishes you to fight alongside us, despite his condemning your misdeed. He suspends a royal judgment until the warring is done."

Gorinna the Grin laughed. "He has already lost one Giantess on this march," she said. "He does not wish to lose any more of us! Not before the battle is joined."

Dahrima turned her face to the sea again. "So this is why you have raced ahead of the legions," she said. "To tell me that Vireon gives me his permission to die for him."

I will if I must.

"What did you expect, sister?" asked Chygara. "The blue witch had it coming."

The Uduri laughed, filling the quiet valley with the thunder of their mirth. Dahrima could not help but join them.

"Come," she said when the guffaws subsided. "There are fish in the river. One cannot fight a war with an empty belly."

Not long after their morning meal, the first of Vireon's legions topped the ridge.

The Northern Kings had arrived.

The hooves of Tyro's charger stamped along the muddy riverside trail leading into the wild green valley. Mendices rode nearby, a sodden cloak billowing about the shoulders of his golden corslet. They followed a torn track that used to be a road running from the city to the farmlands upriver. The wind was at their backs, blowing strong from the Sharrian delta. It carried the odors of fish, brine, seaweed, and horse dung. Soon it would reek of blood and death.

Behind the King and the Warlord of Uurz, the despondent Undutu rode at the front of nine surviving Mumbazans, all on borrowed warhorses. Their armor and swords, too, were on loan – the metal of Uurzian soldiers. Undutu had given the nine men leave to return to their homeland, but all of them chose to stay here with their lord. Tyro admired Undutu's ability to inspire men to die in his name, if not his appetite for rash action.

Let them wear the green and gold, Tyro had decided. *Let them fight for Uurz, knowing that if the City of Sacred Waters falls, it will not be long before Mumbaza falls as well.*

At the Mumbazan King's side rode D'zan, looking like a man who had lost his own name. Not a single Yaskathan mariner had escaped Zyung's wrath. Tyro wondered how D'zan himself had become the exception, but he supposed the Feathered Serpent had plucked the monarch out of the burning ocean, as he had plucked his own King from death's jaws. The Southern Kings had lost their crowns along with their ships, but at least D'zan had managed to hold on to his greatsword. Legend had it that the Sun God himself had blessed that blade. Its power had guided D'zan to victory over the Usurper Elhathym. Tyro also shared in that glory, for he was the one who had taught young D'zan to wield the big blade eight or nine year ago. He was glad that D'zan had survived the smashing of his doomed navy. It seemed that everyone else Tyro cared for was either lost or dead these days.

What about Lyrilan?

This was no place for thoughts of his exiled brother. Already Tyro's dreams were haunted by Lyrilan's face. He could not allow his waking hours as well to be occupied by guilt. For the same reason, he put Talondra from his mind, yet that wound was still raw and stinging. He would lose its pain in the red rush of battle, where wholly greater pains would emerge to drown it. Until he was victorious or dead, he would not dwell on his wife's tragic demise, or the loss of his unborn son. If he allowed himself such weakness, he would not have the strength to sit atop this horse and drive his sword into the guts of his enemies.

He hoped that Undutu and D'zan were making similar decisions. The Mumbazan's dark face was empty of hope, as if he was already dead. The Feathered Serpent had spoken with Undutu at length, urging him toward the strength of a King. As for Tyro, it was Mendices who had talked him back from the edge of despair two nights ago. D'zan had spoken to nobody, only nodding his blond head when addressed. He insisted upon riding with the cavalry instead of returning to Yaskatha.

Tyro had advised D'zan to go home and gather his remaining legions for the defense of the southern realms, and he offered the same advice to Undutu. Neither man would listen. Perhaps they both wished to die in the coming battle. A warrior must accept death before he ever raises a blade, but not with the resignation of despair. He must accept death so that he can overcome it, with joy and fury and ruthless determination. Perhaps the Southern Kings would find these things in the heat of battle. It was their choice to ride and fight with the northern hosts.

The green banner of Uurz fluttered above the three Kings' heads, followed closely by the purple standard of Udurum. Behind them came the combined forces of the two nation's cavalry. Two Legions of Uurzian horsemen totaled upwards of six thousand riders. Vireon's horse legions were half that number, but his true strength lay in the Giants who were stationed at the ruined city itself. Still, the riders of Udurum meant that Tyro commanded a blended cavalry force of nearly ten thousand on this day. They moved in two columns along the bank of the Orra to position themselves behind the hills north of the ruins.

"What do you think of the Giant-King's strategy?" Tyro asked Mendices. He spoke loud enough to be heard above the clattering of horses' hooves and the clanging of spear, shield, and harness.

The Warlord turned his head, squinted eyes peering from the shadows of his greathelm. "It seems wise enough," he said. "Let the Giants bear the brunt of the invasion."

"Are you surprised that Vireon suggested it?"

Mendices shrugged in the saddle. "I am grateful," he said. "Those behemoths are far harder to kill than Men. Let them face the onslaught of Zyung before we do. Let us hope they succeed in knocking a few hundred ships out of the sky."

Back in the valley proper, the Udvorg, Uduri, and Uduru were gathered among the stones of the dead city. Nearly three thousand Giants would draw the God-King's attention. The allied host could not ask for a better vanguard. It was now midday, and Khama's magic had told the Kings that the airborne fleet would arrive soon. How much chaos the legion of Giants could inflict upon it remained to be seen. Yet the powers of both Vireon and Khama stood with the Giants. This gave Tyro some measure of confidence that Zyung's invasion would be well met. Perhaps Vireon would grow tall as a mountain, as he had done in the Khyrein Marshes, and snatch the flying galleons from the air with his fists, cracking them like walnuts. Tyro shuddered as the vision entered his mind. What if Zyung and his legion of sorcerers could grow as large? Or even larger? Such sorcery boggled his mind; best leave the details of its working to sorcerers and the sons of sorcerers.

This brought Iardu and Sharadza to mind. Where were they? The Shaper had promised more sorcerers to stand against the invaders. He had told Vireon they would meet him here, but there was no sign of any reinforcements, sorcerous or otherwise. Sorcerers could never truly be trusted. Mendices certainly did not trust Vireon any longer, now that he had seen evidence of Vod's power in the Giant-King. Yet it was this power that gave them a glimmer of hope against the overwhelming odds the Men of Uurz must face.

On either side of the ruins the valley ridges were lined with twenty thousand archers, more than half of them Uurzian. Behind the bowmen the bulk of the northern forces waited for their signal to rush the lowland. Fourteen combined legions armed with sword, spear, axe, and mace.

With cavalry stationed upriver, archers and infantry above the vale, and Giants straddling the ruined city, the armies of the north were ready for battle.

Tyro chose a wide, flat area of the river basin to assemble the ranks of horsemen and their captains. The Orra raced blue and silver across the grassy tableland, winding between a league's worth of rocky hills before feeding the delta. This was once a place of fertile plantations whose produce fed Shar Dni and was traded across the Five Cities. Now it was untamed grassland again, save for rotted fences and the fallen timbers of corroded manor houses on the hillsides. How quickly the verdant earth had risen to erase all signs of agricultural development. Eight years of neglect and steady rains would do that to any land. Fear of the haunted ruins downriver kept even the most stubborn farmers from resettling here. There were no more Sharrians in this country, and likely never would be again. Their bloodlines had been absorbed into the populations of Udurum and Uurz.

When the signal came, the cavalry legions would thunder along the abandoned river road and join in the great slaying. Until then, Tyro must wait in the grave company of D'zan and Undutu. Their sorrow seemed as deep as his own, but he dared not speak of their common grief. They were three Kings wrapped in shrouds of pain and loss, ready to spit in the eye of death and take their place among the legends of the world.

Tyro closed his eyes and tried not to think of his dead wife and child.

You will see them again when you enter the valley of death.

Lyrilan's dream-words echoed inside his skull. His horse whinnied, eager to run and break the tension of stillness. All about him men whispered assurance to their steeds, patting necks, securing lances, loosening blades in their scabbards.

Tyro knew the meaning of his brother's words.

I will see them again when I die.

Was the dream an omen, some vision sent by the Gods of Earth and Sky? Gods rarely spoke so directly to Men. Perhaps it was simply his own sadness and guilt mocking him. If he had remained at Uurz instead of pursuing the war with Khyrei – a war that was abandoned for the one he now must fight – he might have protected Talondra from whatever it was that murdered her. It could have been only a dream born of grief.

Or was it something altogether different?

Tyro had lied and called his brother a sorcerer to discredit and humiliate him. Could Lyrilan actually be what he was accused of being? Could he have called upon some dread power to slaughter Talondra and send Tyro a warning of his coming death?

Lyrilan was a scholar, not a wizard. He was sitting right now in some comfortable Yaskathan library, probably drunk and overpleasured by southern whores.

Damn these thoughts . . .

Tyro shook between visions of Talondra and visions of Lyrilan, both lost to him.

There was nothing to do but await the smoke and thunder of battle, and the signal that would send his legions riding to red glory. He only wished his head would clear and leave him free to focus on the ordeal to come.

Undutu and D'zan sat quiet on their mounts beside him. Mendices rode about the ranks, correcting formations and giving courage to the men. Tyro should be doing this as well. Yet his dark thoughts kept him where he was, watching the riverwater splash over rocks in swirls and eddies as it ran toward the sea, where it would be lost forever, subsumed by the great expanse of the Golden Sea.

There was nothing to do but wait.

*

High cliffs to the east and west enclosed the great bay beyond the
delta. This made the bay and its crescent coastline the most likely
place for the sky-ships to dock. So the Feathered Serpent had told
the Giants, gliding in gentle circles above their heads.

"The ships and their crews have endured a long journey," said
Khama. "They will be nearing the end of their power and ready
to descend. I do not think they are built for resting upon land.
They will crowd the bay and the waters outside it, then pour forth
their legions to take the valley. We must not strike until Vireon
gives the command. Then our battle begins according to the plan
of your King. Strike fast and hard, break as many of the vessels as
you can. When the Manslayers and the silver sorcerers venture
among us with blade and spell, they will see our true ferocity.
Remember that you are the vanguard. Others will come to your
aid, once you have prepared the way for them. Look to the Giant-
King for wisdom and courage!"

The blue-skinned Udvorg stood about the ruins with swords,
axes, maces, and spears at the ready. At their very center, a core of
pale flesh and blackened bronze, stood the sixty-odd Uduru and the
twenty-eight Uduri. Ahead of them all, gazing across their ranks
with his glittering black eyes, stood Vireon Vodson. A Giant
among Giants, his head rose higher than anyone else. Along the
ridges to left and right, thousands of human bowmen crouched,
awaiting targets. Beyond them, out of sight of the Giants, the footmen of the north were assembled for charging. Only the sound of
Vireon's horn would bring them pouring into the valley, along
with the horsemen beyond the hills.

Dahrima stood among the Uduri, neither greater nor lesser
than any of her spearsisters, and admired the proud face of
Vireon. He might have been an icon chiseled from stone,
sheathed in dark bronze, a cloak purple as the sea flapping
about his mighty arms. The hilt of his greatsword gleamed

above his shoulder, and the crown of black iron shone on his brow.

"We fight for both Men and Giants this day," said Vireon. "For the Land of the Five Cities. For the Frozen North and the sun-kissed Southlands. For the wild High Realms and the thundering Stormlands. We fight first today because we are greater than Men, who are brothers to us. My father opened the gates of Udurum to Men because he saw the greatness of their kind. In his wisdom, he believed a better world would arise from the alliance of our races. *This* is that world, swordbrothers and spearsisters. We come here to defend it. Udurum and Uurz and the Icelands stand together on this day. Our children and our children's children will speak of this day a thousand years from now. They will say 'Giants and Men stood together and cast down the Hordes of Zyung!' Let us make them proud, People of Hreeg. These lands belong to us. Let us show Zyung what that means!"

The cheers of the Giants rattled the valley, and Dahrima smiled at her King. He could not see her, not this far back in the ranks. She had taken this position intentionally, for she would not face him until his judgment was made. She would slay and die for him, but she would not endure his scolding or his scorn. That would pierce her more surely than any spear or blade. She would regain Vireon's favor only by destroying his enemies. Then he would love her, as she—

"They come!" The Feathered Serpent shouted his warning. Vireon turned to face the open sea, and his Giants did the same. A storm gathered far above his head, gray and black clouds swirling in to fill the sky from every direction. Dahrima did not know if it was Khama's magic or Vireon's power that brought the stormclouds. Perhaps both.

Cold rain fell in sheets and the wind rose to howling as the first ranks of sky-ships appeared on the horizon. They flew in a

line that stretched from east to west as far as the eye could see,
though as they came closer their lines converged. There were
thousands of them, floating, flying miracles of varicolored sails
and golden wood. Each one sported two sets of wings like those
of great, white bats, flapping against the wind. Dahrima had
never seen so many ships assembled anywhere, let alone among
the clouds.

The vessels grew larger and larger, until the true size of them
became apparent. Even the Giants drew in their breath at the
sheer scale of the dreadnoughts. Each vessel was large enough
for a hundred Giants to board, but they did not engage in such
travels. The Uduru and Udvorg must remain close to the earth;
they braved neither sea nor sky.

The glinting of spears and armor along the dreadnoughts'
railings became visible, yet their decks were still unseen thanks
to their great altitude. The armada slowed as it came closer to
the coastline, each row of ships dropping lower to the sea, followed closely by the one behind it. Now their numbers filled
perhaps a quarter of the visible sky, stretching back to the flat
horizon.

Khama had said there were three thousand of these ships, each
carrying a thousand warriors. If each Giant in the valley could
bring down a single ship, that would leave only a handful.
Dahrima joined them now in hefting great blocks of masonry,
clumps of ruined walls, the stems of broken pillars, and other
great fragments of earth. The very stones of Shar Dni would be
their weapons against the armada. But not yet. They awaited
Vireon's word as the Feathered Serpent glided above, drawing the
armada's attention with his gleaming rainbow of plumage.

Vireon grew even taller as the dreadnoughts drew closer and
sank lower. Now the Giant-King towered twice as tall as any
other Giant, yet his great fists were empty, the greatsword still

sheathed upon his back. The Feathered Serpent, too, grew larger. It hovered above Vireon's crown, coiling to face the armada with feline head and amber eyes. Thunder and rain filled the valley while Zyung's armada filled the bay. A flash of lightning flared amid the sky-ships, but struck none of them. Khama had made it clear that the magic powering Zyung's ships made them incapable of burning, and the sorcerers on board would keep them free of his lightnings. Dahrima saw none of the globes of light that were their primary defense, but she soon learned the reason for that.

A vast flock of winged creatures leaped from the decks of the sky-ships. Some sorcerous signal must have called them into the sky. Armored lancers rode in saddles on the backs of the flying lizards. The long beaks of the beasts gleamed wet and yellow, shod with sharpened bronze, or steel, or some alien metal. The metallic beaks would make them even more deadly, capable of snapping a man in half, or shearing off a Giant's arm. Dahrima watched the flock fill the sky before the galleons. So this was to be the armada's vanguard. Men riding beasts through the sky. Khama had guessed as much. She was learning to trust the wisdom of the Feathered Serpent.

Vireon lifted a massive marble pillar from the rubble. He raised it high in both arms as every Giant behind him lifted a section of the shattered metropolis. One shout from the Giant-King's lips and his people hurled their stones as one. The massive volley flew across the sky, arcing above the ranks of lizard-riders toward the amassing dreadnoughts.

The splintering of wood filled Dahrima's ears above the storm. Masts, decks, and hulls exploded as the great stones found their marks, tearing through the golden galleons. Many in the front ranks went down immediately, smashed to bits by the fury of Giants hurling earthy destruction. Other ships lost wings, masts, sails, or endured massive holes in their forequarters. Dahrima took great pleasure in seeing at least twenty of the impossible vessels crash into the storm-tossed sea. Yet now the globes of light appeared as Khama had said they would, blinking to life about every ship that was not already lost.

The Giants picked more slabs of marble and granite from the earth, shedding moss and mud as they tossed them high. Yet the second volley was aimed at the flocks of winged lizards, which were almost upon the valley now. The lances of the beast-riders were long enough to skewer Giants, and their reptiles' great claws would be as deadly as their razor beaks. Dahrima hurled a block of stone at a diving lizard-beast. It crushed both rider and beast at once, sending them into the shallows of the sea. Hundreds of stones flew from Giant fingers, and hundreds of the winged lizards died along with their riders.

Yet now the beasts flew among the Udvorg, passing by Vireon and the Feathered Serpent as if ordered to avoid them. Lances, beaks, and claws struck at shoulders, arms, and heads. The Udvorg struck back with spear and sword, swiping men from the backs of their mounts and cleaving the sky-beasts' wings and heads. As the winged host descended, Dahrima imagined the Giants as wolves set upon by a vicious flock of ravens. She avoided the plunging lances of two riders and drove her spear through the belly of the nearest lizard. The beast screeched and flew on, trailing a string of entrails. It did not fall from the sky until Vantha's longspear impaled it, as well as the body of its rider.

In the bay now the glowing galleons were sinking out of the sky to sit gracefully upon the water. As each ship became water-borne two things happened: Its double set of wings withdrew into its hull, and the sphere of golden light protecting it faded. The first rank of dreadnoughts approached the shoreline, sailing on water instead of air.

Vireon blew a single note on the great war horn that had belonged to Angrid. He had inherited it along with the Udvorg King's crown. Along the ridges ten thousand archers of Uurz and Udurum let their arrows fly toward the flying lizards and their knights. The sky was so thick with them that the archers could hardly miss. Across the breadth of the valley man and beast glided among a hail of black-feathered shafts.

Dahrima laughed as her axe clove a swooping lizard-knight in two, and arrows bounced off her thick skin. The arrows of men could not pierce the thick skins of Giants. Knowing this, Vireon had commanded the bowmen to await his signal. The Giants were impervious to the death raining about them, but the winged lizards were not. Peppered with biting shafts, scores of the beasts fell from the sky. Some of their riders survived the fall; their armor defied arrows almost as well as Giantskin. However, these knights soon found themselves afoot among a legion of Udvorg who crushed them like insects, or sliced them apart before they could raise a lance.

A second volley of arrows filled the valley, and more beasts fell from the sky. Dahrima killed three more lizards struggling to stay airborne, then her axe took the lives of five lancers who fought her on the ground. They were fierce enough warriors for Men, but they could not stand against Giants. No human could, except perhaps a sorcerer.

The legions of lizard-riders were soon routed, and the storm broke overhead. Rays of sunlight poured through the clouds as dreadnoughts crowded the bay. Their broad decks swarmed with silver-mailed Manslayers. A few hundred flying lizards escaped the continuous rain of arrows and the flashing spears of Giants, returning now to their water-borne ships.

The archers along the ridges cheered, and the Giants in the valley laughed. Shafts of sunlight fell across the bay, and the dreadnoughts gleamed bright as gold. The first rank of vessels made the shallows, three hundred of them at least, and a series of ramps sprouted from each middle deck. Manslayers streamed from them like swarms of silvery ants, running up the beach to throw their lives away against the army of Giants.

More companies of Zyungian warriors came rowing to the beach on lean landing craft deployed by the dreadnoughts stationed further out. Hundreds of these lesser boats glided between the massive vessels like canoes through canyons.

The Giants let them come. Vireon stood still at the head of the Udvorg ranks. His legion awaited the onrushing hordes as he had directed them to do. From the decks of the dreadnoughts arose smaller globes of light now, each one with a silver-robed sorcerer floating at its center. The God-King would send the bulk of his forces against the Giants now, including his wizards.

Which one was Zyung's ship? Dahrima could not tell the dreadnoughts apart. The main sail of each vessel bore the face of Zyung with his eyes of fire. Would the God-King come forth to face the Giant-King himself? Or would he let others do his fighting? She lost count of the sorcerers gliding from the anchored ships into the valley. There were hundreds of them. More ships rested along the base of the cliffs to the east and west of the Sharrian harbor, and more eager Manslayers rowed from them with spears, blades, and shields reflecting the sun's fury.

They were tall, these Manslayers. Not Giants, but taller than normal Men. From their forward rush and the dark eyes behind their visored helms, she could tell they did not fear the Udvorg, the Uduru, or the Uduri. That meant they did not fear death.

They must be taught fear this day.

The archers along the ridges directed their volleys at the swarming Manslayers. Perhaps one shaft in ten found its mark, while most were deflected by armored plate or shield. Like the sails of their ships, the invaders' shields bore the face of Zyung, his eyes those of a raging God.

As the first of the Manslayers met the Giants, the Feathered Serpent rose from Vireon's shoulders and flew into the ranks of gliding sorcerers. Now Vireon blew two more blasts on his war horn, and the Legions of Uurz and Udurum footmen poured down the sides of the valley, twin floods of purple and black, green and gold, to meet the swirling silver of the Manslayers.

Dahrima waded among the Zyungians, turning the wicked blades of their spears with her shield, slicing them neck to groin with her axe, stomping on the corpses of dead men, hewing down one challenger after another.

Now a new kind of rain fell in the valley, a rain of blood spraying from the burst flesh of men as they died. The Giants waded through a sea of rushing Manslayers. They could not kill all of the invaders; the foes' numbers were too great, and they would not stop flooding into the valley.

Dahrima saw the first Udvorg fall, his eye and brain pierced by a Manslayer's flashing blade. She hacked her way toward the Giantslayer, but he was lost in the mêlée before she could avenge the blue-skin. She killed five other men trying to reach him. Their blades were uncommonly wrought, made with curling and jagged designs, and at times they hooked and scored her flesh, though none managed to deliver a serious blow. She killed and killed again. Their armor split like the shells of insects beneath her sweeping axe.

The legions of Men blended with the legions of Manslayers, and Dahrima saw Vireon crushing Zyungians by the dozen beneath his colossal feet. Yet his eyes were upon the sorcerers floating and swarming above the battle. Khama was a raging ball of fire, chasing the wizards here and there across the valley. He caught one in his coils and Dahrima heard the wizard's globe of light shatter like glass above the noise of battle. The Zyungian's flesh burned away and his bones fell to ash as Khama darted toward the next one. The silver-robes cast burning light at him, but the Feathered Serpent brushed away their power like it was nothing. He belched lightning bolts that shivered and cracked their protective globes.

Vireon grew larger still, towering above the valley. He plucked sorcerers from the sky with his bare hands and squeezed their glimmering globes in his fists until they shattered. The men inside died screaming as he crushed their bones and hurled their remains at the dreadnoughts. Those who avoided his grasp cast bolts of light at him like burning spears. Vireon ignored them as he yanked another sorcerer out of the sky.

The thunder of horses' hooves joined the clanging of sword and shield. The cavalry legions led by Tyro crashed into the spreading ranks of Manslayers, none of whom had the advantage of horse power. Did they even ride horses on the other side of the world? No, they rode flying lizards. Yet they had not brought enough of those winged terrors.

The valley became a sea of blood and metal and swirling death. The archers along the ridges fired the last of their arrows, then drew their longblades and rushed down to join the mêlée. Still the Manslayers poured ashore from their golden ships. The Men of the Five Cities were outnumbered thirty to one, not counting the legion of sorcerers. Yet the defenders had known this would be the case.

Dahrima fought on, pulling a lance from her shoulder after killing the man who put it there. Every now and then a Giant fell, but it often took several Manslayers to kill even one of them. In such cases the enraged Udvorg fell upon the slayers and tore them to bits. Yet there were always more Manslayers rushing forward to take their place.

She could not see how well the Men of the Five Cities were faring against the Men of Zyung. She could see nothing anymore but a red haze of muscles, entrails, and mangled armor. Broken shields and rolling heads. Severed limbs and howling wounded. Cracked skulls and crushed ribcages. The red rain continued to fall beneath the relentless sun.

There was only killing and more killing to be done.

Dahrima howled in the deluge of steaming crimson.

"For Vireon!"

Tyro was the spearhead at the front of the cavalry wedge that pierced the ranks of Manslayers. The momentum of the charge trampled hundreds of invaders beneath a wall of mailed horseflesh. Skulls and corselets were punctured and crushed by iron-shod hooves. Tyro's lance punctured a scaled Zyungian breastplate and caught fast in the dying man's ribs. He cast the broken shaft aside and laid about him with broadsword and spiked shield.

Each of the Zyungian warriors stood head-and-shoulders taller than any man of Uurz. Whether they were drawn exclusively from a race of massive Men, or grown to mighty proportions by sorcery, Tyro neither knew nor cared. His rearing warhorse struck at them with its hooves while he clove their metal and flesh with his heavy blade.

Undutu drove his spear through the chests, necks, and faces of a dozen foes before turning to his longblade. D'zan had not bothered to carry a lance; his greatsword flashed down upon beaked helms and spiked shoulders, wreaking havoc on the flesh beneath. The Yaskathan's horse was the first to go down, impaled by a trio of Zyungian spears. Yet D'zan fought more fiercely with two feet on the ground, his iron blade spinning in red arcs.

The Manslayers hardly screamed as they died; they grunted and gurgled and sucked in their last breaths like any dying man must, but they never screamed. Tyro pondered this in the calm chamber at the back of his mind, while his sword set blood and brains free of their fleshy prisons. The red fury fell upon him as it always did in battle. He turned the crooked blades of Zyung or stayed them with his shield, searching and finding the small places where his blade could slide home. When he failed to find such openings, he hacked through metal with repeated blows until soft flesh was exposed, and his final strike stole another life.

The formations of horsemen had broken rapidly into chaos. The valley was full of screeching, thundering death. Across a sea of swords and spears Giants smashed Manslayers by twos and threes, pinning them on longspears like insects, sweeping torn bodies into the air with flailing maces and hammers, slicing men in half with greatswords and axes. Beyond the marauding Giants the silver masses of Manslayers continued pouring onto the shore of the bay. Vireon towered above the battle, a bronze colossus snatching Zyung's wizards from the air like fluttering moths. The Feathered Serpent seethed with flame and light, hurtling among those same sorcerers and drawing their wrath to himself.

Yet so many of the silver-robes flew above the valley now, the majority of them escaped Vireon and the Serpent. A ray of light brighter than a sunbeam shot from a floating sorcerer's globe, igniting a company of Uurzians and the Udvorg fighting alongside them. The warriors turned to ash in a moment of unearthly heat; even their bones and armor were consumed in the blaze. Men ran now from the path of sky-borne wizards, breaking their formations and spreading panic. Giants hurled spears and chunks of stone at the silver-robes, but these assaults failed to break their glassy orbs. They only defense against the legion of sorcerers was the intervention of Khama or Vireon. And neither Giant-King nor Feathered Serpent could be everywhere at once.

A blazing column of light fell next to Tyro, its heat washing over him like a furnace. He watched those caught directly in the glow, men and horses alike, wither and burn away. Before their bones hit the ground, they too were blackened dust.

There are too many of these lightbringers!

Tyro wanted to shout this in his terror, but he drowned the compulsion and fear by lunging at the nearest Manslayer. A lance ripped through the guts of his horse, pulling him down into the filth and pulped bodies. A silver-mailed brute stood over him, raining blows against his backplate. Tyro rolled over and blocked the curved longblade with his shield. His broadsword was caught beneath the dead mount, and there was no time to pry it free. Another blow clanged off his helm as he pulled a dagger free of its sheath. He rolled inside the man's next blow and drove his short blade into the exposed sliver of belly between belt and breastplate. It sank deep. Tyro swept the dagger sideways, eviscerating his opponent. Gore and entrails spilled across his shoulder.

Another Manslayer rushed forward as Tyro grabbed the broadsword and pulled it free of the twitching horse's bulk. He parried a downswing and sent his boot into the assailant's crotch, tipping him off-balance. He drove the blade upward, into the flesh below the chin, where the straps of his enemy's helmet were the only protection. Tyro grabbed the man's belt and used the corpse's backward fall to pull himself upward. On his feet now, he freed his blade from the dead man's skull and spun to meet a new attacker.

The baroque blades of the invaders were marvels of design. While contending with a Manslayer, foiling any major blows, a man could be cut a dozen times by the curling lesser blades or the barbed fringes of their hilts. The Zyungians wore scalloped metal gauntlets and arm guards not only to protect them from enemy blows, but also to avoid injury from their own spinning weapons. Tyro endured more small cuts than he could count as the battle raged, but he also learned how to avoid those lesser cuts with certain lunges and feints. The Men of Zyung were teaching him a new dance.

Still the annihilating bolts of light fell across the legions, killing entire squads of men at once. Only those who were deeply mingled with the ranks of the Manslayers were safe from the sorcerers' killing lights. Tyro guessed that their power could not discriminate between ally and enemy when it fell, and the silver-robes must be under orders not to send their own Manslayers to ash. Tyro shouted this knowledge to all those about him, and drove deeper into the ranks of bloodied silver. Better to die at the end of a man's blade than be reduced to nothingness by a sorcerer's deathlight.

Once again he caught sight of Undutu, who somehow had remained upon his horse. The Pearl King could fight. Tyro was impressed. He drove through the scarlet fray toward the Mumbazan, but found himself stayed by a forest of blade and shield. Up ahead the blond locks of D'zan were visible, slinging blood like rainwater. The black blade rose and fell, rose and fell. Then he saw no more of the Yaskathan, as the Manslayers closed on him from left, right, and behind.

A column of deathlight flared beyond Tyro's immediate foes. He saw the rearing steed of Undutu caught in the rush of white heat. Undutu's dripping blade was raised high when the sorcery fell upon him. The Mumbazan had killed so many Manslayers that a wide ring of bodies lay about him, separating him from the fray as his steed tried to find level ground. Tyro realized too late that this bit of open space was what killed the Mumbazan. The withdrawal of Zyungians from any sector of the field was a signal that they needed a sorcerer's aid. They had receded from Undutu and opened him to assault from above. His flesh curled into strips and wafted away. For a timeless moment his skeleton sat whole upon the raised saddle, proud as a living warrior, blade clutched in fleshless fingers of bone.

Then the bones of man and horse fell together into spinning clouds of dust.

Tyro's blade stole an arm, then a head. He dipped beneath a spear meant to pierce his back, so that it skewered his armless foe instead. He whirled, hacking deep into the spearman's armpit. The man fell, and Tyro finished him with a downward thrust beneath the visor. The blade sank through skull and helm into the muddy earth below.

Undutu is gone. Like his proud and mighty fleet before him.

There was no sign of the nine Mumbazan soldiers. Tyro hoped they were as good with a blade as their King. He fought his way toward D'zan now, Uurzians and Udurumites gathering about him. They needed to stay deep inside the Manslayers' ranks to avoid the sorcery that killed Undutu. If Tyro could reach the Yaskathan King, the two might drive forward and reach Vireon's shadow, where there was at least some defense against the throwers of deathlights.

Three more Manslayers died beneath Tyro's blade as he hewed his way toward D'zan. Along the way he saved the lives of two Uurzians and a man of Udurum who were overmatched by the invaders. The men about Tyro formed a wedge and drove toward the King of Yaskatha, whose battle cries rose above the fray now.

All color drained out of the world, replaced by crimson. The ancient reek of death choked Tyro as his own blood flowed to mingle with that of his enemies.

He drove his blade deep into the groin of a fallen foe and raised his eyes to see Talondra.

She stood in a pocket of calm as the carnage raged about her. The splashing blood did not touch her; she was unstained and clean. Her sad blue eyes flashed at him through the red torrent. Her hands were on her swollen belly. He called her name, but his voice was lost amid the ringing of sword against shield.

You will see them again when you enter the valley of death.

She could not be here, not in the midst of this great chaos. None but Tyro could see her there, or she would have been sliced to ribbons in an instant. He raised a dripping hand toward her, his cheeks ripe with tears among the sweat and blood.

My wife and my son.

Talondra smiled at him, but it was a sad smile.

Her eyes turned toward her pregnant belly.

A blade sank between his shoulders, slowed only by the metal of his corslet. The pain awoke him from the spell of his vision. He swirled about and killed the man who had stabbed him. He was lucky the blade had not reached his heart. Yet the sight of Talondra had pierced it as surely as an arrow.

Tyro took off another rushing Manslayer's head, then turned back to find her gone.

Only a vision. A mirage of battle.

He fought on, ignoring the spike of pain between his shoulders. D'zan was not far away now. Men and Giants died in blazing fury all about him. None of it mattered. He must reach D'zan and they must reach Vireon.

A light flared above him, only for a moment. He expected the deadly heat to fall upon him now, but instead a shadow intervened. The Feathered Serpent glided above him, a mammoth viper that grabbed the sorcerer's globe in its fangs and took the blast in its gullet. Khama swallowed the deathlight and vomited it back at the wizard who created it. Globe and sorcerer were reduced to cinders.

"D'zan!" Tyro killed another man and found himself only yards away from his fellow monarch. "Undutu is dead!" he shouted. "We must make for Vireon!"

D'zan nodded and raised his blade to counter a blow. His helm had been lost, like his crown, and he bled from a dozen wounds. Tyro marveled that the Southern King was still able to fight with such terrible rents in his flesh. Then he remembered the wound in his own back and cut down a man rushing at D'zan. A ring of Uurzians gathered about the two Kings. They stood deep amid the ranks of Manslayers.

Tyro thought of Mendices. He hoped the Warlord had maintained his command position on the slope of the nearest hill, where he could dispatch orders and command troop movements free of immediate danger. Then he remembered the flying sorcerers. If Mendices and his cohort stood in open view, then they were a prime target for the deathlights. He could not see the hill now, so dense was the battle. There was no patch of ground left to stand on in the valley. They fought balanced on the bodies of dead men, or atop the hills formed by the carcasses of winged lizards.

Suddenly night fell across the world, though it should have been hours away. It did not come as a creeping cloak of darkness, but all at once. Tyro's stinging eyes sought the sun and found only a disk of darkness surrounded by a corona of brilliant flame. He looked away, nearly blinded, and endured a stab in the shoulder for his distraction. The Manslayers were not fazed by the loss of daylight, yet the Men of the Five Cities knew a sudden confusion.

Tyro had seen eclipses before, but they had lasted only a handful of seconds. This was no natural event. It must be Zyung's sorcery, stealing the light and forcing them to battle in the gloom. Now the only lights were the blasts of annihilation falling from the airborne sorcerers.

Tyro's legs were caught now in an iron grip. Clawed arms of solid darkness emerged from the blood-soaked ground, wrapping about his lower body, tearing at his skin. All about him men suffered the same fate. Devils of shadow poured from the cursed earth of the valley, tearing at throats, chests, and necks. A cold mouth latched over the wound in Tyro's back, sucking out his blood like a great leech. The shadows clutched at his arms, digging fangs into them as well.

Only D'zan was untouched by the swarm of shadows. The blade of his greatsword gleamed with a pale light now, and he slashed apart the shadows instead of living men. The Sun God's blade tore through their substance where all other blades did nothing. D'zan carved a man free of shadows, only to see him subsumed again by a fresh cluster of the devils.

Tyro cried out. D'zan turned to face him. The fangs of a dozen shadows sank deep into Tyro's body. Their claws tore his armor away so they could dig into his flesh. D'zan swept his blade across the knot of darkness that overwhelmed Tyro, shredding some of the devils. Yet more of them sprouted from beneath the mangled bodies and pulled Tyro lower. Men howled and were torn to bits in every direction.

Tyro's broadsword fell free of his numb fingers. He lay naked and writhing now among a swarm of feasting shadows. Manslayers rushed at D'zan, who turned to defend himself. Tyro knew the bloodshadows feared nothing but the sunlight and D'zan's holy blade. It carried the Sun God's sigil, and they could not touch D'zan while he wielded it. But how long would it be until the Manslayers killed D'zan, now that everyone who did not serve Zyung was being devoured by shadows?

D'zan fought alone, surrounded by the blades of Zyung.

This was the last thing Tyro saw as he drowned in a sea of ravening shadows.

You will see them again when you enter the valley of death.

The words rang in his dying head. Tyro knew that his brother would never forgive him, but he hoped Lyrilan would prove a wiser Emperor than himself.

The last drops of blood left his body as his every bone splintered.

I will see them again.

Now.

12

Colossi

Above the surging tides of metal and flesh a ring of sorcerers converged on the Feathered Serpent with light and flame. Khama's flashing coils drank in their light and his eyes cast it back at them in flaring volleys. He grabbed them in his fanged jaws, cracking their crystalline spheres one by one, tearing their bodies to ribbons. The black stinger at the end of his tail flashed like a spear, piercing globes of light to impale chests and bellies. Still they came, shredding his hide with blazing whips of sorcery.

The rest of Zyung's silver-robes hovered above the battleground like sunbursts, dropping columns of stellar heat to disintegrate Men and Giants. Khama broke free of his assailants several times to allay the slaughter as best he could. Yet always a cadre of silver-robes converged to smother him again, pummeling him with bolts of brilliant agony. Most of his feathers were burned away, and his scaly skin was charred and blistered. It hung in tatters like the torn banners of the desperate Kings below.

The death of Undutu had nearly felled Khama as well. The young lion died instantly, caught in a blast of sorcery from above. Khama's foes were too thick in that moment, or he might have

saved his King. Later he managed to spare Tyro from a similar
fate, obliterating the Sword King's would-be slayer with a
reflected torrent of power. Tyro and D'zan fought their way toward
the heart of a Manslayer legion. Khama lost sight of both Kings
as the silver-robes swarmed him yet again, lacerating his flesh
with their cruel magic. Their sorcery had no finesse or creativity;
they were trained only to be destroyers, murderers, bringers of
death.

Vireon tore them from the sky, crushing sorcerers like beetles
in his fists. More than once the Giant-King saved Khama from a
blast that might have been the end of him. Vireon stood tall as a
mountain above the bay, his feet planted among the wreckage of
dreadnoughts he had stomped to twigs. Piles of pulped
Manslayers lay about him like a range of red hills, even as more
of Zyung's legions streamed across the heaps of dead to join the
fray.

The Giants fought in the shadow of their titanic King, yet even
they were helpless against the flashing bolts that incinerated flesh,
bone, and metal in the blink of an eye. Hundreds of Udvorg had
already been slain by the silver-robes, but the bulk of them
remained, smashing Manslayers into heaps of pulped flesh and
steel. When the sorcerers had eliminated Khama, they would turn
all their efforts to burning away the rest of the Giants.

The Giant-King's flesh was blackened from the same searing
spells that tore at Khama's body. Yet Vireon's great mass was
infused with a dense sorcery that these petty wizards could not
truly harm. Where the Vodson's skin had gleamed bright as polished bronze, it was now soiled with blood and ashes. Yet Vireon
himself did not bleed, or cry out in pain. He had broken a dozen
dreadnoughts, crushed at least forty sorcerers, and trodden ten
thousand Manslayers beneath his boots before Zyung's eclipse
stole the sun.

The gloom of early night fell across the valley and the world beyond it. The only lights were those of sorcerers locked in combat with Khama, or flitting between Vireon's mighty fingers, or raining devastation upon the ranks of Men and Giants.

The valley filled with a flood of deeper darkness, and the howls of dying men grew louder. A second horde, one of blood-hungry shadows, invaded the battleground. They pulled men down and drank their lives, ripping flesh and shattering bone as they feasted.

Bloodshadows! Remnants of Ianthe's sorcery!

Khama had not expected this danger in the middle of the day. Yet Zyung had outsmarted him by ridding the sky of sunlight. The God-King had awakened these nocturnal beasts by offering them a red feast with the blessing of a false night. His Manslayers must be protected by charms engraved into their armor. This was his true reason for choosing the ruins of Shar Dni. The bloodshadows were an extra weapon in his arsenal.

Blots of darkness flowed up the legs of Giants, pulling them down among the dying Men. Neither sword nor spear could touch the bloodshadows. Only Khama had the power to end this attack against which there was no defense but sorcery. The battle would be lost right here and now if he did not dispel the swarming shadows. Every second a hundred more men died beneath masses of writhing darkness. One tiny light persisted in the false midnight of the battleground: D'zan with his bright sword, somehow slicing shadows to bits. Again the Feathered Serpent wondered at the Yaskathan King's powers. D'zan was no sorcerer, but he surely carried sorcery in his body, and in his blade.

Khama whirled in a spherical pattern, releasing the energies at the core of his being. He ignored the hail of biting, burning bolts his enemies cast again and again through his spinning body. In seconds his light had grown bright as the sun, as it had done above the Jade Isles. The silver-robes recognized his power and glided away from him. They had seen Damodar and several dread-noughts reduced to nothingness when his sunburst erupted over the Golden Sea.

Zyung had stolen the true sun, so Khama took its place.

He spun faster and faster, losing all sight and sound, retaining only a core of formless awareness. His golden light flooded the valley, but he did not see it. Neither did he see the bloodshadows curdling and disappearing in the glow of his cleansing light, or the thousands of lives he saved from their clutches. Yet he sensed the dark spirits burning away like torched parchments. He burned and spun until the last of the bloodshadows was gone.

Then his coiled body slowed, warped, and fell.

His inner fires were spent. He plummeted into the corpse-choked valley, striking the ground like a felled tree. The many agonies that he had kept at bay now washed over him. His great eyes closed. About him Men and Giants cheered and picked up their blades, charging once more into the Manslayers whose numbers dwarfed their own. Khama lay among the piles of dead as the battle coursed around him.

A number of silver-robes descended to stand upon the mounds of corpses. Khama could not raise his head or open his eyes, but he sensed them closing in on him. If they killed him, his spirit would return to his hidden sanctum in distant Mumbaza, although manifesting a new body might take days, weeks, months, or even years.

Yet he knew they would not kill him now. They would capture him for Zyung's pleasure, keeping him trapped in this powerless, broken body that was little more than a tube of shredded flesh. Soon Zyung would tear Khama's spirit from this ruined shell and trap it inside some sturdier prison. Or, Zyung might choose to devour Khama's essence, granting him oblivion at last. This was how the Old Breed, who could not truly die, warred upon their own kind.

The silver-robes wrapped him in chains of congealed light, searing his flesh further. Like spiders spinning webs of flame, they encased his helpless form. Perhaps this had been the true reason for summoning the shadow horde. Zyung knew Khama would spend the reserves of his power to drive out the bloodshadows. And Khama had done so, sacrificing himself so that Vireon's legions were free to fight on.

A fair trade.

Consciousness faded as the silver-robes carried him above the swirling red chaos.

The shadows devoured Chygara and Alisk alive while Dahrima watched, unable to help either of them. Neither her blade nor her fingers could find purchase in the non-solid flesh of the devils. She waved the Sky God's amulet among the clawing shadows, but it did not drive them away. It had not saved mad Pyrus either, when he had taken it from his own neck and shoved it into her hand. The stone's protection extended only to the one who grasped it or wore it.

Dahrima tried forcing it into the Windcaller's hand as Pyrus had done to her. She would gladly sacrifice herself to save her dearest spearsister. But the devils pulled Chygara's hand into shadow and Dahrima could not find it. The snapping of Uduri bones rang louder than the clangor of steel and bronze. Many of the Udvorg, also, died screaming in the grip of shadows. Dahrima could do nothing but watch Giants and Men die together, while the Manslayers laughed and brandished their blades in triumph.

She looked toward the mountainous Vireon. His steaming, blackened fists clutched at the sorcerers who assaulted him. The greatsword in his scabbard had grown large enough to slice a city in half, yet he had not drawn it. If not for the ever-present threat of the sorcerers he might take that massive blade and sweep it across the legions of Manslayers still charging up the beach. Yet even Vireon could not rid the valley of the bloodshadows that stole the life from his legions with such terrible speed.

Only the amulet kept Dahrima from death in that moment. She contemplated casting it aside and giving in to the hungry shadows. Her eyes caught a gleam of sunfire in the unnatural darkness. The King of Yaskatha moved alone through the shadows, slicing them apart with his gleaming greatsword. A pale fire ran along the edges of the iron blade as he saved soldier after soldier from death. In the heat of panic, Dahrima considered taking the enchanted weapon away from the Yaskathan and using it to aid her sisters.

Yet she never had to make that terrible decision. A new sun erupted into life above the valley. Dahrima stared into the glare with a bloodstained hand shielding her eyes. The after-image of the Feathered Serpent swam at the heart of the blazing orb. Its light fell across the valley and made the shadows howl. In a blinding instant every one of the formless devils was obliterated. Men and Giants rose up bleeding and grasping for their swords. Yet far too many would never rise again. Dahrima did not recognize the faces of Chygara and Alisk when she saw what a ruin the bloodshadows had made of their bodies.

Now the Khama-sun dimmed and fell from the sky. The Manslayers renewed their mad onslaught, and Dahrima clove a man in two with her axe. Vantha, bloody and smiling, lopped off a silver-helmed head. These Manslayers were enemies they could fight. Dahrima's grief turned to rage as she waded into an armored mass of Zyung's warriors. There was no more sign of the Feathered Serpent in the dimming sky, but the sorcerers in their flying globes of light darted above the slaughter, releasing blasts of death wherever they chose.

Dahrima killed eleven men before she heard the metallic

thunder of Vireon's greatsword leaving its scabbard. Her eyes looked up through a red haze. The monolithic Giant-King marched forward, moving deeper into the bay, smashing dreadnoughts against one another and sending waves against the arriving hordes with every step.

The true sun returned to the sky as Zyung's eclipse faded. A strange hush fell over the battling legions. Every living eye – Men's, Giants', and sorcerers' – turned toward the sea. A second colossus towered now above the armada in the bay, facing Vireon and matching his gargantuan stature.

Zyung the Conqueror was a titan draped in silver, his hair a nimbus of dark light, his face terrible to behold. His eyes pulsed like violet stars above his face of chiseled marble. He raised a great blade of licking flames, pointing its tip at Vireon's heart. Dahrima could feel the heat of that burning blade even from where she stood.

Vireon's greatsword glimmered blue as ice to match the God-King's fiery weapon. Thunder split the sky above the two colossi, and a sudden deluge of rain washed the soot and gore from Vireon's body. The Giant-King stood whole and gleaming before his enemy.

The great moment of reckoning had come.

The storm washed over the valley as Zyung struck his first blow. Vireon's blade met the flaming sword with a crack of thunder. As if this were an unspoken signal to resume the slaughter, Men and Giants fell to battling once more in the shadow of their dueling lords. Dahrima watched the clashing behemoths between blows of her axe. She took more cuts and wounds than she should, but she could not tear her eyes from the Giant-King's duel for long.

Vireon slashed at the God-King's chest. Zyung caught the blade in his fist and hurled it back. The flaming sword thrust at

Vireon's head, but his knees bent and the weapon failed to touch him. He countered with an upward swing but the God-King was no longer standing before him. Zyung had somehow repositioned himself behind Vireon.

The Giant-King whirled to parry the arc of the flaming sword, and he spat thunderbolts into Zyung's face. The dreadnoughts at their knees moved out of the way as best they could, canvas wings carrying them above the churning waters and away from the colossi.

The clashing of the mammoth swords sent fresh thunders across the valley. Men killed and died in the tempest, while sorcerers cast rays of deathlight into their midst. More Giants perished, caught by the falling beams of sorcery. They died now as easily as Men.

Soon Dahrima would find herself trapped inside a burning column, and she knew her amulet would not protect her against such magic.

If not for this legion of sorcerers, we might win the day.

The silver-robes were specifically targeting Giants now, letting Men fight Men. The sheer numbers of the Manslayers would guarantee a victory as soon as the last of the Giants were gone.

More Udvorg burned to death every second this conflict continued.

Yet Dahrima knew that the true outcome of the battle lay in Vireon's great hands. If he struck down the God-King, these sorcerers might flee and abandon their invasion.

The world shook again beneath the titanic blades.

Dahrima leaped away from a shaft of deathlight meant to end her. The Manslayers fleeing her proximity had warned her just in time. A great mound of bodies turned to ash in the glow, and she ran toward the thickest ranks of Zyungians. If the sorcerers became desperate enough, they might start burning away their own men in order to slay Giants. Until that moment, Dahrima would continue her death dance in the very midst of her smaller foes.

More of the flying wizards converged above her. They had taken special notice of her and awaited now the perfect moment to strike. Without Vireon or Khama to occupy their attentions, that moment would not be long in coming. In a matter of moments the Manslayers would realize what was happening. They would run from the raging Giantess in their midst, leaving their sorcerers free to incinerate her.

Her axe was a spinning wheel of death. She would take as many of them with her as she could. It was all up to Vireon now. She would not live to see his victory.

She saw the Giant-King's cobalt blade plummet toward the God-King's head. A gout of seething light erupted from Zyung's eyes, catching the greatsword in mid-arc. The steel turned to molten scarlet, pouring along Vireon's arm. The Giant-King roared in agony as his flesh steamed and bubbled.

A grin empty of mirth spread across Zyung's face. His flaming blade shot forward to take Vireon in the gut. It emerged from the seared flesh of the Giant-King's back. Impaled on the great fire-brand, Vireon's head fell back on his shoulders.

A last peal of thunder rocked the valley. The sword's unnatural fires were quenched as Zyung pulled it free of Vireon's body. The God-King's blade gleamed black as night now, and constellations of stars glimmered in its alien metal.

Vireon staggered backwards, his right foot finding the debris-littered beach. His great form dwindled, growing somewhat smaller. Black blood poured smoking from his terrible wound. The stormclouds parted above him, the rain ceased all at once, and Dahrima screamed as the Giant-King began to fall. Men, Giants, and sorcerers rushed from his looming shadow as it cast the valley once more into darkness. When his gargantuan body met the earth, thousands upon thousands would be crushed.

Dahrima stood still among the carnage. The battle was replaced by running, howling men. Even the Giants ran from the teetering colossus. She did not move.

Let me die with him.

I will perish beneath the mountain of his greatness.

Yet Vireon was not wholly dead yet. She knew this as he fell because his size continued to change. His great body contracted, shrank, reduced itself to the size of an Uduru so that the last half of his fall was through thin air, his legs having left the earth and sea. He fell upon a pile of charred bones and torn corpses, no larger now than any other Giant.

Zyung too seemed to shrink, but still he towered above the valley. He stepped onto the beach, his blazing eyes searching for Vireon's diminished form. By his keen gaze, and the burning intent of his face, Dahrima knew that Vireon was still not dead.

Dying, yes, but the God-King would finish him with a final blow.

Again the battling armies became spectators, captured by the spell of Zyung's greatness, awaiting the final blow that would end all resistance to their invasion.

Zyung raised his starry blade, his eyes fixed upon the fallen Vireon.

No!

Dahrima raced across the scattered mounds of dead to her dying King.

Zyung's voice was a new kind of thunder. He pronounced a final judgment of death in his own language as his arm raised high the dark blade.

A tiny figure appeared out of nowhere at Vireon's feet. A lone Man, his face turned up to meet the God-King's terrible eyes.

Dahrima did not stop to consider his courage, but scrambled on toward Vireon. She would either carry him from Zyung's wrath, or die at his side.

The stranger wore a black hood and a dark robe set with flashing emeralds. He raised a thin arm at the same moment that the God-King's blade began its descent. He spoke a single word that rang as loudly as Zyung's own voice.

The silver colossus slowed and stiffened to a dull shade of black. Even the glimmering sword lost its shine. The God-King and his blade stood completely immobile above the battleground. Zyung was an effigy of dark iron, like the statue of a grim God built too large for any of the world's temples.

The stranger was gone.

Gleaming sorcerers buzzed like flies about their petrified God-King.

Dahrima grabbed Vireon's body into her arms. Now he was only the size of a Man, yet the wound in his gut was a mortal one. She ran toward the river, clutching him to her chest like a sick child. The battle resumed behind her, the clashing of metal replacing the stunned silence. Now, while the sorcerers were distracted from pouring out their deathlights, she must escape with Vireon's body.

The Uduri gathered about her, unwilling to let their spearsister bear this burden alone. They hacked through a formation of Manslayers and gained the riverbank. When the Udvorg had first arrived, they had constructed a crossing out of great, flat blocks of masonry. Dahrima and her sisters ran across these uneven stones toward the slope of the western ridge.

Bodies choked the sluggish red river as it spilled toward the crowded bay.

Dahrima's great axe lay somewhere among the heaps of dead. She did not need it. Her sisters cut down the foes who charged into her path.

She ran from the valley of death, Vireon's blood spilling along her arms and legs.

Khama.

Awake, Feathered Serpent.

Khama opened his eyes. A blur of colors and shapes.

A man's voice.

"Listen to me. We must be quick. I cannot free you from this cage while you wear this form. You must become a Man again."

Khama tried to focus. There was no strength left in him. The furnace of his heart was a flickering candle. The unsteady shapes refined themselves. An orange glow filled a wide chamber of smooth, yellow substance. It felt and looked like wood, but there were no seams or boards.

A hooded figure stood facing Khama's disfigured snout. Khama's coiled body was a mass of agonies. The scent of his own blood filled his flaring nostrils, as well as the scent of the one who spoke to him. He smelled southern perfumes and the fragrant oils of nobility. And the salty tang of brine underlying it all.

How can I smell so superbly when the rest of me lies senseless and broken?

Two piles of silver cloth lay in the chamber, each with a heap of white sand (or salt) at its center. About the walls stood barrels, crates, and chests. He lay aboard a ship; they had carried him into the cargo hold of a dreadnought. A prisoner to torment and pry for secrets when the battle was done.

The orange glow came from the chains of clotted light twisted about his serpentine frame, trapping and sustaining him at once. Their links were instilled with sorcery. He smelled that indescribable odor as well.

"Do you hear me, Khama?" said the hooded man. His cloak and robes were sable, with the green glint of emeralds about neck and sleeves. "Take the form of a Man once more. Do it now. Zyung will soon break the spell of iron."

Khama did not understand. He closed his eyes again. The magic of the spellchains was drawing him back toward a deep slumber.

"Khama!" A small hand slapped his great, torn jaw.

"Too weak . . ." he mumbled. His forked tongue rolled out of his mouth.

The stranger placed his hands upon Khama's great eyelids. He sang an ancient refrain, and Khama's inner flame rekindled for a moment. His eyes reopened, but he could not see the face hidden in the shadows of the hood.

"Now, Khama," said the stranger. "You must become a Man, if only for a few seconds."

Khama seized the borrowed flame and drew upon its power. His ragged, bleeding flesh warped and shrank. His skin once again acquired the rich brown hues of a Mumbazan man. Yet the red wounds across his body remained. The gleaming chains fell to the deck about his smaller form. They were made of a size to encase his Serpent body, not his human aspect.

Khama coughed and spat blood across his bare chest. He could raise neither arm nor head. The energy lent him by the stranger was used up by the transformation.

The stranger sang another incantation, lifting Khama lightly in his arms. Khama recognized the old language now, though he had not heard it in ten thousand years. The walls of golden wood faded, and the world shifted in some imperceptible direction. He was not falling, but something very much like it.

The urge to sleep was still heavy upon him. Or perhaps it was the urge to die.

He had little choice but to accept it.

13

Citadel of Bone

The Almighty shed his prison of iron as a viper sheds its brittle skin.

Flakes of black metal large as the shields of Giants broke from his limbs and fell into the bay, crumbling to dust before they met the water. Flame erupted once more along his great blade and in his eyes. Scores of Seraphim flitted about him like a swarm of nervous wasps.

The battle had not ended, but the defenders were nearly conquered. The Giant-King had fallen, and the Feathered Serpent was captured. A third of the Giant legion had perished in bursts of Celestial Light or were devoured by bloodshadows. Some had even died beneath the unrelenting blades of the Manslayers.

Sungui stood with Ianthe, Gammir, and Lavanyia on the forward deck of the *Daystar*. Captain Ajithi and a legion of anxious Manslayers stood in formation along the middle deck. The flagship had dropped anchor at the outer edge of the bay, placing a thousand ships between itself and the valley. The foremost ranks of dreadnoughts had suffered losses, yet less than a tenth of Zyung's legions had taken to the shore.

Vireon and Khama had slain a dozen High Seraphim and at

least fifty Lesser Ones. A hundred others floated still above the battleground. The main ranks of the Holy Armada had not even entered the bay yet; over two thousand dreadnoughts were anchored in the sea outside it.

Without Kings or sorcerers to lead them, the defenders of the valley could not last much longer. The highest cost of the invasion to Zyung thus far was the loss of three Trill legions. Yet seven such legions remained, and plenty more of the flying lizards could be bred. There were always Manslayers eager for the honor of riding them.

"You see?" Ianthe smirked. "I told you we need not intervene. Zyung shatters his iron skin as easily as he struck down the Giant-King. Now he will finish the slaughter . . ."

Sungui wore his male aspect today. He bristled at Ianthe's false familiarity with the thoughts of His Holiness. Sungui had learned long ago never to second-guess or predict what the Almighty would do. Zyung was often as unpredictable as he was powerful. He had proven that fact once again by allowing Sungui's treasonous yearnings to exist.

He tests me. He tests my loyalty and my wisdom. These qualities he places above even faith, which is only a tool he uses to dominate lesser beings. By giving me a choice, he proves himself worthy of my continued support.

Yet still I remain Diminished, like the rest of the High Seraphim.

And Ianthe is persuasive.

"Are you certain that Vireon is slain?" asked Gammir. "The God-King does not deliver a deathblow after all." Above the mass of corpses and shattered vessels Zyung's flaming sword faded like a snuffed torch. The Seraphim gliding about his colossal body turned their attentions once more to the embattled legions at his feet. New flares of Celestial Light leaped from their hands, burning Men and Giants alive.

Sungui saw no sign of the fallen Giant-King. Vireon's rapid decrease in size meant that he fell into a red haze of carnage and was lost.

"He *must* be dead," said Lavanyia, "or His Holiness would now be correcting that mistake."

Do not be too sure. Zyung's choices are his own.

"Was that Iardu?" Gammir asked.

He meant the stranger who had briefly sent Zyung to iron.

Ianthe turned her black diamond eyes to the Wolf. "Iardu would not strike and disappear as that one did."

"It makes no sense," said Lavanyia. "Why would the Shaper and his cohort of sorcerers not come in full force to face Zyung here?"

Gammir stroked the goatee decorating his chin. "Perhaps Iardu wishes to lull the God-King into false confidence. Let him win the day and strike later, when Zyung least expects it."

"No," said Ianthe. "Iardu's heart is soft. He would not endure a massacre of his own people simply to fuel some greater strategy. Yet the Shaper loves Uurz above all other cities. He will face the God-King there. I am certain of it."

Ianthe stared far beyond the ravaged coastline and its green hills. Her eyes narrowed.

"Iardu seeks the aid of a power greater than Zyung," said the Panther.

Lavanyia gasped. "You speak heresy! There is no power greater than Zyung. Best mind your tongue, Panther."

Ianthe laughed. "You have forgotten too much, Lavanyia. There are beings in this universe that even your High Lord Celestial respects and fears."

"Will Iardu be able to harness such power?" Sungui asked. His tone did not display the hope that lurked in his breast. The more resistance Iardu provided to Zyung, the better for Ianthe's plan.

Lavanyia's gaze was sharp as a dagger. She did not like Sungui's question, despite the reality behind the Panther's words.

A fresh sea wind tossed Ianthe's white locks about her shoulders. Sungui ached to taste her red lips again, as he ached now every night and day. Gammir avoided Sungui's male form, as Mahaavar had done. Sungui expected this with men. His male body was not attracted to other males, so why should they be attracted to him? Yet he had never met the male equivalent of Ianthe. Zyung was perhaps the closest he had found to her, and he had never considered the Almighty as a sexual being. Zyung kept no wife, harem, courtesan, or lover. His only love was his Living Empire.

"Iardu is bold and clever," Ianthe admitted. "Yet his weakness is his affection for living things. It has ever been his undoing, and will be again."

"Look!" Gammir raised his hand, pointing a bony finger at the legions in the valley. "They retreat!" He grinned, lupine incisors gleaming white as ivory in the sunlight.

The legion of Manslayers upon the *Daystar*'s deck raised spears and shields, cheering the victory of Zyung. On the surrounding dreadnoughts men did likewise, and the sounds of triumph spread across the bay to the outer ranks of ships. The defenders of the valley were broken, their Kings defeated, their sorcerers missing or captured, and their numbers decimated. Among the cheers floated the notes of distant war horns signaling retreat along the western ridge. Great bands of soldiery ran toward the river, abandoning heavy armor and weapons to swim or wade across it, while others bounded across on piles of waterlogged corpses.

A cadre of blue-skinned Giants ignored the retreat order. They were caught deep in the red madness and would not abandon its berserk pleasures. Or perhaps they sought to distract the sorcerers and Manslayers, giving their allies a better chance at escape. It made little difference. The flying Seraphim blasted them to bits, two and three at a time, while the eyes of the Almighty watched from on high. Zyung stood smaller now, but still he towered above the ruins and its multitude of dead.

Again the horns blew their desperate warning, a chorus of pleading voices.

Flee! Run! All is lost!

Men obeyed the call in droves, yet once more the blue Giants were more reluctant to abandon the valley. They charged entire companies of Manslayers, who withdrew and left them to the cruel mercy of the Seraphim. A dozen more Giants were burned to ash as Sungui watched.

The Almighty waved a great hand over the battleground. His voice rang deep and clear above the screams of dying men and the clamor of escaping legions.

"Let them go."

The Seraphim in their bright globes fluttered about Zyung's person once again. Now even the last of the Giants were fleeing the valley, wading across the river and pouring up the western slope. Zyung could have ordered his sorcerers to pursue and burn every last one of them to ashes. He chose instead to let thousands live when tens of thousands had died.

The battle was won. There was no need for further carnage this day.

These survivors would carry the tale of Zyung's victory to Uurz and Udurum, and even to the rest of the Five Cities. Every village and town would know that the Conqueror had come to claim this half of the world. They would know his power, and they would fear it.

Sungui saw the brilliance of his strategy.

Gammir cursed and Ianthe chuckled.

Lavanyia sighed. "His Holiness is ever merciful."

Sungui sensed Gammir holding his tongue. The Wolf's appetite for blood was exceeded only by Ianthe's. When he ruled these lands there would be no mercy at all. No enemies left alive to whisper of his power. Gammir could not see the wisdom of Zyung's mercy because he understood only cruelty. This lack of understanding was his weakness. Sungui saw this now and realized why the Panther had so wholly dominated the Wolf.

Sungui observed the red valley and its blackened river. So much rotting flesh and mangled metal. The reek of decay already filled the evening air. Flocks of gulls and crows came to pick at the bloody remains. The valley and its ruins now belonged to Zyung. The Lesser Seraphim would spend the entire night burning away mounds of corpses to prepare for the building of a new Holy Mountain.

The sun was a swollen red eye spilling its blood in the west. The world itself had been bloodied by the day's battle. Purple darkness rose in the east and crept forward.

Suddenly Zyung stood upon the foredeck, returned to his usual hulking stature. His eyes reflected the scarlet sunset, and his silver vestment was unspoiled. His deep calm remained intact, as if it were some other being that had grown to monolithic proportions and cast down the King of Giants. His face turned from the tangled battleground toward the Golden Sea, where the rest of his armada sat waiting for orders.

Sungui, Lavanyia, Ianthe, and Gammir bowed low in his presence, as did every man upon the decks of the *Daystar*. "We hail your great victory, Holiness," said Lavanyia.

Zyung's hands were folded at his back. "Send the Lesser Seraphim to cleanse the valley of flesh. Spare the bones of every fallen Man and Giant. I have use for them."

"It shall be done," said Lavanyia. She rose to implement his command, but he spoke again before she departed.

"A hundred thousand Manslayers will garrison the valley under your supervision, Lavanyia. Have them ashore by dawn. You may keep one hundred Lesser Seraphim with you as well. The rest of the legions are to remain aboard the dreadnoughts. In seven days we cross the Stormland plain and take the city of Uurz. Tomorrow we raise the new Holy Mountain."

Lavanyia bowed once more and glided toward the foremost ranks of ships. She would gather the Lesser Seraphim to her by spell, but orders for the Manslayer captains must be delivered in person.

Zyung's eyes lingered upon the darkening sea. Perhaps he saw all the way across it and past the Outer Sea as well, into the very heart of his distant empire.

"How may we serve you this night, Great Zyung?" asked Ianthe. By *we* she meant only Gammir and herself.

The Almighty gazed at her and ran his massive fingers across her white mane. Sungui was reminded of a man stroking a lion cub.

"I will have need of you," he said, "at Uurz."

Ianthe nodded in a perfect simulation of fealty. She and Gammir departed silently.

"Sungui," said the Almighty.

"Yes, Holiness?"

"Do you recall my conversation with your other self?"

"I recall every word, Almighty."

"Then look upon the death lying in the valley there," said Zyung. "Open your nostrils and breathe deep the stench of it. Taste it on the wind. This is our true enemy. If the stubborn Kings of these Men and Giants had surrendered to order and embraced the peace of submission, none of them would have died today. The Jade King's isle would still sit above the waves if he had chosen the path of non-resistance."

Zyung paused to let the import of his words sink deep.

"Do you understand, Sungui?"

"I do, Holiness. I understand your wisdom and your power. Your mercy and your grace."

"Yet still the seed of doubt grows in your heart."

Sungui shrugged. "Perhaps to doubt is simply my true nature."

Zyung smiled then, something he did rarely. His smoldering eyes turned to Sungui.

"Perhaps it is," said the Almighty.

A Lesser Seraphim rushed across the deck with an urgent expression. He sank to both knees before Zyung and waited for permission to speak. Zyung waved a finger.

"Holiness! The Feathered Serpent! He was confined as ordered in the hold of the *Heaven's Blade*, awaiting your attention. Yet . . . somehow . . . he is gone."

Sungui's anger rose at the incompetence of the Lesser Ones.

"Were there no guards with him?" He spoke for the Almighty.

The man turned his eyes to Sungui, a different sort of fear swimming there. "Two of the Lesser Ones," he said. "Both have been sent to salt."

Sungui started. How could such a thing happen in the midst of the armada? Perhaps the battle had claimed the attention of those who should have been focused on shipboard duties.

"Devoured?" Sungui asked.

"No," said the Lesser Seraphim. "Their salt remains."

Lesser Seraphim were never sent to salt. They were only Men and thus could be killed, unlike the High Seraphim, who were of the Old Breed and could not. Sending a High One to salt, as Sungui had done to Mahaavar, was only a precursor to consuming his essence. To do this with two Lesser Ones, without even troubling to consume them, made no sense at all. It would have been easier to kill the guards in any of a hundred other ways.

Unless someone with great power meant to mock the High Seraphim.

"You may go," said Zyung. The Lesser One departed in relief.

"Salted but not devoured," Sungui said. "Who would do such a thing?"

"The same one who sent me to iron," said Zyung.

Sungui examined the inscrutable face of the Almighty.

"Who ... ?"

If Zyung knew the answer, he did not share it.

The conspirators no longer met in person.

They met in spirit while they slept, slipping one by one into Ianthe's Red Dream.

They floated like phantoms draped in moonlight, gathered above a black abyss of stars. A city of black, barbed towers flamed in the distance, a red jungle steaming about its walls. A river of blood ran from the city, flowing through the air above the abyss. In the crimson flow dark shapes floated like corpses, an endless parade of the dead that reminded Sungui of the slaughter in the valley. Perhaps this river was the dream version of the tainted Orra. The corpses here must then be the souls of those who died today.

Of the one thousand and twenty High Seraphim in service to Zyung, thirteen were currently between physical forms, their spirits trapped in their private sanctums back in the Holy City. One of these was Damodar, who was bested by the Feathered Serpent at Ongthaia. That left a thousand and seven possible additions to Ianthe's plot against the Almighty. She had approached them all in dreams the night before the battle, save for the four who had already joined her. Now five hundred High Seraphim floated above the river of blood, their silver robes painted in shades of rose and scarlet.

Sungui, Durangshara, Lochdan, and Bahlah hovered near to Ianthe. The Panther stood handsome as a Goddess and tall as Zyung in the dream, looking over the faces of those she had won to her coven. Gammir wore his wolf form, his fur dark and ruddy, his eyes red as flame. Ianthe caressed his shaggy neck as she greeted the dreamers with a smile.

"Children of Antiquity," said the Panther. "Brothers and Sisters of the Old Breed. You have entered this dream to seal our pact. The Living Empire is rightfully yours, and so it shall be. You have remembered the taste of unfettered liberty, the joys of serving only yourself, and you will do so again. When Zyung falls, his Living Empire is yours, as the Land of the Five Cities will once again be mine."

The five hundred faces stared at Ianthe with sparkling eyes. There was no sound in the Red Dream but Ianthe's voice. The corpses floating down the blood river sometimes displayed open mouths, but their screams were silent. They could not escape the red current, if that indeed was their desire.

"Seven dawns from now we sail for Uurz, where the sorcerers of this land will make their stand against Zyung," Ianthe said. "Remember what I have told you. Look to me in the hour of Zyung's challenge. You must withhold your aid and strike down those of your brethren who would defend the High Lord. Yet many of those who resist now will join us in the final moment, when they see that Zyung's fall is inevitable. You must be prepared to send them to salt if they do not. None can be spared."

Durangshara moved forward from the masses. "We should have struck today, when the Giant-King faced Zyung and sent him to iron."

Ianthe faced him as a tiger faces its prey. Gammir growled and bared red fangs.

"You are a fool, Sweet One," said Ianthe. "It was not Vireon who imprisoned Zyung in iron, nor could that prison hold him for long. The God-King has not truly been challenged yet. You will see the true power of the Five Cities when Iardu the Shaper rises against him with his own coven of Old Breed."

Durangshara dropped his eyes, embarrassed. Only the Panther could do this to him. Anyone else would have drawn only his wrath.

Sungui gazed across the phantom faces. All of Those Who Remember had come with the exception of Lavanyia, whose devotion to Zyung was flawless. Yet here stood broad-chested Eshad, golden Myrinhama, the alchemists Gulzarr and Darisha, and the triple-bonded Johaar, Mezviit, and Aldreka, along with hundreds of their kind.

How does she sway them so deeply, when my ceremonies have only failed to do so?

A pang of jealousy poisoned Sungui's dreaming thoughts.

Why was Ianthe's power to stir rebellion so superior to his own?

Because she has never been Diminished. She has not spent thousands of years in the presence of Zyung, sinking ever deeper into the pattern of his Great Idea. She was not part of the Living Empire. Of course her powers are greater.

She is closer to what we all were in the Age of Blood and Flame.

To what we will be again.

"Patience," whispered Ianthe, yet every dreamsoul heard the word. "Iardu has not come yet ... but he will come. Zyung expects to face him, knows the depth of his power. This is why he brings every High Seraphim to Uurz, save for a single one. Zyung knows that the conquering of the green-gold city will be done not with spear and sword, but with sorcery. Yet he does not know that *he* will fall instead. And that you, his rightful heirs, will claim his great continent."

The five hundred faces were silent, smiling, hungry with memory. Like a pack of wild dogs, they would be set loose upon the earth. To rend and run and slay and feed as they once did. Sungui felt that same hunger, the lust for a return to independence. The thirst for power and glory and the advent of red chaos. Today's battle had been the merest taste of the grand slaughters that would come when the Old Breed were free of Zyung's long dream.

Damn these Men and Giants! Let them grovel and crawl like ants before us, as their predecessors did when the world was young and burning.

"Look to me in the hour of Zyung's challenge," Ianthe said again. "Wait for my signal. Until then, serve your God-King faithfully. Forget this dream and this pact. You will remember it when the time is right, as you remember your own natures."

Ianthe raised her pale arm and the Red Dream faded. Like a splinter it would remain buried deep in the heart-mind of every conspirator, to blossom like a stoked flame in the hour when Zyung must fall.

Yet Sungui would remember it all. Ianthe's spell was not meant to affect him as it had the rest of the coven. Sungui's thoughts needed no protection from Zyung. Yet Ianthe had no idea that Zyung already saw the betrayal in Sungui's heart. What would the Panther do if she knew? Destroy Sungui, or wipe the knowledge of the plot from his mind? Or perhaps she would allow Sungui to continue in uncertain allegiance as Zyung did.

She would never allow me a choice the way Zyung does.

Had Ianthe enchanted the five hundred to join her scheme, or won them over with memory and promises? Nearly half of the existing High Seraphim were hers now. Did it truly matter if she'd ensorcelled them or persuaded them? Sungui must be careful to take charge of the rebels at some point, before Ianthe bound them to herself as Zyung had done ages ago. Such treachery was not beyond the Panther, despite what she claimed as her true goal.

Sungui awoke inside his own cabin. Ianthe lay beside him in the dark. The dawn was only a few hours away. Outside the porthole the distant lights of the Lesser Seraphim flared in the valley, while the campfires of a hundred thousand Manslayers lined the riverbanks and ridges beyond the ruins. In the morning there would be no trace of decaying flesh left upon the battleground. Only a range of bleached bones.

Ianthe sensed Sungui's waking and pulled him close to her. In the delights of her embrace he found no answers to his lingering doubts, but he lost the compulsion to consider them further.

Afterwards, the bliss of a dreamless sleep.

At mid-morning Lavanyia's legions gathered in formation along the hillsides and ridges. Zyung stood in the middle of the ruined city, surrounded by a dozen new white hills: the heaped bones and skulls of Men, Trills, and Giants that had died in yesterday's battle. The dead of Uurz, Udurum, and the Living Empire were treated as one, the raw materials of Zyung's design.

The Lesser Seraphim had spent the night burning the flesh from these bones. There would have been even more than this, but the Celestial Lights of the Seraphim had turned every part of their victims to dust. Yet these mingled bones would be enough. They lay atop the weather-worn stones of the dead city. Stone and bone would be the bricks of Zyung's new temple-palace. Sorcery was the mortar that would hold them together.

Sungui and ninety-nine other High Seraphim – most of them belonging to Ianthe's secret coven – hovered in a steady ring about the Almighty, prepared to give his vision form and structure. Sungui retained his male aspect today. It seemed to please Ianthe best, and his female aspect had grown tired of Gammir's torrid mating.

From the slopes, hills, and the decks of anchored ships, the eyes of the Holy Armada were upon the Almighty and his chosen builders. Zyung's will reached out to them like a guiding hand, and a current of light gleamed between each of the floating Seraphim. Zyung was the spoke of their wheel, directing their power as an archer directs his arrows.

It began with the scattered stones of the dead city. The ones that were wholly or partially buried beneath the red earth began to rise. The sections of city wall that still stood now crumbled into fragments and floated to join the rest of the levitating rock.

Zyung's soundless symphony played on in their minds, shifting from key to key. The hills of piled bones began to leap and dance. The rattling remains ascended and spun about the wheel of power like a swarm of white flies. The stones began to melt without heat, flowing like water, and the bones added their pale presence to the liquid substance. Stones and bones blended, becoming a single essence that reminded Sungui of the pearly clouds hanging above the bay.

The raw granite that had been the bones of a city combined with the whiteness that had been the bones of living creatures. Together they formed a new kind of stone, pale as marble yet without a single vein or blotch. The symphony of thought rose into a new pattern, and the power of the High Seraphim cast the new stone upward, a rising mountain bright as cloud yet solid as crystal. The white mountain took shape about Zyung's figure, obscuring him from sight as it encased his body and towered above it. The wheel of Seraphim spun in unison about the bubbling paleness as it grew harder and denser. They sculpted the outlines of curved walls and soaring towers, arching bridges and impeccable domes.

The summit of the white mountain rose high above the ridges of the valley. Sunlight struck prismatic auras from its flawless skin. A great arch appeared in the western side of the edifice. Zyung emerged from this arch, leaving the hollow heart of the embryonic citadel. The Seraphim lingered about the pale immensity they had erected. The foundations of the new Holy Mountain completely smothered the grounds where Shar Dni had once spread its streets and gardens.

Zyung looked toward the top of the structure, which grew angular and flattened itself out at the zenith. Twelve snow-white towers sprouted sleek and graceful from its base. The Almighty spread his arms and ascended to float level with the summit. The symphony of sorcery reached its climax and fell into silence. The ring of High Seraphim paused and descended to the earth about the circumference of their creation.

Twin rays of starfire poured from Zyung's eyes, washing across the western face of his temple-palace. When the light faded, the white stone had reshaped itself into a perfect likeness of his face. The deep sockets of the stone eyes burned with inextinguishable fires.

The mountain's interior halls and chambers would be carved and sculpted to perfection over the next few days by the Lesser Seraphim under Lavanyia's charge. They would plant gardens and orchards, growing them swiftly with clever earth-magic. The beauty of this new Holy Mountain would eventually rival or exceed that of the original in the Celestial City.

Yet none of these Lesser Ones knew that the first Holy Mountain would soon crumble beneath the wrath of the unleashed Old Breed. Sungui's skin tingled in contemplation of such delicious blasphemy.

Now a mighty roar shook the valley – the cheering of the Manslayer legions upon the hills and the armada beyond the shore.

This new Holy Mountain was not only the heart of Zyung's Extended Empire. It was a testament to his peoples' victory over their foes. A tribute to their loyalty and bravery. A memorial to all those who had given their lives to make it possible. Within its gleaming substance lay the bones of their brothers along with those of their enemies.

Sungui pondered the symbolism of this blending of bones. It evoked the Living Empire itself, which blended all cultures and nations into one monolithic shape.

It was tyranny and oppression given form, a monument to Zyung's dominance.

Perhaps I will carve my own face on a mountain someday.

Someday soon.

14

The Gates of Uurz

The dream is one with the revolving world itself. We are currents of air gliding across stone and carving ancient patterns into the rock. We are the rock itself, born of heat and slowed to form and weight and density by time and forces unseen. We are the ocean and its waves, the storms tearing trees from the soil and the grass sprouting from mounds of black earth. We are the deep gorges and ice-crowned peaks, the parched and steaming deserts, the verdant fruits ripe with sunlight, the moldering bones of graveyards, and the living blood that courses through living things.

There is only the dream, which encircles and gives birth to the dreamer. We are motes in the great field of consciousness that is everywhere, all at once, rising and subsiding in an endless dance of creation and destruction. We are made from the light of stars and spread by the gusts of eternity.

Time and space are fleeting concepts in the greater dream, and we are their reflections, staring back at ourselves, often without recognizing our true nature.

We are patterns, like everything born of the great world-dream, spinning, churning, producing further patterns. Patterns within patterns.

This is wisdom. It is the light of the dream we inhabit.

This is peace. There are no distinctions here between what is and what has been and what will be. This is the All, and it is the center of existence.

And yet . . .

A glimmer of something separate intrudes on this panorama of boundless unity.

This is memory.

It floods into us like warm blood, pouring from a wound in the substance of the living world. Black talons rip at the dream, shredding it like supple flesh, bleeding awareness into our communal soul. Suddenly we remember . . .

I remember.

We are not one soul, but four.

This dream is not ours after all. It belongs to Udgrond. Its patterns spin across infinity, but we lose sight of them as we sink into those that are most familiar to us.

This is *now*.

Yes, we have awakened from Udgrond's world-dream. Is it time?

The leaden weight of urgency falls upon me like the blow of a great hammer. How long has it been? Udgrond drew us into his dream and kept us there. But for how long?

My eyes open. I see a network of cracks and fissures like translucent veins. The crystalline quartz of our prison shatters. The great pillar in which Udgrond trapped our spirit-selves falls to pieces as our souls leave his world-dream. A fleeting vision of oneness, the dream has already left our minds.

"Iardu . . ."

A voice calls my name, confirming my identity. Below us the physical shards of our broken prison explode against the cavern floor. The orange flames of deep-earth fires leap from chasms in the darkness. The titan of condensed magma reclines still on his throne. His size dwarfs our floating spirits. Udgrond's flesh has darkened, yet it has not completely cooled. Red veins of molten silver gleam across his chest and limbs. His eyes are closed and dark.

How long have we slept?

"Iardu! Awaken, you fool!"

A specter of red-black flame hovers before me. At first I do not recognize it. I turn instead to the three spirits who were entrapped with me. Sharadza blinks at me like a drowsy ghost. Alua's spirit-self is a figure sculpted of white flame. Vaazhia's forked tongue darts in and out of her mouth as she raises ethereal claws. She already knows who has freed us. I sense the mingled fury and fear that radiates from the lizardess.

Now I see clearly the pale face at the heart of the ebony and ruby flames. White as bone, and cruel in its loveliness. Eyes that resemble black diamonds in the physical world seem more like empty voids in this ghostly state.

"Ianthe." I speak her name with suspicion. She is my enemy.

"Who else could have freed you from this fool's fate?" Ianthe asks. Her void-eyes examine my three spirit companions. I recall our physical selves locked inside my sanctum in the world far above. Through the formless current that connects me to my living body, I sense that it still lives. Therefore, it is likely that my companions' bodies are unharmed as well.

Now Sharadza recognizes the presence of the Claw. "You?" There is horror in her soundless voice. "Blood-drinking monster! Slayer of innocents! You will never reclaim me."

Ianthe laughs. "Nor would I wish to, Daughter of Vod. You are less than nothing to me. I come for the Shaper."

Vaazhia hisses.

Alua forms a globe of white spirit-flame and holds it in her fist like a dagger. The wife of Vireon knows she cannot harm Ianthe in this form, or there would be no stopping her from the attempt. There must be a final confrontation between these two, and it will be terrible. Yet it cannot be here in this forsaken place below the world.

"You freed us from the dream of Udgrond." I say it to remind Alua of this fact, and because I hardly believe it myself. I do not trust this deliverance, yet I must accept it.

"If I had not done so, you would have lingered here for a thousand years," Ianthe says. "You always were a Prince of Fools, but this is your saddest folly."

Ianthe's words should not sting me, but they do. She is right. I should never have come here seeking to wake Udgrond from his long dream. It was a grievous error born of desperation. This one mistake could have meant the end of everything that I worked long ages to build.

"You have my gratitude," I tell her, "if not my love."

"I had that long ago," she says. "You forgot the pleasures we shared when you forgot your true self."

"Say rather when I *discovered* my true self, Claw."

Her smile is beautiful and wicked.

"I do not understand," Sharadza says, hovering near to me. "This creature is the enemy of us all. Why has she aided us?"

Alua's flaming spirit erupts. It rushes toward Ianthe's ghost-self. "Twice you have murdered me," Alua says. "I remember now."

"No, Alua," I warn her. "Today is not the day to pursue the vengeance rightly owed to you. We are weak in this place, and too far from our physical selves. Ianthe is our enemy, yes, but she has saved us."

"Why?" Vaazhia spits like a cobra. If she were inside her body, it would be venom rather than mere words. "Why rescue your enemies, Bitch of Khyrei? We will not serve you. Rather put us back in the titan's prison than ask it."

Ianthe's empty eyes focus on Vaazhia's coiled spirit-self. "We have no time for this, Lizard-Queen," says the Claw. "You are not in my debt, nor would I ever accept your service. I can see that you serve only Iardu. Has he bedded you to earn your allegiance?"

Vaazhia writhes and hisses. I calm her as best I can. A caress of my astral hand pulls her back. I move between the souls of the three women and that of the Claw.

"Enough!" I say. "How long have we slept?"

"I know not when you first stumbled into this trap like a brace of stupid hares," says Ianthe. "My far sight found you down here four days after the taking of the Sharrian valley. A mighty slaughter it was. Your Giant-King fell to the blade of Zyung, and your northern legions were decimated. Three days from now the God-King moves his Holy Armada to take Uurz."

Sharadza cries out when Ianthe mentions the fall of Vireon. She longs to ask if her brother still lives, but she will not lower herself to ask this of the Claw.

"You should have been there, Shaper," says Ianthe. She grins, enjoying the pain her words bring. "Yet you were held fast in the dream of Udgrond while your body lay at rest. You *slept* while thousands of your people died. You abandoned them."

"Stop it!" She has raised my ire. She has known how to do this since the world was a cooling mass of stellar gasses. "Do not tell me of my own failings! They will haunt me enough without your gloating. You say we have three days until Zyung sails for Uurz."

"In the evening of that same day his dreadnoughts will reach the green-gold city," she says. "This time you must be there to face him, along with any of the Old Breed who will stand with you. There are a thousand of our kind who serve Zyung, although they are Diminished in his presence. I have freed you from Udgrond only so that you may stop the advance of Zyung. Never forget that I have done so."

"Do you then stand with us?" I ask. It cannot be so easy.

"No," she said. "I sail with Zyung. Yet you already know this."

"You hide your treachery well." Suddenly it becomes plain to me why Ianthe has rescued us. We must rise and reclaim our bodies now. There will be no aid from Udgrond.

"You have three days, Shaper," Ianthe says. Distant stars blink in the abyss of her eyes. "I could have entered your citadel and destroyed your bodies. I did not. Remember this too."

The red-black flame rises into the raw stone of the cavern roof.

"Come," I say. "We must arise." I steal a last look at Udgrond slumbering on his throne.

Our spirit-selves rush upward far faster than they descended. Thousands of leagues of magma, rock, and glittering earth-crust flash by us like a torrent of waters. Yet it is our souls that move, not the substances about us. The rush of ascension is dizzying. At its end the world of flesh and blood claims us as the earth claims a falling star. Yet we have fallen *upward*, and the star is our united immortal essence.

Our bond fades, and our bodies reclaim their spirits.

Again my eyes open, and this time they are actual eyes. Groggy and unsteady on our feet, we rise up to stand about the circle of power. With a word of dismissal I break the spell, plucking the Flame of Intellect from the circle and restoring it to my chest. Our bodies are sore and stiff after long days of lying inert. Our bellies are empty and growling. A great thirst strikes me like a shot arrow.

"We must refresh ourselves," I say, "then travel at once to Uurz."

When the spirit chamber's doors open, Eyeni greets me by rubbing her cheek against my thigh. "You slept too long, Father," she says. "I was worried." She lopes beside me as we walk the corridor to my dining hall. Her tiny wings flutter upon the glossy fur of her back.

"I am unharmed, child," I reassure her, stroking her hair. I do not mention that Ianthe's spirit-self somehow eluded my guardian's astral vigilance and followed us into the titan's domain. If Eyeni had stopped her, we would still be lost in his long dream. Or Ianthe would have slain Eyeni to reach me. There are some powers that cannot be prevented from going where they wish to go. I recall Ianthe's condemnation of my own foolishness and mentally chastise myself. I cannot afford to make such a mistake again.

Thousands upon thousands have died already, and we are out of time.

My guests gather about the banquet table beneath the tapestries of fallen kingdoms. Invisible attendants bring us a meal of fruit, cheese, fresh bread, and roasted lobster. I drink deep of the wine, a heady Yaskathan vintage, and stuff my empty belly until it is full. Sharadza, Alua, and Vaazhia break their fasts as well, pausing only to ask questions of me. Sharadza eats hardly at all; concern for her brother outweighs even her deep hunger.

Outside the high windows sunlight gleams across the green ocean. The tittering of monkeys in the courtyard mingles with the joyous songs of birds. These favorite sounds revive my spirit as the food and drink enliven my body.

Sharadza speaks first. I already know the worry that darkens her emerald eyes. "Ianthe said that Vireon was dead. Is it true?" She looks at me as a child looks to its father for truth.

"We will know soon," I tell her. "The Claw mixes lies with truth. Nor does she know all. Before the sun sets, Alua's magic will carry us to Uurz most swiftly."

"Vireon is my husband," says Alua, as if remembering this for the first time. Sharadza clutches her hand. There is concern but no sadness in Alua's eyes. I think that she still does not recall her love for the Vodson, although she remembers the man himself. When she sees Vireon in the flesh, that will be the test. And if he is truly dead, then it will be better for Alua that she does not remember too much.

"Why did the bitch truly aid us?" Vaazhia asks. She drinks wine and eats lobster, but has no taste for the other foods. I should have called for red meat to suit her tastes. But there is little time for such indulgence.

"Ianthe seeks to use us," I say. "As she is using Zyung."

"To what end?" says Sharadza. She knows Ianthe's cruelty first-hand. It has left a scar upon her soul that will never be completely healed.

"She wishes to pit me and my allies against the God-King, hoping that we will defeat him."

"Why does she not rise against him herself?" asks Sharadza. "She is of the Old Breed, and no doubt Gammir will obey her."

"Because she fears Zyung," I say. "As great as Ianthe's power is, it is no match for that of Zyung. She must have fled into his service when we defeated her at Khyrei, and taken the bastard with her. These two cannot hope to stand against the God-King and his thousand High Seraphim. A legion of Old Breed has been chained to Zyung's will, as we were chained to the dream of Udgrond for a while. Yet Zyung's long dream is an earthly force, a grand theory put into practice, a dogma of absolute order. The longer Ianthe serves him, the more she is Diminished by his will, as these others have been."

"She would have us rid her of Zyung," says Alua.

"She will break Zyung's hold on her only if we cast him down," says Vaazhia.

"And she will claim his empire for her own," I say. "She will become him."

"Does she put so much faith in us?" Sharadza asks. "Can we defeat this God-King?"

There is quiet about the table.

"We must try," I say. "Perhaps Ianthe will aid us when the time is right. I sense that Khama still lives as well. He lies recovering in Uurz even now, with the rest of the survivors."

"Can you not sense Vireon?" Sharadza pleads.

"Vireon carries the blood of the Old Breed, but he is not one of them," I explain. "My bond with Khama is strong. I would sense his death from any distance. As for Vireon, and the rest of the Kings, we must go to them now."

I stand and ask Alua to work her spell. The power swells deep inside her. Vaazhia, too, seethes with restrained energies. Our return to the sunlit world has awakened her lust for life. We do not have Udgrond, but I am glad for the presence of the lizardess.

Alua spins her white flame about us and we rise, gliding through an open window. The gray-white citadel grows small beneath us. The ocean glimmers in all directions. Alua turns her eyes toward the distant coastline, and her comet streaks across the blue sky.

Sharadza's hand slips into my own. I hold it tighter than I should. In her worried state, she does not seem to mind. If my tragic error has caused the death of her brother, I will never forgive myself.

Hand in hand, we hurtle toward the Stormlands.

The City of Wine and Song prepared for a siege. The folk of a hundred surrounding villages streamed along the Eastern and Western Roads toward the gates of Uurz. Many led entire herds of sheep, goats, or pigs, hoping to find refuge as well as profit behind the city's walls.

From inside Alua's rushing flame we watched the men, women,

and children of the Stormlands converge on the city. The gates would remain open until Uurz had swelled to the point of saturation; those left outside would have to fend for themselves when the Hordes of Zyung came. Very few common folk knew that the sturdy walls of the city would mean nothing to an enemy who could sail above them on currents of wind.

The skies above the Stormlands were cloudy yet calm when we crossed them. If they had been raging with storms or blackened by thunderheads, I would be assured of Vireon's health. Like his father before him, the weather often reflected his temperament. It was Vod who turned black desert to green plain, loosing rivers from the earth and rains from the sky. Vireon held this legacy and more of Vod's magic in his blood. Lately he had discovered this fact and embraced it. Yet he had not learned the full depth of his power. If he still lived, I would show it to him.

The globe of white flame sinks toward the great palace at the heart of Uurz. I look across its jumbled vista of streets, orchards, and commons. Although every tavern and shop is crowded, there is little mirth and far less music than usual. An aura of fear hangs about the metropolis like a cloying fog.

Among verdant roof-gardens the noble families gather to fret and glare at the commoners milling below their walls. In the orchards and vineyards of the palace, groups of servants rush to fill baskets with produce that will be priceless treasures if the siege is a long one. Along the congested avenues, merchants haggle with laborers and ask triple the normal price for their goods. Farmers and brickmakers trade in their shovels and trowels for swords and spears, hiding their families in cellars, rented hovels, or overpriced inns. Legions of soldiers in green cloaks patrol the main thoroughfares while the city ramparts teem with spearmen, their eyes aimed eastward, searching for the first sign of the invaders.

Alua sets us down in the palace courtyard. Wing-helmed guards rush forward waving spears as if we four are the Hordes of Zyung. The white flame fades and I raise my hand, announcing myself and my companions. They usher us toward the Grand Hall, where I expect to see Tyro sitting bandaged and exhausted from battle and flight. Yet the Sword King Emperor is not here. The throne of Uurz – not long ago it was a double throne – sits empty now. In a high-backed chair before the royal dais sits a lean man with a prominent nose. I recognize him as Lord Mendices, Warlord of Uurz. His golden seat is the chair of a Regent. By this alone I know that Tyro is dead.

"Iardu the Shaper," Mendices calls out to me. "We expected you at Shar Dni." A score of guards in golden cuirasses stand between the marble pillars. A crowd of nobles and advisors lingers about Mendices, ready to carry out his orders and impress him with their counsel.

Mendices does not need to condemn me with any harsher words. The simple fact of my missing the lost battle is enough to make me cringe before his hard gaze. His shoulder is wrapped in white linen, yet still he wears the gear of an active-duty legionnaire. A sword hangs from his waist, reminding any who have eyes on the vacant throne that he, Mendices, has control of Uurz's surviving legions. He is the one man standing between the city and a horde of invading Manslayers.

I offer him a bow of respect, yet not the low bow I would offer to a King. "It pains me to say that I was hindered by a power greater than my own," I say. "Yet I have escaped to bring Vireon's sister and wife, along with the sorceress Vaazhia, Queen of the Forgotten City. We stand with Uurz now in its moment of need."

"Where is Vireon?" asks Sharadza. "Tell me he yet lives . . ." She cares nothing for courtly etiquette, and I cannot blame her.

Mendices studies each of my companions for a moment, his

gaze falling at last upon Sharadza. "The Giant-King lives, yet I cannot say for how much longer. He is grievously wounded."

Sharadza falls into my arms, pressing her cheek against my neck. Alua blinks at me.

"What of the Emperor?" I ask, already knowing what the Warlord will say.

"Tyro died bravely," says Mendices. His tone is not what I expected. Instead of an accusation tinged with rage, it is the tenor of a grieving father. I see now that he loved Tyro. "He died in battle, drowned by a sea of foes that his sword could not touch. The bloodshadows of the cursed valley."

"Why does the Empress Talondra not sit upon the throne?"

"She too is dead," says the Warlord. "Though none can say how, I suspect sorcery."

"These are dark days indeed," I say. "There are no words for such deep loss. What of Undutu and D'zan?"

"The first is dead, the second yet lives. D'zan rests now in a palace bed."

Tyro and Undutu. Lost. And Vireon dying. A slab of granite falls from my heart into my stomach. I stagger, but Sharadza's grip keeps me from falling.

"There is no time for tears," I say, as much to myself as to those around me. "The enemy will be at our gates in three days. Show us to the Giant-King. I will do what I can to prevent his death."

Mendices' long face damns me without words. *There are many deaths you should have prevented. You have failed us.* Yet he surprises me again by escorting us personally to the helpless Vireon's chamber. It lies beyond a tall corridor lined with a dozen Giant guards. Some of them lean wearily upon their spears. Their thick skins bear the marks of keen metal, their furs, cloaks, and corslets begrimed with dried blood. Most of them are blue-skinned Udvorg, yet three pale Uduru stand among them.

"The Giants guard their King in shifts," explains Mendices. "Fourteen hundred of them rest inside the palace; they cast lots for this revolving duty. It has been so since we arrived two days ago."

"How many Men survived the battle?" I ask.

We approach the great iron doors at the end of the corridor.

Mendices winces at the pain in his shoulder. "Far too few. Two Legions of Uurz. A single legion of Udurum. Less than ten thousand soldiers, all told."

The sheer depth of our losses steals my breath. Sharadza weeps quietly beside me. Nine out of every ten Men died in Zyung's onslaught, as well as two brave Kings, and possibly a third. How different would the outcome have been, if only I had been there? If I had taken my three companions to the Sharrian valley instead of spirit-roaming into the depths of the earth? I will never know the answer to this question. I cannot let it torment me until I do what must be done.

Vireon must not die.

We stand before the double door now, staring at its inlaid mosaic of curling Serpents and battling Giants. Mendices knocks upon the portal with his golden vambrace. The hall and room were prepared specifically to accommodate visiting Giantkind. There are other lofty places throughout the palace, where the Udvorg have been quartered.

Before we enter I ask Mendices one more question. My voice lowers so that only he and I can hear it. "How many legions does Uurz yet possess?"

"Twelve," says the Warlord. "Yet there is no King to lead them." He walks back down the corridor as the big doors open from the inside. An Uduri spearmaiden stands before us. In the rush of thoughts that fills my mind, I cannot recall her name. Sharadza rushes past her. I follow with Alua and Vaazhia in tow.

Alua's steps are hesitant, as if she were a virgin bride walking to meet her ordained husband for the first time.

The chamber is a broad oval, supported by columns of purple marble veined with black. The colors of Udurum. On a great bed at its far end lies Vireon, as small now as any normal man. Twenty-two solemn Uduri stand about the flame-lit chamber, their yellow braids gleaming like strands of gemstones upon their shoulders. Their faces turn to me, then to Sharadza, and finally to Alua. Recognizing the Queen they all thought to be dead, the awed Uduri fall to their knees. All save one, who was already on her knees at the bedside of Vireon. She weeps, but her eyes are fixed upon the dying King. She holds his small hand in her great one.

Sharadza steps near to her sleeping brother. A thick bandage stained to crimson encircles Vireon's entire abdomen. I recall the name of the Giantess who holds Vireon's hand. It is Dahrima, first among his household guard. She embraces Sharadza as one of her sisters, and the two weep together.

As I approach with Vaazhia at my side, Alua walks more slowly. She does not know how to respond to these Giantesses who seem to worship her. Ianthe stole so much of her memory, I wonder if she remembers any of the spearmaidens.

Dahrima's wet eyes look up from Sharadza's to meet those of Alua.

Whatever emotions glimmer there like doused embers, I cannot name them. Yet the Giantess backs away from the returned Queen, as if in horror. Dahrima cannot long meet Alua's gaze, so she turns away and leaves the bedside. She takes her longspear from the wall and finds her station among the rest of the Uduri, who have risen to their feet again. They stand solid as statues, waiting for their King to rise up and lead them again into battle. Or waiting perhaps to carry his bones toward a distant tomb.

Sharadza takes Vireon's hand. She speaks his name, but his eyes do not flutter. His breathing is shallow, his face pale. There is little life remaining inside his body.

Alua looks at her husband with an impenetrable expression. Is it fear, or love, or both? Her eyes are dry, and as cool as black ice. She remains silent. The sobbing of Sharadza and the crackling of flames fills the chamber as I draw near to the one I have failed.

She had run all night long, and well into the next morning. The blood had dried across her lower body in the first few hours, a second skin of brackish purple.

When the sun arose it was a white disk set in a gray sky. A soft, warm rain fell, washing the gore from her hair and skin as she sprinted. Traces of it remained stuck in the grooves of her corslet and beneath her nails. It had stained her leggings and boots thoroughly. The great wound in Vireon's chest, and the matching hole in his back, had clotted in her tight grip. It oozed darkly now rather than bleeding.

Her spearsisters followed, ragged and exhausted. The ones who had escaped major wounds caught up to her, while the rest fell behind. Twenty-two Uduri had survived the massacre in the valley; six spearsisters had been slain by the killing lights, yet none by the blades of Manslayers.

Dahrima wondered as she ran: How many Udvorg and Uduru had the sorcerers burned alive? Hundreds, at the least, along with thousands of Men.

She had not run toward any specific destination, not at first. She only meant to get Vireon as far away from his enemies as possible. It was a kind of madness that had fallen upon her. The madness of grief.

The soft rains grew into a steady downpour, and the stalks of steppe grass stood as high as the belts of the Uduri. Men could easily get lost in that forest of long grasses, and often they did so. It was Vantha the Tigress who had finally convinced Dahrima to stop and take a moment of rest. Vireon was still breathing, though Dahrima could not get his eyes to stay open. He felt weightless in her arms, and she feared there would be no lifeblood left inside his veins by the next sunrise.

Atha Spearhawk wrapped the Giant-King's chest tightly with a woolen cloak taken from a passing villager. Dahrima had failed to notice the isolated farming villages that dotted the plain. The cloakless farmer ran back to his collection of tiny huts and roused his folk. They fled southwest toward the gates of Uurz. Atha told the farm folk to spread warning of the bloody horde that would soon cross their plain, and she claimed the cloak as payment for the information.

"We also must go to Uurz," said Vantha. She kneeled next to Dahrima and studied Vireon's bloodless face. How similar the peaceful look of dying was to the look of sleeping. "The general retreat began when we left the valley. Any survivors will come to the City of Sacred Waters. The Sword King will have physicians and wizards there to aid Vireon."

"The Sword King is dead," Atha said. "I saw him devoured by shadows."

"Yet the Warlord of Uurz commands his legions still," said Yasha the Flamehair. "He blew the horn that called the retreat."

"Let us await the Warlord here then," said Atha.

"No," said Dahrima. "We must run and bring news of the defeat to Uurz. It will take the survivors at least three days to reach the city gates, perhaps longer if there are many wounded among them. Every second we delay could mean Vireon's death." She stood once more with the Giant-King cradled in her arms. His breathing was faint, his heart barely beating.

There were sighs of weariness and moans of pain as the spear-maidens arose about her. The rain had paused momentarily, but the wind brought it back stronger. It blew cold upon their faces.

"We are Uduri," said Vantha. "Let us run!"

All that day and the following night they sprinted, crossing the very heart of the Stormlands. They waded across the Eastern Flow rather than wasting time to locate one of its five bridges. Always the passing of the Uduri was an unspoken warning to the villages in their path. The plantations sprouted thicker and closer together as the Giantesses neared the walls of Uurz. Sight of the sprinting Uduri convinced even the most stubborn doubters that invasion was nigh. A line of plainsmen with carts, wagons, and herds of livestock lined up before the city's great gate.

Vantha ran ahead, shouting the crowds off the road, clearing the way for Dahrima and her burden. When the gatekeepers saw the Giant-King's limp body, they formed an escort to accompany Dahrima's band directly to the palace. There a nervous steward showed Dahrima to the Giant Quarters and summoned the royal physician to tend Vireon.

"There is little more that I can do," the bearded codger told Dahrima. He had cleansed the wound, wrapped Vireon with white bandages, and poured a foul-smelling elixir down the Giant-King's throat. He told her the medicine was brewed by a clever alchemist who was also a known wizard, and that it would revive Vireon if his spirit had not already fled the body. Yet the potion had done nothing. The next morning Vireon still lay barely breathing, pale as a corpse, and a fever had set his brow to burning.

Dahrima and her sisters had not left Vireon's chamber. Servants brought them wine, food, and the physician treated their wounds as best he could. The more seriously wounded of the spearmaidens arrived with the Warlord Mendices and his retreating forces. The

Uduri respectfully ignored Dahrima's tears. They said nothing of the way she cradled his head in the crook of her arm, or the soft words she spoke into his ear. They stood by her as she sat with him hour after hour. At times they rested on the lush carpets, only to rise and stand at attention once again.

Vireon looked so small in the bed sized for a Giant. Yet he was still the Giant-King, and while in Uurz he belonged in this chamber. Dahrima dozed for a while, her head resting on the side of his bed. When she awoke, she examined his face and saw that nothing had changed.

Come back, Son of Vod. She whispered the words so that none in the chamber would hear them but Vireon. *You have a judgment to pass upon me. Cast me in chains, throw me into the dungeons of Udurum, banish me to the furthest reaches of the Icelands, but come back and sit upon your throne again.*

She fell asleep a second time, dreaming that Vireon awakened, met her eyes with his own, and whispered his love for her. He kissed her while the Uduri knelt about them and hid their faces. Then she awoke gasping and fell into despair once again.

I love you, Vireon Vodson, she whispered. *If this is a crime, then add it to my list.*

She no longer cared if her sisters heard. Surely they must know her feelings, watching her linger by his side. A memory rushed into her head as she held his limp hand, hot as fire. She had been a girl, no more than ten or twelve seasons old, when her mother Khorima had sat beside her dying father in this exact posture. Ingthr the Steelheart had also been pale and fevered in his sickbed. The tusks of a great Udhog had pierced her father's flesh deep in two places. He had lived long enough to be carried on a litter back to Old Udurum. This was seven hundred and fifty years before the Return of Omagh and the destruction of the Giants' ancestral home.

Dahrima had offered her dying father a horn of bittermead, the favored drink of hunters, hoping it would revive him. Her mother had taken the flask and helped Ingthr drink a little, but it only threw him into a fit of coughing. Dahrima had recalled for decades the bloody flecks that flew from his lips during those coughs, and she was sure her well-intentioned act had caused her father's death. Ingthr had lasted until the next morning, and Dahrima had wept for days.

Khorima had taken her daughter aside after the pyre had burned Ingthr's body to smoke and ashes. "You must be strong," she'd told Dahrima. "Nothing that dies is ever lost. Your father's strength lives on in your bones. You are Uduri, and on the cusp of womanhood. Let us be done with weeping. Let the flames of your father's pyre burn away your tears. When you run on the Long Hunt, when you face the Udhog or the mountain lion and cast a longspear, every strike will honor your father's memory."

Dahrima had cried no more after that. Yet her mother had wept in secret. Ten seasons later a wasting disease claimed Khorima's life. The Uduri said she died of a broken heart. Ingthr's wife had lived long enough to see her daughter grown, then departed the world to join her husband.

If you die, I will die as she did, Dahrima whispered now.

Come back to me.

Five days after the great defeat, Vireon lay still at the edge of death. The Uduri spoke in hushed tones about the surviving Udvorg and Uduru, the Legions of Uurz, and the death of Tyro's Empress. Dahrima cared nothing for any of these things. It was the chattering of ravens roosted about her and waiting for death.

She realized then that she, too, waited for death, although she hoped for life.

Come back, Vodson.

At midday the chamber's black doors opened and Iardu the

Shaper entered. Dahrima had slept very little, and she did not have the strength to rage at him for abandoning Vireon to his enemies. Sharadza Vodsdaughter walked beside Iardu, and a strangely beautiful woman with a horned skull and the skin of a reptile. The fourth person to enter was a girl with unbound hair the color of spun gold and eyes the shade of deep night. A great cloak of white fur hung from her shoulders, and a gown of snow-colored fabric hugged her lean body.

Sharadza rushed to embrace Dahrima. If not for the distraction of this embrace, Dahrima would have recognized the blonde Goddess sooner. As Sharadza caressed her brother's brow, the Uduri began dropping to their knees.

"The Queen . . ." Their voices were low and heavy with wonder. "The Queen lives!"

Dahrima wiped her bloodshot eyes and looked into the face of Alua.

You died. I saw your mangled corpse frozen atop the Mountain of Ghosts.

Many of my sisters perished in the quest to avenge your death.

Yet here you stand, watching with dry eyes as Vireon dies.

Dahrima might have screamed at the strangeness of the dead Queen's presence, but then she remembered something that explained all of it.

She is a sorceress. Like Ianthe, she cannot truly die.

Iardu has brought her back to Vireon.

There was no recognition in Alua's eyes when she looked at Dahrima. She stared at Vireon in that same blank manner, as if she observed a sick stranger instead of her own husband.

Dahrima moved away from the bed and took up her spear. She joined her sisters standing at attention between the pillars.

Save him. She watched the sorcerer and his three sorceresses gather about Vireon. It had taken far too long for Iardu to gather these powers. Yet the Shaper and his allies had come at last. The Mistress of the White Flame had returned.

Save him, Deathless Queen, and it will be enough.

He is yours, never mine. I will not forget this again.

He is my King, and I am only his servant. Only that forever.

Rekindle his dying fire with your white magic.

Let it burn away these tears.

It pains me to pull Sharadza away from her dying brother, but I must.

I lead her from the bed so that Alua can approach Vireon. Sharadza presses her tear-stained face to my shoulder. Her hands squeeze my arm. I must be the rock she clings to in this storm of grief.

Alua kneels at the bedside. Her fingers run along Vireon's pallid cheek. Still she does not weep, but I believe she now recognizes him. The strands of her memory are thin and frayed, but not wholly broken.

"Vireon." She says his name like a holy word. "My husband. My King." She turns glimmering eyes to me. "I do remember him."

Do you remember the daughter you had with him? Or the tragedy of that lie?

If she had remembered Ianthe's posing as Maelthyn, a seven-year deception that ended in betrayal and death, she would have tried to battle Ianthe's spirit-form in the underworld. I do not think I could have stopped her. If she remembers it now, it will surely shatter her.

"He loves you," Sharadza tells Alua. "More than anything."

Alua kisses the Giant-King's lips. The kiss is gentle. "I loved him too."

Loved. Has her most recent death stolen that love? If so, can it be restored?

I have no answer for these questions. Yet now is not the time to seek them.

I lean close and peel away the stained bandage about Vireon's midsection. The wound is terrible, a suppurating mass of ruptured flesh. It may go deeper than the flesh.

I take Alua's hand and place it upon the open wound.

"Call upon your white flame," I tell her. "Close this wound, Alua."

Her look says *I will try*. She has no confidence. She remembers Vireon, but she has lost the deep love they shared.

Pale light slips from the skin of her palm, sinking into Vireon's gouged flesh. It erupts into a dancing flame, like the blue Flame of Intellect dancing on my own chest. Alua's power burns without heat. The torn flesh sears and blends, knitting itself back together. When Alua removes her hand, the wound has closed, leaving only a great scar stretching from sternum to navel.

Sharadza breathes a sigh of relief behind me. I touch the new flesh of the scar. Vireon's skin is still pale. Still cold. I feel no heart beating in his chest. His eyes do not flutter.

"Will he live?" Sharadza asks. Her hand trembles on my shoulder.

I must tell her the truth. If he dies it is my fault. I cannot compound my crime with a lie.

"The wound is closed and the flesh is whole," I say. "Yet the blade of Zyung tore through spirit as well as body. I fear the damage is greater than we can see."

"What does that mean?" Sharadza asks. There is panic in her voice. Desperation. Love.

"It means we must wait," I tell her. I hold her hands and bring my face as close to hers as I dare. Her eyes are drowning emeralds. "Alua's presence may call him back. Or his soul may have wandered too far away from his flesh. It may be too late."

"How long?" she asks. Always one for impossible questions.

"I cannot say. But I will not leave his side. And I will do what I can to aid him. I promise you. Try to get some rest."

"I'll not leave this room," she says.

I ask an Uduri to bring a cot for her. It takes a while, but I convince Sharadza to lie upon it and sleep next to her brother's bed. Alua sits near Vireon, his hand in her own. This reminds me of Dahrima, who did the same before we arrived. She stands now among the rest of the spearmaidens, but she does not share their icy detachment. Her eyes are red with weeping. I see the worry that obscures her face like a gray mask. I see also that Vireon is far more than a King in Dahrima's heart.

Servants bring us wine and food. The drink eases my vigil, but the quiet of the chamber weighs upon me like a set of chains. Alua whispers to Vireon, speaking of wildflowers and snowy hillsides. Her voice and touch may be what he needs to bring him back to us.

I watch and wait. Sharadza and Vaazhia sleep.

As I pour another cup of wine, the chamber doors swing open yet again. A wounded warrior stands there. I recognize him as D'zan of Yaskatha when he shuffles into the light of flaming braziers. He moves slowly as an old man, though he is in the prime of his life. Bandages cover his arms and legs, chest and waist. Another dressing winds about his forehead, pushing back his mane of thick blond hair. I am glad to see him alive, yet the number of his wounds is appalling. The great blade of Olthacus the Stone still hangs upon his back. The weapon seems to weigh him down like a yoke of iron, yet his eyes gleam bright as candles. He has come to see his Queen.

"She sleeps," I tell him. I offer him a chair at the table where attendants have placed pomegranates, pears, and a roasted pheasant with black bread. He bends to kiss Sharadza's cheek without waking her, then he sits painfully. His jaw is clean-shaven, and in the absence of a beard he looks as young as a teenager. Yet the lines of worry and pain lend wisdom to his handsome face. His green eyes are troubled, restless, and distant.

"You were right," D'zan says, cradling the cup of wine in his hands but not drinking. "The sea battle was sheer folly. We never stood a chance."

"Undutu has paid the price for his warrior's pride," I say. "I could not make him listen. Khama was swept away by that same pride."

D'zan's face tightens. "Along with several thousand lives," he says. "What of Vireon? Will he recover?"

"That remains to be seen."

D'zan drinks. Words flood from his mouth while tears crawl down his cheeks. "All those men burned and drowned to gain nothing. I could have said no to Undutu. You speak of his deadly pride, yet I am as guilty of it. I should have died with my warriors. Every ship was lost and I could do nothing about it. Nothing but watch them burn and sink."

I say nothing. D'zan needs to tell of these things. He needs me to listen.

"When the *Kingspear* went down, I went with it," he says. "My armor dragged me to the bottom of the sea. I struggled to remove it, knowing I would drown before I could do so. I held my breath as long as I could, fumbling with the straps of my corslet. I even cast aside my crown. I did not want to die, but eventually I had no more breath left. All about me dying men bubbled out their last bit of air and twitched like beached fish. I thought my life was over. My lungs were fit to burst, and still I could not get the metal off my body. Panic had numbed my fingers and made them clumsy.

"So I gave up and inhaled the seawater, knowing it was death. There was nothing else I could do. My lungs filled with brine, my eyes closed. I lay there twitching like the rest of them. *But I failed to die.* At last I lay still, not breathing, the sea filling me up like an empty jar. My panic had been drowned, so I finally removed the corslet and greaves. The surface of the sea above me was on fire, so I could not swim to it. Realizing that I was unable to drown, I walked and sprang across the seabed, stepping over the charred and bloated corpses of Yaskathans and Mumbazans. I passed the broken and tangled wreckage of warships, some of them still burning. Not even the deep water could quench the flames of Zyung's sorcery.

"I walked among the feasting crabs and schools of rainbow fish, through forests of seaweed and coral hills. Far above me the burning went on. I passed legions of drowned men, wondering why I was not one of them. I walked in a daze, astounded at my own existence.

"I came to a black mountain and climbed the slimy rocks. It was an island, so I climbed out of the sea to walk along its shore. I vomited seawater from my lungs and learned to breathe again. There was a broad cove not far from where I surfaced. A handful of Mumbazans had swum there all the way from their lost ship.

"I looked across the waves at the pitiful remains of our great fleet – the greatest armada in history – and I saw thousands of Zyung's ships still blotting out the sky. Then I truly understood how stupid we had been. I called out to Khama, and he came with Undutu to carry us away. We fled like cowards instead of dying with our men."

D'zan falls silent and swallows more wine.

"You did what Kings must do," I say.

"We should have listened to you, Iardu. We should have gone north with Tyro and Vireon."

His cup is empty. I refill it.

"It might have been the same, even if you had done so," I tell him. "Tyro and Vireon both fell at Shar Dni. Tyro will never rise again. Yet you live to fight on."

D'zan drains the second cup of wine in a series of gulps. His breathing is heavy.

"Look at me," he says, moving his hands across the mass of linens that band his flesh. "I saw Tyro die, and Undutu. I took spears in the gut, blades in the chest. Here – see this spot?" He points to a place near his heart. "This was a killing stroke. I bled like a fountain, yet again I did not die. Mendices and I led the retreat. Zyung's wizards could have finished us, but he let us go."

He tells me of the hooded stranger who turned the God-King to iron for a brief moment and disappeared. He asks me who it was, but I have no idea. Ianthe helped us break the spell of Udgrond, but surely she would not move so openly against Zyung. Whoever the stranger had been, D'zan tells me, his spell had allowed Dahrima to save Vireon. Suddenly I recognize the true courage of the red-eyed Giantess who watches over her King. And I know of a certain that she loves him.

I look toward Alua. Her head lies upon Vireon's shoulder.

She too sleeps. Vireon does not move.

"Can you explain it, Shaper?" D'zan asks. "Can you tell me why I am not dead? Is it . . . Is it because of the spell you worked with Sharadza? This body you created to replace the one that Elhathym destroyed? Am I no longer even a Man?"

"You are very much a Man," I say. "Yet your woman-born body no longer carries your spirit. The body you inhabit now is a creation of our sorcery and your own willpower. It is not above death, but it is far more durable than one born of a mother's womb. You did not drown for the same reason you did not die in battle: Your flesh is invested with Sharadza's power and mine. It will not age or sicken. Not while we both endure."

D'zan has lost his words. Perhaps he thinks of the guilt he will carry for the rest of his life. I might tell him that I share that same guilt, but I say nothing. He drinks a third cup of wine. Slowly this time.

He leans in close. "What of my children? Will my son be . . . human?"

I could tell him what Sharadza never has. That his sturdy body is a sterile thing, without the procreative power that comes from a parental bloodline. When his original body died, so did his chance at having an heir.

Yet I know that his second wife carries a child in her belly even now. A child that she says is D'zan's own son, even though this is impossible. D'zan had thought Sharadza to be barren, and she lets him believe it to spare him grief and shame.

Should I tell him the truth? That he cast Sharadza aside for a failing that was his own? That his new woman has lied and betrayed him with a bastard offspring? Should I shatter what little remains of his fractured humanity?

I ask myself what Sharadza would want me to say.

"You need not fear," I tell D'zan. "Your son will be fine. As will any other children you sire. This aspect of your manhood was not affected by our spells."

The lie comforts him.

"Iardu!" Alua calls my name. Sharadza wakes, and D'zan moves to embrace her.

Vireon's body trembles, wracked with spasms. The gaping wound has reopened. Alua's power – Alua's love – is not enough.

I rush to the bedside. Alua moves away, one hand covering her mouth. At last, she weeps.

Sharadza and D'zan draw near to me.

"What is happening?" she asks.

"He is dying," I say. "His wounded spirit seeks to leave this flesh behind."

Vireon does not realize that the choice of living or dying is his own. I must show this to him. "There is one last chance," I say. "Only Vireon can save Vireon. The power of Vod's blood slumbers inside him. He must awaken it."

I lie upon the cot Sharadza was using.

"Watch over my body," I tell her. "Let none enter this room."

"What are you doing?" she asks.

"The only thing left to do," I say. "I will enter the realm of Vireon's spirit."

Sharadza is terrified. D'zan clutches her shoulders as if she is still his lover.

"What can we do?" she asks.

"Hold my hand." She does this. My heart leaps, and my head falls back upon the pillow.

My eyes close, and I gaze inward. As my spirit-self emerged from my body days ago to seek the heart of the world, so now it rises to seek the depths of Vireon's soul.

Time to embrace your true heritage, Son of Vod.

You must learn or die.

I float above the Giant-King's body and dive into the red wound, a swimmer leaping from high precipice to deep ocean.

15

Seven Sorcerers

At first there is only the void.

A vast abyss gleaming with constellations, a mirror of the greater void that lies outside the earth. As above, so below.

I am a racing meteor of awareness, painted indigo by the Flame of Intellect that accompanies me into the astral. Each guttering star is a mote of thought, spiraling in multitudes. Innumerable gas giants of sentience orbit the pathways of wisdom, exhaling luminous clouds of insight. None of these are physical entities, yet each is a facet of Vireon's living soul, which is indescribable in all but the corporeal language of analogy and symbol. The starfields of Vireon's inner being are the manifestations of his unbounded consciousness.

I sink deeper. The void takes on shape and form. There is no actual substance, no confining matter here. There is only a vast matrix of ideas, concepts, and perceptions.

A sky of sapphire swallows my intruding spirit-self. Trees great as mountains rush up to meet me. Each leaf is a jade magnificence, each mighty trunk the ideal of arboreal perfection. A sea of red-barked titans accepts me into the olive shadows of its canopy. Starlight follows me down in lambent beams, and my spirit-self manifests the image of my physical body.

The mosses of the forest floor are silver and golden, gleaming with their own phosphorescence. Motes of sentience flit between the great boles like butterflies, their wings bright with nameless and ever-changing colors.

I have reached the floor of Vireon's soul. I am not surprised to see it as a forest, for his love of the wild places sits at the core of his being. About me spreads no true wilderness, but the ideal version of nature itself, a flawless imitation of the woodlands where Vireon's young heart ran free in decades past. The rare splendors of childhood have a way of sculpting the eternal soul.

A stream of diamond waters cascades through the wood, laughing among the green stones. I follow it toward the lip of a great waterfall, where the torrent spills into a lake far below. I leap above the cataract as a white owl, gliding downward. The lake's waters are silver and emerald beyond the thundering falls. Groves of willows and massive Uygas stand about its shore, and wild chromatic flowers blossom among the trees.

A boy swims in the lake, splashing and diving among the sun-scaled fish. His head rises from the water, tossing back a long mane, slinging droplets like tiny jewels across the surface. He watches me perch on a moss-draped log as big as the pillar of a fallen palace. About the lowland, scattered among the roots of the gargantuan trees, the ruins of such a palace lie smothered in curtains of vine and wildweed. They are the remnants of a life that has crumbled. Already the boy has forgotten their importance, and the secrets of their history.

My wings fade and I sit upon the log in Man shape, realizing that it is indeed a column of toppled marble. The Flame of Intellect burns brightly on my chest, shedding cobalt light upon the lake.

The boy swims to the lakeshore and pulls himself from the

waters. His arms and legs are lean, strong, the color of newly minted bronze. His eyes are the fierce blue of a cloudless sky. The water streams from his limbs as he approaches.

"I know you," he says. It is the voice of Vireon's younger self. The soul is ageless, and while memory and experience sculpt its nature, it has no single true shape.

"And I know you," I say, smiling as I would at any child. "I am the Shaper."

"Iardu," he says, running a hand through his damp hair. He smiles. "You are the friend of my father."

"You are Vireon, Son of Vod. Do you remember this too?"

The soul disguised as a boy nods. "I had a brother, but I lost him. He is on the Last Long Hunt now, with my father." He points toward the deep woodland that goes on forever. The depths of his boundless imagination.

"Tadarus was your brother," I remind him. "Would you remember more of him? More of your father and the world beyond this vale?"

The boy is uncertain. He shivers, arms wrapped about himself. Yet he nods again.

I remove the silver chain that supports the Flame of Intellect and offer it to him. Save for a loincloth of woven leaves and reeds, he wears nothing. "Wear this," I tell him.

He takes the chain from me, unafraid of the dancing flame. He does not think that it will burn him. Instinct tells him it is no earthly fire. He places the chain around his neck, and the blue flame leaps upon his narrow chest.

His eyes grow large, his head falling backward, mouth slack. He gazes past the high canopy of leaves toward the glimmering starfields. For a brief moment (there is no real time here) the blue flame engulfs him, then it recedes back to his chest.

No longer is he a boy, but the full-grown image of Vireon. A black crown set with many sapphires rests upon his head. The pain and wonder of memory shines in his eyes.

"What do you remember?" I ask him.

"Everything," he says. He sits beside me upon the pillar and takes the iron crown from his head. He stares at it, as a man might examine a discovery that may or may not have some value. "A great beast swallowed me. It spoke to me with seven different voices that were the same voice."

"What did it tell you?"

"That I was not the King of Storms," says Vireon. "That I could not end its long curse."

"And what was your reply?"

His blue eyes pierce me.

"That I am the Son of Vod," he says. "That I carry his blood."

"What else?" I ask.

"I called out the name of my father. I called on his power. I rose up . . . I crushed the beast. I ended the curse."

"You awakened the power that lies within. Yet there is so much more."

Vireon's eyes scan the deep forest, the crystal lake, the iron crown in his hands.

"None of this is real," he says.

"Oh, it is," I say. "And it isn't."

He smiles at me, yet his handsome face retains its sorrow. "You always were one for speaking in riddles."

"This place is the seat of your soul. Your body is dying."

"I stood against Zyung and lost," he says. "You were not there to aid me."

"I was . . . delayed. I ask your forgiveness. Yet I am here now to show you the secrets of your inheritance. To help you finish the journey you began in the Khyrein Marshes."

"Why?" His face turns to me, and for a moment I see the face of Vod.

"Because otherwise you will die. The world still needs you. Your enemies march upon Uurz. After that they will take Udurum."

"No, I mean why do you care? You are immortal. The living world passes like a dream. Lives are but waves upon the sea, rising and falling, repeating an endless cycle of conflict and pain."

"There is also joy and love in this cycle," I say. "You cannot have these things without their opposites. Have you lost your thirst for life, Vireon?"

He breathes deep the fragrant air of bodiless harmony.

"By *inheritance* you mean Vod's sorcery."

"Simply another word for knowledge."

"You wish me to be Vod. Yet I am only Vireon."

"I wish you to be yourself. Giant-King, Son of Vod, Brother, Husband, Hunter, Slayer, Lord of Giants, Ruler of Udurum. Your father wished these things for you as well."

"No, he did not," says Vireon. "My father wanted Tadarus to be King after him. I wanted to roam the wild, to be free of walls and thrones and towers. I never wanted the crown of Udurum, and I never wanted this second crown either." He lifts the ring of iron and sapphire. "I am King of two nations, but it has brought me no happiness."

"None? What of Alua?"

"She is gone," he says. "Like my brother and my father."

His eyes turn again toward the deep forest. If he chooses to go there, he will not return to the living world.

"No," I tell him. "Alua is alive. I have brought her to Uurz."

He leaps off the pillar, eyes burning. "She lives?"

"She is of the Old Breed. She cannot truly die. Even now she awaits your return. Let me show you how to heal yourself, and you will be with her once again."

"What of Maelthyn?" he asks.

My hand touches his shoulder, spreading warmth to his soul-form. "Maelthyn was never your daughter. Only a ruse. A lie and an unforgivable crime. A creation of the Claw to house her disembodied essence."

"Yes," he says. The bright thrill of Alua's return is dimmed by a fresh current of sadness. "In my heart I knew this already."

"Here is another reason to return," I say. "To make Ianthe pay for what she has done. She sails with Zyung now. If you choose to live, your rewards will be love and vengeance."

"No!" he rages at me. Again I see the child in his face. "I have had enough of vengeance. I will not make that mistake again."

His words make me smile. "You are wise, Vireon. Udurum needs a wise King. Are you ready to learn the depth of your father's legacy?"

"What if I say no? I could wander those woods until I reach the lands of the dead. My father, my brother, they wait for me there."

"Yet Alua waits for you in the world above, along with your sister Sharadza. And there is Dahrima, who carried your torn body all the way to Uurz."

His eyes flicker. He blinks at me.

"She, too, loves you."

He says nothing.

"Both Giants and Men will suffer if you choose death. Udurum will surely fall."

Vireon turns away from me and stares into the mirror of the lake. Slowly his hands rise to place the iron crown upon his head. He returns to me the Flame of Intellect on its silver chain. I set it once more on my own chest and slide down from the pillar.

The Son of Vod has made his choice.

*

As I once did with his clever sister, I instruct Vireon in the Knowledge Supreme.

With Sharadza I had taken the role of the Crone, guiding her through physical metamorphosis, opening her mind and her senses to the forces that lay beneath the shapes and forms of the living world.

Patterns.

Yet there is no need for such transformations in the case of Vireon, for we do not inhabit the physical plane. These lessons grow from the core of his immortal essence to permeate his spirit and the stubborn flesh that houses it. In this place ideas grow into being instantly and without distraction. In the earthly world these concepts and revelations would require wholly different interpretations. Here at the center of Vireon's awareness, I need only plant the seeds of understanding and bid them to grow.

Sharadza learned much in a period of several weeks, locked into a timeless fugue. Yet her tutelage was limited by the material separation of Master from Pupil. As the wine decanter pours its contents into the goblet, so I poured knowledge into Sharadza's mind. Yet Vireon and I are motes of light glinting on the surface of that wine, and it is a glimmering sea that spreads into infinity beneath us. Where his sister was showered with drops of wisdom, Vireon is *immersed* in the boundless source of that wisdom. I show him how to dive deep and seek out the truths that lie in its depths.

There is no time or space in the realm of pure consciousness. The mastery of all powers lies in Vireon's blood already. He need only call them forth, as he did in the belly of the beast. The spark of his legacy has been kindled, yet was nearly snuffed out by Zyung's blade. I revive that flickering spark and stoke it to a blazing inferno. Vireon will burn in this crucible of transcendence, reforging himself.

We begin with the Lesson of Patterns, followed by the Lessons of Unity, Action, and Elements. Each of these blossoms as a new tree about the lake. Vireon plucks and devours their ripe fruits as a reader devours words, the juices of cognition saturating his thoughts. His skin seethes with fresh colors, and his eyes blaze like the Flame of Intellect.

Lessons that would take days, months, or years in the waking world he learns in an instant. More epiphanies follow, one after the other, a deluge of enlightenments.

He imbibes the Lessons of the Worlds. First the Living, then the Dead, the twin illusions that comprise reality. This knowledge falls upon him as droplets of silvery understanding. He drinks deep of the singular truth beyond duality, and it changes him further.

"Now you see that Vod's power has slumbered within you all this time," I tell him. "You have called upon it often, without even realizing it. Your moods have conjured storms and cleared the skies. These were only the surface traits of your deepest nature. You have learned to be both Man and Giant, which makes you more than either."

"I sensed that this was true," he says. "In the Valley of the Bull I called upon my father's power again. Yet it was not enough."

"Your awareness had not fully blossomed," I say. "Now you *are* that awareness."

The forest of ideas fades about us, replaced by a vast network of constellations, gleaming panoramas of light and energy. Countless forms emerging from a single field of infinite potential. We balance between nothingness and everything, floating at the very crux of eternity.

Vireon inhales the winds of understanding that blow between the stars. We glide formless through the deeps of the astral universe, skirting the edges of reality, soaking in the rays of newborn suns.

I am refreshed. Vireon is transformed.

*

At last we step back into the flow of blood and ages. The world of form, locality, and time emerges from the pulsing cosmos. I guide him toward the threshold of his dying body. Already I am slipping away from him, yet he burns brightly in my wake.

"Use what you have learned," I say. "Weave the pattern of this torn flesh and make it whole again. Distill the light of these stars and fill your veins with their blood. *Heal yourself*, Son of Vod."

I emerge from the wound even as it closes, leaving not even a scar on his broad chest. My spirit-self sinks back into my body, and my eyes flutter open. Still Sharadza holds my hand. The pink light of dawn seeps in through the chamber windows. The braziers burn low.

I stand up between Sharadza and Alua. We watch Vireon's flesh regaining its healthy shade of bronze. Sharadza gifts me with an embrace. Alua squeezes Vireon's hand.

Vireon opens his eyes.

His great arms pull Alua close to him. Their kiss is long and deep.

Sharadza kisses me on the cheek. My second gift, though I am undeserving of it.

D'zan and Vaazhia rouse from their chairs. There is joy in the chamber now, and laughter. Even the Uduri smile as they celebrate the risen King.

Dahrima kneels with spear in hand, her face no longer shadowed by a pall of worry. The tears of a warrior swim in her eyes, yet she refuses to let them fall. The mystery of her emotions is her own secret to keep.

Vireon rises from the bed, whole and full of new strength. He is no longer a Man-Giant caught in the immense shadow of his father's legend. No longer a vessel built to carry the Blood of Vod and wear an unwanted crown. He is reborn.

He is a *sorcerer*, like his father before him.

Servants bring wine, meat, and fresh loaves to quench his hunger. We drink, eat, and forget momentarily that our enemies will soon be upon us.

In the war room of the dead Emperor of Uurz they gathered about a great oval of black marble. Vireon had risen from his deathbed only hours ago. The news of his recovery had spread across the palace, into the courtyards, and along the streets of the nervous city. Dahrima heard the cheers of commoners and soldiers from where she stood before the door of Vireon's chamber.

Sharadza had cleared the room so the Giant-King and his wife might enjoy their reunion in privacy, if only for a little while. The Udvorg guarding the outside corridor were replaced by the Uduri. None of them cared to argue against Dahrima's order that they join the rest of their blue-skin brothers and get some rest.

"Soon you will defend this city against the same forces that slaughtered us in the valley," she told them. "So sleep, eat fresh meat, and swill royal ale while you can." They had not forgotten her murder of their shamaness, but they knew that she had saved Vireon from the God-King's death blow. They took her advice with nary a grumble.

Dahrima had placed her own back to the Serpent-carved doors while her sisters lined both sides of the hallway. Their eyes searched her face for signs of heartbreak, but she gave them nothing. The King and his Queen were reunited, and Dahrima guarded him once again. All was as it should be.

The sun moved slowly across the blue above the golden spires. A sudden shower sent rainbows to gleam outside the corridor's leaf-shaped windows. After the rain the sky turned to shades of pink and purple, a palette of clouds smeared across the heavens. Dahrima tried not to imagine Vireon and Alua making love in the chamber behind her. She heard no sounds of passion seeping through the doors, and she was grateful for a handful of quiet hours. Soon chaos would rise again to deafen Men and Giants with its red thunder.

A herald came when the sun's rim touched the top of the western battlements. The pink sky was crimson now, the purple clouds deepened to the black of bruised flesh. The messenger carried word from Lord Mendices: Vireon and Alua were requested in the council chamber at sunset, to meet with the Warlord and his allies. Now that the Shaper and his sorcerers had finally arrived, it was time to plan the defense of Uurz.

Shortly after the herald's departure Vireon emerged from the chamber. Alua walked arm in arm with him. She looked much the same in her gown of white fabric and cloak of snow-bear hide, blonde hair streaming in wild curls down her back. The King wore his crown of iron and sapphires thanks to Vantha the Tigress. She had taken it from the battlefield while Dahrima had grabbed up Vireon's body.

Vireon wore a corslet of gilded bronze, the rising sun insignia of Uurz set in emeralds across the breast. His broad belt supported a kilt of bronze plaits. His northern-made boots had been replaced with Uurzian sandals. There was much of Tyro about him in these accoutrements, but the cloak pinned at his shoulders was the deep purple of Udurum. He carried no blade or weapon yet to replace his ruined greatsword; the armory of Uurz would soon stand open to him.

Vireon paused as the chamber doors swung shut behind him. His blue eyes met Dahrima's own. He stood at the size of a Man now, yet his aura was still that of a Giant.

"Come with us, Axe," he said. "You too must sit on this council of war."

Dahrima followed him through the winding halls and soaring galleries of the palace, skirting the empty throne room and at times ducking to avoid low lintels. The council chamber lay above the Grand Hall and to its south. Inside it Lord Mendices shared the great table with D'zan, Iardu, Sharadza, Vaazhia, and the Feathered Serpent, who sat at ease in his Man shape.

Khama seemed wholly recovered from his deep wounds. He wore the white-green robes of an Uurzian lord, without his Mumbazan headdress or feathered cloak. The braids of his long, dark hair were thick as adders, and his brown face was lined with worry. Dahrima sensed the grief hanging like a yoke about his thin shoulders. The King he had watched over from boyhood was dead. Khama resembled nothing less than a father who had lost his son.

Crystal flagons of red and yellow wines cluttered the tabletop, along with jeweled cups and jasper bowls piled with grapes, olives, and pears. Iardu was the only one drinking as yet. Sharadza sat between the Shaper and D'zan, though she spoke to neither.

Vireon and Alua took the chairs assigned for them, and the Giant-King announced that Dahrima would share their council. Dahrima wanted to stand nearby as she was accustomed to doing, but Mendices ordered a chair brought for her. Now Vireon sat between Dahrima and Alua. Dahrima displayed nothing at all of the discomfort this placement caused her.

The walls were thick with tapestries depicting ancient battles, including the exploits of Vod slaying Omagh the Serpent-Father. Dahrima did not recognize any of the other historical figures, most of them Uurzian heroes. Two great windows allowed the scarlet sunset to spill within, but the chamber's chief light came from six braziers suspended by chains from the high ceiling. The warm air of evening blew in through the casements, and stars glimmered to life above the rooftops of Uurz.

Mendices the Regent, who was honor-bound to perform the duties of his fallen Emperor, was the first to speak. "Friends and allies," he began. "The Gods of Earth and Sky allow us to assemble here in unity. We have suffered a great defeat and survived it. We have seen two valiant Kings fall at the hands of our enemies. Our losses have been staggering, and we will mourn them at a more appropriate time. Yet our spirit remains unbroken, and we live to face our enemy again. This will happen soon. As the standing Regent of Uurz, I welcome you all in the name of the Stormlands and the City of Sacred Waters."

The Warlord raised his cup and most of those gathered returned his toast. Only Dahrima, Sharadza, and Alua chose not to drink. "First, let it be known that my duties as Regent will last only until the remaining Son of Dairon returns to claim his crown. A delegation sails even now to retrieve the Scholar King from his exile in Yaskatha. Yet we must face a new battle and a siege without him. I will take the Sword King's place at the head of our legions, though I cannot hope to inspire them half as well as Tyro did."

D'zan sat next to Mendices. His bandages were hidden beneath a long-sleeved tunic of black silk stitched with the Sword and Tree insignia of Yaskatha. Mendices placed a hand lightly upon his shoulder.

"King D'zan, who fought bravely in the valley of Shar Dni, chooses to stand with us once again. Yet his Yaskathan legions will not reach us before Zyung's siege, which falls upon us tomorrow. The Feathered Serpent of Mumbaza also stands with us to avenge the death of mighty Undutu, who fell among a sea of enemies. As with Yaskatha, we can expect no aid from the legions of Mumbaza for several weeks. The loss of the great southern fleets means a land-bound journey for both these armies. So we must face Zyung's horde with the twelve Uurzian legions at my command, a single legion of surviving Udurumites, and – our greatest asset – a legion of Giants who march at Vireon's command."

"I have sent word to Ryvun Ctholl for five more legions," said Sharadza. She had married the King of Yaskatha eight years ago, but still she was the Princess of Udurum. It was her right to rally the northern forces while her brother lay wounded. "Yet they will be at least two weeks in arriving, even at a hard march." She turned to Mendices, whose grim nod agreed with her.

Dahrima wondered how many more Udvorg and Uduru would descend from the Icelands if they were summoned by Vireon. There were at least a thousand Uduru living on the northern plateau who had chosen their new blue-skin families above the call of war. Vireon might still rouse them, and perhaps thousands more blue-skins as well. He might promise the Udvorg justice for the death of Angrid, and set them all to marching southward. Yet they would all come too late.

"We have also dispatched an ambassador to the King of New Khyrei," said Mendices, "calling upon him to send what legions he may. As it stands now, our best hope is to endure the coming siege long enough for these southern legions to reach our gates."

"All this talk of legions and numbers is fruitless," said Khama, waving his hand above the bowls and goblets. "Even if we had all the legions of the Five Cities at our command, it would not be enough. Zyung commands a thousand sorcerers. It is plain that military forces cannot win this war."

A moment of heavy silence hung about the chamber.

"Khama speaks truly," said Iardu. His eyes gleamed with an array of shifting colors, twin auroras seething below his brows. He stroked his silver beard. "This is not a war of blade and shield, but a contest of sorceries. Men and Giants are caught in the heart of it, yet the true contest is among sorcerers. If more of us had been present at Shar Dni, the defeat might have been less devastating, or avoided altogether. I take full blame for my absence. I cannot restore the lives that were lost, but I will do what I can to atone for my mistake."

D'zan broke the silence this time. "None of us blames you, Shaper. You have assembled all the wizards at this table to face Zyung's assault. You have our gratitude for this."

"If I had heeded your advice in Khyrei," said Khama, "Undutu and thousands more would be alive today. It is too late for them now, but I am ready to listen."

Iardu refilled his cup and swallowed a mouthful of red wine. "A thousand High Seraphim serve Zyung, who has convinced them of his divinity. Twice that number of Lesser Seraphim attend him, yet their powers are limited – they are trained as war dogs and can be slain with a well-aimed arrow or blade. Most of the Lesser Ones' attention is bent on protecting the dreadnought to which they are assigned, yet the High Seraphim are also scattered among these ships.

"The High Seraphim are of the Old Breed. They can be defeated, but cannot truly die. Ianthe the Claw has also returned to serve Zyung, although she will betray him if given the chance. We cannot count her among our allies, but her presence cannot be overlooked."

"What of Gammir?" asked Sharadza. Dahrima saw fear and guilt in her eyes.

"Where the Claw goes, her pet will not be far behind," said Iardu.

"So it comes to this," said Mendices. "Six sorcerers must stand against a thousand."

"We are seven." A new voice rang in the chamber.

All heads turned to a hooded figure who stepped from the shadows between braziers. Dahrima's hand went instinctively to the haft of her spear, yet none else about the table made any show of alarm.

The stranger's robe was black and hung with a garland of emeralds about chest and sleeves. He stood now between the elbows of Mendices and D'zan, although there was no entrance or window at that end of the chamber. Had he been there all along, lurking in the shadows?

Dahrima recognized the dark robe and its obscure shape. This was the stranger who had stood before Vireon's bleeding body as she raced toward it. He had raised a hand, spoken a word, and turned the God-King to black iron.

The stranger raised his hands, his long fingers heavy with jeweled rings, and pulled back his hood. The face of Tyro stared at the war council. Yet the cheeks were somewhat leaner, the hairless chin not quite as strong. The dark eyes were full of mystery where Tyro's had been full of glinting steel. His black hair was long and curly, wet with the fragrant oils of Yaskathan nobility. Yet this was no southern lord who had entered the palace like a gliding ghost.

"*Lyrilan?*" D'zan blinked and leaped from his chair, wrapping his arms about the Scholar King. D'zan laughed loudly, a strange and merry sound that broke the solemn aura of the chamber. D'zan greeted Lyrilan as if he, rather than Tyro, was Lyrilan's true brother.

Mendices' jaw fell open, his face limp with awe. He sank to one knee before the Scholar King. "Majesty . . . " That single word was all he could manage. The Warlord's head bowed low, and he drew his short sword to lay it on the floor at Lyrilan's feet.

"How did you come to Uurz so swiftly?" asked D'zan, releasing Lyrilan from his embrace. Lyrilan did not laugh, though his eyes gleamed with warmth. He seemed to hardly notice the kneeling Mendices.

"You must have left Yaskatha well before Tyro . . . " D'zan stopped himself.

"My brother, the Emperor of Uurz, is dead," said Lyrilan. His eyes looked past Mendices at the faces gathered about the table. "I come to claim my father's throne. And to stand with you all against the enemies of my city."

"It was you," said Khama, his eyes burning. "This man pulled me from the grip of Zyung's dogs. His magic brought me to Uurz, where I could be healed. I owe him my life."

"As do I," said Vireon. Someone, probably Iardu or Sharadza, had told him of the stranger's appearance in the valley. Dahrima had not known the Scholar King of Uurz was a sorcerer. Yet he must wield great power to quell Zyung in such a way, even for a moment. Her sisters had told her that the spell of iron did not last long, and that after the God-King broke it he had allowed the retreat instead of smashing it. Dahrima knew well that she and Vireon would surely be dead if not for Lyrilan's intervention. He might have saved them all with his secret sorcery.

Iardu and Sharadza rose from their chairs to greet Lyrilan.

"They tell me you sent Zyung to iron," said Iardu.

"Only for a moment," said Lyrilan.

Iardu gazed into his eyes, as if inspecting the light reflected there. "Exile has taught you much," said the Shaper. "How on earth did you manage such a feat?"

"Names confer power," said Lyrilan. "I know the true name of Zyung, and the true names of all the Old Breed. Including yours, Iardu. Yet I promise not to send you to iron. Or salt."

Iardu smiled. Another laugh escaped D'zan's lips as he poured a cup of wine for his friend. Sharadza embraced Lyrilan. Dahrima saw that the two of them were also old friends.

"Rise, Mendices," said Lyrilan, acknowledging the Warlord's presence at last. "Fetch me the crown that Tyro wore."

"At once, my King," said Mendices.

"*Emperor*," Lyrilan corrected him. "There is no time for ceremony.

I will assume my duties and my throne this night. As soon as this council of war is done."

Mendices grabbed Lyrilan's hand and kissed his rings awkwardly. "The Gods have blessed us with your speedy return. I live only to serve your will."

Lyrilan said nothing to this. Mendices rushed from the room to find the crown for him.

"Please, sit," said Lyrilan. He took the chair of Mendices.

"I have many questions for you," said Iardu. "Yet I must ask first: How did you learn the forgotten names of the Old Breed? There is no one alive who retains this knowledge. Even we ourselves have forgotten them."

"One can find even the most esoteric knowledge if one knows which books to read," said Lyrilan. He accepted the cup of wine from D'zan. "I have always been a lover of books. If my brother were here, he would tell you that."

Iardu introduced Vaazhia and Dahrima. Lyrilan greeted them with princely politeness. He shared familiar embraces with Vireon and Alua as well.

The lizardess stared at Lyrilan with interest, her ruby eyes shining. "You are the heir of Imvek the Silent," she said. Her lips formed a flirtatious grin. "I knew him well."

"And you, Great Lady," said Lyrilan, "are as perceptive as you are lovely." He raised the cup and drank deeply from it. All those about the table joined D'zan in a toast to Lyrilan's return, and another to his impending coronation as Emperor.

Soon Mendices returned bearing a golden crown set with three great emeralds. A coterie of astonished courtiers and captains followed at his heels. They peered into the chamber and hailed the name of Lyrilan. The Son of Dairon ignored them all as Sharadza placed the crown on his head.

"Mendices, you shall retain your position as Warlord of Uurz until Lord Undroth arrives from Yaskatha," said Lyrilan. "At such time the office will belong to him." Mendices frowned, but nodded his acknowledgment. Dahrima could see that there was bad blood between these two. She did not understand the politics of Men, nor did she care to learn about it. Lyrilan ordered the doors of the council chamber closed, restoring the room to silence.

"Now," said Lyrilan. "Time enough later for ceremonies, gratitudes, and feasts of friends. Let us speak of Almighty Zyung and his Holy Seraphim."

Iardu's luminous eyes turned to Khama, then scanned those of Vireon, Alua, Vaazhia, and Sharadza. Finally his gaze settled once more upon Lyrilan.

"*We are seven*," said the Shaper. "It must be enough."

16

The Scroll

A blanket of clouds obscured the sun and sky when Sungui first saw the walls of Uurz. All morning she had glided through the mist and rains above the Stormlands. The green plain grew thick with villages, rivers, streams, and roads as she approached the city. Clusters of spires and domes gleamed like wet amber beyond the granite ramparts. Many of the winding streets and broad plazas were as green as the outer steppe. The city's double gate was shut tight, its battlements thick with pennons, spears, and the winged helms of sentinels.

Sungui spotted the palace easily, a glittering hill of pinnacles, minarets, and spiked cupolas surrounded by lush walled gardens. A thousand varieties of tree and flower lined the walkways between courtyards. The Emperor's banner fluttered atop the three highest towers.

Guards pacing the grounds rushed to inform their commander of Sungui's approach. She had chosen her female aspect for this duty, estimating that a male envoy might enjoy less hospitality. She pulled the tube of yellow bone from the sleeve of her vestment and descended feet first toward the steps of the palace proper. A squad of spearmen in gold and green armor moved to intercept her.

When Zyung's attendant had roused her from sleep before dawn, she had met with the Almighty on the middle deck of the *Daystar*. At first she thought he might chastise her for lying with Ianthe. The Panther had still slumbered in Sungui's cabin. Yet if Ianthe's sedition and rebellious activities were hidden from Zyung's eyes, Ianthe herself must be as well. "One does not need to be invisible to remain unseen," the Panther had explained, "but only to redirect the watcher's eye. Even the eye of a God-King."

In that dim hour the sun still lurked below the purple horizon, yet any moment it would rise up red and golden to set the world aflame. Sungui walked into the glow of Zyung's eyes as wind rustled the main sails above them. The dreadnoughts had not yet taken to the air, the oarsmen had not yet begun to flap the great wing-sails, but when the sun arose the Holy Armada would too. Moving at full speed, Zyung's forces would reach Uurz well before dusk.

"You will be my envoy to Uurz," Zyung told her. "A new Emperor sits upon its throne. He is the one who saved the Giant-King from death and set free the Feathered Serpent. His brother was a simple warrior, but this one is clever. He is a sorcerer whose magic hides Uurz from my vision, even as he makes plans to resist us. I offer this new and wiser Emperor the chance to surrender and save his people from further bloodshed. Fly to him, Sungui, and give him this offer. Let him know that we will be at his gates this day."

Sungui bowed low. "It shall be done, Holiness."

"Do not make the mistake of Damodar," Zyung added. "You must enter and leave Uurz without violence."

Sungui agreed. The Almighty disappeared once more into the shelter of his great cabin.

Before departing the ship, Sungui met briefly with Ianthe.

They spoke under the shelter of the Panther's misdirection. Then Sungui flew into the west as the sun climbed over the New Holy Mountain.

A few short hours later her feet touched down on the rose-marble steps of the Uurzian palace. A thicket of spearheads surrounded her on the instant.

"I carry a message for the Emperor of Uurz," she told the spearmen in their own language. "From Zyung the Almighty, High Lord Celestial, Heart of the Living Empire. It must be delivered in person."

She endured the indignity of allowing them to search her for weapons. Finding nothing except the capped tube of bone, they escorted her into the Grand Hall. There sat the ruler of Uurz, an assortment of wizards and advisors gathered about his dais. They watched her intently as she walked the length of the gallery toward the throne.

Four of the eight who stood about the dais were of the Old Breed. Sungui sensed the power seething inside their flesh, like flames dancing inside shuttered lanterns. She recognized Khama the Feathered Serpent in his human aspect. Two of the Old Breed were women, one of them wearing a reptilian aspect. That meant the ageless one in the orange robe and a cobalt flame dancing on his chest must be Iardu the Shaper. Unless they had traded shapes to mislead her.

Vireon the Giant-King stood there, also wearing a human aspect. His Queen, standing pale and silent at his side, was another of the Old Breed. D'zan of Yaskatha wore the marks of battle upon his thick limbs; his invincibility in the face of overwhelming foes had impressed Sungui. The last of the figures Sungui identified was the lean Warlord of Uurz, who had led the retreat after Tyro's demise.

As the Almighty had mentioned, this new Emperor of Uurz

was obviously not a warrior. His arms and legs were thin, his young face dominated by the squinted eyes of a sage or scholar. Yet Sungui sensed his power as she approached. She bowed from the waist, not too deeply, but enough to convey courtesy and respect. This many sorcerers might pounce on her and refuse her return to Zyung. They might salt and devour her easily if they chose to do so. She was overmatched and not a little afraid of the powers assembled here.

A herald announced her presence, dubbing her "The Emissary of the Invaders" as he presented her to "Lyrilan, Son of Dairon, Lord of the Sacred Waters, Scholar King of Uurz, and Emperor of the Stormlands."

"What is your message?" asked the Emperor without formality. His eyes were cold as onyx, deep with mysteries. He seemed to know Sungui. He looked through her as if she were a wraith gliding into his throne room from beyond the living world.

Sungui raised the bone tube and offered it to the herald. "This parchment is for the Emperor's eyes only," she said. The herald took it from her hand with some caution. He walked up the carpeted steps to stand beside the throne. Lyrilan nodded. The herald uncapped the tube, pulled out the rolled parchment, and began to unroll it.

As he did this, Sungui spoke directly to Lyrilan.

"Great Emperor," she began. "Zyung the High Lord Celestial asks for your submission to his rule, your allegiance to his Living Empire, and your complete surrender in his name. In exchange, he promises an end to the bloodshed and a peaceful transition of power. Your losses are already great, while his are miniscule. His power is untold, as is the power of those who serve him. Yet he would rather rule in peace than conquer in war. Accept these terms without condition, and your city will prosper as part of his domain. If you should decline, Uurz will fall into the flames of

Celestial Light. The Almighty's Holy Armada will be at your gates before sunset. I am to return at once with your answer."

Lyrilan took the scroll from the herald's hands. His eyes scanned the parchment carefully while he listened to the words of Sungui. When she fell silent, he continued reading the scroll. Sungui stood wrapped in calm, the eyes of the Emperor's curious retinue upon her. At any second a burst of sorcery might accost her, yet she must not respond to violence. Each of the messages she now delivered was of utmost importance – both the spoken and the written. To negate them with open hostility would serve neither Zyung nor herself. She endured the burning stares in silence.

Eventually the Emperor finished reading, rolled up the scroll, and dropped it into his lap. His eyes fell once more upon Sungui. Lyrilan's gaze carried more weight than all the other stares combined. The balance of the future lay in this very moment. How would the Scholar King respond? She hoped that a lust to avenge the death of his brother would not cloud his wisdom. Yet perhaps there had been no love between the two monarchs. Provincial Kings had often murdered their siblings for power in the Outer Provinces of the Living Empire. The Kings of the Five Cities could not be wholly different.

"Tell your God-King that I reject his offer," Lyrilan said. "Tell him also that I know him for what he truly is. Tell him that soon he will taste the bitter end that has been denied him for ages. You may go."

Sungui bowed, turned, and once again walked the interminable length of the Grand Hall. Rows of spears gleamed between the columns of white marble on either side. At any second she expected the bite of a blade, or the searing touch of sorcery on her back. Yet she exited the hall unmolested and stood again upon the polished steps. She breathed deeply of the citrus fragrance wafting from the gardens, then rose into the sky of gray and gold.

She flew northeast to intercept the Holy Armada.

Once more dreadnoughts filled the sky. Their shadows fell across the emerald plain like rolling thunderheads. The cloudbanks were ever-present here, yet the morning rains were long gone. The sun came and went above the beating canvas wings of two thousand sky-ships.

Sungui found the Almighty in his chamber, planning battle strategies with Eshad and three others. Eshad's concerned face betrayed nothing of his secret alliance with Ianthe. Possibly he did not even remember that alliance. Possibly none of them did besides Sungui. Ianthe would return that memory when the moment was ripe. The moment for revolution was not far away.

"What is the answer?" Zyung asked her.

Sungui shook her head. "The Emperor of Uurz follows the Jade King's path, and vows to end the reign of His Holiness."

Zyung sat silent for a moment in his great chair. He tossed back his head and laughed. "He will end my reign? I thought this Emperor would speak with more wisdom. Yet I did not expect him to submit gracefully. They never do."

"As you say, Holiness."

"Did you bring me his name?" asked Zyung.

"He is Lyrilan," said Sungui. "Son of Dairon, Brother of Tyro."

Zyung nodded. He dismissed the gathered Seraphim to their assigned duties.

"Let the siege of Uurz commence," he said. "We will reach the city within the hour."

They all bowed low and left the Almighty to his meditations.

After a word with Eshad regarding the High Seraphim's role in the coming battle, Sungui went below decks. She found Ianthe in her own cabin, drinking blood from a jeweled bowl. Gammir lounged nearby, doing the same.

Sungui stared at the red fluid when she entered. She could smell its coppery tang.

"Another accident among the slaves," said Ianthe. "We cannot let his diligent substance go to waste." Sungui refused an offer to drink from Ianthe's bowl and took a seat upon the satins of her bed.

"Well?" asked the Panther. "Did he accept the scroll? Did he read it?"

"Yes," Sungui said. "It seems that we have an understanding."

Ianthe and Gammir smiled at one another. Their lips were scarlet, their teeth pointed and feral. "You have done well," said the Panther. "If Lyrilan can send Zyung to iron, he can just as well send him to salt."

"Only for a brief moment," said Sungui.

Ianthe's tongue glided across her lips like the head of a red viper.

"A brief moment is all we need, child."

Sungui considered the boldness of the move they had made this day.

"Are you certain His Holiness knows nothing of this?" she asked.

Ianthe rolled her eyes. "Again you doubt me?" Her taloned fingers glided to Sungui's cheek, caressing it softly. Her touch was a rush of painful bliss. Sungui trembled.

"Zyung can no more see the existence of that parchment than he can see this . . . "

Ianthe bent her white head to kiss Sungui's mouth. The familiar spell of heat and desire arose once more to supplant the world.

Gammir lingered this time, sipping blood and watching like a patient hound.

17

The Siege

Five hours past the sun's zenith, the Armada of Zyung arrives at last.

The great gate of Uurz is fortified with bands of Udurum steel. The flat stones of the northern road glimmer gray as pearls in the sunlight. The clouds have broken above the City of Sacred Waters, and the puddles of morning rain have disappeared.

Vireon stands as tall as the city wall at his back. His new greatsword has grown to match his Giant stature, and so have we. All seven of us stand as tall as Vireon now, placing ourselves between the shuttered city and the approaching dreadnoughts. On the Giant-King's left stand myself, the coiled Feathered Serpent, and Sharadza. Her spear and shield are made of sunlight frozen hard as diamond. On Vireon's right are stationed Alua, Lyrilan, and Vaazhia. The white flame burns in Alua's open palms, dripping like magma between her fingers to sear the flagstones.

Blue-skinned Giants line the ramparts behind us, a thousand hulking Udvorg with spear, axe, sword, and mace. Above the great gate itself stands the band of Uduri led by Dahrima the Axe. The watchtowers are filled with Legions of Uurzian infantry.

Legionnaires peer between the merlons alongside Lord Mendices and D'zan of Yaskatha. Behind the wall ten more Legions of Uurz and the surviving legion of Udurum wait in the deserted streets. Civilians are nowhere to be seen. The last of them have taken shelter in cellars, warehouses, or in the caves beneath the city, where the Sacred River flows.

Uurz has girded itself for war.

The great crowns of Lyrilan and Vireon flash in the sunlight, drawing the attention of the armada's first wave. Vireon raises his gleaming Giant-blade and shouts at the ships above the green plain.

"Zyung!" His voice does not command the thunder that rakes the sky; it *is* the thunder. The God-King *must* hear it. "Our duel is unfinished! Come forth and face me before the gates of Uurz!"

Vireon has made his appeal. Now we wait as two thousand warships blot out the sunlight. They encircle the city in concentric formations, just as Khama said they did at Ongthaia. They might easily begin the assault and ignore Vireon's challenge, but Zyung's pride will not allow it. He must come to finish what was begun at Shar Dni. We have staked our lives on my familiarity with Zyung's arrogance. It is perhaps his defining quality, evinced in the form of a vast empire built in his image, and by the temple-palaces bearing his likeness.

Yet Zyung also waits. His dreadnoughts move like titan hawks about Uurz, turning their beaked prows inward to face the streets full of anxious legions. From the sides of their hulls spring the iron tubes Khama described. Soon, very soon, they will vomit flames of alchemy upon the great walls and the city within. Even the flesh of Giants will burn.

Still we wait. Serene. A wedge of seven monoliths with Vireon at our head.

"*Zyung!*" Once again Vireon thunders at the unseen Conqueror.

There is no telling which of the airships carries Zyung, yet it does not matter.

We will draw him out like a Serpent from its cave.

Sungui had expected the defenders of Uurz to come blazing through the air like ferocious meteors, blasting holes in dreadnoughts as Khama had done above the Jade Isles. Yet the armada had crossed the green plain with no sign of resistance, until the gold-green city came into view. There, like great pillars before the massive gates, stood the sorcerers Iardu had assembled.

Giants, all seven of them now, with the wind in their hair and defiance in their eyes.

Sungui stood on the foredeck of the *Daystar* with Gammir and Ianthe. Zyung remained hidden inside his council chamber, yet his awareness spread across the armada as a stifling pressure in the moist air. Now his mental command rang like a gong in their heads. The captains of the great ships began swinging their vessels into siege formation. The double wings of the *Daystar* flapped in unison with those on either side of her, and the aerial fleet spread itself about the city with practiced precision. The sky-ships fixed themselves between the golden towers and the blazing sun, casting bright Uurz into shadow.

Along the ramparts the ranks of northern Giants were assembled for a fresh slaughter. How eager these brutes were to throw away their lives. They had died in the thousands at Shar Dni, where the New Holy Mountain had absorbed their bones. The Men of the city were far greater in number. They had little choice in the matter of defense, for it was their city that would fall today. The Giants might easily run to their icy northland and leave these humans to their fate. Sungui admired the loyalty of Giants, if not their common sense. They would stay and perish alongside the Men of Uurz.

She expected Zyung to fall eventually beneath the power of Iardu's band, as Ianthe's plan had all but ensured. Yet before that moment came, Uurz would suffer and burn. A flood of death would drown the green plain, no matter who conquered this day. Like the stubborn navies who died in defense of Ongthaia, the defenders of Uurz were bound to enter death's kingdom by the power of their own oaths, their vain pride, and the cruel honor shared by all warriors.

Let them die, Sungui mused. *As long as Zyung falls with them.*

She would help make it so.

Yet first Ianthe's coven must continue the charade of serving the Almighty. Make a show of assaulting his enemies and razing this city. The bones that were scattered across the ruined steppe would not be raised into a Holy Mountain. They would be left to rot in the sun and drown in the mud, until the Land of the Five Cities had entirely forgotten them.

Sungui sighed. The last of the armada had assembled itself about the city, with the *Daystar* floating in the outermost ring. Great, golden birds of prey waiting to strike.

"The Son of Vod will challenge Zyung first," said Ianthe. "His honor demands it." Her hand lingered on Sungui's shoulder. The Panther's touch was a constant murmur of pleasure.

"Vireon is a fool," Gammir said. "He believes that he owns the strength of Vod, and he will prove it by crossing blades with the God-King yet again. Yet even Vod could not stand against Zyung's power."

"And if you were Vireon?" Sungui asked. "What would you do?" Her eyes lingered on the seven patient Giants before the gates of Uurz.

Gammir's lupine face regarded Sungui with contempt. His yellow eyes narrowed. "I would surrender and strike later, when my enemy least expected it."

"Of course," Sungui said. *More likely you would run and hide like a viper in some deep-earth crevice.* She looked forward to parting ways with the Wolf when today's deed was done. She would miss Ianthe's touch, but not the presence of her minion.

Vireon's voice rattled the sky, and Zyung's unspoken command echoed once more in the minds of Seraphim, Captains, and Manslayers. The firing tubes of the dreadnoughts emerged from their glistening hulls, pointed like a million accusing fingers at the city below. Sungui admired the expansive gardens and orchards, the marbled streets and plazas, the sheer beauty of the Uurzian palace. All of this would soon be no more.

As surely as Ongthaia had drowned, Uurz would burn.

She watched the impassive faces of the High Seraphim across the decks of nearby ships. How many would choose annihilation over revolt today?

A second mental command resounded, and the Seraphim floated from their ships into the air, converging above the gates of Uurz and its seven titans. Protective spheres of light blinked to life about each of their hovering bodies. Zyung had called forth his High Ones.

The Almighty was indeed coming to meet the Giant-King face to face one last time.

Be patient, came the voice of Ianthe in Sungui's head. She knew that voice was heard by all the coven. *Wait for my signal. Until then, serve your God-King.*

Joining her brethren in the sky above the doomed city, Sungui waited.

One by one, tiny stars erupt in the purple sky above the gate. Surrounding our group of seven as the dreadnoughts surround the city, a thousand silver-robes appear inside globes of condensed light. They are the size of Men, so to us they are but a swarm of fireflies. Yet only when the last of them appears does Zyung manifest himself before us, accepting Vireon's challenge.

The unspoken rules of Zyung's response are clear: We are not to interfere in this final duel, or his High Seraphim will pelt us with their brilliant destruction.

Giant-King and God-King face one another yet again.

Today Vireon defends a living city, not a haunted ruin.

The Giant-King strides toward Zyung, whose flaming blade ignites from the center of his fist. The Conqueror says not a word. He will let his power speak for him.

Vireon's blade arcs forward, a bolt of lightning against a pillar of flame. There is thunder, and black clouds swirl above the swarm of dreadnoughts. Wind blasts the battlements of Uurz. The gigantic blades howl and collide again.

The Flame of Intellect leaps upon my chest. I sense the presence of Ianthe and Gammir among the legion of Old Breed who watch this contest of titans. They, too, await the perfect moment to strike. Yet all eyes are focused on the two colossal combatants.

The dust along the gate road leaps as the great blades connect. Vireon steps away from the burning blade and parries a downstroke. Zyung moves very little, yet his arm is a leaping cobra with a tongue of flashing fire. Vireon's steel begins to smoke from the touch of the burning blade.

Giant-King circles about God-King, and Zyung swivels to keep his eyes on Vireon. His arm knows no weakness or fatigue. He deflects Vireon's every blow and thrust. His flameblade singes Vireon's eyes, leaving a cut across the Giant-King's cheek that steams and sizzles. Vireon feints to avoid the next blow and locks his left hand about Zyung's right wrist. The flaming blade vanishes, only to reappear in Zyung's left fist. It turns Vireon's blade away and slips upward to catch the Giant-King in his left side, running him through. Zyung withdraws it instantly. Steaming blood spills from the hole above Vireon's hip, spilling down his bronze legs. A more central thrust would have ended the duel at once.

Vireon staggers but does not fall. His blade rises to protect his neck from the flaming sword's arc. The two blades are locked now, emitting sparks and black smoke. The eyes of Vireon and Zyung are also locked. A third deadlock: Their free hands have come together, fingers entwined in a crushing grip.

"Vireon!" calls Sharadza. "*Vireon!*"

It is too late. Stellar flames from Zyung's eyes blast Vireon in the face. The Giant-King howls, losing his grip as his iron-dense flesh melts away from the skull beneath it. Zyung spins his flame-blade and takes off Vireon's right arm at the shoulder. Then the burning weapon arcs upward and sideways, cleaving off the Giant-King's head.

The great crown of iron and sapphire falls free of the head as it tumbles. Vireon's smoking skull never meets the earth. Zyung catches it in his free hand. Vireon's blade falls to join his crown. Yet before either of them hits the ground, the Conqueror's voice rings out. The towers behind us tremble.

Vireon's head is a mound of white salt in Zyung's palm.

The flaming blade extinguishes itself. Zyung's hand touches the chest of Vireon's headless body, which has not yet fallen. It becomes an icon of white solidity now, a great effigy of salt that holds its shape as if wrought of pale marble. Zyung casts his fist-ful of salt — Vireon's pulped head — across the salted body. The scattered grains adhere to the body's surface like thistles in a hunter's cloak. Yet the head does not reform. Nor will it ever. The Conqueror will either consume the salt himself when the siege is done, or give it to his Seraphim to imbibe.

Sharadza cannot find a voice to cry out. Alua stares at her salted husband, tears of white flame drizzling from her eyes. Her mouth is open, but like Sharadza her scream has not yet begun.

All at once it begins. Here is the signal the armada has been awaiting: the Giant-King's death. Orange flames pour from the sky-ships, washing across the ramparts of Uurz into the streets and gardens beyond. The wails of burning Men and Giants rise on currents of stifling air.

The Feathered Serpent leaps at Zyung with Vaazhia at his side.

Sharadza and Alua advance screaming with spear and flame.

Lyrilan and myself circle about to approach Zyung from behind.

A hail of deathlights falls about us as the High Seraphim unleash their power.

A sea of flame deluged the city as the six titans fell upon Zyung.

The High Seraphim needed no command to begin defending the Celestial One. They cast bolts of solar conflagration toward Vireon's rushing avengers.

Again Ianthe's voice rang in Sungui's mind, and in the minds of the five hundred.

Not yet, my children. Do not unleash your true power. Throw beams of gentle sunlight upon these defenders of Uurz. Allow them to weaken Zyung. We must neither prevent nor aid them. Wait for my signal. Be patient . . .

Among the thousand High Ones there remained half who were not among Ianthe's coven. They hurled honest deathlights at the six sorcerers below, and there was nothing Sungui could do to prevent it. Yet Iardu's followers were not so easily ashed as the soldiers who had died by the thousands at Shar Dni. As for the ranks of Lesser Seraphim, their power was directed at the besieged

city. Their sunbolts sent towers and bridges toppling while the
dreadnoughts poured rivers of flame across the battlements. The
Men and Giants there sent up volleys of arrows, burning logs, catapult stones, and screams of hatred. Other than that, they could
only burn and die.

Sungui poured harmless light upon the Feathered Serpent as its
maw struck at Zyung. Ianthe and Gammir floated among the
High Ones nearby, indistinguishable from all the rest in their
silver vestments. The entire coven pretended to defend their
master with impotent rays of light, while the five hundred who
were not among Ianthe's revolution poured raw power upon the
Sorcerers of Uurz.

Each of the loyalists would have one last chance to join the
coven. The wisest among them would choose treason instead of
oblivion. The rest of them would not be missed.

Be patient . . .

We are six now.

Zyung ignores the torrent of starfire rushing from Khama's
jaws, though it burns away his silver raiment. He grabs the
Feathered Serpent by the throat with both massive hands. I have
seen men kill vipers in this way by strangling them to death.
Khama's black stinger strikes home again and again, puncturing
the God-King's marble flesh. The Serpent's convulsions knock
over the salted remains of Vireon, who crumbles to white powder
among the tall grass.

Vaazhia's leap brings her falling upon the God-King's shoulders
like a raging lioness. Her claws rip both sides of his face, carving
rents in his stony cheeks, while the talons of her feet dig deep into
his back. Sharadza's spear of hard light impales Zyung's gut,
emerging bloody from his back. Alua casts streams of flame like
whips about the God-King's legs.

I weave a curtain of sorcery to block the deathlights that rain upon us. Lyrilan does the same as he positions himself behind Zyung.

Beyond the burning walls Giants hurl spears and burning logs at the sky-ships. Volleys of flaming arrows fly upward, but they will do no good. We already know that these ships do not easily burn.

Alua pulls her flame-whips forward and Zyung topples backward. Instead of falling he rises into the air. His voice erupts like a volcano, spilling across the snared Feathered Serpent. Khama's bright coils turn to milky crystal, losing color and flexibility. Like Vireon before him, Khama is sent to salt. Zyung breaks the salt-Serpent in half, hurling both pieces to the ground, where they erupt in clouds of dust.

We are five.

We rise into the sky with Zyung, tearing at him like wolves rending an elk.

Vaazhia sinks her talons into Zyung's eyes, which blast forth sunfire. The blast catches Sharadza, who reels and loses her spear, her skin dissolving. Bolts of deathlight from the High Seraphim pummel the Daughter of Vod. Her scream is one of mingled agony and grief. She becomes a burning, swirling mass of flame that refuses to fall.

Alua's white fires glide up Zyung's naked legs like pythons, devouring his flesh like brittle parchment. In moments it will reach his chest and heart.

Lyrilan and I await our opening.

It will come soon, but now Vaazhia's berserk assault hides Zyung's back from us. His grasping hands reach backward to seize her horned head as she sinks fangs into his throat. He wrenches the comely head away from her shoulders, a gout of crimson spewing across his torso.

The Conqueror's voice rings out again, and Vaazhia's tumbling body is a thing of salt that explodes when it hits the ground.

Two more sorcerers crushed by Zyung's power.

Perhaps there were not enough of them to weaken him after all. Perhaps Ianthe's plan was doomed to fail. Could the Almighty know of the Panther's betrayal as he had known Sungui's dual nature? Certainly he did not trust her. It could be that he *allowed* her to assemble this coven so that he might expose and destroy it during this very confrontation.

The Feathered Serpent was no more. The reptilian sorceress had been salted as well. Iardu had yet to strike. Lyrilan cowered behind the Almighty like a village boy afraid to cast a spear on his first hunt. White flame devoured Zyung's lower half, and the sister of Vireon had become a burning, howling maelstrom.

Was the sacrifice of these allies part of Iardu's plan? Was he waiting, like Ianthe, until Zyung had spent the majority of his power destroying them? Perhaps then the Shaper would strike and Lyrilan could work his transforming spell.

Sungui fretted as she tossed light across the battling titans. Uurz was a wailing holocaust below the dreadnoughts.

"Turn your lights upon the city!" Sungui gave the command to all the High Ones. "Zyung does not need us. Bring down the golden towers! Send the walls to ash!"

Her distraction worked: The High Ones who were truly attacking Zyung's combatants turned instead to the blazing city, casting their deathlights upon it. They could not conceive that the Almighty should need their aid any longer; he was making quick work of the seven sorcerers. The High Seraphim and the Lesser Seraphim would complete what the dreadnoughts had begun. The earth shook beneath crumbling, burning Uurz. The outer walls began to melt and splinter, collapsing across the bodies of Giants and battalions of Men.

The cries of winged beasts filled the sky above the Seraphim. The first rank of dreadnoughts released its Trill Knights, who descended like a flock of vultures into the devastation. Uurzians who fled between the collapsing towers and flaming walls were skewered on the lances of the riders. On the decks of the airships the massed ranks of Manslayers beat swords against shields, anticipating the moment when they would be set to ground, turned loose to plunder the shattered city.

Sungui turned her eyes back to Zyung.

Iardu and Lyrilan pounced on him like tigers.

Be patient . . .

We are four.

Sharadza, torn and blazing from the deathlights, lunges once more toward Zyung. She has armored herself in condensed sunrays, forging a greatsword from that same brightness.

Lyrilan and I strike as one. Our blazing hands dig into the God-King's back, tearing through stony flesh toward the beating heart within. Lyrilan chants a song of annihilation. I join his spell, although it cannot affect the Conqueror unless we claim his heart.

Alua's flame engulfs the lower half of Zyung now. The Conqueror grows even larger, increasing in mass and density. He tosses us from him as a hound slings water from its fur. Even Alua's white flame is cast away.

Zyung's arms move faster than my eyes can follow. He catches Sharadza and Alua in his tightening fists. Lyrilan and I rush through the air at him.

The city burns and shatters below us, and the Seraphim have begun casting their deathlights upon it. A flock of leather-winged lizards rises from the ships, diving in the hundreds toward Uurz's remaining defenders. On their backs armored riders carry Giant-killing lances.

Again Zyung's voice rises above the fray, and two more of our number perish in salt.

The remains of Sharadza and Alua stream like white sand from Zyung's clenched fists.

We are only two.

"Now!" I yell at the Emperor of Uurz.

Lyrilan sings again the ancient incantation that he spoke at Shar Dni.

Yet Zyung mutters his own syllables of power, reflecting Lyrilan's sorcery.

Instead of Zyung it is Lyrilan who whitens and falls to join the heaps of salt.

No . . .

Sungui watched the colossal Lyrilan crystalize and plummet toward the plain, bursting into a cloud of salt before the broken gates. Zyung stood tall as a mountain now, ready to trample the world beneath his heel. Iardu was an insect buzzing about his granite face, avoiding his blazing eyes.

We have waited too long! What hope has Iardu without Lyrilan?

Among the hovering Seraphim, Sungui found Ianthe's stunned face. The Panther turned to meet her, and the panic in her black eyes turned to fury. Gammir growled like a beast in the air beside her, his face gone crimson in the glow of the burning city.

Now! Like shattering glass Ianthe's command exploded inside the heads of the coven. Sungui nearly screamed at the intimate violence. *Turn on your brethren, my children! Let each one choose annihilation or freedom!*

The five hundred seized their fellow High Seraphim, grabbing them by wrists and necks. *"Join us against Zyung, or be sent to salt."*

There was nothing else that need be said. Here, in simple words spoken plainly, was the last chance the loyalists would get to share in the plunder of the Living Empire, once it was broken and divided among the Rebel Seraphim.

Sungui and Eshad grabbed one between them.

"Never!" screamed the loyalist, deathlights flashing from his eyes.

As one, the two rebels breathed their spell, while the loyalist struggled and vomited sorcery at them. In seconds it was over. The loyalist was an effigy of salt. Sungui and Eshad broke him into pieces, stuffing him into distended mouths.

Sungui chewed and swallowed as her fellow rebels were doing in the sky all about her.

The taste was bitter, as it always was. Fleeting emotions and memories, drowned beneath her will. Imbibed power gleaming from mouth and nostrils.

Eshad gave her a nod, turning to exchange bolts with another loyalist. Sungui helped him grab the man, yet before they salted him, he surrendered. He set off with Eshad to salt and devour another. Ianthe and Gammir were devouring Seraphim after Seraphim. Sungui knew these two were offering no last chance for their victims, but she had no time to protest.

The Lesser Seraphim had receded from the battle entirely, seeking refuge on the dreadnoughts. This civil war was not for them to fight. A single High One could destroy a dozen of them in the wink of an eye. They would sit out this conflict and swear allegiance to whichever faction won in the end.

And which faction will that be? Sungui wondered.

A fog of salt dust filled the hot and smoky air. Amid the chaos of battling, consuming Seraphim, Sungui glimpsed Zyung grabbing Iardu in his massive fist.

If the Shaper perishes, so do our dreams of conquest.

Ianthe has used us all, she realized. *Zyung has destroyed her enemies one by one. Now he will devour Iardu. The Panther and Wolf will flee, leaving us to the Almighty's wrath.*

In that moment, she knew herself a fool.

"Iardu." Zyung greets me at last. His quicksilver hand falls fast, snaring me like an errant fly. He will salt me too, but again his arrogance tells me what he will do first. He will gloat over my defeat. He brings me up close to his flaring eyes. He towers above the burning city, his head higher now than his floating dreadnoughts.

The High Seraphim have turned their attention to the city, casting towers into rubble with their gleaming bolts. They are as children entertaining themselves with the slow destruction of an unwanted toy. Yet something new begins among the floating Seraphim. Two of them send a third one to salt, devouring him as I watch over Zyung's shoulder. The same thing happens again and again throughout their swarming ranks. There is strife among the High Lord's servants.

Ianthe's doing.

I sense her and Gammir darting among the legion of sorcerers, singing the songs of transmutation that send the Old Breed to salt; aiding the Rebel Seraphim in the rapid devouring of their stubborn fellows. Ianthe has turned the entire legion against itself. No longer do their deathlights fall upon the blazing towers of Uurz. They strike at each other instead.

A second battle rages now above the first – a revolt of sorcerers.

I knew this would come. It is early, but not surprising.

The winged lizards harass the walls and dive among the streets, snatching men into the air and dropping them into the flames. Further up, Ianthe's rebels annihilate their own kind.

Zyung should never have taken one as empty of loyalty as the Claw into his midst. In a moment he will discover this error, when he has sent me to join my companions in the salt-death.

"I warned you long ago not to resist my vision," Zyung says. I am held fast in his behemoth fist. "There is no redemption for you, Starwing. You will see my wisdom at last, when I have consumed your essence."

I meet his gaze, drawing his attention as deeply as I can.

"Perhaps," I say. "And you will see mine."

In the instant before Zyung's voice can send me to salt, another voice rattles our bones. In that same moment he forgets the nuisance trapped in his fist, and watches the rapid flow of whiteness cascade up his legs. As a rushing wave it comes, a transformation of titanic flesh to marbled salt. A scream of rage dies in his throat as his colossal body goes rigid.

Even as I shatter his salted fist with an eruption of blue flame, he falls forward across the green plain. The thunder of his impact shakes the burning walls of Uurz and flattens an abandoned village.

I descend to find the *true* Lyrilan waiting for me, emeralds agleam on his dark robe.

We are the size of Men once more. He smiles.

"Call them quickly," I say.

Half of the loyalists were salted and consumed in a matter of moments. The black smokes rising from Uurz mingled with wisps of salt from bodies broken and divided.

In the moment that Lyrilan's voice rang across the darkening plain, the struggles of the High Seraphim ceased. The mountain of salt that was Zyung seemed impossible, but there it stood. A frozen moment that would change the shape of the world and those who built it.

How? Sungui could not say.

The earth rumbled as Zyung crashed to the ground.

A green flame flared into the twilight, a beacon that drew the attention of the High Ones and brought an end to their feud. There was nothing left to fight for. No Celestial One to claim their loyalty. The last of the loyalists conceded, joining the rebels in an instant, all of them gleaming like silver motes between leaping flames and floating ships. All of them hearing Lyrilan's voiceless summons, the attraction of his light-burst, the glow that tinted the salt of the titan to shades of emerald.

The Emperor of Uurz lives! Ianthe's plan has worked.

The time for devouring had come.

Now, my children! Now! Ianthe's voice resounded in the heads of the High Seraphim. *Zyung is salted! Feast! Feast! His power and his empire are yours! Take it!*

They swarmed from the sky like a plague of silver locusts.

Sungui joined them gladly. The coven had grown by at least two hundred.

All of them unbound.

All of them *hungry*.

A blast of viridian light spears the sky, and the Rebel Seraphim descend upon the salted God-King by the hundreds. Their mouths open impossibly wide to bite off great chunks of his brittle substance. They cover his massive body like ants upon a pile of sugar, devouring, devouring. Consuming both form and essence. There is Ianthe, and Gammir, along with the rest of them, imbibing Zyung's eternal spirit through his salt.

Vireon and Alua step from nowhere to join Lyrilan and me. Khama floats close behind them. A soft hand takes my own, and Sharadza is there. We watch the long-enslaved Old Breed feed upon the God-King's crystallized soul. They take his diluted power into themselves, spreading it among their hundreds as a legion of warriors shares a keg of ale.

"This is gruesome," Sharadza says. "Must it be this way?"

I cannot tell her what I must do next.

"Yes," I say. "The only way to destroy Zyung's immortal being is to divide it among the others. If not for Ianthe's rebels, we would have to consume him ourselves."

Sharadza shivers. "I would not devour anyone so."

"Then thank our enemy," I say.

"And the envoy who brought her scroll," says Lyrilan. "Sungui the Venomous."

Even as Ianthe's swarm devours the salted colossus, it shrinks to the size of an Uduru. This must have been Zyung's customary size. The Seraphim move quick as spiders, stuffing their mouths and bellies, streaming light from their eyes and throats. Soon there will be nothing left of Zyung.

Vireon turns toward the blazing Uurz. "What of the city?" he asks. There is confusion among the dreadnoughts and the Man-slayers peering from their decks. The silver hordes are ready to storm the dying city. The Men and Giants are finished, the golden towers toppled to dust, the orchards and walls aflame.

"Tell Vaazhia that the time for phantoms has passed," I say. The Feathered Serpent flies off to find the lizardess. I face Sharadza and take both her hands in mine. "I must leave you now, before this devouring is complete. Trust me when I say that this must be done. Wait for me on the island. If you will . . . "

She cries my name as I move away from her, but I do not respond. I cannot.

Vireon grabs her shoulders to keep her from rushing after me.

Floating above the dwindling hill of Zyung's salt, I remain unnoticed by the Seraphim who lick, chew, and swallow their way to his last grain. I close my eyes and begin the most important spell I will ever cast.

The Flame of Intellect on my chest gutters and fades. My hand plunges into my breast, sharp as a blade. It clutches the pulsing jewel that is my heart. With the last of my strength and a shout of agony, I tear it out through the bleeding hole in my chest. It pulses redly in my hand, no larger than a pomegranate, dripping crimson across the salt-mound below. Some of it falls upon the heads of the devouring Seraphim, yet they take no notice.

Only Ianthe senses it. Her weakness for blood aroused, she watches me with eyes of jet. The heart turns to a white rock in my hand, and I drop it into the midst of the salt-mound that is the last of Zyung. Instantly the heart-stone dissolves and merges with the existing grains. My own salt is indistinguishable now from that of Zyung. Ianthe has already returned to devouring him like the rest of her conspirators.

I hover for a moment longer above them, heartless and fading. Then I glide back to Sharadza, streaming blood from my opened chest. I fall into her arms, and she weeps over me. Still I fade, yet the last thing I see is her sweet face close to mine.

I hear her calling my name. I hope she understands.

I die in her arms, at peace with what I have done.

18

Phantoms

Uurz was a great circle of flame and rubble. The bodies of Men and Giants were cinders scattered across its blackened interior. A host of winged lizards spiraled above the flames like black vultures, searching for the wounded and dying. Above the flocking Trills the ranks of dreadnoughts floated among columns of black smoke.

North of the inferno Zyung the Conqueror lay salted and dwindling, sinking swiftly into the stomachs and souls of his most powerful slaves. Yet they were slaves no more. Word of the High Seraphim's betrayal had not yet reached the armada, but like the rising smokes it would soon engulf the dreadnoughts.

Khama soared into the clouds east of the Holy Armada and then sped south across the unspoiled grassland. When the burning city seemed no larger than a bonfire on the north horizon, he opened his great maw and bellowed a roar that shook the plain. His Serpent body coiled and flashed sun-bright above the flatland, the second part of his prearranged signal.

As if some cosmic sleeper had awakened from a dream of flaming death, two things happened at once. First, the walls of the flaming city on the north horizon vanished, along with its toppled

towers, shattered palace, and the charred bones of its Men and
Giants. Second, the granite ramparts of the true Uurz appeared
below the Feathered Serpent, its golden spires gleaming in the
purple dusk. Like a desert mirage it shimmered into existence,
along with the surrounding roads and plantations that had
remained unseen.

Before the city's double gate stood thirteen armored legions of
Men, with a fourteenth legion of Giants. Dahrima and her spear-
sisters stood among the ranks of anxious Udvorg. D'zan of
Yaskatha sat upon a mailed warhorse at the front of the Uurzian
vanguard. Vaazhia the Lizardess stood tall as a Giant at his side.
Her crimson eyes were vivid with sorcery.

The Holy Armada of Zyung floated now above a great, burning
ring of grassland north of Uurz. The phantom city conjured by
Vaazhia had faded into nothingness, along with the phantoms of
the six sorcerers defeated by Zyung. The false city and its defending legions had been as real the Nameless Folk that served the
lizardess during her isolation, yet also entirely unreal. Conjurings
of dust and vapor, shadows and light given substance by Vaazhia's
willpower, guided by her imagination. While the armada had set
the phantom city aflame, the real Uurz and its legions had stayed
hidden beneath a cloak of sorcery a league to the south.

Until Khama's signal, when the lizardess dropped her great
mantle of phantasms.

Of the seven who battled the God-King before the gates of the
phantom Uurz, only Iardu had been more than a clever apparition.
"There must be some truth at the heart of any good lie," the
Shaper had insisted. "Zyung knows me better than any of you.
When he sees my own reality, he will believe these phantoms to
be my true allies. And when they are all vanquished, he will relish
his victory over me. In that moment, when I claim the whole of
his attention, Lyrilan must strike."

The ruse had succeeded. Now, while the devouring of Zyung's corpse claimed the attention of his sorcerers, the true battle for Uurz must begin.

D'zan raised a war horn to his lips and blew a mighty note. The true Men and Giants of Uurz charged across the steppe between them and the burning field. By the time they reached the outskirts of the conflagration, there must be foes upon the ground for them to slay.

Khama swept downward and Vaazhia leaped upon his back. He swung about and flew ahead of the charging legions. Their massed battle cries echoed his roar.

As the burning patch of earth grew nearer, Vireon grew once more to the height of a mountain, his greatsword raised high as both salute and beacon to the advancing legions. Khama sensed terror spreading across the decks of the dreadnoughts. Two thousand sky-ships hovered still above the flames in their concentric pattern of assault, yet Vireon's head and shoulders rose far above them. The point of his blade pierced the clouds, sending a heavy rain to douse the flames at his feet. The befuddled Trills glided about the columns of his legs, a cloud of gnats caught in the tempest.

Vireon wore a crown of stormclouds now, aglow with crimson lightning.

In the moment before Khama reached the outermost ring of ships, Vireon swept his greatsword across the sky. Thunderbolts leaped across the blue blade, and a great wind rushed before it, tearing sails and masts from their moorings. The gleaming razor's edge of the blade sliced through the first rank of dreadnoughts as a scythe reaps stalks of wheat. Golden hulls burst apart like cloven melons, spilling their silvery contents toward the plain. Vireon's arc continued, shearing through the second rank of dreadnoughts, and the innermost third. A single stroke of the behemoth blade slashed half the armada to splinters. A sea of warriors and wreckage fell upon the blackened, muddy steppe. A great number of Trills were caught in the plummeting debris and torn from the sky.

A few motes of light, Lesser Seraphim trained to fly in their crystalline orbs of power, darted between the falling debris, casting deathlights at Vireon. They were less than stinging wasps to him. The Giant-King's arm had reached the end of its arc, pausing before a reverse sweep that would split the rest of the fleet to kindling.

In the moment of that pause, Khama belched lightning toward the first dreadnought in his path, while Vaazhia tossed a bolt of crimson flame. The ship exploded, sending more of the horde plummeting to earth. Khama swung about as Vireon's right arm began its dreadful backstroke. Yet many of the dreadnought captains were swift thinkers. Their unbroken ships dropped downward, as if the invisible strings holding them airborne had been cut. The blade roared past above them, taking down another hundred vessels that were not fast enough to avoid it. A second rain of bodies, splintered beams, and cloven Ethus Trees fell upon the first.

Several hundred ships had reached the smoking plain unharmed, hovering just above the ground. Broad ramps sprouted from their hulls, and ranks of shouting Manslayers poured from their decks. Their commanders had spotted the charging Legions of Uurz, and now the ranks of Manslayers rushed to meet them. The sky was clear of dreadnoughts, but the plain swarmed with the unleashed legions of Zyung. They flooded in thousands from the surviving ships.

The Men of the Stormlands and their Giants were still outnumbered forty to one.

*

Never was there a salt such as this . . .

Sungui filled her mouth with a handful of Zyung's essence, her head spinning, the light of his power streaming from her eyes. She was drunk on his Almighty potency, as were they all. They crawled across the last of his white mound, slurping the salt of divinity and moaning their pleasure. Heedless of those who watched them with silent condemnation, they devoured the one who had Diminished them for so many ages, sick with the boundless pleasure of it.

Her eyes caught Ianthe, spilling a stream of the pale grains into her own mouth, and, beyond her, Gammir biting into a congealed fragment. And there was fat Durangshara, who would not spare a single grain, and mighty Eshad, sweet Myrinhama, the alchemists Darisha and Gulzarr, and the triplets Johaar and Mezviit and Aldreka. And seven hundred more devourers of the High Lord Celestial's immortal essence. The coven had swiftly salted and devoured those High Seraphim who refused to heed Ianthe's call, yet two hundred more had joined the rebels this day rather than face destruction. Consuming the essence of their fellow Diminished ones while Iardu and his allies battled Zyung was nothing compared to ingesting the Almighty himself.

It was almost *too much* power.

The coven's cries of ecstasy rose like glorious songs of shame and debauchery. They gloried in this consumption. If there had been any less of them, Sungui doubted they could have contained the power coursing through their bodies.

Her mind reeled, and she swayed atop the salt-mound. Soon the last of Zyung would be gone. Great thunders broke overhead, and the flames of Uurz were quenched by a torrential downpour, yet the coven paid attention to none of it. They rolled on their backs among the flattened grasses, caught in the terrible, transcendent rush of Zyung's ingested essence. Sungui struggled to keep her feet. The Emperor of Uurz stood nearby with his sorcerer allies, watching as the seven hundred slurped up the remaining salt, which had mingled with the mud and rain.

Visions fell upon Sungui like waking dreams, fragments of Zyung's scattered consciousness. An abyss of stars, seething with stellar eruptions. A primordial sphere of swamps and volcanoes. The dark temples of forgotten ages. A sea of blood and flame. Multitudes of tiny lives, flickering into existence and fading into nothing, numerous as the stars themselves. A continent teeming with savage life, endless wars, rivers of red and collapsing spires of crystalline wonder. Shapes and forms without name . . .

Memories.

She did not want Zyung's memories. Only his power. Only freedom from his long rule, the opportunity to roam this world and beyond as she desired. The shattering of his empire, the death of his great dream. The untold power of her primal self.

Yet there was something else in the salt. Iardu had placed it there.

In the depths of the dark dreams spinning like stormwinds inside her head, there blossomed a deep and abiding warmth. A calm eye in the hurricane of thought and sensation. It grew like a golden lotus, spreading petals across the garden of her mind.

She saw unborn infants sleeping in the wombs of their mothers, like the world itself held in the embrace of the cosmos. The tears of lovers fell like sweet rains across her altering mind. The strong arms of Men building high walls and proud towers, the breath of mercy bestowed from one brother to the next. The innocence of children found in every soul that manifests into the living world. A boundless ocean of light containing all that lives, all that is yet to live, and all that has lived.

A sense of undeniable unity, heavy as the gravity of stars.

Oneness.

I will never be the same . . .

She wept tears bright as quicksilver. Those reeling in the salt about her did the same.

Iardu has poisoned us.

No.

He has enlightened us.

Sungui was on her knees now. Ianthe and Gammir stood over her. They grasped her hands, pulling her up. There were no tears in their eyes, yet they grinned as well-fed wolves must grin over the corpse of their kill. The rest of the seven hundred still lay senseless and dreaming in the rain, intoxicated by the power of guzzled divinity. Lost in the throes of an unexpected enlightenment.

"Is it not wonderful?" the Panther said. "Never have I had such a feast!"

Gammir howled at the storming sky.

Iardu lay nearby in the arms of a weeping girl. Lyrilan stood before them, his crown of emeralds slickened by rain. Thunder and lightning tore the sky where ruined Uurz no longer stood. Only now did Sungui realize that the conquered city had disappeared. Dreadnoughts were falling from the sky like dead birds. A dark mountain in the shape of a Man stood with its back to the coven's feast. A steely whirlwind soared across the sky beyond the titan.

"I have delivered my side of the bargain," said the Emperor of Uurz. "Will you honor yours? Or stay and be salted like your God-King? Make your choice now: Retreat or Annihilation."

Before Sungui could find her own voice, Ianthe spoke for her. "We may do what we please, Scholar King. These seven hundred no longer serve a God-King; they rule the Living Empire now. If we decide to remain and devour Uurz as we have devoured Zyung, then that is what we will do."

Lyrilan's dark eyes flashed. "Then I will send you all to salt."

"No!" Sungui shouted. She raised a trembling hand to stay the sorcerer who was also Scholar and Emperor. "We will honor the words of the scroll, as you have honored them. Ianthe does not speak for us, only for herself. We will take our surviving ships and go now."

Ianthe turned upon her. "You are weak, Sungui. The essence of Zyung should have made you strong. You need not fawn before this overproud boy."

"Leave us in peace," said Lyrilan. "I care not what you do with Zyung's lands, but this land belongs to us. You must never return here."

"Ianthe," said Sungui, "we, too, have an agreement. If you wish to conquer the Land of the Five Cities you must do it without the Seraphim. We will return to our side of the world."

Ianthe laughed. "Your honor is above reproach, Sungui the Venomous. They should rename you Sungui the Honorable. I would return with you now to witness the death of Zyung's dream, and to revel in the red chaos of its dissolution."

Sungui was ambivalent. She would enjoy more of Ianthe's burning passion, yet she would have to endure the icy presence of Gammir. There was no separating the two. Still, the Panther and Wolf were inconsequential in the light of Sungui's newfound state of being.

It does not matter. We have changed, even if these two have not.

"Your decision is most wise," Lyrilan said to the Panther. "For if you remain here, it will be as salt in the bellies of Vireon and the Feathered Serpent. Go with these Eaters of Zyung, or hear me speak your true name as you die."

Suddenly Ianthe was the White Panther again. She roared and snapped at Lyrilan but did not move against him. The dark-haired girl arose to stand at the Emperor's side. The corpse of Iardu had dissolved into blue smoke behind her.

"Go!" the girl shouted at the Panther and the Black Wolf. Hate swam in her green eyes. "Go and never return!" A blade of starlight appeared in her fist. She struggled to resist using the weapon. How she must loathe Ianthe and Gammir. Sungui felt it pouring off her like a raw heat. Lyrilan put his arm around her shoulders. The Scholar King spoke an ancient word, and he was gone from the plain along with the girl.

Sungui turned to the salty-mouthed figures of the New Seraphim. She raised her white palms to them in a sign of victory. Their eyes met her own. Fresh understanding gleamed there. They had shared her dream of change, seen the eye of the storm inside. Even cruel Durangshara was altered. Only the Panther and Wolf remained the same.

"Let us return!" Sungui rose into the sky and the seven hundred followed her. Panther and Wolf sprouted black wings and joined them. Sungui had promised to leave the Land of the Five Cities to Ianthe, and to give the Living Empire over to her brethren.

She had promised Lyrilan an end to this invasion if his power could send Zyung to salt.

Now she promised herself something new.

We will never be the same.

Alua hovered among the darting figures of the Lesser Seraphim, cracking their spheres with blasts of her white flame. They fell dying to join the piles of wrecked dreadnoughts and bodies below. Vireon snatched them from the air in handfuls, crushing them in his great fists, tiny globes of glass popping into red shards. He waded across the heaps of devastation, his feet smashing dread-noughts and Manslayers to pulp.

Khama glided between the low-hovering dreadnoughts like an eel, belching lightning and splitting hulls. Vaazhia laughed upon his back, casting spears of flame at the vessels. Khama was pleased to see that they burned far more easily without the protection of their silver-robes.

The Legions of Uurz and Zyung met in a wave of hammering blades and shields. The Giants ripped diving Trills from the sky or hurled spears to impale them. Now Lyrilan and Sharadza appeared above the battlefield, standing on a platform of solid air. Sharadza swelled to the size of an Uduri and leaped to join Dahrima in tearing through the deep ranks of Manslayers. Khama had not guessed Iardu's apprentice capable of such savage fury. Yet Sharadza had Giantsblood in her veins. To see her wading through a sea of bloodied foes was to understand that she was truly the Daughter of Vod.

A chorus of long, wavering notes rang across the battlefield from a thousand war horns at once. The Manslayer legions, whose vast numbers had already encircled the Uurzian forces, paused and broke away from their foes. The Trills turned back toward the waiting dreadnoughts. The Hordes of Zyung retreated now, as the remnants of Udurum and Uurzian legions had retreated from the Sharrian valley.

Men and Giants rushed to pursue the receding tide of enemies, but now it was Lyrilan's voice that rang across the sky. "Let them flee! There has been enough death this day! We have won!" His magic ensured that every warrior heard and understood his words.

The land battle had not lasted long, and the Uurzian forces had not suffered greatly from it. The legions erupted into cheers at the words of their new Emperor. Khama watched the horde of Zyung-ians streaming toward the hills of smoking rubble and corpses. A million foreign lives and a thousand ships had been lost to the sky-reaping blade of Vireon. As the Manslayers had poured from the few hundred intact dreadnoughts, so they flooded back into them now. The glowing forms of Seraphim floated patiently above the last of the boarding legions.

Vireon no longer towered above the heaps of debris. Alua had also disappeared. Khama imagined them somewhere on the other side of the devastation, sharing a private moment of triumph. Then a pillar of Alua's white flame sprang up and gushed like a torrent across the mounds of bodies and the splintered husks of dreadnoughts. Where the phantom city had stood earlier, there now burned a funeral pyre larger than any in history.

The irony was not lost on Khama: The Zyungians had come to burn Uurz alive, but instead it was their own multitudes of dead who burned.

D'zan sounded his own war horn again. The Uurzians turned away from the rising airships and marched toward their golden city. Floating above the triumphant legions, Khama wondered where the Shaper had gone. Iardu was not among the returning host. Sharadza walked with Dahrima and her spearsisters. The faces of the Uduri were agleam with the thrill of victory, yet the Vodsdaughter's face was grave, her eyes reddened by tears.

Rain and wind had ceased. A bright moon rose over the horizon. Stars glistened as the calm of night fell upon the world.

Lyrilan rode beside D'zan on a steed made of swirling smokes. Perhaps he had learned the art of weaving phantoms from Vaazhia. The lad was a quick student.

Khama flew toward the walls of Uurz, Vaazhia hugging his great neck.

"Does this bold young Emperor have a Queen?" she asked in the rushing wind.

19

The New Seraphim

D ue to the talents of Red Ajithi's piloting, the *Daystar* had avoided Vireon's awesome blade. Like all of the surviving dreadnoughts, the ship had taken to the ground and spilled its legions across the ravaged plain. Now those same legions returned with their battle lust unquenched. The order of retreat had been given by Eshad and spread across the armada by the voice of his sorcery.

There might have been a struggle over who would command the legions now, but Sungui was the tender of the flagship's Ethus Tree, and the *Daystar* was the Queen of the armada. Therefore command fell naturally to Sungui in the absence of Lavanyia, who had remained at the New Holy Mountain. None of the seven hundred transformed Seraphim objected to this. Their minds were still swimming with the ingested power of Zyung and the great revelation of Iardu's heart-essence. As a drop of poison will spread itself throughout an entire bottle of wine or carafe of water, so had the Shaper's salt permeated that of Zyung.

Yet it was a venom sweet as honey and potent as flame.

At the rail of the forward deck Sungui stood between Ianthe and Gammir, watching the Manslayers board the several hundred remaining sky-ships. She sensed Ianthe's brooding discontent long before the Panther revealed it with words. In that same mysterious way, she knew the still contemplation of the High Seraphim as they paced the decks of surrounding vessels. She recognized so much more of *everything* now, in the wake of Iardu's gift.

She knew the confusion of the Lesser Seraphim, who did not understand the retreat any more than the armored legions who obeyed the order. Yet there was relief and fear mingled with the curiosity of the Lesser Ones. The High Seraphim had consumed a third of their own number; however, the Lesser Ones had lost more than half their ranks to the sorcery of Alua and Vireon. The Lesser Seraphim had no idea of the rebel coven's existence until they had witnessed the unthinkable fall of Zyung, and his swift devouring. Yet it was far beyond their power to stop the mutiny, as it was now far beyond them to resist the Eaters of Zyung.

Sungui's sharp eyes scanned the moonlit plain. The true Uurz lay to the south, a mountain of glittering lights rising above shadowed ramparts. Watchfires burned in the windows of its guard towers as the legions of Men and Giants marched through its open gate. By the actions of Iardu, Lyrilan, and their clever allies, the City of Sacred Waters had completely avoided another great slaughter.

"Even now we could turn these dreadnoughts toward the real Uurz," said Ianthe. Her mane rustled like a mantle of white silk in the night wind. "Your legions of Men and sorcerers still outnumber them greatly, Sungui."

Gammir watched Sungui's face for a reaction. He knew that something about her was not the same, but he did not understand the nature of her change. Perhaps he sensed this among all of the High Seraphim. Yet Iardu's gift had not affected the Wolf or the Panther. Possibly they were beyond its reach, as blind cave-creatures are beyond the reach of the sun's glory.

"You already know my answer to that," Sungui said. "I will honor my given word."

"Of course," said Ianthe. "You are anxious to see your homeland again, where you and your cousins will divide Zyung's empire. The Land of the Five Cities is of little consequence with so many other kingdoms awaiting your rule. I understand this. In fact Gammir and I will help you to smash the Living Empire and reforge it in your own image. Then we will return here to reclaim our own lands. After all, we are immortal, and time is of little consequence to us. Let the people of the Five Cities believe us vanquished for a while; we will catch the next generation of Men unawares and take back what is rightfully ours."

Sungui sighed as she watched the ranks of Manslayers file onto the broad decks of ships. At the center of the great circle of dreadnoughts lay the wreckage of half the armada and the bodies of uncounted dead, all withering inside a mountain of white flame. A warm wind blew across the inferno to warm her face, yet there was no smoke rising from this sorcerous pyre. Alua's mystical flame would burn all night, and in the morning there would be no trace of the invaders left upon the spoiled plain. Only a great, leagues-wide circle of charred earth that would grow fertile and green again within a season or two.

She imagined the healthy green stalks of the steppe once more taking root in the black, rich soil. It made her long for the purple plains outside the Holy City. Zyung was dead, consumed into oblivion, but the great land that bore his name lived on.

It *must* live on. It must not burn like these shattered vessels and their crews.

In a moment of outward metamorphosis that strangely mirrored her inner transformation, Sungui shifted toward her male aspect. The silver robe rippled about expanding arms and shoulders. When it was done, he turned to address Ianthe directly.

"I do not think that I – that *we* – shall break apart the Living Empire after all," Sungui said. The minds of the High Seraphim were like the lights of the distant city, gleaming about him with a newfound sense of peace and purpose. He saw them as clearly as any message beacons.

"What?" Ianthe placed a hand on her hip, cocking her splendid head at him.

Gammir growled low in his throat, like a suspicious mongrel.

Sungui crossed his hands behind his back and walked the foredeck to the opposite railing. Panther and Wolf followed him, drawn along by his every word. They ignored his sudden transformation from female to male. It was his mental alteration that concerned them.

They will never understand this illumination. They are incapable of it.

"When we absorbed Zyung's essence, we absorbed also his dream," Sungui said. "His Great Idea. Call it his Wisdom, if that helps you to understand. We spent ages helping to build his great vision of order and peace. Tending the Tree of Empire, he called it. There are millions of people who benefit from the order we have created, perhaps billions. This was an idea born from long ages of chaos, suffering, and war. Zyung sought to end this plague that afflicted humanity." He turned to meet the skeptical faces of his listeners. "For it was the same plague that afflicted us . . . the Old Breed."

Ianthe laughed. "The power of Zyung is intoxicating, and it has made you drunk. Gammir and I have relished its potency as well, yet we did not absorb this dream of which you speak. The absence of Zyung's order – his tyranny to be more accurate – means freedom for those of your kind. Why should you care if this brings chaos to Men, these wretched creatures? Their place is below us, ants beneath the heels of Giants."

"You ate of Zyung's salt as we did," said Sungui, "yet you did not inherit his dream because you never understood it. You cannot. You are too deeply rooted in your own malady. Like Zyung himself, whose entire being was rooted in the empire that he built, you are incapable of change. We are not. And we *have* changed."

Ianthe offered only silence for a moment. Sungui watched the flickering of stars in the black sky. How had he never noticed their sparkling beauty until this moment? The minds of his fellow High Ones shared this thought, as they had come to share so many things since the devouring.

Ianthe smiled and placed her arm about Sungui's broad shoulders. "I see now, Venomous One. You would set yourself above all others as the God-King's replacement. The Almighty Reborn, a whole new High Lord Celestial who will keep the Living Empire alive in your own name instead of Zyung's. And do you expect the rest of your High Seraphim to follow you in this? To worship you as they worshipped Zyung?"

"No," said Sungui. "My fellow Seraphim and I are equals. I would not subjugate them, nor would they accept my subjugation. I am simply a catalyst, an agent of change. Zyung knew this, as he knew so many things. I wonder now if he—"

"Enough!" said Ianthe. Her teeth were bared in a vicious grin, the incisors long and sharp as ivory barbs. "You wished for an end to Zyung's reign, you worked toward this end with my aid, and now you abandon its rewards? Have I wasted my time in serving your cause? I might have taken Zyung's power for myself!"

Sungui tilted his head. "That you could not have done without the aid of the High Seraphim and your own enemies, Lyrilan and Iardu chief among them. Zyung's power was beyond your own. If it had been otherwise, you would not have hidden your subversion from him."

Ianthe withdrew from Sungui. The Panther's narrow eyes were bright with darkness. Gammir leaned against Ianthe from behind, grasping her arm as a child clings to his mother.

"Then all this was for naught?" said Ianthe. "The Living Empire will remain as it was, except ruled by a Council of God-Kings instead of a single one?"

"No," said Sungui. "The Living Empire will remain, yes, but like we Seraphim it will change. Under Zyung it could not do this. Now it shall prosper with new virtues."

"New virtues?"

"An Age of Illumination," said Sungui, "built upon the pillars of compassion, free will, and independent thought, all tempered by the rule of order. The empire preserves the peace, yet it must also preserve the people. Even the lowest of them must be free to walk the path of their own choosing, to worship their own Gods, and sing their own songs. No more slaves. Zyung's greatest mistake was his complete annihilation of freedom. Here in the Five Cities men are free to do as they will, yet their Kings and Emperors keep order and peace alive. The peoples of this land are content, full of joy, and blessed with personal liberty. Still they choose to honor their rulers and serve their kingdoms unto death. This is the true path to the Great Society that Zyung imagined but never perfected. The New Seraphim will not be self-appointed Gods. We shall be Kings and Sages and Healers."

The minds of the New Seraphim gleamed as bright as Alua's white flames across the armada. Sungui knew they all had heard and agreed with his words. This was a shared enlightenment. A transfiguration, and a bond like none other. The path to a glorious future.

"This foolishness was not Zyung's vision," Ianthe said. "He demanded worship and fealty. He ruled with cruelty and ruthless might as the Old Breed have always done."

"Not all of them," said Sungui. "The wisest ones have never done so."

Ianthe simmered, her taloned fists clenching.

"*Iardu . . .* " She said the name as if it were a curse. "The Shaper has reshaped you fools! Now I understand his blood scattered upon the salt of Zyung. You are under his spell even now!"

"No." Sungui stepped close to the Panther. She was beginning to vex him. Yet he had expected this. "Say rather that the long spell of Zyung has been broken by Iardu's sacrifice. His salted heart has permeated our vision, awakened us like cold water poured in the face of a sleeper. He has given us wisdom, an understanding of his own Great Idea, his dream that carved these Five Cities and built this land of wonders. Inside of us the conflicting dreams of Zyung and Iardu have blended into one. The Living Empire will be reborn by this united wisdom, as we ourselves have been. Since you cannot understand this, Panther, bother me no more. You may leave the New Seraphim if you wish. With or without you we sail for home this night."

Sungui turned his back to Ianthe and walked toward the middle deck. He must speak with the captain before the long journey home could begin.

The Panther struck without a sound. She pounced upon Sungui's back and sank her talons into his neck. Gammir in wolf form snapped yellow fangs as Ianthe straddled Sungui and flipped him over to expose vulnerable belly and chest. Ianthe spat a word of power, and suddenly Sungui could neither move nor speak. His connection to the minds of the New Seraphim had been broken, cut from him as easily as sliced threads.

Ianthe peered into his face. She was half woman and half Panther now. Gammir's red wolf-eyes loomed next to hers, which were sharp as black diamonds.

"Now I will drink *your* essence," Ianthe said, panting. "Not through your salt, but through your blood. The poison of Iardu will not harm me. I will take your place at the head of these New Seraphim. They will follow me again as they followed me in this rebellion. I will take these ships and burn this land to ash like the Serpents of old. Then I will rear a throne of white bones in Khyrei and rule a kingdom of the dead from its seat." Her talons dug deeper into Sungui's bleeding flesh. "And when I am done I will come for your Living Empire and tear it to shreds. The dreams of Zyung and Iardu will both die, and only *my* dream will endure. The dream of Blood and Fire and Suffering. The oldest dream of all."

Ianthe's mouth opened wide, and her fangs sank into Sungui's neck. There was little pain, but a great sense of violation. Ianthe sucked greedily upon the open wound she had made, pulling the first glimmers of Sungui's life out in a gush of scarlet fluid. It dribbled from her mouth along her chin and breasts, spotting the golden wood of the deck.

Gammir's fangs sank into Sungui's paralyzed wrist. Now two ragged holes poured out Sungui's lifeblood and soul-essence together. Panther and Wolf suckled at the torn flesh.

Where are my cousins? Where is Eshad, Myrinhama, even Durang-shara? Why do they not rush to save me from these leeches? Where are Captain Ajithi and his soldiers? How can these beasts slay me here in the plain sight of the surrounding armada?

Then the truth of it came to Sungui. Ianthe's magic was hiding her red feast from all those around them, as she had hidden her treachery from Zyung. Nobody on the deck of the *Daystar* saw this feeding, this act of heinous blood magic, nor did anyone else among the legions or the New Seraphim. Ianthe's spell had redirected their eyes and their minds.

How much blood do I have? How much longer until they have swallowed it all?

A sensation of horrid pleasure twisted Sungui's body. He thrashed and moaned, but none would hear it. Now, when he finally saw the beauty of life unfolding into a bright future, Sungui wanted to live more than ever. He had hungered for chaos and glory and bloodletting. Yet now he hungered for life itself, and the chance to make it better. To fulfill the promise of Zyung's imperfect dream by investing it with Iardu's kindness.

Stars dimmed in the upper darkness.

Ianthe drank. Gammir drank.

Sungui withered.

Thunder rocked the decks. The dreadnought trembled in the air. A burst of white light and flames filled Sungui's vision. Two shapes hurtled from the light, colliding with the blood drinkers and tearing them away.

Ianthe screeched while Gammir howled. Their bodies slammed into the forward mast, which rocked the ship again. Four figures, intertwined, fell to the middle deck while soldiers and crewmen rushed away from them. The Panther's spell was broken. Sungui lurched to his feet, still bleeding from neck and wrist. On the scorched deck below the forecastle Vireon grasped Gammir the Wolf by his thick neck. His blonde Queen held the White Panther in a similar deathgrip, white flames dripping from her eyes.

Alua of the Old Breed.

Sungui knew her name because Iardu had known it. The Panther and the Queen wrestled inside a ball of white flame, black claws raking pale skin, bloody fangs gnashing at Alua's face.

Sungui's limbs were numb. He could do little else but watch the conflict.

"Unclean beast!" Alua screamed wrath and flame across the Panther's roaring snout. "Malignant devil! Deceiver! Slayer of

Children! Today you pay for your crimes!" Alua's hands tore at the Panther's snowy pelt, ripping red chunks of flesh from the bone. They burned to ash as she tossed them across the deck.

Vireon said nothing as he wrestled with the Black Wolf. His teeth were gritted, his mighty arms clasped tight about the brute's neck. Gammir was caught fast in the trap of the Giant-King's strength. The Wolf sprouted leathery wings like those of a Trill, flapping desperately. Yet Vireon's weight kept him pinned to the deck. His lupine claws tore at Vireon's chest and legs but could not break the bronze skin.

The New Seraphim began to float across the railings from other ships, gathering about Sungui to watch the spectacle of white flames and dueling enemies. Durangshara raised his hand as if to cast a bolt of deathlight upon all four of them, but Sungui stopped him with a glance. Durangshara lowered the hand, and the Seraphim observed in silence.

The flames burned Ianthe's flesh and charred the deck, but they did not ignite the Ethus wood. Even if they had, the Seraphim could have stopped the burning with a few words. There was little danger to the ship itself, and Sungui understood the justice that had fallen upon Wolf and Panther. Vireon and Alua had suffered much at the hands of these two fiends. This was the moment where the wronged King and Queen would exact their well-deserved recompense.

"You burned me to nothing once before, Ytara!" growled the Panther. "Yet I took refuge in your own belly. Have you learned nothing?"

Ianthe reared up on her hind claws and smashed Alua, who was also Ytara, to the deck. The white flame extinguished itself, except for the fires of Alua's eyes, which burned brighter now. The Panther raked its black talons across her stomach with a splash of crimson. The fanged maw opened wide enough to snap off Alua's head, but her swift hands grabbed the upper and lower jaw. The Panther's fangs hovered a finger's breadth from her face.

"I have learned many things," said Alua. "Including the Bitch of Khyrei's true name."

In that instant the Panther abandoned its attempts to rend Alua's flesh. It tore away from her and sprouted eagle's wings from its back, leaping across the railing toward the night sky. Sungui could almost feel Ianthe's fear from the top of the forecastle steps.

Alua grabbed the Panther's whipping tail and slammed the winged beast against the deck. The dreadnought trembled a third time. Alua's voice rose in a single word loud as a thunderbolt, as if she spoke with the voice of dead Zyung himself. Soldiers and slaves clasped their hands over their ears, so loud was that sound.

Where Ianthe had been scrambling upon the deck, there now stood a statue of opaque crystal in the form of a winged panther. Alua's flame ran along its back, and the frozen wings shattered like panes of glass. Ianthe's essence seethed inside the crystal prison. Alua examined her handiwork as the wounds on her body vanished beneath the power of her flame.

Vireon held the Black Wolf above his head now. The beast erupted with tendrils of darkness like questing black tongues. They wrapped about Vireon's limbs, their thorny tips piercing his flesh where claws and fangs could not. With a great cry of pain and indignation, the Giant-King tore the Wolf's body in half. Scarlet sprayed across the deck, and Gammir's bones cracked like hammered boulders.

The Wolf howled as Vireon stood over its bisected form. The black tendrils faded to smoke and the lupine body parts flowed into the shape of a mangled and broken man. Gammir stared up at Vireon with yellow wolf-eyes that had not changed at all. His maimed arms and legs shuddered, his shattered spine convulsing. A gout of black gore burst from between his lips.

"Brother . . ." gasped Gammir. "Kill me now. You've earned the right."

Vireon grabbed Gammir by the neck and lifted him to dangle like a ruined doll. "I too have learned many things, False Brother," he said. The holes bored into his flesh by the cutting tendrils leaked blood across his stomach and legs. He seemed to feel no pain from these wounds. "I know that you cannot be killed as a Man is killed. You are no longer a Man, but a sorcerer. So are we both now, though spawned by different fathers."

He tossed Gammir's mangled body next to the crystallized Panther. Alua looked upon the wailing Wolf without pity. Vireon walked near and embraced her.

Gammir spat a fresh torrent of blood across the deck. "You will devour us then. Take our essence into yourselves." He smiled through his pain. "There is no other way to end us. I welcome this, Brother. Let me become a part of you, as I was never truly a part of your family. Let me be the memory that will haunt you forever."

"No, Kinslayer," said Vireon. "You murdered my brother and my cousins. The Bitch of Khyrei murdered my father . . . and our daughter. Yet we will not devour you."

"You must!" choked Gammir. "Or we will return, and the killing will begin again."

"There are fates worse than death for immortals," said Alua. "This you will discover, Wolf. You will be bound to your Panther forever."

A fresh blast of the white flame coursed from Alua's eyes. It drowned Gammir's cries along with his shattered body. When the flames faded he, too, was a frozen lump of foggy crystal.

Alua sang an ancient song. Vireon held her left hand as her right dripped molten fires between its fingers. The crystallized pair smoked and steamed and began to merge. In a few swift moments, a single lump of amorphous quartz lay where the Wolf and Panther had been. It was large as a boulder and murky as the waters of a blood-glutted river.

Vireon lifted the boulder of crystal, which darkened now to the color of a purple bruise, or fresh-dried blood. He squeezed it between his mighty hands as if to splinter it, but it did not crack or shatter. It grew smaller instead, and smaller, and smaller still, until it was a single diamond lying in his palm, emitting a residue of sorcerous vapor.

The center of the bright diamond was a drop of crimson.

Sungui saw it clearly, even from atop the foredeck.

The undying spirits of White Panther and Black Wolf had merged – fused like the disparate dreams of Iardu and Zyung – inside a gleaming stone no bigger than a walnut. They would lie entombed in this humble prison until the end of time, unless some great power freed them. Perhaps after a few eons they would become one with the stone, and their living souls would fade into oblivion. Vireon would ensure that the red diamond never saw the light of day again.

Alua took the diamond and sang another ancient song over it, then closed it in her fist. Her eyes met Vireon's, and a moment of understanding passed between them. The two shared a peculiar knowledge, a soul-deep communication that even Sungui's expanded consciousness could not fathom. Perhaps it was that mysterious emotion that Men called *love*. He could not say for certain.

Sungui broke the uncomfortable silence with polite words.

"I thank you for ridding us of these pests," he said. "We also have learned much, though the learning has cost us dearly. So we must depart this land, leaving our dead multitudes to enrich the soil of your plain. We wish only for peace between the two halves of the world."

Vireon and Alua regarded Sungui with keen eyes and stern faces.

"So be it," said Vireon.

A globe of white flame sprang up about the couple. It lifted them into the night and raced like a falling star toward glimmering Uurz.

Sungui turned to the New Seraphim gathered upon the *Daystar*'s deck.

So be it.

The dreadnoughts, full now with Manslayers and Trills, rose into the sky. Wind filled rustling sails, and canvas wings flapped to the rhythms of oarsmen who would soon be slaves no longer. The airships glided east beneath a sea of stars.

In the bloody gold of sunrise the fleet of the New Seraphim entered the valley. A thousand dreadnoughts had remained here, floating like seaborne galleons in the bay with sails and wings furled. A hundred legions of Manslayers were camped across the valley in the shadow of the New Holy Mountain. Orderly rows of canvas tents spread wide from both banks of the Orra, and a new bridge of white stone arced above the river. The delta was no longer stained a deep red; sunbeams gilded the water and danced across the sea.

Lavanyia and her hundred Lesser Ones had been busy. Their spells had sculpted the interior of the temple-palace into twenty-one levels, each with its own set of apartments, pillared halls, galleries, gardens, balconies, terraces, bath chambers, privies, and quarters for a hundred legions of Manslayers. In a few more days they would complete the last of the detail work that must be in place before soldiers and Seraphim could inhabit its airy precincts. Great murals, statues, arabesques, frescoes, and friezes would celebrate the Almighty and his Living Empire. Those who dwelled inside the creation of His Holiness would live in opulence and majesty.

Yet these dedicated sculptors would never finish their great labor.

Sungui pondered the wasted effort of Lavanyia and her charges. It was regrettable, but far less a tragedy than the multitudes of lives lost on both sides of this war. Lavanyia alone had survived the rise of the coven because she was not present at Uurz. She would be the last to choose between loyalty to Zyung or to the New Seraphim. If she resisted this new vision of the empire, then she must be sent to salt. Yet if she chose to join them she had none of Zyung's essence to imbibe. None of Iardu's either. The merged dream, the illumination of her fellow Seraphim, these things would be forever beyond her, no matter what her decision. Unless Sungui found some way to give her that illumination, as Iardu had found a way to give it to them all.

Concern and confusion spread among the encamped legions when they saw less than half of Zyung's dispatched dreadnoughts returning from Uurz. A single day had passed since their departure. This spoke of a quick defeat. Yet the truth was so much more complicated. There had been defeat, that was true, yet there had been a victory as well. That victory belonged to the New Seraphim as much as to the defenders of Uurz. All those who served the empire could be made to understand that in time. But first Sungui must bring that understanding to Lavanyia.

The *Daystar* touched its hull to the water nearest the inland shore of the bay. The hundreds of other surviving dreadnoughts stationed themselves upon the calm sea outside the bay, which was already thick with anchored ships. Like the disembarked legions, those legions aboard the ships grew restless for news of the short Uurzian campaign. It would come soon, but Sungui was in no rush to end their curiosity.

The New Seraphim gathered once more upon the deck of the *Daystar* as the last of the fleet came to rest upon the water. The enlightened ones were seven hundred and twenty in number. Sungui counted them with his mind as they assembled, his eyes unnecessary for the task.

"She comes forth even now," said Eshad. He stood nearest to Sungui on the middle deck. "We will have to send her to salt."

Gulzarr nodded on Sungui's opposite side. "Perhaps not," said the alchemist. "Her loyalty may have perished with Zyung."

Darisha regarded her mate with a half-smile. "Zyung resides within us now," she said. "All of us. If Lavanyia realizes this, it may sway her."

Durangshara shook his round head. "She has always been stubborn. She will call us traitors and choose the salt."

"Only a fool would make that choice," said Eshad.

Brethren.

Sungui's mental plea sent them silent. "I will speak to Lavanyia first. Alone."

Without waiting for their reply, Sungui rose into the sea wind and glided toward Lavanyia, who was flying toward the *Daystar* with a company of twelve Lesser Ones.

"What news?" asked Lavanyia in the air. "You return too soon."

They floated above a forest of masts and sails. Sungui motioned to the Lesser Ones.

"Dismiss them," he said "and I will explain."

Lavanyia's gaze fell to the *Daystar*, where the cluster of New Seraphim stared up at her with an odd serenity. She waved a hand and the Lesser Ones turned in mid-flight, heading back to the nearly complete temple-palace.

"Let us walk the shore," said Sungui. Lavanyia descended with him to the strand of pale sand girding the bay. They strolled there between water and land, armada and mountain, past and future.

The salty breeze was cool against Sungui's skin. He decided to keep his male aspect for this conversation. Lavanyia had always resented the beauty of his female form.

"Where is His Holiness?" asked Lavanyia.

"Gone," said Sungui. Wavelets washed the shore with gentle sighs.

"Do not riddle me," said Lavanyia. "Gone where?"

"Nowhere and everywhere," said Sungui. He stopped, turning to face her. "Gone to salt."

Lavanyia's face went slack as if Sungui had slapped her. She blinked, and a strand of raven hair whipped across her face.

"There has been a coup," said Sungui. No need to be subtle. "We have taken his salt. Shared his essence and his wisdom."

Lavanyia looked toward the *Daystar* again, where the mass of silver-robes stood along the railing, awaiting the answer to a question that had not yet been asked.

"Impossible . . ."

"May I touch your hand?" Sungui asked.

Lavanyia hesitated, but nodded.

Sungui wrapped Lavanyia's fingers in his own, then poured his mind's images into hers. Lavanyia's eyes grew round, then swollen with tears. They streamed down her smooth cheeks. Sungui showed her everything that had happened at Uurz, the battle of sorcerers, the salting, the devouring, the exodus. Yet a mere touch and a handful of visions could not instill the depth of the enlightenment that had transformed the Eaters of Zyung.

Lavanyia fell to her knees on the wet sand. Sungui released her hand.

The last of the High Seraphim glared at Sungui with red rage on her face. "You did this! It's what you've wanted all along! Your hidden ceremonies, your lessons of memory! I should have salted you long ago. You are a traitor. Nothing more!"

"Then so are all of us," said Sungui. "Save you and the three hundred who chose salt instead of revolution."

"So this is the choice that I must make?"

"It is," said Sungui. "But not yet." He grabbed her shoulders and helped her to her feet. She was too weak to resist.

"I would have you walk beside us," he said. "Beside me. Hear my words before you decide."

Lavanyia turned away from him, her eyes scanning the rows of ships. How she must feel as the last of her kind, he could only imagine. Yet more than ever he *could* imagine her feelings. They poured in waves from her eyes and her skin. Sungui had never sensed another's emotions so deeply. This was another of Iardu's gifts, or another facet of the same gift.

His salted heart had taught them empathy.

"Speak," said Lavanyia, her eyes on the blue-green horizon of the sea. She squinted against the sun's brightness.

Sungui explained to her the illumination of the Eaters. The transfiguration of the Seraphim that had altered their immortal selves. The blending of Zyung's and Iardu's dreams. The vision of a Reborn Empire without slaves, tyranny, or conquest. The rise of a new order where free will could flourish and Men could determine their own destinies under the guidance of the New Seraphim. They would not shatter Zyung's empire and abandon his dream. They would improve it, perfect it, replace it with a greater dream, one that served humanity far better than the old one.

Lavanyia listened in silence, and the morning shadows grew smaller.

"As we were Diminished by Zyung, so was Zyung diminished by his creation," Sungui said. "The greater his empire grew, the more it defined him. He was the Conqueror, the Almighty, the High Lord Celestial. Yet he built a vision so powerful that it trapped him within itself. Still the core of his wisdom yearned for what it could no longer have. He longed for change. Yet he could not change, or he would sacrifice everything he had built. He *was* the Living Empire."

Lavanyia turned to face Sungui. "Are you saying that Zyung wanted this to happen?"

Sungui shrugged. "What happens to all empires eventually? Like earthbound trees they rise, grow strong and flourish, but eventually they grow brittle, and entropy claims them like a slow rot. They fall into chaos, which brings war and suffering and the death of peace. All of those terrible things that Zyung built his Living Empire to banish. I believe he knew that his great order must change to survive, as change is the only constant of this universe. Yet how could he change what was an extension of himself, when he was unable to change himself?"

"How can you know all of this?" Lavanyia asked.

"Zyung knew I was going to betray him," said Sungui. "He told me this himself. For centuries he had known about Those Who Remember, and he knew that I led their rites. He could have destroyed me at any time, yet he did not. He told me that the seed of doubt growing in my heart was the test of his Great Idea. He challenged me to see that his wisdom was true. Now, when I feel the last glimmering of his salt inside me, I believe he knew that I would be the one to transform his dream in a way that he could not. I believe he saw at last the wisdom of Iardu's own dream, and regretted that he had not seen it long ago. I believe all of this was meant to happen, Lavanyia. I ask you to believe these things as well."

Lavanyia's thoughts were her own. She brushed the windblown hair back from her eyes.

"I can never be one of you," she said, voice heavy with regret. "For I did not taste his essence with you. I will remain a stranger to this new dream."

Sungui touched Lavanyia's cheek lightly, raised her face to meet his own. "You need not remain so," he said. "If I share my enlightenment with you, if I reshape your heart into that of a New Seraphim, will you come with me across the Outer Sea? If I do this thing, will you help me foster this Age of Illumination?"

Lavanyia regarded Sungui now with fresh eyes. He remained a mystery to her, now more than ever, and he knew that she longed to understand that mystery. Her curiosity was irresistible. She nodded. He smiled.

Sungui drew the black dagger from his inner sleeve. It was the same one that had transfixed poor Mahaavar the Ear not so very long ago. Its edge, tempered by sorcery, was as sharp as any metal could be.

He raised his left hand, fingers spread, holding the dagger in his right fist. Sunlight flashed on the dark blade as it sliced through the smallest finger of his hand. He severed it cleanly at the middle joint. The finger fell in a thin trail of crimson, yet when it landed upon the sand it was no longer flesh and blood.

Sheathing the dagger, Sungui bent and picked up the nugget of salt that had been part of his living body. Instead of blood it dribbled a few loose grains.

"Eat of my salt, Lavanyia," he asked.

She accepted the white nugget from his open palm and raised it to her lips without a word. She paused for only a moment's reflection, then dropped it into her mouth like a grape. She chewed it and the light of wisdom blazed from her eyes.

Sungui ignored the pain of his hand. He conjured a flame to burn the small wound until it closed. The stump of the half-finger was pink and raw, but it would heal.

Lavanyia fell forward, and he caught her. She wept softly, her arms clasped about his neck. They stood this way as seabirds warbled glorious melodies overhead.

White surf washed again and again over the sandy beach.

At last Lavanyia lifted her face close to his and breathed a single word.

"Sungui . . ."

Their lips met, and the heat of understanding passed between them. Sungui's body altered spontaneously, its male and female aspects advancing and receding upon Lavanyia like the waves upon the warm sand.

There was no more salt but that which lay in the sea.

20

Vows

It was the silence of the forest that she loved most of all.

The deep quiet of the glades between the soaring Uygas was not silence at all, if one paid close attention to it. This quietude was a blend of rustling leaves, gurgling waters, singing birds, and the sighing of wind between the branches. Yet after so many months in the cities of Men, and so many nights in the clattering, noisome camps of war, the forest was a golden dream of silence.

The days flowed one into another, a stream of unbroken solitudes. Dahrima hunted the shaggy elk and the tusked pigs of the wilderness whenever she grew hungry. She walked by day beneath the titan trees, rediscovering the hills and grottoes of her youth. Once, while she sat dreaming atop a windswept hill, an eagle landed on her shoulder. It must have mistaken her for a crag of yellow stone. When she turned her head it flew away, yet she saw it later flying above a meadow with the sun at its back.

After the first few weeks she spent most of her time near the Falls of Torrung, where the water plunging into the lake replaced the forest's silence with its own gentle roar. She had come to the falls with her cousin Chygara many times as a girl, hunting the wily tigers that came down from the White Mountains in summer to stalk the elk herds. It had been three centuries since she had seen the place, but it was much the same. A hundred colors of leaf and blossom adorned the cleft hillside and the high cliff beyond it. The great leaves of the Uygas had begun to fall; they floated across the lake in shades of red, yellow, orange, and brown.

At the edge of the lake, at the foot of the ancient falls, she found the peace that had eluded her for so long. She continued roaming the forest, hunting when she felt the call, but always she returned to the sweet thunder of the Torrung. A shallow cave across the lake from the torrent became her sanctuary. She slept there more often than not, on a bed of elk hides and brown reeds.

When the Udvorg had returned to the northlands, she had marched with them across Vod's Pass. Vireon and Alua had ridden upon fine Uurzian steeds at the head of the procession, gifts from the new Emperor of Uurz. Dahrima had not spoken with Vireon since the day he requested that she join the war council, but the promise of his suspended judgment hung over her head during every league of that northward journey. She had never answered for killing Varda of the Keen Eyes, though her spearsisters spoke of it only as a duel of honor. Dahrima herself was no longer sure of the reason for the fight, or the killing. She remembered only the burning rage in her breast and the blue blade of Vireon in the witch's fist. Had she killed Varda to protect Vireon from the witch's influence, or because she was jealous of Varda's closeness to the Giant-King?

Dahrima could not answer that question if Vireon were to ask it. Nor could she answer it in her own heart. Vireon was King of both Uduru and Udvorg now, and he must uphold the laws of the blue-skins. Dahrima's crime had placed him in a precarious position: Pardon her and offend his new people, or punish her and risk losing the loyalty of the remaining Uduri who served his house.

Dahrima knew that she could not bear the chastisement of Vireon, or the loss of her station at his court. So she had done the only thing she could rightly do. When the legion of Men and Giants came down from the pass onto the wide, rolling plain of Uduria, she fled into the night as she had done before. Yet this time she spoke first with her sisters and made them understand. They must stay to serve the King as she could not. She explained her reason, and they grudgingly accepted it. Vantha wanted to come with her, but Dahrima forbade it.

"You have taken the vow," she reminded Vantha. "You must serve Vireon."

"You too have taken the vow," said the Tigress.

"And I have broken it," said Dahrima. "I must be the last one to do so."

Vireon had camped in the shadow of the mountains, within a day's march of Udurum. In the morning they would enter the city gates to cheers and celebrations of victory. Then would come days of memorial services and feasts to honor the fallen Men, Giants, and Uduri who had died for their King. Vireon would bury the red diamond deep in the vaults of his palace. Yet Dahrima would see none of these things.

She ran north while the camp was asleep, and entered the deep forest of the Giantlands well before sunrise. For weeks now she had wandered these wilds alone, regaining the calm that her spirit had lost, and trying to put Vireon's judgment from her mind. She had spared him from a painful decision, and spared herself from humiliation and heartbreak. Yet she had rediscovered the ancient ways of her people, the sweetness of northern rains, the freedom of the untamed woodlands, the scents of bark and leaf and Narill blossoms alive with honey.

The Uygas rising tall in every direction made her feel small as a child again. The walls of moss on their trunks faded from bright green to blue and orange as the summer waned. Beneath their endless canopy of leaves she forgot the bloody slaughters of Khyrein swamp and Sharrian valley.

When winter came full upon the forest, she would find some deeper cave in which to shelter. There would be bears, wolves, and great cats to hunt in the highlands for their thick furs. For now she wore a simple tunic of Uurzian fabric, green as the Stormland grasses, cinched at the waist by a belt of black leather. Her feet were bare against the tufted earth, and she enjoyed the touch of moss and leaf as she walked. Her axe lay forgotten in the shadows of her modest cave, and she carried her longspear when she hunted. There were no enemies to vex her in the forest of Uduria. This, too, she enjoyed.

She was at peace, and completely unprepared, on the day that Vireon found her. She was bathing in the falls when he emerged from between the twisted Uyga roots, his long black hair tangled with leaf and thistle. He wore no crown, but he carried a hunting spear in his fist and a greatsword across his back. He wore his Giant aspect that day, and at first she thought him some lone Uduru huntsman wandered south from the Icelands. She walked from the misty torrent, one arm covering her exposed breasts, the other wringing water from her hair, and saw his face clearly.

"Forgive me," said the Giant-King. He turned away from her like a shy boy who had stumbled upon his first naked girl. "I will wait for you to dress."

Dahrima waded to the lip of her cave and pulled on her tunic and belt. She walked about the rim of the lake to where Vireon sat perched atop a mossy slab. He stared into the evening gloom of the woods. She wondered if he was alone. There was no sign of other Men or Giants. No sign of his fiery Queen either.

Did he track me to this place, or discover it by chance during one of his hunts?

The latter seemed unlikely.

She sank to one knee before him as he turned to face her. He pulled a leather bottle from his belt. "How long has it been since you've had good Uduru ale?" he asked. He offered her the flask. She stood up and drank from it long and deep. It was cold and refreshing, bright on the tongue. She sat on the boulder next to him.

"I am sorry, my lord," she said, her eyes on the purple moss at her feet.

"For what?" asked Vireon. "Drink as much as you want."

"No," she said. "For leaving you. For not returning to Udurum with my sisters. I only wished to . . . spare you a difficult decision. Yet I know that I must answer for my crime."

Vireon sighed. He shed his purple cloak and unlaced the front of his black tunic. "I need a swim," he said. His bare chest and shoulders were unscarred, solid as sculpted bronze. He kept his leggings on but kicked off his boots, then dove into the lake.

Dahrima nursed the ale, finishing half the flask while Vireon swam to the falls and let its chill wash over him. The dirt and bits of foliage were gone from his wet mane when he returned. His hair glittered black as onyx in the sunlight, his eyes blue as midday. He rejoined her on the rock and finished the rest of the ale in a single gulp.

"I love this place," he told her. "I used to stop here on the Long Hunt with my uncle Fangodrim. The sunfish in this lake are fat and tasty."

"I came here with Chygara," she said. "Long, long ago."

She made the sign that honors the remembered dead, and Vireon did the same.

"There are many places like this in the forest," he said. "I'll wager you know more of them than I do, since you hunted here well before I was born. Perhaps you'll show me a few?"

Dahrima forced herself to meet his gaze. "Where is your reborn Queen?" she asked.

Vireon looked toward the falls. Fragments of rainbow glittered there as sunbeams intersected the white flow. "Alua has gone north," he said. "Beyond the Icelands, into the Frozen North. That cold land is her true love."

Dahrima blinked. "But I thought . . ."

"You thought that what I had lost was returned to me," said Vireon. "Or at least part of it. So I thought, too, at first. Yet it was not so."

Dahrima did not quite understand. "You love her. She loves you."

"At one time, yes," said Vireon. "That was true. But our love died with Maelthyn. Or, like our daughter, it was never real. I am no longer certain. Yet together we brought the Claw and the Kinslayer to justice. They will trouble us no more."

"I am sad to hear that you are . . . alone," said Dahrima.

Vireon looked directly at her face. "Do not be," he said. "Alua died and was reborn. I also experienced death of a sort and returned from it. Yet neither of us is the same."

They sat for a while listening to the steady voice of the falls. A fish leaped from the silver lake and splashed back into its depths.

"What of the Udvorg?" Dahrima asked. "Do they demand justice for Varda?"

Vireon shook his head. "Varda should have known better than to take up a sword against a spearmaiden of the Uduri. The Udvorg have mostly returned to their high plateau. All but a hundred or so, who chose to remain in Udurum. I have welcomed them, as I welcome all Men and Giants into the city."

"Why have you followed me here?" Dahrima asked. She held her breath a moment.

Vireon laughed a little and stood up to face her. "You have awaited my judgment for a long time now, Dahrima the Axe. So I have followed you all the way to the Falls of Torrung to deliver it. Are you prepared at last to hear it?"

Dahrima swallowed. She rose to her feet and squared her shoulders. "I will abide by your decision, whatever it may be."

He will pardon me, but I can no longer serve him.

My vow was broken on the coast of the High Realms.

"Then here is my judgment upon you," said Vireon. His eyes locked hers in a steel-bright grip. "I judge that you are loyal and fearless and valiant. A great warrior, a keen hunter, and a born leader of Giants. My fiercest ally, and my best friend. And the most beautiful of all the Uduri."

Dahrima could find no words. The waterfall's roar filled her ears, and the sun's heat filled her face in the dim cool of evening.

Vireon took her hands into his own.

"I grant you pardon for the price of a kiss," he said. "If you will allow it."

She could not move, but her limbs trembled. A flurry of red and golden leaves fell about them as the wind caressed the high branches. At last she nodded.

The beating of her heart drowned the waterfall's song, and his kiss was gentle. She opened her eyes, and his face was still so very close to hers. Uduri were known for choosing their mates with violent passion, yet this tenderness was a new discovery. Now she was the one being chosen. This was not the way of Giants, but of course Vireon was half human. Therein lay his greatness, and his worthiness to rule both races.

"The King of Men and Giants needs a Queen," said Vireon. "I would have you, Dahrima."

She pulled away from him, wrapping her arms about herself. Once again she felt naked before him, although still fully clothed.

"It cannot be," she said. "I bear the Curse of Omagh. Do you forget this? A King must have heirs, and I can give you none."

Vireon walked around to find her face again. "I do not care about that," he said. "I never asked to be King of Udurum. It was my duty when Tadarus died and my mother abdicated. Then again, when Angrid died, another kingship was forced upon me. When the Long-Arm's son has grown of age, I will give him the Udvorg crown. As for Udurum, I am bound by no laws but my own, and I will have no other wife. I will rule alone, and still childless, should you refuse me. You have followed me across a continent. Do not abandon me now to loneliness."

Dahrima looked into the blue of his eyes and saw truth glistening there.

She fell into his arms as he fell into hers.

Together they made a new song to rival the harmony of falling waters.

The marriage ceremony was held in the great hall of Vod's palace, where Men and Giants gathered to see Dahrima replace her old vow with a new one.

Lyrilan came from Uurz with a coterie of green-cloaked noblemen; Vaazhia the Lizardess came with him, arm in arm, a splendor of jewels and gold upon her limbs. Khama the Feathered Serpent arrived alone in his cloak and headdress of crimson plumage.

Vireon's sister brought their mother Shaira home by ship and carriage all the way from Yaskatha. Shaira declared her joy at Vireon's choice. Alua had been a stranger to Shaira, but Dahrima was a long-trusted friend and guardian. The wife of Vod had lost none of her wits as she had grown older. At the banquet it was Shaira who professed the irony of Vireon's path: Vod was born a Giant but took the form of a Man to win Shaira; Vireon was born in the shape of a Man but took the form of a Giant to win

Dahrima. There was much laughter as this observation made the rounds between heavy-laden tables and found its way into the crowded streets.

Two weeks of festivities marked the joining of Vireon and Dahrima. When it was done the visiting dignitaries returned south to resume the business of their own kingdoms. The repelled Armada of Zyung had left a great, unfinished temple-palace in the Sharrian valley. Vireon dispatched a company of Uduru and Udvorg to demolish the abandoned edifice. They hauled blocks of its pale stone back to Udurum for use in public works. From that stone the city's best sculptors crafted effigies of Iardu, Tyro, and Undutu to stand along the Avenue of Idols beside those of Vod and Tadarus.

A contingent of Udvorg brought the son of Angrid south to meet with Vireon. The boy's name was Olgrid, and he was eleven years old. He stood tall as a Man already, but still a third the height of a full-grown Giant. Some of the Udvorg had taken to calling him "Olgrid the Arrow" in honor of his great skill with a hunting bow. Vireon spoke with Olgrid regarding Angrid's bravery and wisdom; the two went on many Long Hunts together. Dahrima saw Vireon begin to think of the blue-skin lad as his own son, and she did as well.

Dahrima found happiness in Vireon's house and in his arms. Yet often she woke late in the night, lying next to him in their great bed, and caressed her flat stomach. She had heard the whispers of palace attendants and advisors; they all spoke of Vireon's lack of an heir. Surely Olgrid, Son of Angrid, would return north when he came of age to wear the Udvorg crown. Udurum would need a new King on that far distant day when Vireon were to pass from the living world. The people of Udurum did not understand that sorcerers were immortal and could not truly die. Yet this misunderstanding did not comfort Dahrima. She thought of her barren womb as an abiding *lack* within herself. Vireon might be immortal, but she was not. So she dreamed of a child born from their honest love.

Dahrima never spoke to Vireon of this matter. Like any Uduri, she bore her sadness in silence. In all other things, she was joyful. In her darkest hours she reminded herself that she was a warrior and a hunter. She did not need to spawn offspring to be whole. Yet the laughter of children running in the courtyards of Udurum was never far from her ears or her heart.

At the end of her first year of marriage she dreamed of the white flame. Inside the dream she lay in the pillared bedchamber next to Vireon, as she did in the waking world. Yet in the dream white flame poured like water from the window casements, spilling across the marble floors and gliding up the columns and walls. Her dreaming eyes opened while her true eyes remained closed. A woman's figure glided through the window like a pale ghost.

The bed now floated upon a sea of white flame, yet there was no heat or smoke. The ghost-woman hung above Dahrima, who could neither move nor speak.

Alua.

Even asleep Dahrima recognized the Mistress of the White Flame whose long blonde tresses flowed and burned upon the silk of the bed. Alua's dark eyes scanned the sleeping face of Vireon, then turned upon Dahrima with a smile both warm and gentle. There was no fear in this dream, only strangeness.

Alua's hands touched Dahrima's cheeks, and the white flame coursed through Dahrima's body like a cool and pleasant wind. It gathered in the space between her hips, churning and burning there with sudden heat. Yet there was no pain.

Dahrima awoke sweating in the dark silence of the bedchamber. There was no trace of flame or sorceress. Vireon's slumber had remained undisturbed. Dahrima laid her face upon his shoulder and returned to sleep. No more dreams came to her that night.

She forgot the dream of white flame until many weeks later, when she discovered her stomach had swollen into a soft yet firm mound. The palace physician, well schooled in the medicine of the Uduru, examined her and confirmed what she already knew.

A child grew in her belly. Nor would it be her last.

There was much rejoicing in the City of Men and Giants.

21

Vengeance

For thirteen days Mendices languished in a dank cell beneath the Uurzian palace. His titles had been stripped, his estate emptied, and his children had fled for the southern cities. There was no way to predict how deep the Scholar King's wrath would run, so in the days before his arrest Mendices had made certain that his progeny were far away. Yet he refused to run from the city he had once helped Tyro rule. He had served his rightful King faithfully, and his reward was a set of rusted chains upon his limbs.

On the third morning after the siege Lord Undroth had arrived from Yaskatha and officially replaced Mendices as Warlord of Uurz. That same day Lyrilan sent a squad of spearmen to take Mendices into custody. A nameless official informed Mendices that he must await Lyrilan's judgment in the dungeon. Mendices neither protested nor begged for mercy. He would not give Lyrilan the satisfaction. So the scholar had learned a few magic tricks from some ancient text of sorcery. That did not make him a suitable Emperor of the Stormlands. Yet with Tyro dead, there was no other choice.

The guards fed Mendices well during his incarceration. The ale was bitter and the bread was stale, but the red meat was well cooked, and there were fruits and cheeses to accompany it. The groans and pleas of other prisoners along the row of iron-barred cells had ceased to bother him after the first three days. Later he realized that this was because Lyrilan had ordered them all released. Most were political prisoners who had spoken out against Tyro's reign. Now they would fawn over the Scholar King and return to life in the city above. Mendices wondered if he would ever get that same mercy. Yet he thought it more likely that Lyrilan would take his head in payment for the death of Ramiyah.

Tyro and Talondra were gone, so there was no one left for Lyrilan to take revenge upon but Mendices. Surely the Scholar King did not know how integral Mendices had been to the plot that had murdered his wife and seen him banished as a madman from his own father's palace. Yet Mendices had always stood high in Tyro's favor; when the Twin Kings had divided the city into factions, Mendices had led the Gold Legions in Tyro's name. That alone was enough to damn him in Lyrilan's eyes.

If the Scholar King was going to sentence him to death, Mendices wished it would come sooner rather than later. Yet Lyrilan obviously wanted to break his spirit, to weary him with imprisonment and humiliation. Perhaps they would soon turn to starving him as well. Anything to make him grovel for a pardon, something Mendices would never do.

When the door of the cell swung open on the thirteenth night, Mendices expected to see that the headsman had come for him at last. He blinked against the torchlight flooding into the black cubicle. A figure in dark robes stood in the open doorway with torch and keys in hand.

"Lord Mendices," said a smooth voice. "Come with me." The man pulled back his hood to reveal a handsome face. He was middle-aged, and his features spoke of Uurzian blood. His dark hair was oiled slick and his beard was tied into six braids secured with gold rings. Jewels glittered on his fingers, and he wore the gilded sandals of a highborn lord.

Mendices staggered to his feet. His legs were weak from lack of exercise; the cell's ceiling was too low to allow for more than a standing crouch. He did not recognize the visitor at all, but it did not matter if he was executioner or liberator. Any chance to leave the cubicle, even if it meant walking to his death, was preferable to lingering a moment longer among the filthy straw and rat droppings. The stranger dropped the keys into a pouch at his belt. He offered Mendices an arm to steady himself.

"Who are you?" Mendices asked. He became suddenly aware that his beard and hair were matted and overlong, his nobleman's robes reeking and stained.

"Consider me a friend of the late Sword King," said the stranger. "One who was as dedicated to his cause as yourself. I come with a message from Lord Aeldryn, who fled the city upon your arrest. You may call me Thaxus."

Aeldryn? If that one had fled the city, then Mendices knew the lords Rolfus and Dorocles must have absconded as well. Along with Mendices they had been the chief captains of Tyro's Gold Legions. Now they were scattered, flying far from Lyrilan's vengeance.

Thaxus helped Mendices walk the corridor of raw stone past the rows of empty cells on either side. "Lord Aeldryn's message is this," said Thaxus, clearing his throat. "'*Hail, Mendices, my Brother of the Gold. I cannot aid you directly. Yet the wizard Thaxus is beholden to me and will serve you well. The future of our noble cause will soon lie in your hand. Follow Thaxus now and trust in my word.*' That is all."

Mendices saw that he had only two choices: Trust Aeldryn via Thaxus, or return to the miserable cell and wait for a death that might be far too long in coming. It was no choice at all.

"Where are you taking me?" Mendices asked. Thaxus led him by the elbow up the stairs at the end of the corridor. Here the smells of human waste and suffering were replaced by the scents of deep earth and ancient stone. Somewhere above lay the splendor of the palace halls.

"Heed the words of Aeldryn and have faith in me," said Thaxus. Mendices asked him no more questions. Soon the prisoner was able to walk on his own, and the stairs had brought them to an intersection of subterranean passages. Mendices followed Thaxus into a labyrinth of corridors, stairwells, and vaulted chambers of granite with little decoration. In a short time he was lost in the catacombs, and only regained his sense of direction when they reached the threshold of the royal crypts. Thaxus' torch guttered, shedding orange light across wall niches filled with sarcophagi and tomb-galleries where generations of royal corpses slumbered beneath the golden lids of a thousand coffins. The smell of ancient rot filled the dusty air.

Thaxus led him into the lowest levels of the crypts, where the most ancient of skeletons had fallen from their niches and mildewed sarcophagi had long ago vomited up piles of bones. Hollow-eyed skulls watched Mendices, and the walls were crusted with nitre, the ceiling sharp with dripping stalactites.

There must be some hidden exit in this forsaken maze of death.

Mendices followed his guide without question. At last Thaxus paused before a great door of black stone. Its edges had been sealed centuries ago, and runes of ancient power were carved across its obsidian face. Despite the portal's impassable appearance, Thaxus waved a hand before it and uttered a few words, causing it to swing open with a gravelly groan. The ceiling trembled, raining dust and cobwebs. Mendices coughed and followed Thaxus into the musty chamber beyond.

The tomb was an oval room with a flat floor and ceiling. A single sarcophagus of white stone sat on a pedestal at its center, carven into the life-sized image of an armored warrior in repose. The dust of ages lay about the place, and the coffin was adorned with inset rubies, emeralds, and purple agates. A tomb-robber's dream, this forgotten sepulcher. Yet Mendices' eyes were drawn instantly from the jeweled sarcophagus toward the room's true treasure.

It lay horizontally upon a double-pronged stand at the head of the coffin. A longblade of ancient make, sheathed in a scabbard of scaly black Serpent-skin encrusted with gray pearls. The sword's iron handle had been dipped in gold, its pommel shaped into an eagle's talon clutching a great fire opal.

Thaxus walked near to the blade but did not touch it. He faced Mendices and held his glowing torch above the sword. "Behold: *Earthfang*, the Blade of Gyron the Protector, greatest warrior of the First Century."

Mendices leaned in close to examine the superb hilt. The dust and spiderwebs of ages lay upon it, yet they did nothing to dim its brightness. He ran a trembling finger along the edge of the sarcophagus. "Gyron . . . " he repeated the name. "This tomb was built in the Age of Heroes. Fifteen hundred years ago."

"Nineteen hundred," said Thaxus. "And it has lain undisturbed since Gyron's death. How well do you know your legends, Mendices? Do you know this blade?"

Mendices shook his head. "I know that Gyron was a slayer of sorcerers. A knight in service to the Third King of Uurz. In the end it was no sorcery that laid him low, but the treachery of his own men who were jealous of his fame."

"I have not led you here to admire the bones of this great hero," said Thaxus, "but to claim his blade. If you would have it."

Mendices looked into the shadowy face of Thaxus. The wizard looked like any normal highborn man; there was nothing of the sorcerer about him. Mendices was certain that he had never seen Thaxus before, but that was not unusual in a city the size of Uurz, where thousands of highborn inhabited hundreds of broad estates.

Thaxus was likely not a true sorcerer, but a magician who had found a modicum of power in ancient texts. Most of his kind were frauds, yet Lyrilan had gained his own very real power in this way. Perhaps Thaxus was more than he appeared. Certainly he had enough power to gain Aeldryn's trust. And there were no other allies looking to aid Mendices.

"The weapon is valuable, I have no doubt of that," Mendices said. "Would you have me rob this tomb to pay for my escape from Uurz? I will die before I flee, wizard."

Thaxus smiled. "You misunderstand Aeldryn's message," he said, "and the import of this relic. We, the followers of Tyro's dream, expect far more from you than simple escape. This sword was forged long ago by a sorcerer friendly to Men. Some say it was the work of the Shaper himself. The warrior who wields it stands immune to even the deadliest sorcery. Surely you understand that Lyrilan is a true sorcerer now. If you were to oppose him with an earthly blade, you would stand no chance. But with *Earthfang* in your fist, the Scholar King cannot harm you. Nor can any other sorcerer. How do you think the great Gyron managed to slay so many of them? It was the power inside this blade that protected him. Now it falls to you, Mendices. You can take the head of Lyrilan with this blade."

Mendices stared at the sword, only half believing what he heard.

"If you have not the stomach for avenging Tyro's death, I can lead you from the palace. You may begin a new life as a commoner in some distant kingdom. I hear Yaskatha is lovely this time of year. What I offer you this day is a choice . . . "

Thaxus took a heavy pouch from his robe and held it in his palm. "Take this gold from Aeldryn and use it to flee the Stormlands. Or take this blade and use it to slay the Emperor of Uurz. If you choose the latter, certain of those once loyal to the Gold Legions will rally to your side. They may even choose you as the next Emperor."

Mendices was reluctant to lift the blade from its stand. "What have you to gain from this conspiracy, wizard? Exactly how are you beholden to Aeldryn? You could take this blade yourself and overthrow Lyrilan without me."

Thaxus smiled. "First, I am no swordsman. I have not the skill or the honor to wield such a weapon. Second, I could never get close to Lyrilan. But you, as the former Warlord of Uurz, have friends among the legions, and even among the palace guards. If you ask, they will disguise you, bring you close to the throne, and rise up with you. Of this I am certain, as is Aeldryn. Yet the final decision is yours. If you choose to leave this blade lying here with the bones of mighty Gyron, then the Scholar King will remain Emperor until his dying day, which will be long in coming."

Still, Mendices hesitated. He thought of his three children, scattered across the southern realms. They would never be able to return to the land of their birth. Not while Lyrilan sat upon the throne. Tyro, who was like a son to Mendices, might have been killed by Lyrilan's own sorcery in the midst of battle, yet there was no proof of it. Mendices was certain that Talondra had been killed by Lyrilan's magic.

"Choose," said Thaxus. He stroked the braids of his beard with nervous fingers.

Mendices wrapped the fingers of his left hand about the scabbard, and those of his right hand about the sword's grip. It was cold as ice against his skin. He pulled the weapon from its sheath with a metallic sigh. The fire opal gleamed in the torchlight, and the black iron blade glimmered as sharp as the day it had been forged.

The words of Aeldryn's message rang in Mendices' head.

The future of our cause will soon lie in your hand.

"I choose *Earthfang*," Mendices told the wizard. "And vengeance for Tyro."

Thaxus smiled and offered a small bow. He led Mendices out

of the deep crypts into a cold night heavy with rain. Mendices turned to offer his thanks, but Thaxus was already gone.

The palace gardens were dark beneath the storm. Mendices knew exactly where to seek refuge among the quarters of the soldiers who had so recently served him. He carried the Blade of Gyron like a terrible secret, one that would soon avenge Tyro's death and free Uurz from the bondage of its Scholar King.

Two weeks after his great victory, Lyrilan greeted the ambassador from New Khyrei in the Grand Hall. The celebrations were long ceased by that time, and the priests had officially ordained him as Emperor of Uurz. The City of Wine and Song was once again living up to its name. The multitudes hailed Lyrilan when he went among them on a palanquin chair, or rode upon a steed hung with golden mail. He kept a high profile in the first few days of his reign. The people needed to know that the Scholar King had won his feud with the hawks of Tyro, and that the city itself was safe from invaders.

Each day brought golden sun and silver rain to the city, and Lyrilan was glad to be back in his own land. How he had missed the bright spires and gardens, the minstrels and orchards, the simple folk that called him their own. He gave three speeches, all proclaiming peace and promising prosperity. He would do his best to keep both pledges, and he was confident in his power to do so. He visited the tomb of Ramiyah with a fresh bouquet of flowers at each sunrise, yet the pain of losing her had faded to a distant ache in the back of his skull.

It had nearly ruined him, yes, but he had found wisdom, strength, and salvation in the *Books of Imvek the Silent*. There he found also the means for vengeance, and a return to the throne that was stolen from him by his brother. He had accepted that the one thing his newfound powers could never return to him was

Ramiyah. When he had acknowledged that fact – and it was much easier once the scales were balanced by Talondra's death – he found himself capable of a far greater understanding. Discovering the true names of the Old Breed in Imvek's final volume had changed everything.

Lyrilan would make sure that Imvek's hard-won knowledge was preserved, never again lost to his people. It was the only power that would keep Uurz from falling prey to the dark whims of the original masters of sorcery. These ancient beings were fonts of untold power, and to master it was to master the Old Breed themselves. Yet contending with the Old Breed was something only to be done in the face of extreme desperation. It was far wiser for Men to make allies of them.

The threat of Zyung was gone, as was that of Khyrei. Lyrilan would not call his present mood one of happiness, but it was close enough to contentment. By joining with Iardu and the other sorcerers to face down the God-King, he had found an unexpected blessing in the company of Vaazhia. The lizardess could never replace Ramiyah. There were none in the living world who could do that. Yet he found Vaazhia fascinating, alluring, and ultimately irresistible.

Vaazhia told him stories of the Ancient World, calling up her memories like lost jewels plucked from the murky sea-bottom. Already Lyrilan had conceived the title of his next book: *Chronicles of the Old Breed*. He had learned many of their secrets from Imvek, and he would learn the rest from Vaazhia. When he was not enjoying one of her spellbinding narrations, he was relishing the splendidness of her lithe body. She was the first woman he had lain with since Ramiyah. Undroth and Volomses had returned from Yaskatha, and both of them approved his dalliance with the lizardess, although they did not quite understand it. Upon their advice he had refrained from appearing with Vaazhia in public, but he would not keep the relationship a secret for much longer. Her strange beauty thrilled him, and he disliked keeping it hidden. Yet there were more important considerations that needed tending before the revelation of his new consort.

Today was a banquet for the Khyrein ambassador, the first to visit Uurz in a century. The slave revolt in that kingdom had brought sweeping changes and a new King who, by all accounts, was a brave and honest man. As a former slave Tong the Avenger was bent on reforming the black city and restructuring its every institution. Never had there been a better time to forge a lasting treaty of peace and cooperation between Uurz and Khyrei.

Lyrilan wore the crown of gold and emeralds as he sat patient and silent upon the throne. The bronze statue of his father looked upon him from between the pillars. He had ordered it moved from the Plaza of Great Ones into the Grand Hall five days ago, so he would be reminded of Dairon's wisdom whenever he sat in the high seat. A statue of Tyro was being erected in the Plaza even now, and it would stay there. Lyrilan would not trouble himself to look upon it. Not for a great while at least.

Sixty spearmen in green-gold corslets and winged helms stood in a double line across the center of the hall. Behind them lingered the usual crowds of courtiers and highborns who perpetually filled the palace. Undroth and Volomses, whose titles had been elevated to that of Warlord and Royal Vizier, stood to either side of the throne. Upon a flower-decked balcony twelve minstrels played a symphony of welcome to honor the Khyrein representative.

Hu Yuan, Hand of the Avenger, Envoy of New Khyrei, entered the hall with a modest retinue of servants as a herald announced his titles. Hu Yuan's robes were crimson and black, trimmed with silver thread, and his almond eyes were dark and keen. His sable hair was tied into a topknot above his head, with a single braid falling the length of his back. His presence might have been menacing but for the pleasant smile on his face. He carried a golden coffer in his hands, a gift for the Emperor of Uurz.

Lyrilan marveled at the man's distinct beauty, for he had seen few living Khyreins up close. Hu Yuan's skin was pale as milk, a striking contrast with his black hair and eyes.

He bowed low and greeted Lyrilan in the common tongue of the Five Cities with a perfect accent. "Great Emperor of the Stormlands, Scholar King of Uurz, Lord of the Sacred Waters, Son of Dairon. This one brings you greetings from the High King of New Khyrei, His Majesty Tong the Avenger. He offers you peace, friendship, and brotherhood."

Lyrilan returned the envoy's smile. "You are most welcome here, Hu Yuan," he said. "Long have I awaited the day when such a message would arrive from the black city."

Hu Yuan lifted the golden coffer. "This one brings also a gift from his King for the Emperor of the Stormlands." One of the envoy's attendants stepped forward to unlock and open the coffer lid. Hu Yuan dropped to one knee, offering Lyrilan a clear view into the box. Precious stones in seven colors sparkled there like frozen flames.

Volomses came down the steps to accept the coffer for Lyrilan. Such a splendid gift was common as the first step in reaching any accord between monarchs. It was a good beginning.

As Volomses took the coffer into his bony fingers, the Uurzian guards on either side of the envoy rushed forward. At first Lyrilan thought they meant to slay his guest, but in the next second he realized they were rushing the dais, not the ambassador. One of their armored shoulders collided with Volomses and sent him tumbling. The box of jewels spilled its contents across the floor of polished marble.

A spearman rushed at Undroth, and two more lunged at the guards stationed directly behind the throne. A fourth man had dropped his spear to unsheathe a dark longblade. A great fire opal flashed on its pommel. As the swordsman leaped up the steps toward the throne, other spearmen behind him turned to strike at their brothers.

Lyrilan saw the face of Mendices beneath the visor of the winged helm. The long nose and heavy brows were unmistakable. The clangor of spears against shields filled the air, and the death grunts of impaled men. The Khyrein envoy and his attendants cowered at the foot of the dais. They were caught helpless in the middle of this sudden coup.

Undroth turned a spear-thrust from his belly with the blade of his broadsword. The dais guards engaged the two men charging at them. Mendices stepped between them all and thrust his blade at the Emperor's heart.

Yet the Blade of Gyron never reached Lyrilan's breast. Mendices drove his arm forward in a strike both straight and true, but his sword had become a pale vapor rising from his fist and fading into nothingness.

Lyrilan smiled at the empty-handed assassin. "You made the wrong choice," he said.

Mendices' eyes grew round as Lyrilan breathed another, less identifiable series of words into his face. He shivered and fell at the Scholar King's feet, a bag of splintered bones and torn flesh. A small cry escaped his lips, and twin streams of crimson spilled from his mouth to run along his cheeks. The winged helm fell from his head.

Undroth struck down the rebel accosting him, sinking his broadsword deep into the man's skull. The dais defenders drove their foes backward with clever spear-thrusts, down to the bottom of the polished steps, where they impaled them almost at once. Only the most skilled of spearmen were selected to stand this close to the throne, and here was evidence of their worth.

Between the avenue of pillars, the remaining rebels were being cut down. Some attempted to flee when they saw the coup had failed. More guards rushed into the hall and skewered them without mercy. In all, fifteen rebels were killed in a matter of moments, with only three of Lyrilan's loyal spearmen lost. Somehow, Mendices had persuaded fifteen men to join his foolish vendetta. The former Warlord lay still alive, yet broken and dying, at the foot of the throne.

Lyrilan sighed. "I gave you a choice, Mendices," he said. "You could have taken the gold and fled my city. Yet instead you took the blade."

Mendices shook his head, spitting blood instead of questions. Yet the questions leaped from his eyes, bright as needles.

A tapestry behind the throne rippled, and Thaxus the Wizard stepped from behind it. He walked to the throne and stood silent at Lyrilan's side. The victorious guards were helping Volomses and the Khyrein ambassador to their feet. The minstrels had ceased playing when the fighting began, but now they started up again as a crowd of relieved courtiers streamed back into the hall.

Lyrilan observed the figure of Thaxus shifting and swirling like a pillar of gray smokes at his elbow, until it coalesced into its true form. Vaazhia leaned against the arm of the throne, her scaled skin bright as the scattered jewels of Khyrei. She lowered her horned head to kiss Lyrilan's lips. The eyes of Mendices rolled backward in their sockets, and he writhed like a dying viper.

"I would have liked to ask what part you played in the murder of Ramiyah," Lyrilan said to him. "Yet upon further reflection I decided that it was not important. You were only doing the work of my brother and his Sharrian witch. Both of them have paid for their crimes. So I gave you the choice to live in peace or die in hate. The enchanted blade, like Thaxus himself, was never real. And if it had been, it still would not have protected you."

Mendices tried to raise a hand, but the shattered bones of his arm would not allow it. His tongue bulged black and swollen from red-stained lips.

"I suppose I owe you my thanks," said Lyrilan. "For here now lie fifteen more traitors who would have lurked among my court until they saw a chance to betray me. I will no longer have to worry about them. Or you. Know that your death has served the Emperor of Uurz in this way."

Lyrilan apologized to the Khyreins, who were unharmed yet shaken. He led them into the garden for a discussion of the great treaty to be signed the following day. Later that evening he walked with Vaazhia across a high terrace, and there he saw the heads of Mendices and the fifteen rebels spiked along the palace wall. Their slack faces were turned toward the streets beyond, where all who entered the royal precinct could witness the fate of traitors.

In the weeks that followed, the people of Uurz stopped referring to Lyrilan as the Scholar King. A new sobriquet had grown to fit him: Lyrilan the Ruthless. Yet at the same time they called him also the Peace Bringer. He had gladly signed the first treaty with Khyrei in all of Uurzian history. During the celebration of that agreement, which fell upon same day as the annual Festival of Ascension, he finally unveiled his new consort to the masses. Vaazhia rode beside him through the roaring streets, her limbs bright with jewels, her horns and hair thick with garlands. A shower of white blossoms cascaded from the walls and towers.

When the festivities ended, Lyrilan returned to working on his new book. Vaazhia told him many spectacular truths long forgotten by mankind. Many of these he recorded in *Chronicles of the Old Breed*, but many of them he did not.

Sorcerers, like Emperors, must keep some secrets.

22

The Truth

Above the rolling swells of the Cryptic Sea the sky was blue and cloudless. There had been no inclement weather or large waves, nothing to make the journey taxing. Yet D'zan stood at the railing of the *Cointosser* and wished he were back on solid ground. Visions of his fleet's destruction plagued him when he tried to sleep, and ever since he had begun this voyage the dreams invaded his waking hours as well.

The many wounds he had endured were entirely healed and had left no scars. Examining his healthy physique in a mirror reminded him that he was no longer fully human. His unblemished flesh was a construction born of sorcery, and after eight years of ignorance he finally understood what that meant. Only his mind and spirit remained unchanged, both of them trapped inside a body that would not age or die. This should have brought him comfort, as most men fear death above all other enemies. Yet so many things which should have made him content failed to do so these days.

D'zan stared at the sunlight broken into flashing diamonds atop the water. The *Cointosser* was a fat-hulled merchant trader with a single sail, less than half the size of a Yaskathan warship.

Yet there were no more Yaskathan warships to carry him north-ward. His own folly had lost every last one of them, along with every member of his royal navy. Yaskatha's treasury would not support the building of another fleet, not without several years of robust trading and exports to fill the coffers with tax revenues. So his closest advisors had informed D'zan on his return from the siege of Uurz. The great harbor of Yaskatha was filled now with merchant ships like this one, the only vessels remaining to serve the realm's interests.

"Perhaps I should avoid building another fleet," D'zan had told Cymetha. "If there is no fleet of warships, there will be no war upon the sea. If I build another fleet, some King who comes after me might commit the same crime of which I am guilty."

His Second Wife, who had become his First Wife in all but name, soothed his pain with kind words and the pleasure of her skilled touch. "You acted honorably," Cymetha reminded him, "and honored our long treaty with Mumbaza. You sought to end the ancient threat of Khyrei. How could you or anyone know that these strange invaders would overwhelm your fleet and that of Undutu as well? I have thanked the Sea God many times that the Feathered Serpent was there to save you. Be glad that you have returned alive and wiser, and that you have a healthy son to carry on your bloodline. The Four Gods returned you to us because Theskalus needs you. He will be a great King someday like his father."

Yes, Theskalus.

Another miracle that should have brought D'zan happiness. Yet when he had returned home to meet his three-month-old son for the first time, when he held the infant in his arms, he had felt only suspicion. He saw none of himself in the child's face. The baby's eyes were blue, yet D'zan had been born with his father's dark eyes. His grandfather had shared those same black pupils. The eyes of his sorcery-built body were green, but that color was only a reflection of Sharadza's power. If Theskalus was the product of D'zan's loins, he should be dark of eye. Cymetha's own eyes were dark as well. Perhaps some blue eye color lay in her family tree somewhere, but D'zan did not ask. He did not want her to know of his suspicion.

The baby was handsome and healthy, but his hair was also dark. D'zan and Cymetha both possessed hair as yellow as ripe corn. D'zan had no dark hair at all in his family, unless it had been so many generations ago that it had been forgotten. All of his living relatives were slain by Elhathym when the necromancer murdered Trimesqua and stole the throne of Yaskatha. In gaining back his dead father's kingdom, D'zan had been forced to surrender his very humanity. Only recently had he realized the cost of that victory.

He loved Sharadza, but she had given him no child. So he had turned to Cymetha. Within months his mistress had grown heavy with child. Sharadza had fled, unwilling to share her husband, even for the sake of royal heirs. Yet now D'zan wondered, not for the first time, if his own seed was barren instead of his First Wife's womb. He had asked Iardu that very question at Uurz, when the Shaper was explaining the truth of D'zan's enchanted body.

You need not fear, the Shaper had told him. *Your son will be fine.*

D'zan believed those words at the time, yet upon his return to Yaskatha they had lingered in his mind. Every time he looked at the round, soft face of his infant son, they rang in his head again. Had Iardu lied? Had Sharadza done the same? It would be just like her to bear the secret of his impotency and take the blame for it upon herself. She was always one to put the welfare of others before her own interests.

Is this truly my son?

The question haunted D'zan even more than the nightmares of his shattered fleet. For three months he sat above the royal court conducting the affairs of state, and he returned to Cymetha and Theskalus every evening. Peace had once again fallen upon Yaskatha. There were rich harvests to swell the pockets of the people and the holds of trading vessels. The merchant houses had actually benefitted from the demise of the royal fleet; the King had no more ships of his own to send on trading missions, so the merchant fleets took up the slack. The Jade Isles were constructing a new capital to replace the one sunk by Zyung's wrath, so Yaskatha had replaced Ongthaia as the central hub of trading among the Five Cities. There was also the newly opened trade with Khyrei, a business which turned minor investors into wealthy men as their ships came in loaded with goods from the black city.

The nation prospered while D'zan brooded.

On the day that Theskalus turned six months old, the King of Yaskatha decided that he could no longer suffer the pain of his own doubt. If D'zan was ever to love his son as a father should – if he was ever to trust Cymetha as a husband must – then he must discover the truth. If Theskalus was a bastard, he would never be heir to the throne. And if D'zan was truly incapable of fathering children, then he would never have a blood heir.

I owe it to my son to find this truth.

D'zan announced his intention, though not its true reason, during a court assembly.

"My mind is troubled by dark dreams and bloodstained memories," he said. The rouged faces of courtiers, advisors, and attendants looked upon him with concern. "In order to find the peace that eludes me, I must speak again with Iardu the Shaper. Although I would rather not sail the unforgiving sea again, I must seek the wizard on his lonely isle. Until I do so, I will know neither peace nor rest."

He expected a deluge of objections, but the court was silent.

The merchant lords in their gaudy robes and jewels avoided his gaze. They knew what he would ask next.

"Since I have no royal ships left," D'zan said, "I require a merchant vessel and its crew for this voyage. I will pay handsomely any sea lord who volunteers. You will also have the glory of serving your King and the interests of the realm."

There was silence between the tapestries decorating the throne room walls.

The graybeard Metricus, who served as Master of Coin for the King, leaned close to whisper in D'zan's ear. "Majesty, you will find it difficult to convince any of the merchant houses to offer up their vessels. This is the busiest of trading seasons after all. And there are other factors as well."

"What other factors?" D'zan asked.

"Forgive me, my King," said Metricus, "but there is a rumor that the Sea God's curse lies upon your house. No other King in our history has lost an entire fleet. Naturally I, myself, do not believe such nonsense, but these merchants are prey to many superstitions. Lastly, it is well known that the Isle of Iardu is protected by sorcery that manifests as a ring of perpetual storms to drive away continental ships. Many men have died while seeking the Shaper's favor."

D'zan leaned his head against the cushioned back of his throne. "So fear and superstition rule the hearts of Yaskatha's nobles." He said it loud enough so that all in the hall could hear him. "If the Sea God's curse lies upon me, then why did he spare me at the Battle of the Jades?"

None of the assembled nobles would dare to answer this question.

"I will pay fourteen chests of gold to the lord who lends me a ship," D'zan said. "Consider this offer as you dine at my table and enjoy the pleasures of my court this evening."

D'zan left the throne and the fawning courtiers, choosing to take his supper on a balcony overlooking the harbor. Sharadza used to sit with him on this same terrace. The young couple had watched the moon rise many times from this perch. Lyrilan had sat here drinking with D'zan during his brief exile. Both D'zan's first love and his best friend were far from him now.

Surrounded by a palace full of people, D'zan was alone.

In the early morning a servant roused him while Cymetha and the baby were still asleep. It seemed that a young merchant lord had come forth to accept the King's generous offer. D'zan dressed himself in a tunic of silver and sable, donned the lightest of his three crowns, and met the merchant in his private study.

Lord Andolon of House Silver was at least two years younger than D'zan, who was still a young King at the age of twenty-four. Andolon was a slim youth with angular shoulders, bright eyes, and a strong chin. His black mustache was neatly trimmed and oiled, and he wore rich fabrics done in a simple style. A necklace of silver links marked the sign of his wealthy and well-reputed house. His father had died only recently, leaving tremendous wealth and status to his eldest son. Andolon's five younger brothers sailed the finest vessels in their house's fleet. D'zan could tell Andolon was also a swordsman by the thickness of his arms and the way he carried himself. The longblade on his hip with its ornate handle might have been worn by any merchant nobleman, but here was a man who knew how to wield such a blade. This was a rare skill among the elite of tradesmen.

After formal introductions, Andolon spoke with candor and grace. "My Lord, I am ashamed of the cowardice displayed by my fellow merchants," he said. "I offer you my house's proudest vessel, the *Cointosser*, and the service of its best and boldest captain, that noble personage being myself."

D'zan smiled. "My gold has swayed you."

Andolon cocked his head. The oiled ringlets of his hair hung below his shoulders. "I will accept no payment, Majesty," he said. "It is my duty to serve you, and in so doing to prove that Yaskathans are not afraid of the sea or its mysteries. My father served your own in the wars of the Southern Isles. It was the abiding pride of his life. I can do no less."

You are lucky that you did not serve me when I sailed to the Jade Isles.

"I accept your kind offer," said D'zan, "and I commend your bravery."

The very next day the *Cointosser* had departed. Cymetha tried to talk D'zan out of making the voyage, and little Theskalus cried the whole morning. D'zan could not explain himself to his wife. Not yet. He simply asked Cymetha to trust him. He kissed the infant on its forehead before leaving the palace.

The *Cointosser* was manned by thirty men, including Andolon, who was its captain. D'zan brought a company of twelve palace guardsmen along, at the insistence of his advisors. The bright sails of the merchant fleets in the harbor grew tiny as the *Cointosser* took to the open sea. On the ninth day they passed the pearly cliffs of Mumbaza, whose harbor sat nearly empty of swanships. Perhaps a dozen of the white ships had remained behind when most had sailed to make war under Undutu's banner. D'zan had considered leaving a few of his own ships in Yaskatha when he had joined the swan fleet, but he knew he would need every single one of them to destroy the black reavers of Khyrei. How could he know that the reavers would end up his allies instead of enemies? Or that numbers of ships would make no difference in the slaughter to come? As it was with Yaskatha, the majority of ships docking at Mumbaza now were merchant vessels.

Word of a new King on the Cliffs had come to D'zan months ago, and then a few months later the news that the Feathered

Serpent himself had removed the new King and replaced him with a bastard sired by Undutu. A strange decision, but Khama must have his reasons. His power would overrule any objections to such an heir. The folk of Yaskatha would never accept a bastard ruler, and there was no revered Feathered Serpent there to change their minds about it. D'zan put thoughts of Theskalus from his mind as the sparkling domes of the Pearl City dwindled in the wake of the *Cointosser*.

Sailing along the established trade routes took longer than braving the open ocean, but it helped ensure the safety of any ship. Today, as in all the nine days previous, the sky and sea were calm and a good wind filled the sails. Soon the ship would turn its prow west toward the wizard's isle, and then would come the ring of storms.

D'zan passed the gentle days reading Lyrilan's biography of Dairon the First. In the evenings he gathered with Andolon in the captain's cabin and played at dice. A minstrel named Yudun entertained them with harp, flute, and bawdy tales as they drank fine wines from the Jade Isles. D'zan enjoyed the young lord's company, and that of Andolon's cousin Hammon. The lad was only fifteen but possessed all the wit of a lord twice his age. Between Hammon's jokes, Yudun's tales, and Andolon's good wine, D'zan found himself enjoying the voyage. Yet at the end of each night he was left alone in his cabin with his churning thoughts, his burning memories, and his doubt.

The evening of the fifteenth day saw a dark wall of stormclouds rushing toward the ship. Rain came in gusts, pelting the decks and ripping at the sails. D'zan spent the next three days inside his cabin while Andolon and his crew battled the storms. They must have come deep into the Shaper's territory by now. A natural storm would have broken after a day or two. The ship rocked incessantly, and D'zan's nightmares rose like Sea Serpents to tear apart his sleep. A sailor was swept over the railing and lost on the third day of storms.

The fifth day into the ring of storms dawned gray and windy, yet calm and dry. A cry from the crow's nest brought D'zan from his cabin, stomach queasy and feet unsteady on the deck. He could still feel the ship moving and swaying beneath him, even though his eyes told him it sat steady upon the water. On the horizon a small green chunk of land had appeared.

Andolon clapped his hands together. "There's your wizard isle, Majesty." The young lord smiled and rubbed the stubble of his chin. "The Sea God smiles upon us."

By midday the *Cointosser* had made the island. Bright birds filled the sky above thick groves of palm and cypress. A citadel of white stone rose from the eastern shore, hemmed by a range of forested hills. Three slim towers stood at the keep's center, their cupolas bright with jewels inset into clever patterns. Pitted stone gargoyles perched on the ramparts.

A long and narrow cove welcomed the *Cointosser*. At its end was no dock or wharf, but only a set of weedy stairs rising from the black water toward the citadel's main gate. There was no sign of guardian or sentinel along the white walls. The sailors eyed the stony grotesques along the battlements as if the monsters might spring to life at any moment. They might indeed do such a thing if Iardu willed it, D'zan mused. He did not share this thought with the nervous crew.

Andolon ordered a rowboat dispatched so that a small party might approach the stair. The forestland was so thick and the cliffs so steep that no other approach to the keep was possible.

"I must go alone," D'zan said. His guards objected, as did Andolon, but he commanded them all to silence. Then he followed the path of their wide eyes past his shoulder and turned to see what had captured their attention. At the summit of the salt-crusted stairway stood a woman in a robe of white silk. Her hair was long, dark, and curly. Even from this distance D'zan recognized the emerald glare of her eyes.

Sharadza. He had guessed she would be here. She had made no secret of her choice to join Iardu on his island. Perhaps it was her magic that had guided his ship through the ring of storms.

The crew lowered D'zan alone into the small boat, seeing now there was no evident threat to his person. He rowed it toward the stair with anxious strokes, then mounted each of the slippery steps until he stood before her. Sharadza's presence stole his breath away, as it had always done. The supple skin of her cheeks held a rosy hue, and he longed to kiss her scarlet lips. Yet he had lost the right to do so. It was perhaps his greatest mistake, letting her go. Greater even than sailing his fleet to its doom at Ongthaia.

She spoke his name and embraced him heartily. There was no longer any heat or passion between them. It was the embrace of a sister, not a wife or lover.

"Why have you come?" she asked him.

Her eyes said: *Please do not say that you have come for me.*

"I need to speak with Iardu," he said. "I must know the truth once and for all."

Sharadza sighed and led him into a courtyard beyond the gate. The trees here were full of tiny, domed huts like oversized beehives. Chattering monkeys pale as clouds darted in and out of them. A lion creature with the head of a beautiful girl watched D'zan and Sharadza approach the doors of the citadel, petite wings fluttering on its tawny back. What other strange beings lived in the Shaper's domain? D'zan could not begin to guess. The scents of the wild garden were overpowering: citrus, jasmine, vanilla, starberry, and a hundred others he could not name. He became dizzy amid the mélange of exotic fragrances.

Sharadza sat beside him on a stone bench before a gurgling fountain carved into the shapes of impossible creatures. "Iardu is not here," she said. "He has not returned from . . . wherever he has gone." Her voice was tinged with sorrow. Yet it was obviously a sorrow she had lived with for some time, not some fresh wound. D'zan could always read her moods.

With careful words she explained to him what he had not understood after the siege of Uurz. The Shaper had sacrificed his own living heart to work a spell that turned the invaders away from the Five Cities and sent them back to their side of the world in peace. Yet it had done far more than that.

"Iardu changed their hearts with the power of his own," Sharadza said. She told him more, but D'zan could not understand exactly what the Shaper had done. Only that he had apparently given up his life to save the Five Cities and create peace between the two sides of the world.

"Are you telling me the Shaper is dead?" he asked.

"Iardu cannot truly die," Sharadza said. "One day he will return."

"When will that be? I must know the truth of what he told me."

"I do not know when," she said. "He has gone beyond my power to reach him."

"Then why do you stay here alone?" he said. "Come to Yaskatha, or return to your family in Udurum. Surely either would be better than this isolation."

Sharadza shook her head. "I wait for him."

He tried once more to sway her.

"I wait for him," she said again.

He gave up and accepted her offer of food and drink. Now that he was on solid ground again, his appetite had returned. The interior of Iardu's manse was as opulent as any palace. The dining hall was thick with ancient silk hangings in colors of mauve, ochre, and gold. D'zan ate roasted fowl and drank an entire bottle of amber Uurzian wine. The lion-lady sat upon a purple rug in the next room. D'zan sensed that the creature was watching over Sharadza. Perhaps it was a specimen of some lost race that Iardu had preserved in his sanctuary. Or the Shaper himself might have created the beast specifically to guard his house.

"What is this truth you seek?" Sharadza asked.

He put down the cup of wine and swallowed a mouthful of meat. He laid his hand upon hers, and the words came tumbling out of him.

"Iardu told me about the nature of this body that you and he created for me. If not for its magic, I would be dead many times over. He told me I will not sicken or age. Yet he also told me that my children would be normal. Human."

Sharadza blinked. Her hand twitched beneath his own.

He understood her enough to know what these small things meant.

"You are not barren, are you?"

She said nothing.

"I must know," he said. The wine had loosened his tongue, and he let the words spill forth. "I look at my son and I do not see myself in him. I remember your pain and my accusation, and it tears me apart. You must know as Iardu knew. Is Theskalus my son? Can I have a son? I must know the truth now or I will go mad. It is why I have come all this way, sailing every league in the shadow of nightmares. I will not leave this place without an answer."

Sharadza took a deep breath and turned away from his eyes.

"You cannot father children in this body," she said. Her voice was only a whisper.

Gods of Earth and Sky, I knew it. Somehow I knew it.

"Then . . . Theskalus is not mine?"

Sharadza shook her head.

"I could not tell you," she said. "I wanted to spare you pain. D'zan, I am sorry."

He grabbed her by the shoulders. The lion-lady sprang up but did not advance. Her eyes were upon D'zan, yet she was a civilized creature.

"No," he said. The tears began to fall and he did not try to stop them. "I am the one who must apologize. I blamed you for not giving me an heir. I let this ruin our love, when all the time it was my own fault. Can you ever forgive me?"

"I already have," she said.

They kissed then, but he did not remember moving toward her. The kiss was a tender one, but she broke it first and moved away from him.

"Come back with me," D'zan said. "Cymetha is not fit to be Queen. You are the only one I love. Let me fix my terrible mistake."

Sharadza shook her head again, and her black curls shuddered. She dabbed at her eyes with a silken napkin.

"Please try to understand," she said. "I do love you. But I am waiting for Iardu."

D'zan could not finish the fine meal. Sharadza held him in her arms for a while, and they said nothing. *She knew Cymetha was unfaithful, but she chose not to tell me. She took the blame to spare me the reality of my impotency.*

Theskalus is not my son.

And I will never produce an heir.

D'zan rose from the table at last and emptied his wine cup. "I came to learn the truth from Iardu, but you have given it to me. I thank you."

"Wait," Sharadza said. "Your voyage was long, and your men are weary. Stay here a few days at least. There is room."

"I cannot," D'zan said. "The longer I am near to you the more I will want you, and the more I will hate myself for what I did to you. To both of us. Yet I am grateful. You have given me a precious gift today, as you once gave me the gift of life inside this body. I may not have a son to bear my crown, but I still live to sit upon my father's throne."

"What will you do?" she asked, one hand on his chest. She meant about Theskalus. Yaskathan tradition did not allow for illegitimate offspring among royal bloodlines. Women and children had been put to death many times over the issue. D'zan knew now how those betrayed Kings of history must have felt. He could not imagine spending another night with Cymetha, or holding Theskalus in his arms ever again. Yet he would have long days of sailing ahead of him. Plenty of time to decide the fate of the liar and her spawn.

My father would have them both killed without another thought.

Trimesqua had been a Warrior King, with a warrior's ruthless nature.

"I do not know," D'zan told Sharadza. He did not want her to bear any guilt for the death of a faithless trollop and a bastard child.

I will do what must be done. As all Kings must do.

He left her standing at the top of the sea-stained stairway and rowed back to the ship with a few hours of daylight remaining. Sharadza waved as the *Cointosser* raised its sail and glided from the cove. Andolon and the crew had not questioned D'zan's orders for an immediate departure. They saw the look on his face and knew that a King's worries were not theirs to share.

There were no storms as they left the isle behind. The sorcery that kept ships away from Iardu's domain must have been configured to assault only approaching ships. Or perhaps Sharadza spread her own magic across the sea to ensure D'zan's safe departure. He sat in the shuttered cabin and drank Andolon's wine until he passed out.

Over the next few days the King rarely emerged from his cabin. He refused the company of Andolon, Hammon, and the minstrel. He drank and read the pages of Lyrilan's book until his eyes grew bleary and his head was too full of wine vapors to continue. The nightmares of marine slaughter returned, but they were distant and blurred now. He was unsure if this was the wine's effect or the result of his new concerns. The weight of what he must do pressing on his soul before he even gave the order.

Bastards cannot be Kings.

A King must have an heir.

D'zan could not unravel the knot in his mind, and his anger grew like a sickness inside his non-human heart. He shouted visitors away from his cabin door and refused the company of anyone but the guard who brought him fresh bottles of wine. This man visited him often.

Mumbaza came and went upon its bone-bright cliffs.

D'zan was lost in a dark dream of flame and smoke when the shouts of men and clanging metal eventually roused him. The wooden deck rumbled with the thundering of booted feet. The voices of sailors and soldiers mingled into a violent cacophony. The sounds of a battle outside the cabin door were unmistakable, and the scent of burning sails filled D'zan's nostrils.

Still drunk, his head pounding, D'zan took up his greatsword and staggered out of the door onto the middle deck. Black, ragged shapes rushed about him, driving silver sabres into the bodies of crewmen and dueling with the skilled Yaskathan guards. The main sail had been set ablaze by a half-dozen flaming arrows.

Along the starboard rail of the *Cointosser* sat a black Khyrein reaver flying a tattered crimson sail without insignia. The free-blood banner of pirates. The immersion into carnage sobered

D'zan instantly. Before he could raise his voice to rally the ship's defenders, a grinning pirate rushed at him with a curved blade raised high.

D'zan caught the downstroke against his greatsword. The pirate was not a Khyrein, but a Jade Islander. His eyes were squinted with bloodlust, his brown face marred by scars and open sores. He screamed something in the dialect of Ongthaia, but D'zan did not understand it. Most likely a curse.

"Protect the King!" someone shouted. The middle deck was a forest of clashing blades beneath a canopy of black smoke.

D'zan's greatsword cleaved his attacker from shoulder to breastbone. The brigand went down howling. The decks were already lathered in blood, littered with bodies and piles of slippery entrails. D'zan's arcing blade took the head of another charging pirate. The raiders were clumsy fighters, used to preying on those that feared them.

Yudun the Minstrel lay dying not far from where D'zan stood blinking. The singer's throat was sliced from ear to ear. Men died every second that D'zan hesitated. The pirates had killed a dozen men already, and now they outnumbered the Yaskathans. D'zan leaped recklessly into the fray, catching a glimpse of Andolon fighting for his life atop the foredeck.

The greatsword that bore the mark of the Sun God cut men down like a great scythe. The points of curved daggers and rusty sabres bit into D'zan's flesh, slicing deep cuts into his chest and back. He ignored them all, knowing that each wound would heal. He could not die at the hands of Men, and certainly not from the blades of diseased vagabonds. He had stood against the Manslayers of Zyung in their multitudes and stolen hundreds of their lives. These desperate thieves were no match for him. He poured his anger upon them like a poison, slicing through arms and ribcages and knees like summer grasses.

The fury of D'zan's assault gave fire to his guardsmen, who shouted his name as they cut down pirates. This in turn inspired the sailors to fight bravely and with confidence. Soon the decks were choked with dead brigands: Khyreins, Jade Islanders, Sharrians, even a few Yaskathan outlaws. The black reaver cut loose its grapples and glided away, the last of its crew no doubt regretting their decision to raid the *Cointosser*.

Andolon Silver raised his dripping longblade and shouted a cry of victory. He bled from a deep shoulder wound, but his fierce skill with the sword had kept him alive. Half of the crew was dead, and only three guardsmen were left standing. The *Cointosser's* losses were great, but it had survived the boarding.

If I had not been a sleeping drunkard, I would have fought sooner. Some of these men would still be alive.

How many times must I fail those who serve me?

D'zan barely heard his name ringing out as sailors rushed buckets of water toward the burning mast and sails. He dropped his filthy blade to the deck and leaned over the nearest railing. His guts rumbled, wanting to spill from his belly into the sea.

With his eyes on the foaming water, D'zan never saw the shaft that flew from the distant reaver's deck. Something slammed into his right shoulder, and the arrow struck with a meaty sound. D'zan fell on his left side into a puddle of congealing blood, and he retched. He rolled away from the stench and discovered Andolon lying near, the black-feathered shaft protruding from his chest. The young lord gasped for air.

He took this arrow meant for me.

Some pirate aboard the departing ship had heard D'zan's name and tried to pin the King of Yaskatha with a well-aimed shot. Andolon had shoved him out of the way, but could not avoid the speeding shaft.

The reaver was too far out now for another shot. D'zan shouted for help. Hammon came running across the smeared planks, crying his brother's name. D'zan sent him for bandages and wine.

"Rest easy," D'zan told Andolon. He examined the arrow. It had sunk deep and pierced the heart. There would be no need for bandages after all. Whether or not D'zan removed the shaft, Andolon would soon be dead.

"Majesty . . . " Andolon's voice was a rasping croak.

D'zan hushed him. "Don't try to talk. You are a hero, Lord Andolon. A statue of you will stand forever in my palace court-yard. Bards will sing of your great deed."

"No!" Andolon spat blood. He waved away those gathering about him, even his brother. "My words are only for the King's ears."

D'zan poured a bit of wine into Andolon's mouth and leaned low to hear him.

"Speak quickly then."

"The child," said Andolon. His eyes burned, drowning in tears. "The boy *Theskalus* . . . He is mine. I am his father." D'zan saw it clearly now, as if a spell of blindness had been washed from him. The face of Cymetha's child mirrored the face of Andolon. The same blue eyes.

"You cried out in your sleep," Andolon breathed. "I heard your pain. Let the lie die with me. Please . . . Majesty . . . Forgive me . . . "

You gave your life to save mine.

You could not know that no arrow can slay me.

You died for nothing. Nothing but loyalty.

"I already have," said D'zan.

Andolon grabbed his King's hand, sticky with blood. He squeezed it with the last of his strength. "I have loved Cymetha . . . since we were children," he wheezed. "I could not forget her when . . . she went to the palace. I have betrayed you . . . "

"And saved me," said D'zan.

Let him believe this. It might have been so.

Andolon smiled through his tears. "You are a great King . . ." He gasped and coughed blood. His flesh grew paler by the moment. "Promise me . . . that you will not slay the boy. Exile him . . . give him to the temples . . . but let him live."

D'zan nodded.

"Promise me!" Andolon's red fingers clutched D'zan's shoulder, the final spasm coming.

"Theskalus will live," said D'zan.

Andolon's head fell back against the deck. His blue eyes were dull glass.

D'zan would never know if the young lord heard his promise.

A King must have an heir.

The funeral of Andolon Silver was a grand affair, and his statue erected in the palace courtyard was of purest white marble. Cymetha wept as D'zan had never seen her weep. He knew her heart was broken. He comforted her as best he could.

The following week he conducted the ceremony that raised her officially to the status of First Wife and Queen of Yaskatha. In the years that followed, he would take many more wives. They too would bear him children: sons and daughters who looked nothing at all like their royal father. Yet only Theskalus mattered to the masses, for he was the first-born heir to the throne.

D'zan saw Andolon in the boy more and more as he grew, yet the King never spoke of the young lord to any of his wives or children. One day D'zan would teach Theskalus the ways of the sword, the spear, and the arrow. Yet he would also insist that the brightest of sages tutor the boy in diplomacy, commerce, and philosophy.

Theskalus would make a clever Prince and a wise King.

Yaskatha deserved no less.

23

The Living Empire

The contents of the messenger's scroll made Sungui's eyes water. His fingers trembled and his female aspect rushed from within to take command of the body. Men should be allowed to weep as openly as women, yet somehow the act always sent his male aspect into hiding as if ashamed of its sorrow. As the metamorphosis finished, she held the ink-scrawled parchment to a candle flame and watched it shrivel.

The first casualties of enlightenment.

There were bound to be more.

Since Sungui had returned from the Land of the Five Cities a year ago, the reformation of the Living Empire had proceeded with hardly an impediment. The millions of families in the Outer and Inner Provinces had been dreaming of such a day, pining for freedom in the midst of oppression, worshipping the old Gods in secret, and praying to them for change. At first Sungui had felt ashamed. Her fellow High Seraphim had never seen this hidden desperation that permeated the empire, never heard the whispers of hope that refused to fade. Yet the shadow of Zyung had blinded all of his servants, even those who stood highest among them.

News of the Almighty's death had spread from the Holy

Mountain like a storm. A day of fear and dread fell across the Celestial Province, while the Inner Provinces remained quiet and the Outer Provinces held blasphemous celebrations. A fleet of dreadnoughts had traveled to every corner of the empire, and the mere presence of the sky-ships had quelled distant revelries.

The New Seraphim agreed that Sungui should serve as High Consul of the Senate that replaced Zyung's rule. During their journey back across the world they had drafted a charter for this new form of governance: Rule of the many by the select few. The Holy Mountain itself would be the seat of this parliament, and its holy shrine would become a hall given to legislative action. The Lesser Seraphim were affirmed as enforcers of Senate law across the length and breadth of the empire. This was not so different from their duties under Zyung, yet their titles and methods would change.

Sungui spoke from the great terrace three days after the Holy Armada's return. She confirmed the news of Zyung's passing and announced the sweeping reforms that would forever alter his empire. First, all slaves were granted freedom; the Slave Estate was immediately blended with the Earthbound Estate. The Lowblood Estate, composed of non-human and semi-human individuals, was also elevated to Earthbound status. All labor performed in the empire must be rewarded with fair wages, according to imperial laws and local statutes. These were delivered at the hands of the Lesser Seraphim, who were now called Magistrates. The penalties for slaveholding in the Reformed Empire were heavy and unpleasant; the wealthy would be stripped of titles and holdings if they failed to comply.

Second, religious freedom was granted to all the peoples of the empire. Although Zyung would remain the chief deity, worship of the old Gods was no longer prohibited, and even new faiths were to be tolerated without persecution. This edict, too, would be enforced by new laws.

Third, the ruling body of the Reformed Empire was the Senate of the New Seraphim, who would hold court monthly inside the Holy Mountain. Every province would be assigned one of these dignitaries, as well as a number of Magistrates.

Fourth and last, voices of dissent would no longer be silenced with death or imprisonment. Any citizen of any province could make his voice heard by filing a petition with the appropriate Magistrate, who would carry his message to the Senate itself. The New Seraphim would make a regular practice of listening to their subjects and trying to meet their needs.

With these four decrees the great reformation of the Living Empire had begun. Across the entire continent voices were raised in jubilation. The New Seraphim were praised and met with reverence when they walked the streets. For centuries they had been icons of terror and destruction, tools used to spread Zyung's wrath. Now they were all saints and heroes.

All of them except for the Thirteen Skeptics.

These were the confederates of Damodar, the voices of malcontent in the Senate. Sungui could hardly blame them. Damodar had been killed by Khama the Feathered Serpent at the Battle of Ongthaia. His physical form had re-manifested here on the other side of the world, in the heart of the Holy Mountain. The other twelve Skeptics had been slain in the Sharrian valley by Khama and Vireon. They, too, had regained physicality months later. By the time they had arisen from the Inner Sanctum of the temple-palace, the armada was already on its way back to Zyung's land.

Damodar and the Skeptics had not faced the ultimate choice of the other Seraphim, and they had not become the Eaters of Zyung. They remained unchanged, and they did not understand the enlightenment that the consumption of the Almighty's salt had delivered. Nor did they share the Gift of Iardu, the birth of

compassion and empathy that evolved the consciousness of the
Eaters to create the New Seraphim. Sungui had sacrificed a small
part of herself to share that enlightenment with Lavanyia, but
there were none willing to make that same sacrifice for Damodar
and his twelve.

Sungui had made her decision to spare Lavanyia the doom of
salt because she did not have the heart to lose Lavanyia. But the
Skeptics were not loved or overly valued among the New
Seraphim. None of the transformed had stepped forward to sacrifice parts of themselves, so the Skeptics were caught in the
middle of the great reform without truly understanding it. Eleven
Senate meetings had occurred since the return, and the Skeptics
had been the voices of opposition at each of them. Yet there were
seven hundred New Seraphim against Damodar's faction of only
thirteen, so they were outvoted at every turn.

"They are a poison in our midst," Lavanyia had told Sungui.
"We must deal with them."

"How?" asked Sungui. "Will you sacrifice your salt to bring
them understanding?"

Lavanyia laughed. "If you asked me to."

Sungui had kissed her for that sentiment. "I will not ask it of
anyone," she said. "I do not even know if such a gift would work,
were it not given freely with the giver's blessing upon the receiver.
Yet perhaps Damodar and his followers will see the worth of what
we are doing. Let them remain among us and take positions in the
Reformed Empire. We changed in an instant. They must change
slowly."

"As to that," said Lavanyia, "it is I who remain skeptical."

Now came the parchment, with its message of tragedy and
doom.

Sungui stood upon the lofty terrace, directly below the great
face of Zyung that dominated the Holy Mountain. From this

vantage point she saw far across the Holy City. She had missed the avenues of pristine marble, the sprawling gardens and orchards, the striped horses and web-footed Snouts that carried men through the streets. The twenty-nine ziggurats grew thick with vine and flower, green hills rising from the cityscape.

Towers of ivory and jade cast their shadows across canals of green water. The great river flowed through arched gateways, bringing merchant vessels from distant provinces. Dreadnoughts floated in lazy patterns across the blue sky, and the distant ramparts about the city were purple in the rising dawn.

Every spot of the Living Empire must be made this beautiful.

This holy.

The laughter of children rose from the gardens of the temple-palace, which had been opened to the public six months ago. Even the great stone face of Zyung seemed to be smiling, its eyes flaming with benevolence now instead of judgment.

Perhaps it was all a matter of perspective.

Lavanyia joined Sungui on the terrace, wrapping her arms about Sungui's neck from behind. "You've been weeping." She knew Sungui's moods better than anyone ever had.

"You were right," Sungui told her. "Something must be done about Damodar and his Skeptics."

"What has happened?" Lavanyia asked.

"Do you know the city of Avantreya?"

Lavanyia nodded, moving to stand beside Sungui at the white railing. "It lies in the Outer Province of Yetva. Not a great city, but well known for its silver mines."

"The population began rioting there days ago, and the Magistrates failed to stop it. The merchant lords who run the mines refuse to pay their former slaves a decent wage, so the Earthbound ceased working. The merchants hired mercenaries to subdue the rioters, and the city became a battleground."

"Yetva was given to Zolmuno," said Lavanyia, "one of Damodar's brethren."

Sungui breathed deep of the flower-scented air. "It was," she said. "Zolmuno must have feared he was losing control of Avantreya. Not only did he murder his own Magistrate, but he called upon Damodar to help him pacify the city. Damodar gathered his Skeptics, and the pacification became a slaughter."

Lavanyia exhaled heavily. "They are prisoners of the old ways," she said. "Zyung's method for trimming the Tree of Empire."

Sungui nodded. "They rained Celestial Light upon the city for a day and a night. The message that I received estimates thirty thousand dead. Men, women, children. The Skeptics did not discriminate."

"So Zolmuno restored order. But who will work his mines?"

"The few thousand men that survived have been pressed into that service," said Sungui.

Lavanyia took her hand, pressed her forehead against Sungui's. "What will you do?"

"What I should have done months ago," Sungui said. "Help me gather an emergency quorum."

"I will send out the voice of my mind," said Lavanyia.

"I will speak with Damodar," said Sungui.

"Be careful what you say to him."

Sungui shrugged. "I will offer him a choice."

Damodar met her in the lower gardens. A dreadnought had carried him overnight all the way from Yetva. Even he did not dare ignore a summons from the High Consul of the New Seraphim. Surely he must have known the purpose of this summons. The dead of Avantreya had not even been buried yet.

Dark eyes glimmered above his hawkish nose. Sungui hated the sight of the silver robe upon him. Yet she hid that hatred, knowing it was her own weakness to feel this way. She must not let it pollute her heart or her judgment.

Damodar bowed briefly and joined her on a bench overlooking a sunken fountain. The sound of gurgling waters brought a welcome calm to Sungui. The early sun was bright above the green canopy. A circle of roses grew about the fountain, spreading petals red as blood. She found it an appropriate venue for this conversation.

"Greetings, High Consul," said Damodar. "You wish to speak of Avantreya."

"You are direct," said Sungui. "I appreciate this."

Damodar smiled. His arrogance was tangible.

"I need not remind you," said Sungui, "that formal executions of imperial citizens are only permitted by consensus of the Senate. Yet you have spat in the face of our laws and executed some thirty thousand without our approval. I know that you do not share our respect for human life, but I had thought you at least respected our laws."

"These were not executions," said Damodar. "They were casualties of war. The people of the silver city were out of control, pulling merchant lords from their houses and putting them to death. Looting, burning, and instigating a full-scale revolt. If there is any fault here, it must be placed upon Zolmuno, who could not maintain order without our help."

"*Our* help?" said Sungui. "You mean the Thirteen Skeptics. It was these noble personages who Zolmuno called upon rather than any number of the seven hundred New Seraphim who might have aided him in a legal manner. I sense a lack of trust among your brethren, Damodar. Or is it perhaps some deeper flaw?"

Damodar brushed a fallen leaf from his knee and shrugged. "You know well that we are not as you Eaters of Zyung," he said. "We remain unchanged."

"And unconvinced?"

Damodar smiled. "If you will."

"Skeptics or no Skeptics, you have broken the law. You must face the Senate."

Damodar's smile turned to a frown. "As High Seraphim we are above the laws."

"No longer," said Sungui. "Once that was true, when there was no law for us but Zyung. Yet none of us are above the laws of the Reformed Empire. If you understand nothing else, you must understand this fact."

Damodar said nothing.

Sungui endured his frosty silence, then spoke again. "We have discussed your fate and decided that we have only two options to address your crime. One, we could banish the Thirteen Skeptics from the empire. Yet if we do this you will only foment rebellion in the Outer Provinces and rise against us at every opportunity. Therefore it would not be a wise decision. Two, we might grant you the enlightenment that we have all shared. In order to do this, each one of you must consume salt from one of us. Not all of it, mind you, simply a portion invested with our understanding. The tip of the smallest finger will do." Sungui raised her hand and showed him the missing tip of her own finger. "Yet who will make such a bold sacrifice? I have already done so, by sharing my wisdom with Lavanyia."

Damodar offered no suggestion.

"Or perhaps there is actually a third alternative," said Sungui. "We greatly outnumber the Skeptics. We might pursue you to the ends of the earth until we have captured and salted and devoured every one of you. Oh, you might evade us for weeks, months, or years, but eventually the seven hundred will catch up with the thirteen, and you will face oblivion. Does this idea appeal to you, Damodar?"

"I would not choose that fate."

Sungui smiled, though it was difficult to do so.

"Well, since you would not choose oblivion, and we would not choose banishment, there remains only the option of sharing our enlightenment. I am assured that if you partake of our salt, you will see the rightness of our reforms. Then there will no longer be conflict between us. Are you agreeable to this remedy?"

Damodar shifted uncomfortably on his seat. He did not truly believe that eating a modicum of salt from a New Seraphim's body would transform him. Sungui saw the doubt in his eyes. She had lived with doubt for millennia, so it was easy to spot. This very doubt was what made him a Skeptic. Him and the twelve like him.

"It seems to be the most preferable of options," Damodar said at last.

"Then I have good news for you," said Sungui. "I have found thirteen volunteers among the New Seraphim willing to share their salt with you. Do you understand the nature of this sacrifice? Such altruism is rare among the Seraphim."

"I understand this," said Damodar.

"Good," said Sungui. "Assemble your Skeptics at once. Tomorrow the New Seraphim will gather at midday. The ritual of salt-sharing will take place on the Senate floor. I trust you will explain the necessity of this act to your brethren?"

"It shall be done," said Damodar.

Sungui left him beneath the sun-dappled leaves, contemplating the change to come.

The great throne room of Zyung had once been dominated by the nineteen-stepped dais supporting his oversized diamond throne. That noble platform had been removed and the high seat broken down to fund the empire's costs of reformation. Yet the great pillars of agate, emerald, and onyx remained standing about the domed chamber. An amphitheater had been sculpted in the exact center of the hall, with enough benches for eight hundred New Seraphim, although little more than seven hundred existed.

At the northern end of the amphitheater's polished floor rose the seat of the High Consul, with an Assistant Consul seat placed on either side of it. Only a hundred Seraphim were required to attend for a Senate session to convene, but all seven hundred were present today. The Thirteen Skeptics stood upon the floor before the High Consul, each of them paired with a member of the New Seraphim who had volunteered for the ritual.

Normally the Senate sessions were open to the public, who often attended in great numbers. Yet today the Senate Hall was filled only with Seraphim. Even the guards had been excused from the hall to preserve the secrecy of today's doings.

Sungui sat in the High Consul seat and watched the faces of Damodar, Zolmuno, and the eleven other Skeptics. She was confident in the choice she had made, but still the seed of doubt lay inside her. There was no other path to walk than this one. The preservation of the Reformed Empire was the most important consideration. The New Seraphim had agreed. Yet something about their choice did not sit well with her. It smacked too much of their old ways. Too late now to change course.

"Skeptics," she called out, her voice ringing upward across the benches and traveling the length of the hall above. "You stand face to face with those who have tasted the salt of Zyung the Almighty, sprinkled as it was with the blood of Iardu the Shaper. You stand on the cusp of ultimate change, the threshold of glory. Are you prepared to accept the gift these New Seraphim will give you?"

Each of the Skeptics responded with a "Yes," beginning with Damodar and moving down the line.

"Givers, are you prepared to do what must be done?" Sungui asked.

The thirteen New Seraphim spoke as one. *"We are."*

"Take up your blades."

The thirteen New Seraphim pulled daggers of black metal from their robes.

"Lift your hands."

The Givers raised their free hands, each displaying spread fingers to the Skeptic who stood before him. Sungui kept her eyes on Damodar. His face was impenetrable. He may not believe in the power of their enlightenment, but like her he knew this ceremony was his only true option.

"Sing your songs," said Sungui.

The Givers chanted their ancient syllables.

The sharp edges of the blades hovered close to the skin of their smallest fingers.

"Strike," said Sungui.

Moving as one, each of the Givers plunged his dagger deep into the breast of the Skeptic before him. The mouths and eyes of the stabbed ones widened in disbelief. Yet there was no sound from any of those mouths, and not the slightest of movements.

The Givers stepped back, leaving their blades transfixed in the hearts of their victims.

Sungui stepped down from the high seat and walked across the floor. She paced along the line of immobile Skeptics. Traces of crimson ran down the chests of their silver robes.

"Each of these blades has been aligned with the Ninety Aspects of Higher Being," she told them. "Your positions in the universe are now fixed. We might keep you like this until the stars shift themselves into new patterns. Yet we are not so cruel. Not anymore."

Sungui reached Damodar at the end of the row. She stood with her face close to his unblinking eyes. An expression of shock was frozen there. The last expression he would ever wear.

"As I explained to Damodar, none of us are above the law," Sungui said. "The New Seraphim must be held to the same standards as their subjects, or the law itself is meaningless. The old days are gone, and the old ways with them. For the massacre of Avantreya and for the memory of its thirty thousand dead, we the Holy Senate condemn you. In honor of our shared heritage, we will accept you in the Ancient Way."

Sungui raised her arms and began the Song of Salt. The silver robes of the paralyzed Skeptics paled, their flesh turning white as bone, their fleshy substance altered to saline crystal. Thirteen statues of salt stood before her with the hilts of black daggers protruding from their chests. She finished the song and a moment of silence lingered above the Senate floor.

She walked back to the high seat as the seven hundred came down from their benches. One by one they tore away pieces of Damodar, Zolmuno, and the eleven others, stuffing them into their mouths, chewing and swallowing their salted essence. The light of ingested souls streamed from the eyes and mouths of the Eaters.

These Skeptics will serve the empire yet, as they have become part of us all.

Word of this punishment would spread throughout the land. Men would know that the New Seraphim held fast to their own laws. There would be no more slaughtering of citizens, no more of Zyung's heartless cruelty. The law of the Holy Senate was now the heart of the Living Empire. Only Sungui refused to take part in the mass devouring. The others accepted her refusal as the express right of the High Consul.

In the end there was little left of the Skeptics but a few grains of loose salt sprinkled across the marble. These were swept up by attendants, carried to the summit of the Holy Mountain, and scattered to the winds.

extras

www.orbitbooks.net

extras

about the author

John R. Fultz lives in the Bay Area, California, but is originally from Kentucky. His fiction has appeared in *Black Gate*, *Weird Tales*, *Space & Time*, *Lightspeed*, *Way of the Wizard*, and *Cthulhu's Reign*. His comic book work includes *Primordia*, *Zombie Tales*, and *Cthulhu Tales*. John's literary heroes include Tanith Lee, Thomas Ligotti, Clark Ashton Smith, Lord Dunsany, William Gibson, Robert Silverberg, and Darrell Schweitzer, not to mention Howard, Poe, and Shakespeare. When not writing novels, stories, or comics, John teaches English literature at the high school level and plays a mean guitar. Visit his website: www.johnfultz.com

Find out more about John R. Fultz and other Orbit authors by registering for the free newsletter at www.orbitbooks.net

if you enjoyed

SEVEN SORCERERS

look out for

VENGEANCE

by

Ian Irvine

Chapter 1

"Matriarch Ady, can I check the Solaces for you?" said Wil, staring at the locked basalt door behind her. "Can I, please?"

Ady frowned at the quivering, cross-eyed youth, then laid her scribing tool beside the partly engraved sheet of spelter and flexed her aching fingers. "The Solaces are for the matriarchs' eyes only. Go and polish the clangours."

Wil, who was neither handsome nor clever, knew that Ady only kept him around because he worked hard. And because, years ago, he had revealed a gift for *shillilar*, morrow-sight. Having been robbed of their past, the matriarchs used even their weakest tools to protect Cython's future.

Though Wil was so lowly that he might never earn a tattoo, he desperately wanted to be special, to matter. But he had another reason for wanting to look at the Solaces, one he dared not mention to anyone. A later *shillilar* had told him that there was something wrong, something the matriarchs weren't telling them. Perhaps—heretical thought—something they didn't know.

"You can see your face in the clangours," he said, inflating his hollow chest. "I've also fed the fireflies and cleaned out the effluxor sump. Please can I check the Solaces?"

Ady studied her swollen knuckles, but did not reply.

"Why are the secret books called Solaces, anyway?" said Wil.

"Because they comfort us in our bitter exile."

"I heard they order the matriarchs about like naughty children."

Ady slapped him, though not as hard as he deserved. "How dare you question the Solaces, idiot youth?"

Being used to blows, Wil merely rubbed his pockmarked cheek. "If you'd just let me peek . . ."

"We only check for new pages once a month."

"But it's been a month, look, *look*." A shiny globule of quicksilver, freshly fallen from the coiled condenser of the wall clock, was rolling down its inclined planes towards today's brazen bucket. "Today's the ninth. You always check the Solaces on the ninth."

"I dare say I'll get around to it."

"How can you bear to wait?" he said, jumping up and down. "At my age, the only thing that excites me is soaking my aching feet. Besides, it's three years since the last new page appeared."

"The next page could come today. It might be there already."

Though Wil's eyes made reading a struggle, he loved books with a passion that shook his bones. The mere shapes of the letters sent him into ecstasies, but, ah! What stories the letters made. He had no words to express how he felt about the stories.

Wil did not own any book, not even the meanest little volume, and he longed to, desperately. Books were truth. Their stories were the world. And the Solaces were perfect books—the very soul of Cython, the matriarchs said. He ached to read one so badly that his whole body trembled and the breath clotted in his throat.

"I don't think any more pages are coming, lad." Ady pressed her fingertips against the blue triangle tattooed on her brow. "I doubt the thirteenth book will ever be finished."

"Then it can't hurt if I look, can it?" he cried, sensing victory.

"I—I suppose not."

Ady rose painfully, selected three chymical phials from a rack and shook them. In the first, watery fluid took on a subtle jade glow. The contents of the second thickened and bubbled like black porridge and the third crystallised to a network of needles that radiated pinpricks of sulphur-yellow light.

A spiral on the basalt door was dotted with phial-sized holes. Ady inserted the light keys into the day's pattern and waited for it to recognise the colours. The lock sighed; the door opened into the Chamber of the Solaces.

"Touch nothing," she said to the gaping youth, and returned to her engraving.

Unlike every other part of Cython, this chamber was uncarved, unpainted stone. It was a small, cubic room, unfurnished save for a white quartzite table with a closed book on its far end and, on the wall to Wil's right, a four-shelf bookcase etched out of solid rock. The third and fourth shelves were empty.

Tears formed as he gazed upon the mysterious books he had only ever glimpsed through the doorway. After much practice he could now read a page or two of a storybook before the pain in his eyes became blinding, but only the secret books could take him where he wanted to go—to a world and a life not walled-in in every direction.

"Who is the Scribe, Ady?"

Wil worshipped the unknown Scribe for the elegance of his calligraphy and his mastery of book making, but most of all for the stories he had given Cython. They were the purest truth of all.

He often asked that question but Ady never answered. Maybe she didn't know, and it worried him, because Wil feared the Scribe was in danger. If I could save him, he thought, I'd be the greatest hero of all.

He smiled at that. Wil knew he was utterly insignificant.

The top shelf contained five ancient Solaces, all with worn brown covers, and each bore the main title, *The Songs of Survival*. These books, vital though they had once been, were of least interest to Wil, since the last had been completed one thousand, three hundred and seventy-seven years ago. Their stories had ended long before. It was the future that called to him, the unfinished stories.

On the second shelf stood the thick volumes entitled *The Lore of Prosperity*. There were nine of these and the last five formed a set called Industry. *On Delven* had covers of pale mica with topazes embedded down the spine, *On Metallix* was written in white-hot letters on sheets of beaten silver. Wil could not tell what *On Smything*, *On Spagyric* or *On Catalyz* were made from, for his eyes were aching now, his sight blurring.

He covered his eyes for a moment. Nine books. Why were there *nine* books on the second shelf? The ninth, unfinished book, *On Catalyz*, should lie on the table, open at the last new page.

His heart bruised itself on his breastbone as he counted them again. Five books, plus nine. Could *On Catalyz* be finished? If it was, this was amazing news, and he would be the one to tell it. He would be really special then. Yes, the last book on the shelf definitely said, *On Catalyz*.

Then what was the book on the table?

A *new* book?

The first new book in three hundred and twelve years?

Magery was anathema to his people and Wil had never asked how the pages came to write themselves, nor how each new book could appear in a locked room in Cython, deep underground. Since magery had been forbidden to all save their long-lost kings, the self-writing pages were proof of instruction from a higher power. The Solaces were Cython's comfort in their agonising exile, the only evidence that they still mattered.

We are not alone.

The cover of the new book was the dark, scaly grey of freshly cast iron. It was a thin volume, no more than thirty sheet-iron pages. He could not read the crimson, deeply etched title from this angle, though it was too long to be *The Lore of Prosperity*.

Wil choked and had to bend double, panting. Not just a new book, but the first of the *third shelf*, and no one else in Cython had seen it. His eyes were flooding, his heart pounding, his mouth full of saliva.

He swallowed painfully. Even from here, the book had a peculiar smell, oily-sweet then bitter underneath, yet strangely appealing. He took a deep sniff. The inside of his nose burnt, his head spun and he felt an instant's bliss, then tendrils webbed across his inner eye. He shook his head, they disappeared and he sniffed again, wanting that bliss to take him away from his life of drudgery. But he wanted the iron book more. What story did it tell? Could it be the Scribe's own?

He turned to call Ady, then hesitated. She would shoo him off and the three matriarchs would closet themselves with the new book for weeks. Afterwards they would meet with the leaders of the four levels of Cython, the master chymister, the heads of the other guilds and the overseer of the Pale slaves. Then the new book would be locked away and Wil would go back to scraping muck out of the effluxors for the rest of his life.

But his second *shillilar* had said the Scribe was in danger; Wil had to read his story. He glanced through the doorway. Ady's old head was bent over her engraving but she would soon remember and order him back to work.

Shaking all over, Wil took a step towards the marble table, and the ache in his eyes came howling back. He closed his worst eye, the left, and when the throbbing eased he took another step. For the only time in his life, he did feel special. He slid a foot forwards, then another. Each movement sent a spear through his temples but he would have endured a lifetime of pain for one page of the story.

Finally he was standing over the book. From straight on, the etched writing was thickly crimson and ebbed in and out of focus. He sounded out the letters of the title.

The Consolation of Vengeance.

"Vengeance?" Wil breathed. But whose? The Scribe's?

Even a nobody like himself could tell that this book was going to turn their world upside-down. The other Solaces set out stories about living underground: growing crops and farming fish, healing, teaching, mining, smything, chymie, arts and crafts, order and disorder, defence. They described an existence that allowed no dissent and had scarcely changed in centuries.

But their enemy did not live underground—they occupied the Cythonians' ancestral land of Cythe, which they called Hightspall. To exact vengeance, Cython's armies would have to venture up to the surface, and even an awkward, cross-eyed youth could dream of marching with them.

Wil knew not to touch the Solaces. He had been warned a hundred times, but, oh, the temptation to be first was irresistible. The book was perfection itself; he could have contemplated it for hours. He bent over it, pressing his lips to the cover. The iron was only blood-warm, yet his tears fizzed and steamed as they fell on the rough metal. He wanted to bawl. Wanted to slip the book inside his shirt, hug it to his skin and never let it go.

He shook off the fantasy. He was lowly Wil the Sump and he only had a minute. His trembling hand took hold of the cover. It was heavy, and as he heaved it open it shed scabrous grey flakes onto the white table.

The writing on the iron pages was the same sluggishly oozing crimson as on the cover, but his straining eye could not bring it into focus. Was it protected, like the other Solaces, against unauthorised use? *On Metallix* had to be heated to the right temperature before it could be read, while each completed chapter of *On Catalyz* required the light of a different chymical flame.

A mud-brain like himself would never decipher the protection. Frustrated, Wil flapped the front cover and a jagged edge tore his forefinger.

"Ow!" He shook his hand.

Half a dozen spots of blood spattered across the first page, where they set like flakes of rust. Then, as he stared, the glyphs snapped into words he could read. Such perfect calligraphy! It was the greatest book of all. Wil read the first page and his eyes did not hurt at all. He turned the page, flicked blood onto the book and read on.

"I can see." His voice soared out of his small, skinny body, to freedom. "I can see."

Ady let out a hoarse cry. "Wil, get out of there."

He heard her shuffling across to the basalt door but Wil did not move. Though the crimson letters brightened until they hurt his eyes, he had to keep reading. "Ady, it's a *new book*."

"What does it say?" she panted from the doorway.

"We're leaving Cython." He put his nose on the page, inhaling the tantalising odour he could not get enough of. It was ecstasy. He turned the page. The rest of the book was blank, yet that did not matter—in his inner eye the future was unrolling all by itself. "It's a new story," Wil whispered. "The story of tomorrow."

"Are you in *shillilar*?" Her voice was desperate with longing. "Where are the Solaces taking us? Are we finally going home?"

"We're going—" In an instant the world turned crimson. "It's *the one*!" Wil gasped, horror overwhelming him. "*Stop her.*"

Ady stumbled across and took him by the arm. "What are you seeing? Is it about me?"

Wil let out a cracked laugh. "She's changing the story—bringing the Scribe to the brink—"

"Who are you seeing?" cried Ady. "Speak, lad!"

How could *the one* change the story written by the Scribe Wil worshipped? Surely she couldn't, unless . . . unless the Scribe was *fallible*. No! That could not be. But if *the one* was going to challenge him, she must have free will. It was a shocking, heretical thought. Could *the one* be as worthy as the Scribe? Ah, what a story their contest would make. And the story was everything—he had to see how it ended.

Ady struck him so hard that his head went sideways. "Answer me!"

"It's . . . it's *the one*."

"Don't talk nonsense, boy. What one?"

"A Pale slave, but—"

"A *slave* is changing our future?" Ady choked. "Who?"

"A girl." Wil tore his gaze away from the book for a second and gasped, "She's still a child."

"What's her name?"

"I . . . don't know."

Wild-eyed and frantic, Ady shook him. "When does this happen?"

"Not for years and years."

"When, boy? How long have we got to find her?"

Wil turned back to the last written page, tore open his finger on the rough edge and dribbled blood across the page. The story was terrible but he had to know who won. "Until . . . until she comes of age—"

"What are we to do?" said Ady, and he heard her hobbling around the table. "We don't know how to contact the Scribe. We must obey *The Consolation of Vengeance*."

The letters brightened until his eyes began to sting, to steam. Wil began to scream, but even as his vision blurred and his eyes bubbled and boiled into jelly that oozed out of his sockets, he could not tear his gaze away. He had longed to be special, and now he was.

She tottered back to him, wiped his face, and he heard her weeping. "Why didn't you listen to me?"

He took another sniff and the pain was gone. "Stupid old woman," sneered Wil. "Wil can see so much more clearly now. *Wil free!*"

"Wil, what does she look like?"

"She Pale. She *the one*."

"Tell me!" she cried, shaking him. "How am I to find this slave child among eighty-five thousand Pale—*and see her dead*."